Silent Lies

BY

Mel Parish

Mel Parish

ISBN-13: 978-1470125387

Cover design: Jonny Gillard

For Cerianne

For reminding me of childhood joys

Chapter 1

Cal Miller could sense the crowd's anticipation. He was one point away from making history: the oldest man ever to win the US Open tennis title and against the reigning champion at that. He bounced the ball twice, took a deep breath and tossed the ball high into the air, only to be immediately knocked off balance by his wife's insistent shaking.

He groaned. Even in his dreams success eluded him.

He mumbled into the pillow and pulled the sheet over his head. If he concentrated hard enough he might just make it back to that winning point.

Lily pulled the sheet back down. "Cal!" Her voice was an urgent whisper. "Two policemen are downstairs, asking to see you."

Cal tried to pull the sheet back up. "It's Sunday. Tell them to come back later."

"Cal! You don't tell the police to come back later."

The police? Did Lily say the police? He rolled onto his back and forced his eyes open. Now he could see the concern on her face.

"What... what do they want?"

"They wouldn't say, just that they wanted to speak to you."

A flicker of fear jolted Cal upright. "Has there been an accident? Is someone hurt?"

"I don't know."

"Where are the kids?"

"Downstairs in the den watching cartoons. I asked the police to wait in the living room." Cal realized she was still whispering. And not just for the kids' sake. She was scared.

He grabbed his shorts from the chair next to the bed. It had to be about his parents or one of his siblings. Or maybe even one of Lily's relations. And the police didn't want to tell her without someone else present to comfort her. As he pulled a T-shirt over his head he prayed he could be strong enough to support her.

He tried to give her a reassuring smile. She looked pale and shaken. What else did he expect? There was only one reason the police came to the house early on a Sunday morning. Bad News. He gave her a quick kiss on the mouth and then took her by the hand.

"Let's get this over with," he said, leading her out of the bedroom.

Cal stopped just inside the living room. The two officers stood across the room by the patio doors, looking out onto the deck, talking in hushed voices. They weren't in uniform. Was that a good sign? For some reason he'd always imagined it was the uniformed police who were sent out to dispense the bad news, but maybe it was different on a Sunday.

They turned when they heard him enter. One was tall and lean, his long thin face softened by gentle eyes and upturned lips that gave the impression he was about to smile. The other man was younger and sturdier, but his surly expression only made Cal feel even more on edge. Luckily, in his three years in Leyton he'd managed to avoid any contact with the local police force, so he'd never seen either of them before.

The older man flipped open an ID wallet and stepped towards him. "Mr. Miller?"

Cal just nodded, the enormity of the moment silencing his vocal cords.

"Detective Pearson." The detective motioned to the guy behind him. "My partner, Detective Rigby, from Lewisville HQ."

Lewisville. Cal tried to swallow the lump forming in his throat. This was something worse than an accident. These guys were from the central division, not members of the town's local police force. He squeezed Lily's hand and braced himself for what he was about to hear.

"What do you want?" The words came out rude and brusque, but these guys would understand, wouldn't they, at a time like this? He just wished they would hurry up and get on with it.

Detective Pearson gave him a hard stare before replying. "We'd like to ask you a few questions."

"What?" Cal looked from Pearson to Rigby then back to Pearson. "What?"

"We'd like to ask you a few questions." Rigby enunciated the words carefully, like Cal was having a problem with English.

Cal snorted with relief. "You mean nobody's dead?"

Pearson and Rigby exchanged glances. Cal didn't care. Nobody was dead. He flashed a grin at Lily then exhaled with a small whoop and smiled at the officers.

They weren't smiling back.

"Why should anyone be dead?" Pearson said.

"Because you're here. In my house. On a Sunday morning."

"To ask you a few questions," Rigby said. "So what makes you think someone's dead?"

Cal hesitated before replying. Amazing! These guys had just given him one of the worst few minutes in his life. They should be apologizing, not hostile. He glared at Rigby. Rigby didn't look like the kind of person who did much apologizing. Or smiling, for that matter.

"What the hell did you expect me to think?" he said, "two policemen turn up on my doorstep on a Sunday morning?"

Lily tugged at his arm.

Rigby gave him a look of pure disdain. "We're detectives, Mr. Miller. It's how we work."

"Well excuse me, but if it's just a few questions you want answering, why couldn't you ring up and make an appointment instead of turning up unexpectedly like this?"

"Hey Pearson, there's an idea." There was no mistaking the sarcasm in Rigby's voice. "Oh I forgot... people generally aren't that keen to make appointments to see us."

Cal sniggered. "Yeah, I could see how you would have that problem." He felt another tug on his arm.

"Okay." Pearson stepped between Cal and Rigby. "Let's calm down, shall we?" He cast a warning look at Rigby, staring his partner down until Rigby rolled his eyes and moved back a couple of paces.

Pearson turned to Cal. "I'm sorry if we inconvenienced you. We'd like to ask you a few questions, that is all." He glanced towards the couch. "Why don't you have a seat and we can get started?"

Cal shook his head. "Why don't you sit down? This is my home. I don't need you to tell me when I can sit down."

There was a momentary tense silence before Pearson crossed to the couch and sat down. Cal waited. Rigby just leant up against the patio door, suggesting he was taking a back seat role for the time being. That was fine with Cal. He moved towards an armchair opposite Pearson. Lily followed. As she was about to sit, Pearson spoke.

"Mrs. Miller, we'd like to speak to your husband in private." He gestured over at Cal. "If that's all right with you."

"In private?" Lily looked at Cal.

Cal nodded as he considered the implications of Pearson's request: something to do with him personally rather than the family. He grimaced. Business. It had to be. He mentally checked through his client list, a list made up of small local business owners and a few wealthy individuals. It was hard to imagine any of them involved in a serious crime. He looked at Pearson expectantly. So which one was up to no good?

Chapter 2

As the door closed behind Lily, Pearson turned to Cal. "Mr. Miller, you have an assistant in your office called Katy Shore, is that correct?"

"Katy? Uh... yeah, that's right."

"When did you last see her?"

"Why?"

Rigby cut in. "When did you last see her?"

"Friday! Has something happened to her?"

"Mr. Miller, please just answer our questions," Pearson said, "and then we'll answer yours."

Cal's stomach cramped. "Something's happened to her?'

"Mr. Miller."

Cal slumped back against the couch. He had to calm down until he knew how much they knew. It had to be a coincidence that they were here asking about Katy. He combed his fingers through his sleep-ruffled hair. He should have taken the time to rinse his face, freshen himself up a bit before rushing downstairs, but how was he to know he would have to answer these questions already? And to the police of all people?

"What time on Friday?" Pearson asked.

"Ten."

"Ten a.m.?"

"P.m."

Pearson frowned.

"Ten p.m.?"

Cal knew what Pearson was thinking. He could have cleared that matter up then and there, but Pearson had said just answer the questions and under the circumstances that was beginning to look like the best strategy. That way he wouldn't say anything he shouldn't.

"Yes," he said.

"Working late, were you?"

There was an edge to Rigby's question that Cal didn't like. He glared at Rigby. "Yes."

"So you were both in the office until ten o'clock in the evening?" Pearson said.

"Yes."

"Anybody else with you?"

"No."

"Did you leave the office at ten?"

Cal thought for a moment. "I finally left the office about midnight."

"About midnight?"

Cal shrugged. "I wasn't clock watching. About midnight is the best I can do."

"You always work this late?"

"No."

"So why Friday?"

Cal sighed. "When my wife and I moved up here three years ago I promised her there'd be no more weekend working. When I've got a big job on, I stay late in the evenings so that I can keep my promise.

"And Katy stays too?"

"She volunteered to this week, thank goodness, or I would have been there until way past midnight."

"But she left before you."

"I told you already, she left at ten."

"Katy Shore is missing."

The abruptness of Pearson's statement caught Cal unprepared. "Missing?'

"As in disappeared," Rigby said.

The guy was beginning to rile Cal.

"She hasn't been home since Friday morning," Pearson said.

For the second time that day a wave of relief washed over Cal. So that was what this was about. Heaven knows why the police were involved, but this was an easy one to solve. Cal couldn't help but smile.

"She went to stay with a friend for the weekend," he said.

It was Pearson's turn to look puzzled. "A friend, which friend?"

Cal shrugged. "I don't know. She just mentioned she was going to see a friend for the weekend." He smiled again. "I'm her boss not her father, she doesn't tell me everything. I think someone's set you off on a wild goose chase."

Pearson shook his head. "Seems like you know more than her father. It was the family who reported her missing. They knew nothing about a weekend visit to friends."

Pearson's words sent a chill through Cal. Katy had told him that her family thought she was going away for the weekend. Why would she lie to Cal? But if she hadn't, why had her family reported her missing?

"Maybe they forgot."

"Don't you think they would have remembered when she didn't come home?" Rigby said. "At least considered the possibility?"

Cal wanted to say that anything was possible with a family that dysfunctional, but he kept quiet. A strange sensation was beginning to build inside, the feeling that he was teetering on the edge of an abyss, and his next few sentences would determine whether and how far he would fall. He shuddered. Pearson and Rigby were staring at him, waiting for his answer. He had to get a grip. They were only asking him a few simple questions.

He gave the detectives a bemused grin. "Isn't this all a little premature? After all Katy's a grown woman, not some little kid. Maybe she thought she'd told them and forgot. You'll see, by tomorrow this will all be sorted out."

"Wouldn't you be concerned if it was your daughter," Pearson said, "no matter how old she was?"

"Well, yes of course." Cal shuffled uneasily in his seat. "But I'd check with her friends first before getting the police involved."

"Her father did," Rigby said. "She wasn't with any of them,

so her brother called it in."

Cal leant forward resting his elbows on his knees. "I thought a certain amount of time had to elapse before you guys would get involved in cases of missing adults?"

Rigby gave him a knowing grin. "Did you now?"

"Technically, yes." Pearson ignored Rigby's remark. He flashed an apologetic smile at Cal. "But when it's one of our own...."

Cal tried to hide his shock with a look of mutual understanding. "One of your own?"

Pearson nodded.

"Dennis Shore still works out of the station house here in Leyton, but Brad Shore has moved across to Lewisville HQ. The Shores are a real close family, so of course the boys were concerned when their little sister didn't come home Friday night."

Cal winced at the words. Little sister—she was twenty-one for God's sake. That was part of the problem. They kept her on a real tight rein. He remembered the mixture of excitement and nervousness in her eyes on Friday night when she'd hugged him, the trembling in her limbs as he hugged her back. What should he say?

Hell, what had he gotten himself into? Why hadn't Katy mentioned her brothers were cops? Had she deliberately not told him, knowing it might have made a difference? He didn't think she was capable of such duplicity, but the police were here in his living room and they had already offered two potential instances where she might not have been totally honest with him.

It just didn't make sense. The weekend away was the first stage in the plan. Everything else followed on from it, so why should she risk messing it up? He thought again of her desperation, her fear that she would be followed. That hadn't been an act. Damn! The police didn't need to be involved in this. These guys were only here because her brothers were police officers.

He just had to keep quiet a little longer. A few half-truths, no harm done and by tomorrow it would all be irrelevant.

"I'm sorry I can't be of more help," he said trying to look apologetic, "but as I said, I haven't seen her since Friday night either."

Pearson looked disappointed.

Rigby stepped away from the wall. "You're sure there's nothing else you could tell us?"

The abyss opened.

"No," Cal said, making his voice as firm as possible. "Nothing."

Pearson stood up and moved towards the door. Rigby looked thoughtful as he followed Pearson. Cal got up to see them out. As Pearson opened the living room door, Rigby turned back.

"Just one more thing Mr. Miller," he said. "Were you and Katy Shore having an affair?"

Cal heard Lily's gasp before he saw her. She was standing outside the door, a large tray bearing coffee and mugs in her hand. She stared open mouthed at Cal.

Cal was rooted to the spot, rage building inside him. Rage and fear.

The cups rattled as Lily held the tray out to Cal. "I... I thought you might like some coffee."

Cal avoided her gaze as he took it from her. "Thanks, but these gentlemen are just leaving."

He scowled at Rigby. The officer's mouth turned up in what Cal took to be his attempt at a smile. Cal hesitated for a second contemplating the satisfaction he would get from smashing the tray into Rigby's smug face. Instead he slammed the tray onto a nearby side table and pushed past Lily to the front door, yanking it open before turning back to the officers.

"Sorry ma'am," Pearson said to Lily as he left.

Sorry for what, Cal wondered. That she'd heard Rigby's question? Or for the effort she had wasted on the coffee?

Rigby stopped in front of Cal. "Mr. Shore and the boys said Katy was acting rather strange the last couple of weeks, as if something was going on."

Cal ignored him, concentrating on keeping his face impassive.

"But apart from work she never much left the house." Rigby shrugged nonchalantly. "So I thought maybe something at work was getting her a little excited." He glanced back at Lily and then leant nearer to Cal and whispered, "All those late nights you know."

Pearson grabbed Rigby by the elbow and pulled him away.

"Excuse him. He's just concerned about Katy's safety."

"As am I," Cal said, indignation surging through him, "but if you have any other questions, call me first." He nodded at Rigby. "And leave him in his cage."

Rigby gave him a menacing glare. "We'll be back Mr. Miller, you can be sure of that. What you don't seem to realize is that you're the last known person to have seen Katy." He shook Pearson's hand off his elbow, straightened his jacket and started down the path. "Besides, you didn't answer my last question."

Cal slammed the door.

Chapter 3

Lily disappeared into the living room without a word. Cal remained at the front door, hesitant to follow her. His mind kept replaying Rigby's sneering grin, Lily's shocked response, and how easily she believed the worst of him. Surely she should give him some benefit of the doubt?

He could hear her fiddling with the dishes on the tray. Tentatively he crossed the hallway and stood at the doorway watching her. Best to deny it right now, but somehow he couldn't get the words out.

Lily's hands shook as she picked up the coffee pot. She took a long time pouring out the coffee, adding the milk and sugar. All the while she kept her head bent forward so that her shoulder length auburn hair created a curtain across her face. But Cal didn't need to see her face to know what her expression would be.

He hated it when she was like this, closed up tight and silent, her lips clenched, cheeks sucked in as if she was trying to swallow the hurt or the anger. Why couldn't she just let rip and give him hell so that they could clear the air? Instead, she left him without a clue how to deal with it but the sense that whatever he did would be wrong. He sighed silently, about to turn away.

"What did they want?" she asked suddenly, holding out a cup of coffee without looking up at him.

He took the coffee. "Katy never came home after work Friday."

"Her parents must be worried," she said turning towards the

patio doors.

"Father," Cal said, "her mother died a long time ago. She lives with her father and four brothers."

Lily didn't even look as if she was listening to him. She just stared out through the glass door.

"They're very possessive," Cal said. "She can't do anything without their permission."

Lily took a sip of her coffee.

"I thought I'd told you about her." He knew he had, but he had to say something to get her talking.

Lily remained silent.

Cal took a gulp of his coffee, the heat burning against his throat. Should he deny it now? Or if he brought the subject up, was he making it a bigger deal than it really was? Or should he cross the room like he wanted to, take her in his arms and hold her tight so that she could feel how much he loved her, the love that outlasted the moods, forgave the doubt?

He'd been smitten the moment he'd set eyes on her and six years of marriage had done nothing to change his feelings. But in the beginning, he'd had to almost lose her to understand how much she meant to him. He wished he could be sure the feeling was mutual. Most of the time he assumed it was, but what if she brushed him away? What then?

He stayed where he was.

"So what did they want from you?" Lily asked again.

Cal shrugged. "Seems like I'm the last person to have seen her."

"At the office? Late on Friday night?"

"That's right." He didn't want to lie to Lily but it seemed safer to stick to what he'd told the police. The question of where Katy was would blow over in the next couple of days. His immediate concern was the effect of Rigby's comments; those insinuations could linger far longer.

Lily finally turned to face him. "Do you know where she is?"

"No." At least that wasn't an outright lie. "She mentioned going away but she didn't say where."

"It must be worrying," Lily repeated, turning back towards the door.

12

Cal took that as his cue. He put his cup down, crossed the room and wrapped his arms around her, pulling her back up against his chest. She was tense and ungiving. Not a good sign.

"She's a grown woman," he whispered as he nuzzled his face against her hair. "She'll be okay."

"You can say that now. Just wait until ours are that age."

Cal shuddered at the thought. He remembered how he had been at twenty-one, but at least he'd had the decency to be away at college so that his parents had no idea what he was up to. On occasional trips home, he'd been a model of sense and responsibility and his quick brain had given him grades that supported the studious front. He dreaded to think his kids might turn out the same way.

Still, three and a half years of carefree existence had been his, living life to the full. And then, the week after graduation, he had sold his soul to the highest bidder, traded in his jeans for a suit and joined the ranks of model citizens. Hell, the way the accountancy firm worked him and with the additional exams he had to pass there wasn't time for him to be anything else. It was okay though, he'd had his wild years, got it out of his system. Katy, on the other hand, had led a sheltered, ordered life, little chance of her having a wild time here in Leyton. Didn't she deserve her opportunity?

He kissed Lily on the top of the head, hoping the gesture would make her turn round so he could kiss her again on the lips. It didn't work. She continued to stare out the door.

"What you thinking?" he asked at last.

She was silent for a while. Then she sighed. "I'm wondering why that officer should even think to ask such a question."

Cal released his hold on Lily and took a step back. She still didn't turn around. It was quite possible that she was crying. The bastard. One vindictive little statement and he'd hurled them back four years in time.

"It's not true," Cal said.

Lily turned without looking at him and picked up the tray. "That's what you said last time." She paused at the door. "I'm going up to take a bath. Keep an eye on the kids."

She was gone before he could think of a reply.

Chapter 4

Tuesday morning the police were back. This time to his office, a few minutes after he'd opened for business. It was as if they had been outside waiting for him, but he hadn't noticed them in the street as he arrived. It spooked him to think they might have kept deliberately out of sight. Did they think they were being discrete, doing him a favor by not hanging around his doorstep?

Maybe. He assumed they'd come to offer an apology. They certainly owed him one. He could hear them in the outer office talking to Betsy, his secretary. The door to his office was open so he could have just sauntered out and spoke to them then and there, but he was still pissed off at them for the way they'd behaved on Sunday so he was going to make them jump through all the hoops. Besides the last thing he wanted was for Betsy to overhear the conversation. At sixty she had a heart of gold but one of the loosest tongues in Leyton. He'd often wondered about the wisdom of employing her as his secretary, but as there wasn't exactly a line of other applicants he just had to make do.

So he waited while she went through the motions of asking them their names and if they had an appointment, even though she knew fine well they didn't. He pulled a blue file from a pile on his desk and opened it, picked up a pen and tried to look busy for when the detectives walked in.

He almost dropped the pen when Pearson started asking Betsy questions about Katy.

The tone of the queries was wrong. It sounded like they

were still looking for Katy but that couldn't be right. By now the family should have received the letter. They might be angry about it but there was nothing the police could do for them.

Damn, maybe the postal service had let her down. That had to be the reason. The letter would turn up today or tomorrow at the latest. So what should he do? If he came clean about the situation he could save the police time and effort. But then his role in the plan wouldn't make him very popular with the Shores, and the police would be onto him for not telling them all this on Sunday. He could just imagine Rigby's delight. He'd slap Cal with a charge of obstruction of justice before lunch. No, the only thing to do was to keep quiet a little longer and he'd be in the clear.

Betsy appeared at the door. "Detectives Pearson and Rigby are here to see you Mr. Miller."

Cal made himself look surprised. He glanced at his watch. Thirty five minutes until his ten o'clock appointment with Marc Coulsen. Ample time to get rid of the police.

Betsy came across to the desk, leant forward and lowered her voice to a loud whisper. "It's about Katy. They're saying she's disappeared." Cal could hear the shock in Betsy's voice. Such events didn't happen in Leyton. "Can you imagine? I told you we should have checked when she didn't ring in sick."

"Betsy!" Cal jumped in before she said anything that could be conceived as damning. "I think the officers are waiting to come in."

Betsy blushed at the rebuke. "Shall I make some coffee?"

"No," Cal said, "they won't be staying that long."

Betsy regained her composure and went back into the outer office. "Mr. Miller will see you now."

Cal tried not to smile. When she wanted to be Betsy was a paragon of etiquette. Mostly it infuriated him but today it suited him perfectly.

"Morning, Mr. Miller," Pearson said as he walked in. "Sorry to have to bother you again."

Through the open door Cal saw Betsy's face light up. Now she knew there was more to the story. Her mind would be working overtime to fill in the gaps.

"Can you shut the door please Betsy," he called out.

She blushed again and quickly complied. Cal stared at the

door for a moment. He was tempted to rush across and pull it open to see if she was listening, but caution warned him against providing any strange behavior for the police to pounce on.

"Have a seat," Cal said to Pearson, indicating the solitary chair opposite his desk.

Pearson ignored the suggestion and stood surveying the office as if he might find clues to his problem in the bare blue walls or in the overflowing bookshelves. Eventually he gestured towards the outer office. "Katy didn't come in this morning."

"No."

"I guess she didn't come in yesterday either?"

"No."

"Has she called in and explained why?"

"No."

"Doesn't that strike you as odd?" Rigby said.

Cal looked perplexed. "What? That she hasn't rung in to say she was missing?"

Rigby was across the room in a flash, his face like thunder. He struck his hand down on the desk with such a crack that Cal jumped, even though he knew it was coming.

"Not funny, Mr. Miller. Weren't you concerned yesterday when she didn't show up for work?"

Cal hesitated. Rigby was pushing him into a corner. Of course he hadn't expected Katy to be at work yesterday, or any day for that matter, but he couldn't tell the police that without admitting the truth. On the other hand, if he had been expecting her in, it was only reasonable to assume he would be concerned by her no show, especially after the police visit on Sunday; concerned enough to at least mention it to Pearson. Problem was he'd assumed that things were going according to plan and nobody would give any more thought to his involvement.

Damn! If he had just thought to call Pearson and mention Katy hadn't shown up. It wouldn't have cost him anything and he wouldn't be in this spot.

"You already knew she was missing." It was a lame excuse but the best he could come up with.

"Not according to you," Rigby said, smirking, "you were insisting she'd gone away for the weekend. In fact you even said that on Monday we'd be wondering what all the fuss was about, weren't they your words?"

Cal remained silent. He remembered his words only too well.

"Isn't that right?" Rigby said.

"Because that's what she told me."

"What? That on Monday everything would be okay?"

"No. That she was going away for the weekend."

"So why didn't she tell anyone else?"

"How the hell am I supposed to know?" Cal said, "I assumed it was general knowledge."

"Betsy didn't know."

"What?"

"Your secretary." Rigby's smirk became a sneer. "She didn't know anything about Katy going away for the weekend."

Cal didn't know what to say.

"Don't you think that's odd?" Rigby said. "She would tell you, her male boss, about her plans for the weekend but not the woman whom she shares an office with."

"Enough," Pearson said. "I'm sure Mr. Miller is wishing he'd phoned in his concern yesterday morning." He gave Cal a strange smile. "But that's not why we're here."

"It's not?"

"No," Pearson said, "we just wanted to take a quick look at her desk. See if she left anything there that might help us work out where she is."

"No problem." There was no point trying to stop them, so Cal stood up and led the way back into the outer office. Betsy looked up from her computer screen, startled by their sudden appearance, or was she covering up for the quick sprint from his door to her desk?

Cal gestured towards the desk opposite Betsy's. Apart from a computer monitor and a telephone, the top of the desk was bare.

Rigby strolled around to the other side of the desk and opened the top right hand drawer.

"Half used pencils, an eraser." He shut that drawer and opened the middle one. "A box of tissues." He dropped the latter onto the top of the desk then silently opened and closed the other four drawers. "Nothing else. No personal effects of any kind."

Pearson gave a bemused look round the room as if he

thought he might find a third desk that was really Katy's.

"My wife reckons," he said, "that every woman's desk has at least one drawer that she treats like her purse." Neither Cal nor Rigby pressed him on the point but he continued anyway. "Has everything but the kitchen sink in it." He fingered the box of tissues. "On that basis this desk would seem a little bare."

Cal shrugged. The empty desk was a dead giveaway. Another mistake.

"Not even a diary," Rigby said.

"Betsy keeps the office diary," Cal said, "Katy didn't need one."

Betsy, who of course was listening in, dutifully held up a thick black book.

"So why the empty desk?"

"She was a very private kind of person," Cal said, "Maybe she didn't want to leave anything personal lying around."

If looks could kill, he would have been dead. He could sense rather than see the outraged glare from Betsy's direction. He should have known she would take a comment like that personally. Thankfully he was saved from further explanation by the outer door opening.

"Hi, Cal." Marc Coulson stepped into the office. His face lit up in recognition as he took in the other people standing with Cal. "Pearson!" He gave Pearson a chummy handshake. "Don't tell me they're paying you guys so much now that you need an accountant."

Pearson laughed. "That'll be the day. No, it's strictly business today."

Coulson winked. "Not been cooking the books have you Cal? At least I hope not my books." He nodded towards Pearson. "I tell you, I know this guy, be warned, the last thing you want to do is get on the wrong side of him."

Cal forced a grin. The one thing he hated about small town living; everyone seemed to know everyone else. First Betsy, now Coulson, soon the whole town would know Katy was missing. The situation was turning into a small town drama and he was positioned right at the center of it.

The sooner he split this reunion up the better. "Betsy, could you show Mr. Coulson through to my office. I'll be with you in a

18

moment Marc. We're just about through here." He hoped Pearson—or Rigby—would not contradict him.

The two remained silent.

Betsy led the way into Cal's office. "Coffee," he heard her ask.

Cal turned back to Pearson and Rigby. "Are you finished, gentlemen?"

Pearson stared at him thoughtfully then said, "Please, don't let us keep you from your work." He leant back against Katy's desk. "But we'll stay a little longer. I'd just like to ask Betsy a few more questions."

Cal felt his stomach sink. He tried to stay calm. Betsy didn't know anything, so she couldn't tell the police anything, so he had nothing to be concerned about, did he? Still he would rather the police left then and there.

"That's fine with me," he said as he went back into his office. "Ask away."

"What would you gentlemen like to know?" he heard Betsy say eagerly as she closed the door on her way out.

Chapter 5

Cal worked late in the office all week. Not because he had to, or even wanted to, but because he wanted to give Lily some space. The atmosphere in the house was heavy, at least when he was around. Even the girls sensed it, keeping out of their parents' way, playing together without the usual sibling squabbles. It wasn't a healthy situation, but he was damned if he knew what to do about it.

Katy, Katy, Katy. She could have no idea of the hassle she had caused him. He had the police on his back, his wife in a deep sulk and to top it all he was short an assistant and couldn't start looking for a replacement. Until Katy's departure was official he had to maintain the façade that she was coming back. If this had been Manhattan, he would have easily solved the problem with a temp, but such creatures just didn't exist in a place like Leyton.

He looked at his watch. Only seven o'clock. Should he go home? A tense weekend loomed ahead of him and he was in no hurry to start it any sooner than he had to. He slammed the file in front of him shut. He'd had enough of work, but he could waste a couple of hours at the bar before he went home. Who knows, he might even hear the latest gossip about Katy. If Betsy was to be believed, the whole town was talking about it, thinking the worst. He sighed. He'd worked hard since the move to prove he was a regular guy rather than some Manhattan hotshot who thought he was better than them all. To come out with the truth now would ruin his credibility. He had no choice but to stay silent on the

20

subject.

It was a warm September evening, the light just beginning to fade as he stepped outside. Despite the time the streets were fairly busy, one of Leyton's attractions being that the downtown area didn't become a ghost town after six. A couple of first class restaurants brought evening customers from the neighboring villages and there was a diner, a couple of bars, an ice-cream parlor and even a movie theater.

It hadn't been easy making the adjustment from Manhattan to Leyton, but as time passed he had to admit there were plenty of advantages to living here. His morning commute was less than ten minutes; he lived in a five bedroom house with an acre of land and no mortgage. He had breakfast with his wife and kids and, when life was ticking along nicely, he was home before dinner at six.

Cal crossed at the main intersection and headed north. The downtown area of Leyton was centered on a crossroad. Shops and restaurants occupied the blocks closest to the junction. Small family businesses offering everything from computer repair to pet grooming spread out for a couple more blocks, their homely exteriors gradually blending into the residential part of the village, the size of the houses and yards expanding the further one moved from the intersection.

The buzz of a busy bar greeted Cal as he opened the door, but as he made his way to the last remaining barstool he could swear the volume dropped. As he sat down he looked for a familiar face. There were one or two people he was on nodding terms with. Friday night and all his real friends were at home with their families, looking forward to the weekend.

Without being asked the barman plunked a bottle of Budweiser down in front of Cal, turning away without any form of greeting. For a moment Cal thought that maybe the barman was having a bad day too, but as he took a slug of beer he reconsidered. He was being watched. Not openly, but he could see the side-way glances, the quick straightening of the eyes as the watchers realized they were being observed. He'd seen this sort of thing all week, when he went to collect his lunch time sandwich or picked up his dry cleaning. Nobody approached him, nobody said anything, but they were all looking.

He took another swig of his beer.

What the hell were they thinking? Had they put two and two together and come to the conclusion that he'd enticed Katy away to some quiet spot and taken her life, perhaps raping her first, before hiding his handiwork in some deep trench in the forest? Is that what they thought?

He slammed his bottle down on the countertop.

Conversations stopped mid sentence, and for a second all eyes turned towards him, hopeful, perhaps, that he was about to make some grand confession in their midst. As he met their looks with pretend insolence the noise level began to rise again and, disappointed, they turned back to their idle chatter.

Goddamn small towns. In Manhattan he could easily have found a bar where he could forget his troubles. Here, they were just rammed down his throat. Was it purely because he was a relative newcomer and therefore easier to suspect? Or would they dole out this kind of behavior to a native too?

Cal glanced around the bar. Smithson's was a tiny place, favored by the men of the town. Decorated in beige, with a long thin bar that took up almost half the room, a few battered stools alongside, and a narrow shelf-like ledge along the wall opposite to hold the drinks of the standing customers, there was little to entice a woman in. At first Cal hadn't liked it, thinking it old fashioned and chauvinistic, but it slowly became his place of choice when he was on his own.

Cal picked up his beer again.

"Not working tonight, Mr. Miller?"

Cal froze at the sound of the voice behind him. So, it seemed, did everyone else in the place. He stared straight ahead then decided to ignore Rigby's question and carry on drinking. He could see some of the other customers watching, sensing the friction, interested to see it play out. He prayed Rigby wasn't about to create a scene in the bar.

The silence dragged on. Cal resisted the growing temptation to turn round until suddenly Rigby moved away without further comment.

Cal allowed himself to relax. Too soon. A few seconds later Rigby appeared at the opposite end of the bar, in Cal's direct line of vision. There were two other men with him, one of whom looked vaguely familiar. Cal tried to remember where he had met the guy before but came up blank. Were the other two policemen as well? Was this meeting an accident or were they following him?

Rigby grinned and winked at him, then said something to his friends that caused them all to laugh out loud. If they were trying to make him feel uncomfortable they were succeeding, but he was damned if he was going to let them know that. He signaled to Mr. Smithson for another beer.

If Rigby's presence was not a coincidence, it meant the police were watching him. And if they were putting that level of surveillance on him, what conclusions were they coming to? The wrong ones, obviously.

Cal took a large swig of beer. The whole situation was ridiculous. He had to stop it. He'd give it until Monday morning and then he'd call Pearson and tell him the whole story. That would put an end to all this shit. He took another swig of beer.

Rigby was staring at him. Cal held his stare while he finished the remainder of his beer, then signaled to Mr. Smithson for another. Rigby turned to his pals and laughed again. The third beer was plunked in front of him with even less grace. He was getting the impression Mr. Smithson wanted him to leave too. Cal took a mouthful of beer. To hell with the lot of them.

He looked up at the television. There was a college football game on. Not his favorite sport, but it gave him a reason to look up rather than across. Before he knew it he was holding another empty bottle. Three was usually his limit, but Rigby was still at the other end of the bar, chatting and laughing and watching him. No way was he going to let Rigby think he had driven him away. He ordered another beer.

Several beers later, Rigby still showed no signs of leaving. Cal had had enough. He paid his check and headed for the door. There were no farewell comments, not even from the barman.

It was dark outside and the streets were quieter now, the diners, drinkers and moviegoers all inside. Only a small group of teenagers loitered outside the ice cream parlor, their lively chatter and laughter reinforcing Cal's awareness of how isolated he was.

He crossed the street and headed back to his office to collect his car. At the junction he glanced back over his shoulder to check for traffic just in time to see Rigby and his pals emerge from the bar. Halfway to his car he looked back again. Now they were standing at the junction, looking in his direction.

Cal stopped walking. Rigby had been watching him all evening. If he got in his car now Rigby would know he was over the limit. He could have him arrested for drunk driving; possibly even get him locked up for the night.

Cal looked back again. The three men were still there. With a sigh he started walking again, straight past his car and on down the road, past the patrol car waiting just out of sight down the first side road on the right.

He sighed again. It was going to take him a good hour to get home now.

Chapter 6

Lily was downstairs playing with the children when the phone rang. Cal answered it.

"Mr. Miller, Detective Pearson here. I have a few more questions for you about Katy Shore. I was hoping I might be able to talk with you this morning."

Childish giggles drifted up the stairs. Cal imagined Lily's response to another police visit.

"It's not convenient for you to come to the house at the moment. Can't it wait until Monday at the office?"

"Actually, Mr. Miller, I was hoping you'd come down to Leyton station house."

Cal tried to hide his fear. "Why should I do that?"

"Just to help us with our inquiries, that's all. Katy's still missing. It's been over a week."

Cal paused. He was tempted to refuse but then remembered his decision of the previous evening. If he didn't go now, how would it look on Monday when he tried to tell them the truth? He might as well get it over with. But going to the station house? That would just make him look guilty. He decided to offer a compromise. "Why don't we meet at the diner?"

There was a momentary silence before Pearson replied.

"Where ever you want, Mr. Miller. I just thought that after last weekend you might appreciate the privacy of the station."

His words caused a flicker of unease in Cal. What kind of questions were they going to ask? He knew he didn't have anything to hide, but all the same Pearson was right. If he met with the police in the diner, the news would be all over Leyton tonight, adding more fuel to the fire of intrigue ignited by Katy's disappearance. If he was lucky he might be able to get in and out of the station house without anyone noticing. He also might just get away without having to tell Lily about it.

"Okay." He let his reluctance come across loud and clear. He wanted them to know he was doing them a favor. "The station house it is." He looked at his watch. "I should be there within half an hour."

"That's great, Mr. Miller. Thanks."

The phone went dead.

On his way to get his car keys, Cal considered where he should tell Lily he was going. He stopped short and cursed silently. His car was still outside his office. He was either going to have to get Lily to give him a lift downtown or walk.

Or run. He grinned to himself. Of course, there was his answer. He changed into shorts and a T-shirt, pocketed his keys and some cash, and headed down to the playroom. Lily was sitting in the centre of the room with the girls in the midst of a doll's tea party. She looked over at Cal, her expression turning to puzzlement as she took in the way he was dressed.

"I need to clear my head, get some exercise," Cal said. "I thought I'd go for a run." He didn't mention the car. He hadn't had a chance to tell her about his walk the previous evening. By the time he'd arrived home she was already in bed, pretending to be asleep, no keener than he to have the inevitable confrontation, so he'd let it pass. He'd tell her about it later, if he needed to.

She gestured with her head in a way that he took for acknowledgement of his plans. Her silence made him feel wretched. As soon as he got back from the police station he was going to have to put the matter to rest once and for all. They couldn't go on like this. Rather than risk rejection, he blew them all a kiss goodbye—an action that was enthusiastically copied by Amanda and Sophie but ignored by Lily—and hurried out of the room.

Cal pushed open the door of the station house and slipped inside. He was in a gray, functional reception area. Light gray walls, medium gray industrial carpeting and dark gray reception desk. Someone had even painted the wooden bench opposite the desk gray. It might have been meant to look modern and efficient. Actually it was clinical and depressing. A solitary officer sat behind the desk reading a newspaper. He looked young enough to be a boy scout.

He glanced up as Cal approached then eyed Cal's sweaty appearance and breathless demeanor. "Can I help you sir?"

Cal wiped the sweat off his forehead with the back of his hand. "I'm here to see Detective Pearson."

"Mr. Miller?"

Cal nodded. Probably not too many people turned up at the station for interviews in running gear and out of breath. He was already regretting the decision. It was unseasonably hot outside, and after his three mile run he needed a shower, not a confrontation with the police. The station house didn't offer much relief. It was hotter inside than it was out. One slow fan rotated above the desk, its motions barely ruffling the air. Cal hoped it would be cooler in the back office.

The officer picked up a phone, mumbled a few words, listened for a moment and put it back down. He looked across at Cal.

"Detective Pearson will be with you in a few minutes. Why don't you have a seat?" He motioned towards the wooden bench and then went back to his paper.

Cal paced, too much on edge to sit. The run hadn't proved as much a palliative as he'd hoped. While eager to get this whole business behind him, he didn't relish having to admit to Pearson that he had not been strictly honest earlier. He read the posters on the walls, desperate to take his mind off the matter at hand. Neighborhood watch, don't drink and drive, missing children, wanted felons. It made for grim reading.

The outer door swung open with force and Rigby hurried across the room straight to the inner door.

"Any messages?" Rigby hurled his question at the officer as he passed the desk, barely waiting for the answer. If he noticed Cal he didn't give any indication of it.

Cal slumped down onto the bench. He'd harbored the hope that it would just be Pearson he'd be seeing. He was inclined to think that Pearson would be understanding. Not Rigby. Never.

The few minutes became forty-five. He'd had time to stroll to the station, never mind run. He was on the point of walking out when the inner door opened. Another young officer appeared.

"Mr. Miller, can you follow me please?"

The officer led Cal through to a large back room. A series of doors were spaced along the left-hand side. A couple of them had glass panes in the upper half, the rest were solid wood. In the far left-hand corner of the back wall there was an archway closed over with a full size metal gate. The sight of the bars gave Cal the shivers. Old memories never died, they just faded away until some untimely event forced them to the forefront again.

The room itself held four desks, all currently unoccupied, although the mess on one suggested that someone had been working earlier. A half-empty coffee cup stood amongst files and papers, an empty sandwich wrapper and… a photocopied picture of Katy.

The officer gave a sharp tap on one of the solid doors then pushed the door open, gesturing for Cal to go inside. Pearson and Rigby were seated at a small table in the interview room. There were no spare chairs. Rigby leapt up as Cal entered and gestured towards the chair he'd just vacated before propping himself up against the wall. Cal wondered whether the guy was capable of standing up straight unaided. He turned the chair at an angle so that when he sat down his back was towards Rigby. He nodded across to Pearson. "You had some more questions?"

He'd decided on his run in that he'd let the police have their say first. That way he might have a chance to slip the real story in without making too big a deal of it.

Pearson stared at him. There was a hint of disdain in his look. "Mr. Miller, we've reason to believe you haven't been completely honest with us."

Cal forced a contrite look. So much for plan A. It was time for plan B; tell them everything as quickly as possible.

"No, I guess I haven't. I'm sorry."

Behind him Rigby snorted. Cal ignored him. He shuffled uneasily in his chair wondering where to begin.

Pearson beat him to it. "Were you and Katy having an affair?"

"No!"

Pearson raised his eyebrows. Cal stared back. He knew he was on safe ground here.

"Were you and Katy having an affair?" Pearson said again.

Cal exhaled impatiently. If they continued this line of questioning he was just going to get up and walk out.

Pearson looked grim. He pulled a file towards him, extracted a hard-bound blue book decorated with yellow moons and stars, flipped it open to a page marked with a small Post-it note, removed the note and looked across at Cal.

"Let me read you something," he said.

Chapter 7

"January fifth," Pearson read. "Started a new job today working as an Accounts assistant for Cal Miller here in town. Not exactly what I want to do but better than working behind a supermarket counter. Besides, Mr. Miller is kinda cute."

Cal grinned, flattered to know that someone so much younger could still refer to him as cute. Okay, so they'd found Katy's journal. Maybe she'd put her plans in there, so now they knew what was going on. But why the questions about an affair?

Pearson flipped forward to another Post-it note marked page. "March fifth, Mr. Miller took me out to lunch today to talk about my first months on the job. I think he likes me, the way he talks to me—*to me* rather than down to me—the way he looks at me. I love his smile. Shame he's married."

Pearson paused.

Cal stayed silent. So, she'd written that she liked him. That wasn't a crime. Still he could feel heat spreading across his cheeks.

Pearson flipped forward a few more pages.

"March thirtieth. I think I am in love. Every time I see him I feel strange inside. My heart flutters, as if it is trying to get out of my body. Even when I am supposed to be working I find myself thinking about him. Sometimes I imagine telling him what I feel, and his response. How terrible not to tell him and then find out he felt the same way."

Cal thought fast. Katy in love? He hadn't noticed any change in her work. She'd always appeared very efficient and

30

reliable.

Pearson flipped forward again. "May first. I still haven't told him my feelings. I hate myself for being so timid but what if he rebuffs me? Not that I really think he would. He is showing a lot more interest in me now. He uses all sorts of pretexts to talk to me even when he doesn't need to. He seems so relaxed and easy to be with."

Cal shook his head. What was the point of this?

"May fifteenth," Pearson read. "I don't know what to think. Today he brushed against me when we were discussing my work but instead of moving away he moved closer, so that we were touching, arm against arm. Is he sending me a message? Surely if he wasn't interested he would have moved away?"

Cal gulped. He had no memory of the event she was referring to. If he had brushed against her it was unintentional. He liked Katy; she was a nice girl and he felt sorry for her given her family circumstances, but he'd had no idea she was harboring such thoughts about him. Before he could say anything Pearson continued.

"May twenty-second. Today Cal asked me if I would be willing to work late occasionally, as there is a back log of work building up. Work late! I guess with being married he's trying to be discrete, but I can see where this is leading. Of course, I said yes. It's perfect because my family won't ask any questions either if I tell them I'm working late."

Cal covered his face with his hands. The girl was obviously infatuated. How could he have not noticed? He'd made a simple request to her and she had built it into something so much bigger, something it wasn't. No wonder the police thought he was having an affair. More than that, thank God they hadn't brought this to the house. Pearson had been doing him a real favor insisting they meet here.

He looked up, shaking his head. "I had no idea she felt this way about me, believe me. I can't think why she should have thought such things." He gestured helplessly. "I'm a married man. I love my wife. Having an affair with my assistant was the last thing on my mind." He rubbed his forehead with his hand. "Jeez, what did I do to make her think like that?"

"Oh you did plenty," Rigby said from behind him.

31

Cal started to turn, an angry denial on his lips, but stopped as he noticed Pearson shaking his head. At Rigby. "What?"

There was silence in the room, a heavy uneasy silence. With a sinking stomach Cal realized that there was worse to come.

"June eighth. Today he put his arms around me. It felt so good I didn't want him to ever let go. I wish that I could push the relationship forward but feel that he's the one who must do it as he's the one who's already married. I wish he weren't! He held me for a long time, stroking my neck and back. I wanted him to move his hands elsewhere but couldn't get up the courage to ask. We talked about the future and made plans. I feel so happy!"

Pearson paused.

Cal slumped forward, leaning his elbows on the table and resting his head in his hands. What the hell was she talking about? Why had she made this kind of stuff up? He could feel both Pearson and Rigby staring at him, taking in his reaction. He hoped they could see he was as flabbergasted as they must have been on first reading it.

He suddenly jerked upright in his chair. He remembered it. He couldn't be sure of the exact date, but it sounded about right. They'd been working late and he'd come out of his office to find Katy in tears at her desk. He knew she was having problems at home but it seemed it was all coming to a head. He hadn't known what to do, but as she blurted out her story amidst her tears, it had seemed the most natural thing in the world to try and comfort her by putting his arms around her. She had offered no resistance so he'd held her while she told him everything.

He let his mind drift back. How could he have been so blind? He'd leant against the edge of the desk to support himself while she leant against his chest, her tears creating small damp patches on his shirt. He'd had to lean forward to hear her sobbing explanations and, yes, he had memories of gently stroking her neck and back. But in a calming reassuring way, like he would do with Amanda or Sophie. Sex was the last thing on his mind. He was worrying about what he could do to help her.

"Look," he said. "She was distraught. She had problems at home. I comforted her, that was all, plain and simple. I had no idea she was reading anything else into it."

Pearson raised his eyebrows. Cal didn't even dare to turn

and see Rigby's expression. Why were they so reluctant to believe him?

Pearson flipped forward several more pages to the last Post-it note in the book.

"June fifteenth. Tonight we made love."

Cal froze. He could feel the color draining from his face.

"He called me into his office," Pearson read. "He said my name in a teasing, languid way. I knew that something was going to happen."

Pearson glanced up at Cal. Cal looked away, swallowing hard to regain his breath.

"He told me to close the door even though there was nobody else in the office then he got up from his desk and took me in his arms. His first kiss was divine, starting off tender, becoming hungry, as if he couldn't get enough of me. I put my arms round his neck and while we were still kissing he started exploring my body with his hands. I thought I would burst."

Cal looked down at his feet. He didn't want to hear any more.

"He slid his hands up my sweater and released my bra with a deft expertise."

Cal closed his eyes.

"When his hands eventually touched my naked breasts explosions of sensation rippled through my body. I had waited so long for this. He stopped kissing me for only as long as it took for him to pull my sweater over my head and move his lips from my mouth to my nipples. His hands then took up their search on my thighs."

"Enough!" Cal couldn't bear to think what else she might have written.

"Well?" Pearson said.

"It's not true." Cal shook his head. "I don't know why, but she's made it up."

"It goes on for quite a few pages." Pearson flipped forward through the pages again. "She remembers it all in great detail. It was obviously a very big event for her."

"It never happened."

Pearson gave him a sly smile. "She's quite complimentary about your technique, you made quite an impression."

"Goddamn it, I said it wasn't me."

"She only had one job, who else could it have been?"

"She must have made it up, imagined it or something. I don't know."

Cal covered his face with his hands again. This was all too much. He had to get out of here as soon as possible. He was aware of movement at his side but he ignored it. How could he convince them he was telling the truth?

Rigby's voice cut through his thoughts.

"Afterwards we lay on the carpet together," Rigby read, "spent and satisfied. I have never felt so happy. We didn't talk; just lay in each other's arms until it was time to leave. When Cal stood up I noticed he had a birthmark above his left buttock, a birthmark in the shape of a C. We laughed about it. He told me very few people knew he had it."

Rigby thumped the book shut. "So what do you think our next question might be?"

Chapter 8

The question was a rhetorical one. Cal ignored it and the police didn't push it, maybe because they already knew the answer from his expression. Rigby dropped the book down on the table in front of Cal. Pearson stood up.

"There's more," he said, "but perhaps you'd rather see for yourself. We'll be back in a few minutes."

Pearson and Rigby left the room, slamming the door behind them. Cal turned at the sound, stared at the door. Was it locked? If he wanted to could he just walk out? Where would he go? This would follow him until he sorted it out. He turned back and looked down at the book; an innocent looking journal, a book that could blow his life apart. He couldn't bring himself to pick it up.

Why had Katy written such things? All he'd done was to try and help her, give her a little support and look how he was being repaid. If this got out to Lily, they were finished. She'd never trust him again. She'd been willing to give him one more chance. He doubted she'd offer a second.

The book lay there on the table, its very presence taunting him. He shut his eyes to block it out. He didn't want to read any more.

But maybe there was something else in there, something that would explain it, something that only he would recognize, but that would show Katy for the liar she was. He opened his eyes and grabbed the book.

At the beginning, which was when she had started working

for him, the entries were repetitive and boring. The one glaring omission, any reference to the problems she was having with her family. Maybe she was afraid they would find the journal. But if she was afraid of that, how come she'd been so open about her supposed relationship with Cal? Had she wanted them to see that? Based on what she'd told Cal, she had to know that it would cause a major crisis when they found out. But to what end?

He flipped forward, past the Post-it notes to the last piece Pearson had read. His throat tightened, his breath became more erratic as he read. She had been quite explicit about what they had supposedly done that night. Even though it wasn't true, the idea of Pearson and Rigby reading it made him shudder.

He continued on through the journal, skimming the pages. His heart sank. According to her, there had been similar trysts at least twice a week since. She'd recorded them in detail in her rounded clear handwriting.

He tossed the book back down on the table and sat back staring at it. He could deny having an affair until he was blue in the face, but why should the police believe him? It was his words against hers. She was a child of the town, born here, grew up here, brothers in the local police force. He was a relative newcomer, of unknown past. He was there, she was missing. In their shoes, who would he believe?

He was beginning to feel like someone had slipped a noose around his neck and, with every revelation, the knot got closer and closer to his throat. Should he be asking for a lawyer? But how could he do that? He hadn't done anything wrong. A lawyer would complicate matters; make it look as if he might be guilty. Besides if he hired a lawyer, Lily would have to know and she would have to know why. No, he had to sort this one out himself.

After all he was innocent. He had to remember that.

He sat and waited for Pearson and Rigby to come back. He tried to be patient, but the mounting rage at the injustice got to him. He'd had enough. It was now almost two hours since he'd left the house. Much longer and he'd have to make up another story for Lily. He knew he was innocent; the police would just have to think what they wanted.

Despite his fears, the door to the interrogation room was not locked. Cal stepped out into the back office. Pearson was sitting at the messy desk. Rigby was perched on the corner of the next desk, swinging his left leg like a pendulum. They both turned to look at Cal.

"Ready to talk now?" Pearson said, as if they were waiting on Cal.

Cal shook his head. "There's nothing to talk about." Then he remembered why he had come to the station house in the first place. "Okay, yes, I do have something to tell you, but it's not related to what's in that book." He shuddered, "That's all a figment of her imagination."

"Some imagination," Rigby said.

Cal glared at him. What on earth was this guy's problem? It was almost as if he had a personal ax to grind.

Pearson led them back into the interview room. Cal slumped down into his chair. Pearson sat opposite. Rigby leant against the wall directly behind Pearson so that he was in Cal's line of vision.

"We're listening," Pearson said a hint of impatience in his voice.

"Katy Shore is not missing." Cal took a deep breath. "She ran away."

There was an audible snigger from Rigby.

Cal ignored him, focusing all his attention on Pearson. "After that day in the office when she broke down, she told me how terrible her home life was, how over-protective her father and brothers were, how she couldn't do anything without them knowing in advance. She felt she was too old to be treated like that, so she decided to leave home."

Cal paused. Pearson nodded at him.

"She knew if she just moved out, her family wouldn't leave her alone. She said she had to leave town, to get away without them knowing, or they'd try to stop her, so she told them she was going to stay with friends for the weekend." Cal paused again. Pearson looked distinctly unimpressed. "Or at least that's what she told me she was going to tell them. Also that she'd written them a letter which she was going to mail on Saturday, which they'd receive on Monday, explaining everything, telling them she wasn't coming back. She figured the weekend would give her long enough to get far enough away without them being able to go after her."

"There was no letter," Rigby said.

"So where is she?" Pearson said.

Cal shook his head. "I don't know. She wouldn't even tell me where she was headed."

"But she told you she was leaving?"

"Yes."

"So why didn't you tell us this last weekend?"

Cal looked down at the floor. "She told me in confidence. I assumed by Monday her father would have got her letter and no harm done."

"But you spoke to us on Sunday," Rigby said.

"Yeah, so?"

"So even if the letter had turned up on Monday, you could have saved her family twenty-four hours of worry."

Cal exhaled heavily. Rigby had him there. "I suppose. But given what she had told me about her family I didn't have a lot of sympathy for them. I guess I was more concerned about protecting Katy."

"Or maybe you hadn't had a chance to think this story up at that point," Rigby said.

"I didn't make it up, it's true."

"Which one? That she had gone away for the weekend or that she's run away from home?"

"Both."

"Both! And you just happen to be the only one who knows anything about either." Rigby laughed. "You're going to have to do better than that, Mr. Miller."

"What do you mean by that?"

Rigby pushed himself away from the wall, crossed the room and sat down on the corner of the table next to Cal. There was a moment of silence while he looked at Cal as if he were weighing him up and not liking what he saw.

"Let's recap, shall we? Katy's your assistant. She claims you were having an affair. You deny it. You tell us Katy went away for the weekend but it seems she forgot to tell anyone else. Then you tell us that that story was only a cover for the fact she's run away, but you can't tell us where to, which means we can't verify your story. So where does that leave us?"

Cal stared straight past Rigby in silence.

"It leaves us with a missing girl and only your word for the fact that she's safe. Rather convenient, don't you think. We believe you, we stop looking for Katy."

Cal looked down at the floor again. He could see only too clearly the police point of view. He would probably think the same if he were on the other side of this. How was he going to get them to believe him?

"How do you think her family would react to that conclusion?" Rigby said. "What are we supposed to do? Go to them and say, o*h, its okay, Mr. Miller says she ran away.*" Rigby leant towards Cal, far too close for comfort. "What the hell makes you think they'll believe you?"

Cal ignored him. He had to get his mind around this. There had to be a simple solution. Just with the pressure of the moment, he wasn't seeing it.

Pearson was watching him intently, judging his every reaction to Rigby's statements, probably already deciding his guilt or innocence right there, from the flicker of Cal's eyes, or the curl of his lips.

Cal forced himself to keep his face straight. He must look innocent.

There was a long silence. Cal sat it out. He didn't have anything else to say so what was the point of talking?

Suddenly Pearson picked up the journal and pushed it back into the file. "That's all you want to say?"

Cal thought of the one other piece of information he could give the police. Problem was, with the current state of affairs it would only make his situation worse. He couldn't be sure whether the police thought they had any grounds for arresting him, but he was not about to give them any additional fodder.

"Yes," he said with more conviction than he felt.

"Well, you'd better start praying that Katy makes contact, and soon, because that sounds like one very dubious story."

"It's true."

"So you keep saying." Pearson nodded towards the door. "You can go." He glanced at Rigby. "See Mr. Miller out, will you."

Cal was taken aback at the abrupt dismissal. Relief at being let go mingled with anger at the inconclusive nature of the meeting. He'd wanted to go home with a clear conscience. He'd been prepared for a reprimand. Instead he was leaving under a bigger cloud of guilt, the hurdles to clearing his involvement in Katy's disappearance looming larger and larger.

Chapter 9

"Clear your head?" Lily spoke to the potato she was peeling, a sure sign that she was still mad at him.

"What?"

"The run, did it clear your head?"

"Yeah." Cal hesitated. Now was the time to tell Lily the truth, explain about Katy's journal. The news of its existence could already be all over town. If she heard about it from someone else and then found out he already knew, hell, her wrath would be so great, he'd be wishing he was a potato.

He watched as her hand moved back and forward across the potato, every other pass revealing what lay beneath the skin. If only it was as easy as that to reveal what he needed to say.

"No." The contradiction came out unintended, but it had an effect. Lily stopped peeling and gave him a puzzled glance. It was now or never. He took a sharp intake of breath. "I've been down to the police station."

"Dressed like that?"

"Pearson called, asked me to go down."

"You ran to the police station?" Lily shook her head. "No you didn't, you've just come back in the car."

Cal grimaced. Why had he thought she wouldn't notice?

"I left the car outside the office last night."

Lily gave him a knowing glance. "So you weren't working late last night?"

"I stopped off for a drink on the way home."

"One drink never stopped you driving before."

"Okay, okay, I had a few."

He had to cut this conversation short. If Lily got upset about his drinking, how would she react when he told her about the police station?

He walked across to Lily, took the potato peeler out of her hand, dropped it in the sink, and put his arms around her. She didn't resist but she didn't yield either. It was like hugging a tree. He kissed her gently on the forehead.

"I love you, you know that?" he whispered.

Lily remained silent.

Cal nestled his cheek against hers. "You know I wouldn't do anything to hurt you."

Lily pulled away. "But…?"

Cal looked at her face. Her eyes were full of pain and fear, had been since last weekend. What kinds of scenarios were running through her mind? Damn it. They should have talked about it straight away, got it out in the open. He remembered back. He'd been willing. It was Lily who'd closed the door first on their conversation. It was Lily who put the barriers up.

Lily took a step backwards, the color draining from her face, and covered her mouth with her hand. Her eyes widened. "Oh my God! Cal, what have you done?"

"Nothing!"

"Cal?"

"I swear to God, I haven't done anything."

"It's rude to swear, isn't it Mummy?"

Cal and Lily spun round at the sound of Amanda's voice.

Amanda raced across the kitchen and flung her arms around Cal's legs, lifting her head back to look up at him with a cheeky grin. "Daddy's being naughty, Daddy's being naughty." She giggled. Cal tried to extract himself from her clutches but Amanda took his actions as a game and clung on tighter. Cal tussled with her for a couple more minutes before his patience snapped.

"Amanda! Let go now!"

Startled by his ferocity, Amanda sprang back. Her lips puckered into a pout and tears welled in the corners of her eyes. She gave her mother a bewildered glance. "Can I have some milk please?" The words came out as a frightened whisper.

There was silence as Lily poured a glass of milk. Amanda gulped it down, her sidelong glances like daggers in Cal's heart. Was he was a monster to be afraid of? Or was she hoping that the monster in front of her would turn back into her daddy?

As she handed the empty cup back, Lily gave her two small bags of chocolate. "Here, take one of these to Sophie."

Amanda's face lit up at the unexpected treat. She took the chocolates from her mother and skipped out of the room.

Cal watched with envy. If only his problems could be so easily dismissed.

Lily swung round, looking angrier than Cal had ever seen her. "You shouldn't take your frustrations out on the kids."

"No? But it's all right for you to use bribery to get them out of your way?"

"I want to know what the fuck's going on Cal, and now."

Cal was stunned into silence. It was the first time he'd ever heard Lily use the F word.

"And I want the truth."

He felt a twinge in his chest. There was a hint of a threat in her tone. The threat he'd lived under for the last four years, his ongoing punishment for the mistake he'd made. He swallowed hard. Whether he told the truth or not he was probably going to lose her. The tension increased. The idea was unbearable.

"You have to believe me. I haven't done anything wrong." Cal looked down at his feet. "But the police may have a different idea."

"They think you're involved in Katy's disappearance?"

Cal looked back up. "They haven't said as much, but yes, that's the impression I get."

"So what did they say? This morning, I mean?"

Cal took a deep breath. "They showed me Katy's journal."

Lily frowned. "Why would they do that?"

"She mentioned my name."

"You're her boss, that's not too surprising." Lily gave him a weak smile. "Wasn't it very complimentary?"

"It was... in a sexual context."

The smile vanished from Lily's face. Her lower lip dropped open.

"She made it sound as if we were having an affair," Cal said, rushing the words out.

Lily let out a half-strangled sob. Her gaze never left Cal's face.

"She made it all up Lily, I swear."

Lily was silent.

"It's not true, believe me. God knows why, but she made it all up."

Lily still didn't speak.

"Now she's disappeared it's my word against hers." He wished Lily would say something, anything, rather than standing staring at him as if he was an apparition. "It… it doesn't look good, does it?"

Lily began to shake her head.

"I don't know what to do," Cal said, "how to get them to believe me."

Lily let out a full sob. Cal stepped towards her. He wanted to embrace her, tell her it would be all right, but even more, for her to tell him it would be okay.

She brushed straight passed him on her way out of the kitchen.

Chapter 10

Cal listened to her slow, heavy footsteps as Lily went up the stairs. There was a moment of silence and then a door slammed, the sound reverberating through the otherwise quiet house like a gunshot. Cal slumped into the nearest chair, elbows on knees, head in his hands. If Lily wasn't even willing to listen to his explanations, what was he to do?

It was his fault, he couldn't deny that. Four years ago it was all so different. Married to Lily for two years, baby Amanda was almost a year old. He had a demanding but satisfying job, a decent sized apartment on the Upper West side and enough income for Lily to stay at home with the baby and yet for them still to enjoy a decent life. And he'd blown it. From this perspective it was hard to understand why.

True, he'd been under a lot of stress. Pressure at work was at a peak, twelve to fourteen hour days were the norm. At home they were adjusting to being parents. They were sleep deprived, still a little scared at the responsibility of having this new life so dependent on them and, at the same time, resentful of the demands and changes required of them.

Cal knew Lily struggled with the isolation of being a stay-at-home mom after her high caliber marketing job. She hadn't complained, but he'd seen a gradual withdrawal from all the activities they'd enjoyed together. He began to feel excluded, like he shouldn't bother Lily with his work problems or office politics. It was easier to confide in others at work, and he found a very willing listener.

Sheila Blane was a junior accountant in his department, although only a couple of years younger than Cal. Single, vivacious, quick witted and intelligent, Cal found he could talk to her about all the subjects Lily had lost interest in or didn't have time for any more. At first it was an occasional sandwich together at lunchtime, then the odd quick drink after work. All very harmless. Lily knew all about Sheila. They had even met on one of Lily's infrequent visits to his office. It was an office friendship, plain and simple, and it should have stayed that way.

It was the end of a difficult assignment with a cantankerous client. To celebrate, the whole team went out for a drink, leaving the office at five rather than the more normal eight of recent weeks. They found themselves a table at a small bar that opened out into the sidewalk. It felt good to be sitting there, early evening, job well done, watching a city of people pass by. So good it was difficult to leave. As the evening wore on the initial party of eight dwindled until there was only Cal and Sheila left. At some point after that their conversation switched from worldly affairs to personal affairs and, without either of them quite knowing how, they ended up in bed together at Sheila's apartment.

Afterwards Cal was mortified. He'd believed he was the faithful type. That he would never cheat on Lily. He told himself it was a terrible mistake. That he should put it behind him and get on with his married life with a little more vigilance in the future. Sheila agreed. Her dreams of the ideal man didn't include someone already married. Their parting was friendly, let's forget this happened and go on as before. Two weeks later Cal was back in Sheila's apartment. As hard as they tried to keep their friendship on the level the more they found themselves drawn to each other sexually. And sex with Sheila was fun, unfettered by tiredness, crying babies or household chores.

Cal cursed his weakness and daydreamed about Sheila announcing that she was changing jobs, freeing him of all temptation. But there was less at stake for Sheila. She wasn't about to give up a good job for his convenience. So he struggled with his conscience and failed, hated himself for what he was doing, but kept doing it anyway.

Then Lily found out.

Sheila lived in Battery Park. Far enough from Cal and Lily that, except for work, it was unlikely their two worlds would ever collide. Cal didn't know anyone else who lived in that part of town, but Lily had a friend who did. One Monday evening Cal found himself being accused of having an affair. He denied it, and continued to deny it, praying that he would get away with it, vowing to himself that he was finished with Sheila from now on, but all the while digging himself in deeper. Lily gave him about ten minutes to make his excuses. Then she told him about the friend.

He came clean, telling Lily the truth, feeling that with every sentence he was plunging a knife into her heart. She didn't speak, just listened to his flimsy excuses and his declarations of love for her. When he stopped talking, Lily went into the bedroom, packed a bag, picked up Amanda and walked out of the apartment. She didn't even need to use words to tear his heart in two.

The next few days passed in a fog. His secretary called when he didn't show up at work the first morning. He was still sitting in the living room, had been all night, so he told her he was sick. It was true enough.

There was a well-stocked refrigerator and pantry but he barely ate, surviving on coffee, beer and, when the pain got too much, whiskey. When the whiskey ran out he switched to brandy, then vodka, then gin. At some point he put the television on and left it on so that in his moments of wakefulness he could stare at the pictures even if the words didn't make sense to his drink addled mind.

In one of his more lucid sessions he sat through a movie about a couple's marriage breaking up, tears spilling down his cheeks. The stupidity of it all overwhelmed him. He'd had everything and he'd thrown it all away.

Lily saved his life, although at the time he didn't realize it. After four days she came back and found him asleep on the couch, dirty, smelly and unshaved, possibly wearing the same clothes as the day she left. She took in the array of empty liquor bottles, beer cans and unwashed coffee cups, noted that the food supplies were virtually untouched. She collected a few more belongings and, without waking him, left. He might never have known she was there, but after she left she called his brother and on her way out ensured that the apartment door was unlocked so Kieran could get in whether Cal wanted him to or not.

Kieran told Cal exactly what he thought of him. Cal tried to ignore him, but Kieran wouldn't go away. He camped out in the apartment and ordered Cal around like a sergeant major. The dose of tough love was enough to get Cal back to a semblance of his former self and into the office on Monday morning. Cal wasn't sure what the point of being back at work was. It wasn't as if he was doing any. He spent most of the day avoiding Sheila and writing long letters to Lily, telling her how much of a fool he had been and how he couldn't live without her, before putting them through the shredder.

"We've grown apart," he told Kieran that evening. "It's as simple as that."

"Grow back together," was his brother's unhelpful response.

He thought it was the stupidest piece of advice he'd ever heard— and coming from Kieran that was saying something—but it stuck in his mind and took root.

With work and the baby, he and Lily didn't have time for each other any more. The baby was a constant so his work had to be the variable. That was a tough decision. He'd spent the last couple of decades aiming for the top and now he was about to make a deliberate detour. But if that's what it took to get Lily and Amanda back, it was a sacrifice worth making.

He toyed with the idea for days, afraid to call Lily, not knowing whether she'd be willing to hear him out and even less sure of how his plan would work financially. Their lifestyle had a hefty price and given the economic climate it was hard to imagine anyone would be willing to pay him his current salary for less effort.

Another week passed. Lily left a message on the answering machine to tell him she would be bringing Amanda over to the apartment on Saturday for the afternoon while she did some shopping. He saw it as a small window of opportunity to talk to her, ask for forgiveness, tell her his plans and ask her to at least think about it. When the day came he was struck dumb as she walked in, handed over the baby, a baby bag and a manila envelope and then left. She looked pale, tired and upset, but mostly nervous. It was obvious she had made a decision and that her decision was inside the envelope.

It took him a full hour to work up the courage to open it. An hour spent bouncing Amanda on his knees, singing silly songs and letting her crawl all over him as if he were a climbing frame. Eventually she curled up on his knee, put her thumb in her mouth and went to sleep. He waited a good ten minutes before daring to lift her gently from his knees to the couch and then spent another ten minutes staring at the envelope.

The contents made him cry.

Lily was offering him a reprieve, but it came at a price. She wanted them to move out of the city, somewhere small, upstate New York, where they could have a house and Cal could get a less demanding job and they could have a real family life together. Lily was chasing a dream, but Cal was prepared to let her if it gave him a second chance. If she'd suggested they move to Alaska he would have agreed.

Leyton wasn't Alaska, although sometimes it seemed that it might as well have been. Decent accountancy jobs were hard to come by so Cal decided to have a go at working on his own. It had been a gradual build up. He'd nervously watched their savings slowly dwindle until finally he had enough clients to keep the bank manager happy and, more importantly, the flexibility to help make Lily's dream come true. Her dream became his.

The underlying tension the affair left behind was hidden at first by the excitement and hard work required in order to bring off this change. By the time they were settled into Leyton, their renewed happiness was sealed with the arrival of Sophie. Family became their purpose. They were hopeful that there would be a third child, even a fourth. The affair was never mentioned again. The dream had come true. They were both happy.

"Daddy?"

Cal turned at the whisper. Amanda stood wide-eyed and concerned at his side.

"Daddy, why is Mummy crying?"

Chapter 11

"Wow, that's a nasty one," Kieran said after Cal recounted his predicament.

Kieran was a lot more sympathetic this time, but Cal needed more than sympathy.

"Could they arrest me?" he said.

"What for?"

"Katy's disappearance."

"What have they got? A missing girl and a boss who could be lying through his teeth to save his marriage."

Ripples of anger coursed through Cal. "I'm not lying."

"Whatever, I believe you, but think how it must look from their point of view. It's not a crime though."

"What?"

"Having an affair."

"Dammit, I said I wasn't having an affair."

"Calm down Cal, I never said you were. I just said having an affair's not a crime, not in this country at least, so they have no grounds for arrest."

Cal exhaled with relief. He'd just allowed himself to get a little worked up about it all, lost perspective. He could rely on Kieran to lay it all out.

"They were probably just hoping that if they got you down the station, you'd confess," Kieran said.

The anxiety came back full force. "Confess to what? That I was having an affair?"

"No. Your part in Katy's disappearance."

"I told you I had nothing to do with her disappearance."

"Yeah, but why did you lie to the police in the beginning?"

Cal hesitated. "I thought I was helping Katy. I thought they were making a fuss over nothing, so that it didn't matter."

"For a bright guy, sometimes you can be really stupid."

"Yeah, well, it's easy to say that in hindsight. Look Katy confided in me. I thought I was doing her a favor. I just wanted to keep her confidence."

"She hasn't done you any favors by the sound of it."

Cal thought of the journal. "It's almost as if she was trying to set me up."

"Had you given her any reason to?"

"What do you mean?"

"Did she make any advances to you, advances that you may have rejected, made her upset?"

"Advances?" Cal laughed. "You don't know Katy, Kieran. She just wasn't that type of girl."

"On the contrary, I think it's you who didn't know Katy. Sounds to me like she's taken you for one hell of a ride."

Cal was silent. That was exactly the conclusion he had come to. He wanted Kieran to rebut it though, not confirm it.

"You've told them everything now though, the police I mean," Kieran continued.

Cal hesitated. "Yes."

He heard a loud sigh of exasperation from Kieran. "Not fast enough Cal. There was a whole second there that screamed no before you said yes. What haven't you told them?"

"Nothing."

"What's wrong Cal, you think I'm going to go running to the police?"

"I... don't want to get you involved."

"So why'd you call me in the first place?"

"Because I needed to unload on someone."

"You try Lily?"

"Not funny."

There was a pause.

"How's she taking it?" Kieran said.

"She hasn't left me."

"That's a good sign."

"Yet."

"She doesn't believe you?"

"I'm not sure. It's opened old wounds, wounds that weren't healed as well as I'd hoped. I think she doesn't know what to believe." Cal felt himself choking up. "I think she's prepared to believe the worst."

"Shit, I'm sorry."

"My fault." Cal sighed. "They say your past will come back to haunt you. I guess it's my turn. The stupid thing is that I thought we were doing so well." He stared unseeing out of the window. "How can you be so wrong?"

"Yeah, well, just make sure you're not wrong about coming clean with the police. I don't want to be visiting you in prison the next time I see you."

"You've just said they had no grounds to arrest me."

Kieran laughed. "It was a joke Cal, just a joke. Don't go losing your sense of humor on me. Then you'd really have me worried."

"Worried! You should try living under suspicion."

"Feeling sorry for yourself?"

"Fuck it, why shouldn't I be? You have no idea what it's like."

"Cal!"

"I live in a town where most of the population thinks I had something to do with Katy's disappearance. They don't even know me and they're imagining… imagining God knows what."

"Has someone said something?"

"No, but it's there in the air. They even look at me different. As if they're frightened to come too close. The town's suspicious, the police are suspicious, even my goddamn wife's suspicious."

"Maybe you should try and get away for a while. Let this whole thing die down a little."

"Won't that make me look even guiltier, if I disappear too?"

"Not disappear, Cal. Just take a break."

"Besides, I can't. Who'd look after the business? As it is I have to cope on my own."

"Well take a few days off. You and Lily go away. It'll do you good. Give you a chance to talk without interruptions. Leave the kids with Mom and Dad. You know they'll be delighted to have them."

"I'm not sure Lily would agree to go anywhere with me at the moment."

"It would be good for everybody."

"Tell me this, Kieran. What happens if Katy never turns up? What then? How can I prove to Lily that I wasn't unfaithful? How can I get the police off my back, the townspeople to stop thinking I'm the potential murderer in their midst?"

Kieran was silent.

"You haven't got an answer for me, have you?"

"A couple of suggestions."

"This should be interesting. Fire away."

"Move away. Start again where nobody knows about this."

"Great, so I get to live under a cloud of suspicion for the rest of my life. And the other alternative?"

"Find Katy yourself."

Chapter 12

Cal stared at the figures in front of him. They were meaningless, just columns and columns of numbers.

He glanced at his watch then rubbed his face with his hands. He had to concentrate. These numbers meant a lot to Marc Coulson. They were projected income and expenses for a business plan to extend his gardening business. With any luck they would convince the bank to loan him the capital he needed. The figures were a numerical representation of his dreams.

The two men had worked long and hard to put the loan application together, Cal shaping the numbers, Marc the words. They should mean a lot to Cal too. If Marc was successful there would be plenty more work for his accountant. He just had to concentrate.

Find Katy yourself. What kind of advice was that? The police had been looking for a week with no success, so what chance would one individual have? Even if he did know something the police didn't.

He'd toyed with the idea of putting a notice in a newspaper, but which one? The chances of a particular person picking up a particular paper on a particular day were off the scale. He couldn't recall ever seeing Katy read a newspaper, but it would show willingness on his part.

Or would it? Why should he have to prove anything? He ditched the idea.

A movement at his office door distracted him. Betsy stood

there, the black diary in hand. "Ed Jones just called. He's canceled the meeting for tomorrow morning."

"Okay," Cal said. "When's it been rescheduled for?"

"It hasn't. He said he'd have to get back to us, he wasn't sure when would be convenient."

Cal frowned. Two weeks ago Ed had called, pushing for a meeting as soon as possible, some kind of problem with the IRS. He'd finally agreed to wait until Cal could fit him in rather than go elsewhere, so after waiting why would he cancel the day before and not reschedule? It didn't make sense.

"Let me have his number, I'll give him a call."

"I asked him if he wanted to speak to you." Betsy's tone dared Cal to doubt her efficiency. "He said it wasn't necessary, he only called to cancel the meeting."

"The number, Betsy."

"Leyton, four, three, zero, two."

Cal scribbled the number on his pad.

"I'll be leaving in a few minutes," Betsy said.

Cal looked at his watch. Almost one o'clock? Where had the morning gone? Four hours and he hadn't done any productive work. He had to concentrate.

"That's fine, thanks Betsy." Cal forced a smile. "See you tomorrow."

Betsy started to walk away and then stopped. "Oh by the way, there are some messages in Katy's mail box. I thought you might want to take a look. Not all the clients know she's not here. There might be something important."

Cal scribbled the word *messages* under Ed Jones' phone number. "Okay, I'll check them out," he said looking back down at Marc Coulson's figures. The figures unsettled him. He was sure there was something wrong, but he couldn't see what.

He sighed. He had to concentrate.

Two hours later Cal tossed his pen down on the desk. Coulson's report was as good as it was going to get. He needed a break. He slipped his jacket on and headed out to the deli opposite his office. With only a few minutes to closing time the place was empty except for the owners. Jim Grainger was in front of the counter, a broom in hand, while his wife Peggy sealed containers of food and transferred them to the giant refrigerators at the back of the store.

"You've only just made it today," Peggy said rinsing her hands at the sink. "What can I get for you?"

Cal glanced at the tubs of food still on display.

"Chicken salad with lettuce on brown." He smiled at Peggy. She smiled back. The small gesture cheered Cal. He realized that one of the reasons he'd left lunch so late was that he wanted to avoid the other customers. It wasn't that they said anything to him. Most of the time they went out of their way to pretend they hadn't noticed him. What could he say to make them change their attitude towards him?

Jim stopped sweeping and looked over at Cal. "Any word from Katy yet?"

Cal shrugged and shook his head. "Nothing."

"I hear the police were going to search the woods north of here today."

A cold shiver enveloped Cal. "Search the woods?"

"Yeah, they were asking for volunteers to help this morning."

Cal nodded. He didn't have to tell Jim that he hadn't been asked to help. "They're wasting their time."

"I guess they've got no choice," Jim said. "She's been gone over a week. They have to be seen to be doing something. I guess they think if she were still alive she'd have made contact with the family by now, she must know they'd be worried." He pursed his lips. "One small phone call or a letter, it's not going to give her ultimate location away is it?"

"There was supposed to be a letter."

Jim propped the broom against the wall and sat down in a nearby chair. "Let's face it Cal, there's no letter."

"She said she was going to send one." Cal glared at Jim through narrowed eyes. Jim and Peggy were two of the few in town who'd bothered to ask him his side of the story. He'd thought they were willing to believe him. Apparently he was wrong about that too. Come to think of it he was proving to be a lousy judge of character these days. "So now you're saying you don't believe me?"

"I didn't say that. I just said there's not going to be a letter. Even if she mailed it from California on Saturday it would be here by now."

"Maybe it got lost."

"Maybe, but that would only make the situation worse." Jim leant back and crossed his legs. "If she thinks they've received the letter she's not going to be in a hurry to make contact, is she?"

"She might never know that anybody's looking for her," Peggy said as she put Cal's wrapped sandwich on the counter. "Not unless the family gets some publicity."

"Publicity?"

"In the papers. Or on the nightly news." Jim paused. "Of course if she's left the area it would have to be the national news."

Cal blanched. Local suspicion was bad enough. If this went national he could find himself being judged on television before there was any evidence a crime had been committed. He shuddered to think of the impact on Lily and the girls, not to mention the rest of his family and friends.

"It would be for the best," Jim said. "Either Katy will see the report and come forward or someone else will recognize her and notify the police." Jim smiled. "End of problem."

Was Jim kidding? End of problem for whom? Sure Katy needed to be found, but not in the glare of national publicity. The media would stick him with enough mud to last a lifetime.

He closed his eyes. For a moment he could see a tabloid spread of Katy's journal outlining the supposed affair. Lurid black headlines sensationalizing the story; an out of focus picture of Cal taken by some snoopy photographer as Cal left the office, home or even the deli; the inadequate disclaimer underneath, *Mr. Miller denies the affair.* He shuddered. He opened his eyes and realized he was standing, shaking his head at Jim.

"This is a nightmare." He turned towards the door. "An absolute nightmare."

"Cal, your sandwich," Peggy called out.

Cal looked back over his shoulder. Peggy held the sandwich out towards him. Chicken and lettuce on brown. Katy's favorite.

"I've lost my appetite," he said and walked out before Peggy could insist.

Chapter 13

Cal checked in both directions for possible photographers before he charged across the street and into his office. He took the stairs two at a time, slammed the door behind him, flicked the lock and rushed to close the blinds at the windows. Only then did he allow himself to relax a little. His heart pounded, more than was justified by his short sprint from the deli. He took off his jacket, perched on the corner of his desk and sank his face into his hands.

What was he going to do? How could his life turn upside down so quickly? It had to be a nightmare. He pushed his face further into his hands. In a moment he'd wake up, find himself in bed next to Lily, their legs entangled. He'd kiss her gently; give her a good morning hug before getting up to start his day. He'd arrive at the office, Betsy would be checking the diary, Katy booting up her computer. Everything would be normal, and when he remembered his dream he would be grateful for the good life he had.

His fingertips were tight against his eyelids. He took two deep breaths, shook his head and ordered himself to wake up. Slowly he dragged his fingers down his face and opened his eyes. He slumped. He was still in his office.

His mind went blank. It was all too much to comprehend. He switched his gaze to his desktop; Marc Coulson's report, Ed Jones' telephone number, the reminder to check Katy's messages. Given what he was going through did any of it really matter?

He debated packing up and going home. He was going to

have to tell Lily about the police search. Unless some neighbor had already taken it upon themselves to enlighten her. She would want some answers.

He didn't have any.

Without thinking he picked up the phone and dialed the police station. His call was connected immediately to Pearson.

"I hear the police are searching the woods," Cal said.

"Just part of the investigation," Pearson said.

"You're wasting your time."

"Where is she?"

"I told you. I don't know. But I do know she's alive."

"At the moment we only have your word for it."

"All you're doing is increasing public curiosity. Searching the woods. You're making people think something has happened to her. And the finger of suspicion is pointed at me."

"Is it?" Pearson said dryly.

"You know dammed well it is. Why else wasn't I asked to help in the search?"

Pearson laughed. "You're joking, right?"

"You think I might try to deliberately sabotage the hunt, don't you? Tell me, are her father and brothers helping with the search?"

"Of course they are, her friends too. This is a small town, Mr. Miller. There are families who've been here a long time. They know each other, look out for each other. Something happens to one of them, they want to be involved."

"Does that make them all above suspicion?"

Pearson sighed. "Mr. Miller we've interviewed everyone who knows Katy or might have been involved in her disappearance. That includes family, friends and work colleagues. Nobody else claims to have any knowledge about plans to run away, not even her best friend or her boyfriend. Only you."

Cal frowned. "She had a boyfriend?"

"Does that surprise you?"

"Yes... No... I mean, she never mentioned one."

"Perhaps she had a reason not to."

"Why would she..." Cal broke off mid-sentence as he remembered the journal.

"Not tell her lover about her boyfriend? Oh I'm sure it's a

fairly common ploy," Pearson said, not bothering to hide his sarcasm.

"I'm not her lover." Cal struggled to keep his temper. "I'm not now and never have been. Why don't you go and bug her boyfriend. Maybe he knows something he's not telling."

"Her boyfriend's been questioned. He has a watertight alibi for Friday night. As far as he's concerned, she was planning to work late and then go straight home." Pearson paused. "He's devastated by her disappearance."

"Is he helping with the search today?'

"No."

Cal smirked. "That devastated? Or is he suspect number two, watertight alibi or not, and therefore not welcome either?"

There was a silence for a moment that gave Cal a spark of hope that he might be onto something, but when Pearson spoke again his voice was cold and hostile.

"Here's a question for you Mr. Miller. Why would you want to volunteer to help in a search when you're so adamant that we're not going to find anything?"

The phone went dead.

Cal sat with the phone to his ear for several seconds. He was beginning to think he should crawl into a small dark space and stay hidden until this was resolved. He'd allowed his paranoia about being under suspicion to totally cloud his thinking. Pearson was right. Who was going to volunteer for a search they knew was futile?

He put the receiver back. He had to develop a thick skin about this. Concentrate on the work, let the police do whatever they needed to do to justify their existence and somehow pretend that it had nothing to do with him.

He picked up the phone again, exhaled heavily and dialed Ed Jones' number. He got a voice mail answer. He waited for the beep.

"Hey Ed, this is Cal Miller. Sorry to hear you had to cancel the meeting tomorrow. Give me a call back and we'll reschedule as soon as possible. Having the IRS on your back is no fun. Speak to you soon."

He scratched through Ed Jones' telephone number on his pad. Maybe he'd be able to help ease the burden off someone else while he waited for his own burden to be lifted. He put the receiver down and glanced at his watch. Five o'clock. Too early to go home. He might as well do the messages too.

While he waited to get online he walked round the office switching on lights. With the blinds down and the daylight fading, the office had a gloomy air to it. Or maybe it was his mood. The lights didn't help.

"You've got mail," his computer told him. He returned to his desk and clicked the box. There were two messages. One from Marc Coulson checking on the status of his report, the other from Mrs. Sanderson, just to let him know that she and her husband had decided to switch accountants, no reason given. Could he forward their files to the new guy and send the Sandersons a final bill.

The Sandersons had been one of his first clients, a sweet elderly couple who definitely needed his help with their finances. It had given him a lot of satisfaction to sort it all out, even getting tax refunds for them from earlier years. Three years developing a good relationship and suddenly a curt note saying thank you and goodbye. Except when he re-read the message, Cal realized there was no thank you.

He was tempted to pick up the phone and call them but decided against it. After his call to Pearson he was still feeling antagonistic. The last thing he wanted to do was to say anything that would upset Mrs. Sanderson. Better to wait until tomorrow when he was feeling a little calmer. Besides it would also give the Sandersons a chance to sleep on their decision after sending the email. Tomorrow they might feel differently.

He switched screen names and entered Katy's password. "You've got mail," the computer told him. There were four messages. Cal scrolled through them, three were work related. He printed them off to remind himself to answer them. The fourth was personal. A friend named Barbara complaining that she hadn't heard from Katy in a while and would Katy please call her.

Cal stared at the message. The email account was meant for work only; that was why he knew Katy's password, but Katy had obviously told some of her friends the address. What were the odds she would try to check it from where ever she was? Incredibly slim, but right now he was willing to grab any lifelines offered. He switched back to his own account and started typing.

Katy, Very Urgent you contact me. Your disappearance has sparked a police investigation. Your letter did not arrive. Please ring asap. Cal

He clicked send, watched as the little egg timer told him to wait and sighed with relief when the computer confirmed the message had been sent. For the first time in days he felt as if he was doing something to help himself.

He checked his watch. Almost six. He shut down the computer. His mood was much lighter now. He knew what he had to do. He had to go home and clear this up with Lily once and for all. Tell her the whole story, let her ask questions, reassure her. He could make her understand. With her support he could get through this ordeal.

He left the three work emails from Katy's account on the centre of his desk for the morning, picked up his jacket, switched off the lights and left the office, locking the door behind him. As he ran down the stairs he slipped his jacket on. Outside on the street he paused for a moment. Should he buy Lily some flowers? No. It would look like a peace offering, an attempt to woo her over, soften her up for what he was about to say. He wanted their reconciliation to be from the heart.

Better to save the gestures for tomorrow. He smiled to himself at the thought as he crossed to the car.

Chapter 14

Cal stacked the plates and a couple of pans in the dishwasher and wiped down the table. Then he glanced around the kitchen looking for other ways to be helpful. As usual the kitchen was spotless; Lily's ability to clean up as she cooked a silent taunt to those, like him, for whom even making a sandwich left the kitchen in need of major attention. He rubbed at an imaginary spot on the counter while he planned his next move.

Dinner had almost been a disaster. His attempts to be cheerful and talkative were met with either stony silence or begrudging grunts. Any illusions he'd had that she'd be pleased he was home on time rapidly disappeared. She looked exhausted. That had to be the problem. He suggested he bathe the girls while she had a break, but she refused his offer and disappeared upstairs with them as soon as dinner was over.

This all didn't lend itself to the heart-to-heart he'd planned. It was going to take a concerted effort to get through to her, but he was still determined to go ahead.

He went into the living room, dimmed the overhead lights and turned on a couple of table lights for ambiance. Then he returned to the kitchen and checked out the pantry. There were several bottles of wine including a couple of Merlots, Lily's favorite. He opened one, put it on a tray and added a couple of crystal wine glasses from a rarely used collection that they'd accumulated as wedding presents. The glasses were dusty from disuse, a sign of how their pre-marriage dreams of entertaining as a couple had gone out the window with the birth of Amanda. While he rinsed the glasses out, Cal considered how many other dreams they'd abandoned.

Lily was still upstairs when he went back to the living room. He set the tray down on a table between two armchairs and paced around the room waiting for her. Much as he tried to think of Lily, his thoughts kept turning to Katy.

Had she tried to set him up?

The idea seemed outrageous. There was nothing to indicate that she harbored any grudges against him. They'd worked well together and despite what she'd written in her journal she'd never given any indication that she was infatuated with him. A sudden shiver coursed through his body. Was it possible she was seriously disturbed and had taken his inability to guess as a form of rebuff? Were the tears and stories about her family an attempt to solicit more than just sympathy? Would that explain why there was no mention of family problems in her journal?

Lily poked her head around the door. "The girls are in bed, will you go and say goodnight." She withdrew before he could answer.

Cal stared at his reflection in the window. He wished he'd never heard of Katy Shore, never taken her on as his assistant, fallen for her stories, tried to do her a favor. If he'd told the police everything on that first morning he wouldn't be in this mess. The police would have no reason to doubt his story.

He frowned.

His thinking was becoming confused. He wasn't in this mess just because of his lack of honesty. For a start the police didn't know some of the… half-truths, as he liked to think of them, that he'd told. Not yet at least. Besides, he was the only one claiming Katy had run away, the only one she claimed to be having an affair with. Even if he'd been upfront the suspicion would still be there.

"Cal." Impatience made Lily's voice strident. "The girls are waiting."

Cal turned at her voice. He wanted her to understand how he was feeling, how desperate he was for her support, but she'd called the words out in passing. There was no one at the door.

Cal trudged upstairs and into the girls' bedroom. They each

had their own room, but since Sophie had moved out of her crib she more often or not ended up sleeping in Amanda's room. Cal and Lily had agreed that, as long as they slept, it seemed pointless to make an issue out of it.

He knelt down beside Sophie's bed and leant over so she could wrap her small warm arms around his neck. He took in the sweet scent of clean child, the baby softness of her skin and listened to the self assured words, "Night, Night, Daddy, I love you," and he wanted to weep in her arms.

"Goodnight Sophie." He disentangled himself from her arms, stood up and pulled the bedcovers up to her chin. "Sleep tight."

He paused for a moment, blinked to dry his eyes, cleared his throat and hoped that the older and wiser Amanda wouldn't notice anything was amiss. He sat down on the edge of her bed. Only her head was visible above the bedclothes. Her eyes were closed. He kissed her on the forehead. Her arms stayed beneath the sheets, her way of showing she was upset. Guilt surged through him. What was he doing to his children? He stroked her forehead.

"Night, night, sweetie," he said.

"Night, Daddy,"

He let his fingers trace gently round her face, across her chubby cheeks. She opened her eyes a fraction and gave him what might have been a smile. His heart skipped a little. With a minor sense of elation he kissed her again on the forehead.

"Sleep tight," he said as he rose and left the room. It was a ridiculous situation. His level of happiness now depended on the responses of a five-year-old.

Lily was in the living room when he went back in, curled up in her favorite chair, a glass of wine in her hands. She had poured the second glass and placed it on a side table on the other side of the room.

She looked up as he entered. "We need to talk," she said before he could speak.

Cal's elation disappeared. Given the severity of her voice he wondered where he might be spending the night. He sat down in the chair Lily had selected for him; one as far away as possible, not a good sign.

"Thanks." He raised his glass towards her in a salute. He took a sip of wine and waited for her to begin. Better to let her set the tone of the conversation.

Lily put her glass down with a sigh.

"I need to know exactly what is going on here," she said. "If you've been having an affair with Katy, I want to know the truth." She put her hand up as Cal made to speak. "I want to know why the police think you're involved in Katy's disappearance, if that is what it is." There was a slight croak to her voice. "And I want to know where you think we, as a family, stand in all this."

"I promise you I am not and never have been having an affair with Katy."

Lily's nod in response was barely perceptible.

"Do you believe me?"

"I'll try," Lily said.

"When you confronted me about Sheila I told you the truth, didn't I?" Cal pleaded, desperate for her outright approval. It was pitiful to beg like this, but where Lily was concerned he already knew he had no dignity. "I'm doing the same now, please, please believe me."

"I said I'll try. What more can you expect?"

Expect? This wasn't about expectations, this was about needs. He needed Lily to be by his side, going through this with him. With Lily there was a reason to fight, however big the odds against him. Without her what was the point? He might as well walk into the police station with his hands in the air and let them do what they wanted with him.

"I learnt my lesson with Sheila, Lily. You're too important to me."

"I learnt a lesson too," Lily said, "only a different one. Harder to absorb."

"You don't trust me?"

"I want to." Lily hesitated. "I used to."

"I did everything you asked, gave up my job, moved here, away from friends, family."

"So you did. You changed your life." Lily turned her head away. "But have you changed?"

"What do you mean?"

"You always said that you didn't love Sheila, that you just found yourself sexually attracted to her." Lily took a large gulp of wine. "How do I know it wasn't the same with Katy? Did she offer and you couldn't say no?"

"No!"

"Did she run away because of you?"

Cal started at the question. "No! She ran away from her family. They were stifling her lifestyle."

"Did she write about that too in her journal?"

Cal shook his head. "That's the one thing I don't understand, there was no mention of her family problems."

"And you know why that is?" There was an element of triumph in Lily's voice, the kind that comes from knowing something someone else doesn't. Cal sensed it was probably the last thing he wanted to hear. "She didn't have family problems, not like the ones you mentioned anyway."

"How would you know?"

You'd be amazed at how many people have felt the need to tell me things about Katy. It's hard to tell whether they are telling me because they think they're helping me or whether they're trying to hurt me." Lily took another large gulp of wine. "After all, it does seem like my husband is the main suspect in the disappearance of a village girl. Do you feel sorry for the wife or do you think her guilty by association."

"Lily! What have they told you?"

Lily took a deep breath. "The Shore family has been well-respected in Leyton for generations. So it was a bit of a shock when the current Mrs. Shore ran off and left her husband."

"She died," Cal said. "She died when Katy was eleven."

"No, she didn't, she left. Abandoned her husband and kids and took off to be with some other guy. The family was devastated. I think the only way they could deal with it was to act as if she had died."

"Katy told me she died."

"Katy was probably the hardest hit. She was still a child. Her brothers were all several years older." Lily shook her head. "How could someone abandon their children? It's beyond me."

Cal wondered whether Lily harbored any sympathy for the husband or just assumed he must have done something to deserve it.

"For a couple of years Katy withdrew into herself," Lily said. "She was quiet, well behaved and doing well at school. Then all of a sudden she changed. Whether it was hormonal or what nobody seemed to be sure, but within a few months she was in all sorts of trouble."

"Don't tell me. She let her imagination get the better of her."

Lily grimaced. "Worse than that. She had baby-sitting jobs. She was stealing from the families. At first just small amounts of cash that they left laying around but then other small valuables, the kind of thing you might not immediately notice, so it was difficult to link the disappearances to Katy's baby-sitting."

"Katy? A thief?"

"Not just a thief. One night the parents came home early and found her in bed with a boy from school."

"Whoops," Cal said.

"Not whoops, Cal. This was worse than whoops. Turned out she'd done it several times before and that she was charging the boys."

"Katy?" Cal almost choked on his wine. "Are you sure this isn't all gossip?"

"No. I've heard snippets of the same story from about three different people. As you can imagine the baby-sitting work dried up, so Katy turned her attention in other directions."

"Such as?"

Lily shrugged. "The story gets vague there, but it appears she had some run-ins with the local police. There was talk of her being sent away to one of those special schools for unruly kids, but after missing a couple of weeks of regular school she reappeared as quiet, hardworking Katy Shore again. Never caused another bit of trouble after that."

"Quite the little chameleon, our Katy, isn't she?"

Lily made a face at him. "She went through a tough patch, maybe a bit worse than most, but given her circumstances, is it surprising?"

Cal looked askance at Lily. Sometimes he just didn't understand female logic. "So now you're feeling sorry for her?"

"No, I'm just trying to understand what might make a

68

young girl behave like that."

"Why, so you can believe she threw herself at me and I was too weak to resist?"

"Is that how it happened?"

"You're not even prepared to give me the benefit of the doubt, are you?"

"I told you I want to believe you."

"But you don't."

"I want to," she said, "but I don't know that I can."

They sat in silence.

"Mummy." Sophie's plaintive voice drifted down the stairs. Lily stood up without speaking and left the room. Cal watched her go. He wondered if he called Lily's name she would stop half way up the stairs and come back to him. He doubted it, so he didn't.

So Katy had a past. Was he surprised? Not really. Kids would be kids, trying out new personas, shredding previous ones like discarded skins. Hell, he had quite a past himself. It was all part of growing up. It didn't mean anything much.

Or did it?

Could that have been why her family was so watchful, so restrictive? He couldn't really blame Katy for not wanting to talk about it, it was hardly suitable material for a resume, but it would explain the family situation. He was buoyed for a second until he realized it didn't affect his position one bit.

It wouldn't convince anyone he wasn't having an affair.

More importantly, it wouldn't convince anyone that Katy was alive and well.

Chapter 15

Lily was gone a long time. Cal waited a while before going upstairs to see what was happening. The two girls were asleep. Lily was sitting in a rocking chair in the corner of the room, the rockers creaking rhythmically against the wood floor. At first he thought she was asleep too but as he stood in the doorway she looked up at him.

"Are you coming back downstairs?" he said.

She continued to rock, all the while staring at him as if she was seeing him for the first time.

"Come back downstairs Lily." Cal whispered so as not to disturb the girls. "We can't go on like this."

She nodded.

"I need your help." He paused. "And support."

She nodded again.

He crossed over to her and caught the arm of the chair to stop it rocking then leant over and kissed her on the forehead. "I love you, you know that?"

She looked away.

He put a finger under her chin and turned her face towards him. "I need you Lily. If we don't talk about this now we'll never sort it out." He held out his hand to her. "Come on, let's go back downstairs."

He held his breath while she made her decision. He could see a glisten in her eyes.

"Please," he said.

To his relief she took his hand and allowed him to pull her up. He put his arm around her waist and guided her out of the room and downstairs. There was a robotic gait to her movements that made him uneasy. Maybe she had decided it was easier to just go through the motions with him but had already switched off emotionally.

In the living room she made as if to move away from him and then suddenly flung her arms around him and pulled him close.

He hugged her back. Even in her vulnerability Cal could derive a source of strength. Together they could get through this.

Lily pushed back after a few minutes and moved towards the couch. Cal went with her, sat up close and put his arm around her shoulder. She nestled her head against his left shoulder.

"At the playgroup this morning, everyone was talking about Katy." She let out a deep sigh. "That's when I got all the low down on Katy's past. Some of the moms seemed disappointed that I didn't know more about recent events. As if because she worked for you I had some kind of direct line to what was going on. I explained that I'd only met her briefly a couple of times in the office, but you could sense them digging, trying to work out whether I knew more than I was letting on."

She snuggled up closer to Cal. "It was awful. I wished I hadn't gone. I thought about leaving early but that would just seem to confirm their thoughts, and besides the kids were having a good time."

She paused. Cal knew not to interrupt.

"I guess this kind of thing doesn't happen often in a place like Leyton," she said. "It's become an obsession. Every time the conversation moved onto another subject it ended up back on Katy."

She paused again. "I think they've lost their sense of security. They take their safety for granted here, but if Katy's disappearance was the result of foul play then that safety is shattered. If it could happen to Katy, it could happen to them or their children."

Cal didn't like what he was hearing. "Didn't the possibility that she had run away come up?"

"Tania Shore mentioned it, said that her brother-in-law Brad said the police had to consider it but..." Lily's voice choked up. Cal waited. "A lot of the others were doubtful. After all it's not like she was a teenager. Why does a twenty-one-year-old need to run away? If she wanted to leave Leyton she could go. Legally nobody could stop her. Think of the worry she's causing her family. Why would she do that?"

Cal closed his eyes for a second. It all came back to the missing letter. He offered up a silent prayer. One little letter would clear this up in an instant.

"I don't think she intended to worry her family," he said. "She just wanted to get away. It was an oppressive life. I think she really believed they would try and stop her so she had no choice."

"Tania didn't think so. There was talk of marriage. You know Katy had a boyfriend?"

There was a slight barb to the end of her sentence. A question asked out of politeness, assumptions already made about the answer.

"I didn't, not until today when I spoke to Pearson."

Lily frowned. "You spoke to the police again today? What did they want this time?"

"I rang them."

"You rang them? Why?"

Cal told her as gently as he could.

"I heard about the search," Lily said, "Tania told me, even asked if you were helping."

A spiteful sounding lady, this Tania. "Who's the boyfriend?" he said, hoping to change the subject.

"Some guy called Paul. Seems she's known him a long time, met him through her brothers. He's a policeman too."

So that explained the watertight alibi. The boyfriend was probably on duty on Friday night. Would also explain why he wasn't part of the search. Too much personal involvement to be included on the case. Cal's heart began to pound a little faster. Could also explain why Katy was so keen to run away. A boyfriend who's a friend of the family, and a cop to boot. Maybe he was only her boyfriend because the family had imposed him on her. Maybe the talk of marriage, with its relative permanence, scared her enough to want to leave.

Lily lifted her head from his chest. "What is it Cal?"

He told her.

Lily looked doubtful. "I think you'd have a hard job getting the family to accept that, or the police for that matter. For a start, why wouldn't Katy have told you about her boyfriend and the marriage plans if it were such a big issue to her? You said she told you everything else."

Did she though? Cal thought of Pearson's answer to that very same question. If Lily had not got there on her own yet, now was not the time to enlighten her. Damn, he was doing this all wrong. He wanted to be honest with Lily, but it was harder than he thought. He was trying to convince her of his fidelity. Adding extra doubts wasn't going to help his case any.

He wrapped his right arm across Lily and hugged her tight.

"I'm beginning to feel I've stumbled into some surreal world where I'm fighting a one-sided battle. Everybody against me." He let out a deep breath and waited for Lily to contradict him. "But I know what's right and I know I haven't done anything wrong. What I don't know at the moment is how to prove it." He tightened his grip on Lily. "I hate to think that I'm causing you or the girls any anguish or discomfort." Another deep breath. "Everything I've told you is the truth. I need you to believe me. Somehow this will work itself out."

He loosened his grip and pushed Lily back a little so he could look straight into her face. "Please, please don't give upon me now."

Lily stared into his eyes as if she could see the answer there. She stared for a long time until he started feeling uncomfortable but he didn't flinch. He wanted to put the words into her mouth to make sure they were the right ones but he kept quiet. She continued to stare. She was taking too long to answer. His hope began to fade. Yes was a quickly given answer. It was harder to say no.

Lily gave a little cough to clear her throat, shook her head a fraction. His hope faded even more.

"I love you more than you can know," she said.

It was there, invisible but present. *But*...

"I don't know what to make of Katy's disappearance but I can't believe for a moment that, even if she'd come to any harm, you had anything to do with it." She paused then continued in a lower voice. "I pray to God that I'm not wrong."

Cal shook his head, eager for her to continue. That but was still there.

"I want to believe you haven't had an affair with Katy. A few years ago I'd have sworn you weren't that kind of guy either." She looked at him with such pain in her eyes he had to turn his head away. "I would have been wrong then."

Cal's chest began to constrict. It was coming, any minute now. *Sorry, but...* He held his breath.

"I hope I'm not wrong now. I don't want to leave you, give up on everything we've worked so hard for."

Cal exhaled with relief. Lily continued.

"I'll fight for us, for our marriage, but you have to know this. This has to be all, it has to be the truth. If there's anything else, any more surprises, it's over."

There it was. His lifeline. The first tangible sign of support in over a week, and from the most important source. True it came with conditions, but under the circumstances what could he expect? He'd lost the right to unconditional trust.

He pulled Lily into his arms and held her tight.

"Thank you," he whispered into her ear, "I won't let you down."

He was glad she couldn't see his face now. Concern had overtaken the initial elation. No more surprises, she'd said.

There was a tight knot already forming in the base of his stomach.

They sat side by side on the sofa sipping their wine. They were all talked out. Neither one had been able to come up with a solution that would put this matter to rest once and for all, but at least they were both on the same side. After a lengthy but comfortable silence Lily kissed him goodnight and went to bed.

Cal was going to follow suit, he just wanted to catch some evening news. He turned on the TV and flicked through the channels. It was the usual round of heated studio debates on all the cable channels. He watched for a moment, lost his patience with the verbal diatribes and turned to the local channel.

"And in other news, police in Leyton today began searching the woods round the town for missing resident Katy

Shore."

The visual switched from a studio shot of the female anchor to a taped scene from the woods. The voice over continued. "Concern has grown for the woman who has been missing for over a week now."

Cal watched mesmerized as several of his neighbors appeared on screen, eyes to the ground, slowly moving forward, prodding any suspicious bumps or piles in the undergrowth with sticks. "The search is believed to have been prompted by the discovery of Miss Shore's journal, which police say could shed new light on the investigation."

Cal's jaw fell open.

A picture of Katy flashed up on the screen. "Miss Shore was last seen on Friday September 5th at the offices of accounting firm Miller & Associates where she worked."

The outside of his office appeared on screen. Cal watched as he came out of the office, paused, smiled and then crossed to his car. He didn't look like a man who was concerned about the whereabouts of a missing employee. He looked like a man who was feeling pleased with himself.

"Mr. Miller is assisting police with their inquiries," the voice said. "Finally in Chichester…"

Cal sat staring at the TV screen, unaware that the image had changed, so strongly was it etched in his mind. The publicity had started. The press was out there, outside his office today. Where would they be tomorrow?

He looked over his shoulder towards the door and the stairs beyond. He felt sick. He thought of Lily lying in bed upstairs waiting for him. Did this count as a surprise?

Chapter 16

Cal smiled as he turned off the alarm, rolled over and snuggled up to Lily. Ed Jones had canceled their morning meeting so there was some unexpected clear time in his diary and his newly improved relationship with Lily would benefit from a day spent at home. He thought of the reporters waiting outside his office. They were in for a long wait. He smiled again, nudged Lily. She was still in that state of not being quite awake but not fully asleep. His smile broadened. He slipped his arms around her and set to work with his fingers.

Sure enough within minutes Lily was smiling too.

Cal got to the office early the following morning ready to make up for his day off. He unlocked the door, keeping an eye out for approaching strangers, especially ones with microphones or cameras. He was in luck. They hadn't expected him to turn up this early. Not that he was going out of his way to avoid them. He'd made a definite decision the previous day. He was an innocent man, he had to remember that. People could think what they liked. He would just go about his life as normal. This would eventually blow over and until then it was business as usual.

He put the brown paper bag containing his sandwich next to the coffee machine. He would be too busy to stop for lunch today so he'd brought it with him. Amanda had offered him her lunch box but he didn't think pink plastic with a princess on it quite fitted his image. He was a successful self-employed businessman, with a loving wife and two adorable children. He had everything going for him. He couldn't let a small town intrigue knock him off balance.

He set the coffee machine up, taking pleasure from its familiar gurgle. It was the small things in life that brought the most satisfaction. Better to concentrate on those than worry about the larger events over which he had no control.

He switched on his computer and flicked through the pile of yesterday's mail that Betsy had left on his desk. As he finished he noticed the envelope set off to one side with his name inscribed in Betsy's neat script. He ripped it open. The note was very short. He read it twice before letting the paper fall from his fingers to the desk. In a daze he went back to the outer office and looked around, taking in Betsy's desk, clear save for the office diary opened to today's page. He checked the drawers. They contained only office supplies.

He went back to his desk, flopped down in his seat and picked up the letter again. She was sorry, but she didn't think it was appropriate to be working for him at this time. She was giving him a week's notice but she had over a week's holiday due so she was taking that in lieu. Could he forward her final check?

The bitch.

He tossed the letter back down. Three years and she just walked out, just like that. He'd paid her well, knowing that despite her age she needed to work. He'd let her pick her hours, gave her paid leave when she had to visit her sick sister, and this was how he was repaid?

He slumped lower in his chair. Betsy needed to work. Resigning was not a decision she would have made lightly, but having made it, it spoke volumes about what she was thinking of Cal. What kind of message was this going to send to others?

The phone rang. It took Cal a couple of rings to realize that he had to answer it.

"Hey Cal, Bud Laker." The pharmacist sounded surprised to be talking to Cal. No doubt he'd expected Betsy. "You're an early bird."

"Well, you know how it is. Pressure of work." Cal forced a laugh, "Got to keep the clients satisfied."

"Glad to hear you're busy," Bud said.

Cal frowned. Bud's voice didn't sound glad.

"Look, about that work I was going to send over this week." Bud hesitated. "We've got a few problems. We'll have to hold off for a couple of weeks or so."

"What kind of problems Bud, maybe I can help?"

There was an uncomfortable silence before Bud replied. "I don't think so. Not at the moment. We need more time. More time to get the information together."

"I thought it was all ready."

"Yeah, well, so did I." Cal could almost hear Bud choosing his words. "But I was wrong. And the shop's so busy I don't have time to deal with it right now."

Cal sighed. Why didn't Bud just come right out and say it? "Okay, but we shouldn't wait too long to get started. You've got reporting deadlines to meet."

"Of course, a couple of weeks should do the trick."

A couple of weeks? Is that what they thought, that in a couple of weeks he'd be proved innocent or guilty but until then they'd rather not know him?

"Okay Bud, you get back to me when you're ready."

"Will do. Bye."

The speed with which Bud hung up confirmed Cal's misgivings. He'd be lucky to hear from Bud again. Another client lost, the third in three days. At least Bud had the decency to speak to him direct unlike the others. Or had he? Cal looked at his watch. It was only eight. He didn't normally start until nine. Bud had even made that early bird remark. Damn him, he'd probably been hoping to just leave a message.

The coffee machine let off a final loud gurgle.

The buoyant mood was gone. At this rate the cup of coffee could turn out to be the highlight of the day. Cal filled his mug, opened the counter-top refrigerator and cursed.

There was no milk.

Of course. No Betsy, no milk.

The deli would have milk. If he could face going out. He crossed the room and tweaked the blinds so he could peer through

78

the slats. The street looked deserted, but then again he hadn't seen the cameraman two days ago either. Who knew where they were hiding? Maybe they weren't even at street level. He scanned the windows opposite. Most were shaded. No obvious sign of life.

He let the blind drop back into place. It was a toss up between the risk of being seen or black coffee. Black coffee won easily. He sighed. Cowardice maybe, but it was easy to be full of bravado about something until you actually faced it. He added an extra sugar to his cup to make up for the lack of milk, took a taste and grimaced. Disgusting. Still he needed the caffeine boost. It would have to do.

On his way back to his office he retrieved the diary from Betsy's desk. Jones and Laker were both immediate jobs so their cancellations left holes in his work schedule. That would mean lost income a couple of months down the line, income he could ill afford to lose. He needed to bring some of his work load forward and hope that he picked up more clients later on. Yeah, right, as if anyone was going to pick him as their accountant while he was under suspicion. And how many more of his clients were going to go elsewhere? Just what he needed. Financial worries on top of everything else.

With a thick black marker he crossed out all the time slots allocated to Jones and Laker. The result was a mess, a depressing mess, so he stuck white labels over the blacked out spaces. By the time he finished there were more white spaces than he cared to see, including the whole of the following week.

A week free. Kieran's words came back to him. *Get away for a while.* It was a tempting thought. He could take Lily and the girls to some resort where he could lie by the pool and forget his troubles. He frowned. Could he? Would the police let him go? It would only be a vacation, he would come back, but would they see it like that or would they assume he was about to flee? He could clear the trip first with Pearson, but damn it, why should he have to? On second thought it would be easier to stay home. Besides, the way things were going he doubted they could afford to go away for a week.

The phone rang again. This time he was on the ball.

"Miller Associates," he said, praying it wasn't another departing client.

"Mr. Miller?" The voice, female and confident, was not one he recognized.

"Speaking,"

"Mr. Miller, Judith Knowles of the Leyton Times. I wondered if I could ask you a few......"

Cal slammed the phone down. It rang out again. He stared at it, his mind racing. There was no way the reporter could have dialed the number again so quickly. He grabbed the receiver. "Hello?"

"Cal." Lily's voice was high pitched and agitated. "I thought you should know. There's a group of reporters outside the house."

Chapter 17

It was worse than he thought. Lily told him a full-blown television crew had set up camp outside his house. She'd locked herself and the girls inside and refused to answer the door or the telephone. Cal debated going home. He could tell his side of the story and run the risk of having what he said taken out of context so he looked guilty or stay silent and be assumed guilty because of it. Whatever, it seemed like a no-win situation to him.

He told Lily to sit tight then called Pearson to complain about the reporters, asked him to send a car around to chase them away. Pearson told him that if they weren't breaking any laws or harassing anybody, there was nothing the police could do. Cal argued that he thought Lily was feeling pretty harassed seeing how she had locked herself in the house, but Pearson wasn't having any of it.

"Look, publicity could work in your favor," he said. "The more publicity the case gets, the greater the chance Katy will come forward."

For a moment Cal thought maybe Pearson did believe his story about Katy running away after all.

"Assuming she's in a position to do so," Pearson said, deflating Cal's optimism like a balloon.

So, he was damned if he did and damned if he didn't. What difference did it make? He pushed a few papers into his briefcase, switched off his computer and headed out the door. Pearson's attitude had pissed him off. He wasn't going to let a few media people intimidate Lily. He almost hoped he'd bump into a reporter or two outside of the office. He would enjoy giving them a piece of his mind.

He made the distance to his car unmolested and drove home at twenty miles an hour, only speeding up as he turned the corner into his street. The van, white with a red stripe around the center, Leyton TV in large black letters above the stripe and a large satellite dish perched on the roof, was parked near the end of his drive. The back doors were open wide. Two casually dressed guys sat in the opening. Another leant against the left-hand door. A smart suited woman stood off to the side. Cal slowed down again as he approached.

One of the seated men shouted something and all four leapt into action. The man who'd spoken hoisted a video camera onto his shoulders, the other two disappeared into the van pulling the doors closed behind them, while the woman, as if by magic, produced a microphone and stood in front of his driveway talking to the camera. Cal was forced to stop although the temptation to run her over was strong.

The woman finished talking and walked towards the car. She was middle aged and over made up. Cal recognized her from the local early news show. She gestured at him through the windshield, pointed to the microphone, inviting him to speak. Out of the corner of his eye Cal saw a movement at the upstairs window. Lily's face appeared. She looked tired and frightened.

That decided it for him. He was going to put on a good show for her.

He slid the window on the driver's side down a fraction and spoke through the gap. "Let me park the car and I'll come back and speak to you."

The woman looked back towards the house and then at Cal as if she was weighing up whether she could trust him.

"I want to answer your questions," Cal said.

The woman relented and stepped aside. Cal drove forward and parked in front of the double garage. The cameraman, who had already moved up to the side of the car, kept pace with him. Cal turned off the engine and tried to exit the car in what he hoped was a dignified manner. Not easy when you knew you were being filmed.

"Mr. Miller, do you have any idea what's happened to Katy Shore?" The reporter's first question came at him like an unexpected jab.

Cal took a deep breath. Here was his chance to put over his side of the story. He couldn't afford to blow it. He tried to pick his words carefully. "My understanding is that Katy has left Leyton."

The reporter smiled. "Can you tell us where she is?"

Cal smiled back. "If I could I don't think the police would be conducting the search of the woods, do you?"

"But you have spoken with the police, isn't that correct?"

"Yes."

"Several times, in fact?"

Cal paused. She was trying to lead him in a direction he didn't want to go. "I've done my best to give the police any assistance I can. Like the rest of the residents of Leyton, I'm keen to see the matter resolved as soon as possible."

"The police are still searching the woods."

Cal paused again. That wasn't a question, it was pure insinuation. He glared at the reporter.

"Doesn't it suggest that the police have doubts about the evidence you've provided as to Katy's whereabouts?"

What evidence? There was no evidence. That was the whole goddamn problem. It was his word against others. But if these people didn't already know that he wasn't about to tell them.

"I'm sure the police are just carrying out their job to the best of their ability."

The reporter's lips curled upwards in a tight smile. She looked rather pleased with herself. "How would you describe your relationship with Miss Shore?"

"There was no relationship."

The reporter's smile widened. "I meant your work relationship. She was your employee, right?"

"Yes, she worked for me for several months. She was hardworking and reliable."

"So you would describe her disappearance as out of character?"

"I don't think her work had anything to do with her wish to leave Leyton. Her decision was personal and I can't comment on that."

"Can't or won't?"

Cal had to swallow back a curse. The damn woman was enjoying this. He could tell by the body language, the gleam in her heavily made-up eyes. She thought she was winning this encounter but all she'd done was ask some pointless questions. Or so it seemed. Had he missed something? Whatever, he'd said enough.

"I have no further comment." He turned towards the front door. He wanted to run but made himself walk, shoulders straight, head high, like the innocent man he was. The crew made no attempt to follow him but he could still hear the whirring of the camera. He took out his keys, praying he wouldn't fumble with the lock. As he stepped onto the stoop, the front door opened. He slipped inside, closed the door gently behind him, resisting the urge to slam it, and exhaled with relief. He stood for a moment, drained of energy, then let his briefcase slip from his hands and embraced Lily.

"Thanks," he said, "I was so nervous I'm sure I would've dropped the keys."

Lily just clung to his chest. Cal held her for a few minutes then pushed her back so he could look into her face. Her eyes were red and puffy, her cheeks tear stained and pale. Cal pulled her back towards him.

"I'm sorry, darling," he said, "I am so, so sorry."

Chapter 18

He looked guilty. There was no doubt about it.

Cal sat open mouthed on the sofa, staring at the television. He thought he'd been direct, calm and collected. Instead, there he was, gaze shifting all over the place, responses curt and full of condescension, like a man with something to hide who mistakenly believes he might be clever enough to get away with it.

It was that reporter's fault. Her manner, her attitude, even her looks, had put him on edge. They assumed you were guilty, made you feel guilty and then showed the rest of the world how guilty you looked. He'd seen her do it to other interviewees on television and now she was doing it to him. Whatever happened to fair reporting?

Lily swore he'd come across well but her tone lacked conviction and she struggled to find the right words to console him. If the interview had that effect on his wife, it was hardly going to garner him any new support elsewhere.

As the late news switched to another topic, Cal flicked the television off and stretched out on the sofa, propping his feet up on the arm. Lily had already gone to bed, claiming exhaustion from her stressful day, but Cal suspected she really wanted to put some distance between them. He could tell that privately she was having doubts about the whole business. He wanted to be mad at her. She should have unqualified trust in him. But he only had himself to blame for the fact she didn't.

She'd suggested that she take the girls to stay with her

parents for a couple of days. Cal had asked to think about it, though he knew he would agree in the end. It was only a matter of time before the girls caught on that something was wrong. How could anyone explain what was happening in a way a three or five-year old would understand?

The TV crew had packed up and left after they got their interview, sated for the time being. But, unless events came to an abrupt conclusion within the next twenty-four hours, Cal knew they would be back. Today it was just the local news. It could get worse. On a national scale a missing woman barely registered as newsworthy, but who knew what made one story worth telling while many similar ones slipped through the cracks of public consciousness? Tomorrow he might wake up to find he had CNN or Fox camped on his doorstep.

For a brief second Cal considered whether they shouldn't all go to stay with his in-laws. An image of the TV crews tracking him down jolted him back to reality. His mother-in-law would never forgive him. Such things did not belong in her tidy, ordered life. He doubted even Lily would tell her mother the real reason for her visit until she was forced to.

He sighed, disconsolate. Lily and the girls would go. He would have to stay.

The next few days without Lily and the girls seemed empty and pointless. He went to work as normal, finding excuses to stay late in the office rather than return to a quiet house. Once home he survived on TV dinners in front of rerun movies and the late news. Locally, Katy was still the main topic of the day. The search in the woods continued, but so far all they had found was a couple of old dog bones and a decaying deer's corpse.

The national news still showed no interest in the story. Cal prayed it stayed that way. There had been no sign of reporters, either outside the house or his office, since his television appearance, which in hindsight made him feel that Lily's departure was a little premature. Still, there was no denying that she was more relaxed at her parents' house. When they spoke on the phone she asked only about his work, his meals and whether he was remembering to water the plants. Katy was never mentioned.

On Saturday he couldn't think of anything else to do so he went into the office again. At this rate he was in danger of running out of work. He stayed until six before deciding he'd had enough. On the way home he stopped to pick up a case of beer, a four seasons pizza and an assortment of candy bars. He hadn't eaten candy since he left college, but standing at the check-out with his beer he found himself unable to resist. A sure sign his life needed a little sweetening.

He drove home, deliberately averting his eyes away from the restaurants. Saturday night was family night out, a chance to give Lily a break from cooking and, since their move to Leyton, the highlight of their weekly social calendar. He didn't need any reminders that tonight he was spending the evening at home, alone.

Luck was on his side at last. As he sat down with his impromptu feast he was just in time for the beginning of a Clint Eastwood movie marathon. Five movies in a row, just what he needed to switch off his thoughts and get some inspiration. Clint wouldn't let shit like this happen to him. He'd take action.

Three movies later and the only action Cal had taken was the walk between the sofa and the refrigerator to top up with beer, with the occasional detour to the bathroom. Sometime during the fourth, or it may have been the fifth, he woke up cold and stiff. Dirty Harry was dispatching yet another baddie. It was so easy in the movies—you just took out the enemy and got on with your life. But what happened if you were the enemy?

Cal looked back at the screen. Dirty Harry morphed into Rigby, scowling at him face on. Startled, Cal hit the power button on the remote. The image disappeared into a dot. He stared at the blank screen, daring Rigby to reappear. He didn't. Quite right too, the bastard. Coming round here, stirring up old emotions. Cal would give him more than a piece of his mind the next time he saw him.

That decision made, he staggered up stairs to bed.

He woke to the sound of the telephone. Before he could get his mind round the idea that he should answer it, it stopped. Relieved, he rolled over and went back to sleep. A few minutes later it rang again. He groaned. It stopped. He slipped into a half-doze, half-wakeful state, trying to block out the dull throbbing in his head. The phone rang again.

He fumbled twice before he got it to his ear. "Lo?"

"Cal! Where have you been? This is the third time I've rung since nine o'clock."

Lily.

"I was asleep."

"Asleep! Do you know what time it is?"

With the phone in one hand, he rubbed at his gritty eyes with the other before focusing on his watch. It was one-thirty. He closed his eyes to lessen the tension in his head. "Yes I do."

He could hear Lily's exasperation in the ensuing silence.

As he waited for her to speak he pictured the living room as she would see it. The empty pizza box lay on the coffee table along with candy wrappers and beer cans. There were coffee mugs on the mantel and side table, half read newspapers strewn over the floor. It was a good job she was on the other end of the phone. He had some tidying up to do before she got back. It would take a good hour or so to clear up to Lily's standards. The bathroom and bedroom would no doubt need some attention too. And the kitchen. Two hours.

"What time are you coming home," he asked at last.

"I don't know," Lily said, "that's why I'm calling."

Cal smiled. He was in luck. If she hadn't left her parents yet he had at least three hours before she'd be home.

"I spoke to my parents," Lily said. "They've suggested the girls and I stay a bit longer."

"What?"

"Would you mind if the girls and I stay on?" Now Lily sounded nervous. "You seem to be busy at work at the moment, so it's not as if you'd miss us that much. By the time you get home the girls are often already in bed."

"What did you speak to your parents about?"

A forced laugh came down the line. "You know how much my parents enjoy having the girls with them. They're always complaining they don't see enough of them."

The blood was pounding in his head. "Lily, what did you say to your parents?"

"I told them what was happening."

Cal swallowed hard. "And?"

There was a pause. "They were shocked."

"But supportive?"

"Of course." Lily said too quickly. "That's why they asked me if I wanted to stay up here for a while longer."

"No, Lily. I meant me. Are they supportive of me? Would I be welcome to come and join you on your extended stay?"

There was silence.

Cal sighed. "Well that tells me exactly where I stand with your parents."

"I didn't say anything."

"You didn't have to." Cal could hear the anger in his voice but he did nothing to play it down. "I'm clever like that you know."

"What do you expect them to think?"

"How about that I'm innocent? That they know I'm far too nice a guy to be mixed up in anything like this?"

"They were stunned Cal. They couldn't believe something like this could happen. They didn't know what to make of it."

"Perhaps you didn't do a very good job convincing them."

Lily gasped. "What's that supposed to mean?"

"It's obvious, isn't it? It's hard to convince somebody of something if you don't believe it yourself."

"I can't believe you just said that."

"It's true though, isn't it? What exactly did you tell your folks?"

"Everything."

"Everything?"

Lily didn't respond.

"You told them about the journal?"

Lily didn't respond.

"You told them about the journal." Cal let himself crumple down onto the nearest armchair. "You didn't have to tell them about that."

"Cal, I needed to talk to someone."

"You could have just told them my assistant had disappeared."

"What difference does it make?" Lily was yelling now. "They would have found out about it eventually."

89

"What difference does it make?" Cal raked his hand through his hair. "It only raises the question of whether their son-in-law is cheating on their daughter. Amongst other things."

"I told them you denied there was anything going on between you and Katy."

"Oh, thanks."

"There's no need to be sarcastic."

"Sure there is. I bet your father's already lining up divorce lawyers for you."

"That's a mean thing to say Cal. My father's not like that."

"He didn't ask you to stay, did he? He told you to."

"I'm going to hang up if you don't stop this Cal."

"Why? The truth too hard to take?"

The phone was slammed down. Cal stood with the receiver to his ear long afterwards.

"I would like you to come home now," he murmured down the empty line.

Chapter 19

He called back, got the answering machine. He spent the whole message asking Lily to please pick up the phone. He could imagine her standing beside it, torn with conflict, hand hovering over the receiver. The machine cut him off. He dialed again, openly begged this time. The machine cut him off. The third time, he almost cried. He didn't care if her mother and father were listening. All he wanted was for Lily to pick up the phone. The machine cut him off. The fourth time, his heart leapt as the receiver was picked up before the message could click in.

"Lily!"

"Lily will speak to you tomorrow when hopefully you'll be feeling a little calmer," her father said. "Please do not call again today."

The phone went dead.

Cal hurled the receiver down. It bounced off the coffee table taking a small blue and white china bowl of pot-pourri with it. Fragments of china and dried flowers scattered across the rug. He looked at in despair. One wrong move and the bowl had shattered. One wrong move and his life had shattered.

Cal knew he needed to get out of the house. If he stayed in, all he was going to think about was Lily and the girls. He looked outside. Rain streamed down the windows. It wasn't a day for running or tennis.

He could jump in the car and drive to his in-law's. Yeah, right, and cause a scene in front of the girls. How stupid would that be?

He stood up and retrieved the phone, dialed Kieran's number. His brother would cheer him up.

He got a voice mail. He might have known. Why should a single thirty-year-old male be home on a Sunday afternoon?

He mooched round the house hoping for inspiration. He wasn't in the mood for tidying up. It would have to wait. The house was dark and dreary, matching the sky outside. He didn't bother to switch on any lights. The gloom suited him. Maybe some coffee would help. While he waited for it to brew he surveyed the notices pinned to the refrigerator; preschool schedules, party invitations, dentist appointments and a purple post-it-note in Lily's handwriting saying the library books were due back on Friday.

The girls loved books, often bringing back a dozen at a time. Lily kept a basket in the kitchen especially for them so that they wouldn't get mixed up with their regular books. Cal was sure the library was open on a Sunday afternoon. That was it—he could take the books back, it would be an excuse to get out, and maybe he'd find something diverting to read too.

The library surprised Cal. It was a hive of activity. Parents with preschoolers sat on huge colorful floor cushions in the children's section leafing through picture books. Teens studied at desks in the reference section, and all but one of a bank of computers by the check out desk were being used. He was amazed so many people would use a library on a Sunday. He couldn't remember the last time he'd even been inside one at all.

With a sigh of relief, he put the huge pile of books he'd found in the basket down on the counter. An elderly lady smiled at him from behind the desk.

"They're overdue, I'm afraid," he said, smiling back. "I guess there's a fine due."

The lady looked at the spine of the books. "No, all children's books. No fine."

"Doesn't that encourage people to hang on to the books?"

The lady shook her head. "Most people keep them only as

long as they should." She picked up a book from the pile. "You new here in town?"

"No," Cal said, relieved that he wasn't instantly recognizable everywhere he went. "My wife normally brings the girls to the library."

"I thought I hadn't seen you before." The lady smiled again. "I pride myself on recognizing the regulars."

Cal turned away from the counter before the woman could say anything else. Next she'd be asking who his wife was. He would rather remain anonymous.

"Mr. Miller."

Startled, Cal looked back.

The lady held a blue plastic card out towards him. "I think this must be your daughter's card. It was inside one of the books."

Cal took the card. Sophie Miller was printed in big bold letters above a bar code and the name of the library.

"Thanks," he said, slipping the card into his jacket pocket. The lady continued to smile at him. She hadn't made the connection yet. Before she could Cal gave her a quick salutary wave and crossed over to the fiction section, choosing an aisle where he knew he would be out of her sight.

He browsed through the books on the shelves without seeing the titles. It didn't matter where he went, he felt uncomfortable. After that one interview was repeated several times, he was sure everyone would know who he was, be pointing their fingers at him and whispering behind his back. Perhaps he should have left town.

He tried to concentrate on the books in front of him. He pulled a few out at random and read the jackets. Too many of them were detective novels, ugly crimes often involving young women, the last thing he needed. Finally he settled on a couple of spy thrillers. By the time he was ready to leave, the rain had turned to hail. Pebble-sized drops hit the ground with ferocious intensity. A huddle of people stood near the door, nobody wanting to venture out in the sudden onslaught.

Cal went to the check-out desk. The elderly lady had gone, replaced by a young girl, probably a high school student. He handed the books and Sophie's ticket over the counter.

"This is a child's ticket," the girl said.

"Yes, it's my daughter's."

"You can't use a child's ticket for adult books."

"Why not?"

The girl shrugged. "Library rules. Don't you have your ticket with you?"

"I don't have one."

"I can give you one now if you have your driver's license with you."

Cal hesitated.

"It'll only take a minute." The girl looked towards the door. "You don't want to go out in that anyhow."

Cal handed over his license. The girl went into a small back office, returning with a green card.

"Nice name," the girl said as she waved the card in front of a computer before handing it across to Cal. "Callum. Irish is it?"

"Scottish actually." Cal smiled. "Not that we are Scottish, but my mother always had a soft spot for Celtic names."

The girl laughed. "Mothers are like that, aren't they?" She pushed the books across the counter. "Three weeks, ten cents a day if they're late. Enjoy."

It was still raining pebbles outside. Cal joined the group of people at the door waiting for a break in the storm so they could dash out to their cars. After a few minutes he decided it was pointless. The sky gave no hint of a break anytime soon. There were now a couple of computers free. He could always kill some time on-line.

He scanned the news headlines, national then local, by-passing the one that read 'Hunt for missing woman postponed by rain' then checked the financial pages. Waiting for a download he looked at his neighbors. Two young boys, a couple of students, a woman about the same age as Lily and an elderly man. The download was slow. Cal checked his watch. Four-thirty. The library would be closing in another half-hour. He wished the rain would stop. He wished he had some good news to give Lily.

He wished she were home.

Suddenly he had an idea. He canceled the download and logged onto his email account.

Chapter 20

"You've got mail."

Cal glanced up at his office computer, reached for the mouse and clicked on his mailbox. As he waited for the screen to change he looked back down at the reports in front of him. The figures made dismal reading. Unfortunately they were his. Unless things improved, he and Lily were going to have to make some sharp cut backs in their expenditure. He didn't relish the idea of having to explain it to her. He had yet to mention that he was losing business.

He shifted his gaze back to the screen and his heart skipped a beat. There was one message. From an address called shorekaty.

Barely daring to breathe Cal clicked on READ.

Hi Cal
   Sorry for causing you a hassle. Will be contacting my father today. Hope all's well.
   Katy

He read and reread the message, his smile broadening as he did so. It was over, all over. Katy had made contact. She wasn't missing anymore.

He leapt up, dashed to the window and yanked the blinds open with a crash. Typical, there were no reporters to be seen when he wanted them. He wanted to rush out and wave the message in front of their faces. Who were they to try and tear him down?

Lily. Lily. He had to speak to Lily. He dashed back to his desk, his fingers shaking as he punched in the numbers. "Pick it up, pick it up, pick it up," he mumbled under his breath as the phone rang again and again. "Damn." His father-in-law's monotonous tones told him to leave a message. "Lily! You've got to ring me back as soon as possible. Katy's made contact. It's over darling, it's all over. Ring me back as soon as possible."

Cal cut the connection and dialed the local police station. Pearson wasn't there. The officer on duty asked if it were an emergency. Cal grinned. He couldn't be any more euphoric if he'd been saved from the hangman's noose. He wanted to yell it from the rooftops, tell the whole town that Katy had made contact, but he made do with leaving an urgent message for Pearson.

He paced back and forth across the office, willing the phone to ring. Every few minutes he stopped in front of the computer and stared at the message. This was it. This was going to put him in the clear. Amazing how one little email could have so much power.

He clicked on the print button. Better to have a hard copy just in case. The printer whirred and clattered into action. Four short lines. As the printer fell silent Cal pulled the sheet from the out tray and brought the paper to his lips. Short but sweet, oh so sweet.

All thought of work was forgotten. This was a day for celebration. He'd wait until Lily and Pearson called back, and then go home. He still had that tidying up to do, and he wanted to find the largest bunch of flowers to welcome Lily back.

He hummed as he made himself a coffee. It would be so good to have life back to normal. Just in time too. He might be able to persuade some of his clients against taking their business elsewhere. The figures showed he needed them.

Thoughts of his clients soured his joy. He took his cup and leant against the corner of the window, staring out into the street. Did he want to work for people who could assume he was guilty so easily? Who were prepared to cancel their dealings with him on a whim? He needed the work for sure, but could he forgive Bud Laker or Ed Jones? He would feel uncomfortable sitting opposite the Sandersons discussing their finances, just as he would be facing his neighbors in the street. The mystery of Katy's

96

disappearance might be over, but it had left a huge question mark over his future in Leyton.

And then there was Lily. He loved her with all his heart, but was that enough without trust? A relationship without love might survive—God knows he could think of several loveless marriages just amongst his own family and friends—but without trust the relationship was doomed to either failure or a lifetime of angst and uncertainty.

He had to remember, though, that he'd brought some of this on himself. If he'd never had the affair with Sheila he would have had Lily's unfailing trust. And he could have been more honest about that last evening with Katy.

But to suspect him of murder? He may have managed to fool himself before but now he knew for certain that Lily thought he might have done it. She didn't want to, but she did. And every day from now on, no matter how well their relationship was going, he would have to live with the seeds of doubt that she believed what he told her. What basis was that for a relationship?

He took a large gulp of coffee. He was doing it again. Instead of letting the embers of happiness burst into flames he was busy dowsing them with pessimism. It was because he was on his own. He needed to surround himself with people.

He glanced at the silent phone. So where were they?

An hour passed. He was onto his third cup of coffee. The phone had remained silent. He was on the point of packing up and going home when there was a knock on the outer door. He'd forgotten the door was still locked. There was no need for it now. In a couple of hours he would be old news.

"I got your message. I was passing." Pearson shrugged as if Cal could work the rest out for himself. He appeared disgruntled, not at all like a detective who had just found out that his largest case had been resolved. Cal smiled. Maybe he didn't know.

Without a word he walked across to his desk, picked up the printed email and handed it to Pearson. "It's over."

Pearson took the email without comment. For a short email he took a long time reading it. He looked at his watch, then back at the piece of paper, a frown spreading across his face.

"Well?" Cal said. He looked forward to seeing how Pearson would admit he'd been wrong.

Pearson looked up at Cal. "This is dated yesterday."

There was silence. Pearson didn't need to say any more and Cal couldn't. He was dumb struck by his stupidity. He'd never even looked at the date. He'd read Katy's 'today' and assumed she meant today. But her today was yesterday, and if she'd spoken to her father yesterday he would surely have told Pearson, who would, in turn, have told Cal. Told Cal yesterday, before Cal had even had time to read the email.

"She… didn't speak to her father yesterday?" Cal had to force the question out.

"Her father's out helping with the search this morning."

"Maybe she couldn't get through. Maybe there's something wrong with their phone."

"I've had no trouble getting through."

"Perhaps there's a problem at her end."

Pearson was silent.

"Why would she send me an email saying that if she had no intention of doing it?"

Pearson still didn't speak.

"It's proof that she's alive though. It's dated yesterday, so she had to be alive yesterday to send it. Right?"

"Why would she send you this message at all? How does she know that there's been," Pearson looked back down at the paper, "a hassle, as she calls it?"

"I sent her an email."

"You sent her an email?"

"Last Monday."

"You didn't tell us that."

"It was a long shot. I didn't know I had to."

"We're all working for a common cause."

Were they? Pearson was trying to pin a murder on him. He was trying to find Katy. Some common cause.

"You have a copy?" Pearson said.

"What?"

"Of the email? The one that you sent."

Cal crossed to the computer and pulled up his internet files. He scrolled through his messages, offering up silent thanks that he hadn't deleted it. Pearson peered over his shoulder and read the message.

"It's from a different address."

"What?"

"The address on the reply. It's not the same as the one you sent it to." Pearson waved the paper email. "This says ShoreKaty, that one is ksmiller."

"ShoreKaty must be a personal address. Ksmiller was her work address. It was the only email address I had so I sent my message there. That's why I thought it was a long shot."

"So why didn't she reply from there if she read it there?"

"How the hell should I know?" Cal turned on Pearson in anger. "I'll ask her when I see her, shall I?"

"She also took a week to reply."

"Maybe she only got the message yesterday."

That shut Pearson up. He stared straight at Cal, forcing eye contact. Cal waited for him to back down.

"You have access to Katy's work account?" Pearson said, not shifting his gaze.

"Yes."

"Could I have a look?"

Cal hesitated.

"I can always get a warrant." Pearson shrugged. "If you insist."

Images of policemen carting away his computers and files flooded into Cal's mind. He really would be ruined then. He didn't see he had any choice.

He switched screen names to Katy's account and logged on. Pearson watched his every move. There was mail waiting. Cal clicked on the mailbox. There was one unread message. Cal closed his eyes. The message was his.

Pearson gave him a sarcastic smile. "Any more ideas?"

"There has to be an explanation," Cal said.

"So explain," Pearson said in a tone of voice that sent a shiver down Cal's spine, "how does someone reply to a message they've never even received."

"I don't know," Cal said.

Pearson raised his eyebrows. "I think you can do better than that."

Cal frowned. What was that supposed to mean? He tried to think rationally, difficult with Pearson staring at him. "She must have heard from someone else."

"So you think someone else knows where she is and isn't telling?"

"It's possible."

"Why would they do that?"

Cal couldn't think of one good reason.

"Maybe… maybe she heard about the searches on the news or in the local papers."

"So you think she might still be in the local area." Pearson's expression suggested he didn't think much of that idea either.

"She could have been online, seen something about it on the web, so sent me that email." Cal liked it, it sounded plausible.

"But forgot to contact her father?"

Damn, that was the weak link. Why would Katy say she was going to contact her father and then not do it?

"You look disappointed Mr. Miller."

"What the hell do you expect? I thought this whole nightmare was over."

"Of course you did."

For a second Cal thought there was an element of sympathy in Pearson's tone.

Pearson stood up. "Life's never quite as easy as you'd like, is it?"

Cal didn't reply. He was thinking about Lily and the message he'd left her.

Pearson waved the printed sheet at him. "I'll keep this."

Cal noticed he didn't bother to ask whether he could. "Suit yourself."

"Let me know if you get anymore of these." Pearson folded the message and placed it in the inside pocket of his jacket. "Any help you can give is greatly appreciated."

Like hell, Cal thought as Pearson disappeared through the door without waiting for a reply.

He switched back to Katy's message to him and hit the reply button.

Katy, if you cannot speak to your father please call Detective Pearson at Lewisville police department asap to let him know you are okay. Your disappearance is causing huge problems for me. Cal

He clicked send and watched the egg timer until the message had been sent. Okay, it might have been a complete coincidence that Katy emailed him yesterday without first reading his message, but if that was the case then now she would hopefully realize the mess she had created. There had to be some simple, logical explanation as to why she hadn't spoken to her father. Damn her!

He had to stay calm. Katy was out there. She was alive. He was innocent. He just had to be patient a little longer.

The phone rang. Cal stared at it. It rang again. Pearson calling to apologize because Katy had called her father? It rang again. More likely a nosy reporter who'd managed to get the inside scoop on the email and wanted his personal comments. It rang again. Whatever, it would be bad news. It was turning into that kind of day.

Betsy's efficient tone interrupted, telling the caller that no-one was available at the moment, please leave a message. Cal slumped down in his chair. Much as he hated answering machines, sometimes they were a blessing in disguise.

"Cal, it's Lily, I got your message." He could hear the cautious optimism in her voice. He was torn between the desire to pick up the receiver and seeking solace from her and the dread of her response when she heard that his news was not as good as he'd hoped.

He sat immobilized. How could he be so sure that this whole nightmare was over one minute and plunged further into the puzzle the next?

He let Lily continue, her faltering words indicating that she had expected him to be there. She finished up by telling him she assumed he'd gone home and would phone him there.

Cal sank his face into his hands. She wasn't going to reach him at home either. Not until he could figure out how to explain this latest fiasco. He wanted to reach out, pick up the phone, tell her he loved her, hear her say she loved him back, but he didn't dare. As if to back up his thoughts, Lily rang off without mentioning love at all.

He sighed. A short time ago such a thing would be unthinkable.

Chapter 21

"Sit down."

It was an order not a request, just like the demand that he come back to the station house had been, but at least this time it didn't have threats attached.

Cal remained standing. "What the hell's going on?"

"We'll ask the questions," Pearson said, not bothering to look up from the file he was reading.

Cal glanced round at the officer who had shown him into the interview room. The young guy stood by the door staring at a fascinating invisible spot on the opposite wall.

Cal thought of Pearson's empty threat on the phone. That if Cal wasn't at the station house within half an hour, a couple of officers would be along to escort him. "And believe me," Pearson had added, "they won't try to be discreet."

Cal knew enough about his rights to know the police couldn't force him to go to the station house, not without arresting him first, and what possible grounds could they have for that? Still, he didn't want to risk flashing lights and sirens or the inquisitive press that such an event might drum up, so he complied. But if they wanted his cooperation they were going about it all the wrong way.

He sighed and turned back to Pearson. "Quit with the games."

"You want to talk about playing games?" Pearson said fixing Cal with a glare that made Cal swallow hard. On a scale of one to ten Cal would have rated his current anger at the way he was being treated at about eight. At a conservative guess Pearson had already reached ten. Marc Coulson's joking warning about crossing Pearson flashed into Cal's mind. At least he'd thought it was a joke at the time.

Cal crossed his arms to show that he wasn't about to let Pearson intimidate him then quickly dropped them to his sides as he remembered that crossing your arms in front of your chest was regarded as a defensive gesture.

Pearson waved a piece of paper at Cal. "Let's talk about this one."

Cal recognized Katy's email. "What about it?"

"What kind of game is this?"

Cal frowned. "I'm not sure I follow."

"Is it to show how clever you are, or how stupid we are?"

"What?"

"Didn't you think we'd be able to work out where it came from?"

Cal gasped. "You know where Katy is?"

"You know we don't."

"But you just said-"

"I know what I said." Pearson dropped the paper down onto the table. "I want to know what you think you're doing."

"You tell me, because I sure as hell haven't a clue what you're talking about."

His remark brought a sneer to Pearson's lips. "You like to read, Mr. Miller?"

"What? What's that got to do with anything?"

"How long did you say you'd lived in Leyton?"

"I didn't."

"How long?"

"Three years." Cal sat down in exasperation. "Pearson, where are you going with this?"

Pearson thought for a moment. "How long have you been a member of the library?"

"What has…?"

"How long?"

The curt tone chilled Cal. "A couple of days."

His response elicited a smile from Pearson, who looked at a

hand written note on the desk in front of him. "That's right. Sunday, wasn't it?"

Cal frowned. "How would you know that?"

"I called by first thing this morning."

Cal frowned again. It was only ten-thirty now. The library didn't open until nine. What could have happened at the library to justify this? Pearson was acting as if he was out for blood.

"You a member too?" Cal tried to act casual. Inside he felt anything but.

Pearson scowled. "Why Sunday?"

"Why not?"

"Why, after three years, did you suddenly decide to join the library on Sunday?"

"It doesn't cost anything," Cal said.

"Why Sunday?"

Cal exhaled in frustration. "Because I wanted to take out some books. And they wouldn't let me use Sophie's card." He paused to give Pearson time to understand. "Is that good enough for you?"

Pearson gave an encouraging nod. "That's exactly what the lady in the library said."

Cal stood up, shaking his head. "If you already knew, why the third degree?"

"She remembered you straight away, something about the name."

"What is this all about?"

Pearson was silent for a moment. "Consider it a test."

"A test?"

"Just wanted to see how easy it was for you to tell the truth." Pearson flashed a smile. "Relax, you passed. So far."

Cal glared at Pearson. Maybe he should just walk out. Pearson was the one playing games and Cal was in no mood for it.

"It's amazing what you can do with technology nowadays," Pearson said.

Cal ignored him and turned towards the door.

"Take this email from Katy, for example," Pearson said.

Cal spun back round. "You DO know where she is."

"Don't ask me how they do it," Pearson said. "My wife says I'm technically challenged when it comes to computers, but those guys over in head office, they're pure genius by my standards."

Cal stayed silent, sensing that he was about to hear something that he wasn't going to like.

"Do you know," Pearson said, "that they can tell the exact computer from which an email message is sent?"

Cal didn't say anything.

"For example," Pearson bounced his finger on the email for emphasis. "This one came from the third computer on the right in Leyton library. Late Sunday afternoon." His smiled widened. "Isn't that interesting?"

Cal was speechless.

"Game over." Pearson stood up. "Sit down."

Cal sat.

The two men stared at each other in silence. Cal had no idea how he was supposed to react to Pearson's revelation. All he knew was that Pearson's anger quotient was rocketing ever upwards and he was going to be the target of the ultimate explosion. What could he say in his defense? Did he want to say anything? This misplaced suspicion was beginning to piss him off immensely.

"So let's sum it up," Pearson said, "You receive an email from Katy which has been sent from the local library on the one day and at approximately the same time that you just happen to be there." Pearson put his hands down on the table and leant across so his face was close to Cal's. "I'm right in assuming that you didn't see Katy in the library on Sunday."

Blatant sarcasm. Cal didn't even bother to answer.

"Of course not. Or why would she have needed to email you?" Pearson paused, looking up at the ceiling as if he was deliberating the next point. "So, if Katy didn't send the email, then someone else must have."

Cal looked away.

"You were using the computers," Pearson continued, "this I know without having to ask because that very helpful young lady in the library told me so. She said she thought you'd left, but then she noticed you sitting at the computers." He leant closer to Cal. "Remember?" He lowered his voice as if about to share a confidence. "I think you made quite an impression on her. You seem to be quite an attraction to the young ladies."

Cal glared at him. "Get to the point Pearson."

"Did you send that email to yourself?"

"No."

"I thought you might say that. Is that your final answer?"

"Do I need a lawyer?"

"Do you?"

Cal made as if to stand up. "I'm going."

"No you're not."

"So I do need a lawyer?"

Pearson shrugged. "Not necessarily. But if you didn't send that email then someone else did and chances are you saw them." He turned to the officer at the door. "Bring Mr. Miller a pad of paper and a pen." The officer left. Pearson turned back to Cal. "I want your best description of the other people using the computers at the same time as you."

Cal thought of the kids, the teens, the lady, and… was it one other man? Lily always complained he was shockingly unobservant and apparently she was right. The officer returned, placing a pen and paper in front of Cal before taking up position by the door again.

"I can't remember what they look like."

Pearson slammed his palms down on the tabletop. "This is how I see it. You either sent that email yourself or someone else in the library did. Now if you sent it yourself, you must have been trying to mess up my investigation. People lie to us all the time, it comes with the job, but if you sent that email, that crosses a line. And why would you want to do that?" He paused. "You can see what I'm thinking?"

Cal could see exactly what Pearson was thinking.

"I'll give you a few minutes. Maybe you'll remember better without me around."

The officer stepped aside to let Pearson out and then resumed his position.

Cal scowled at him. "Aren't you going too? I think better on my own."

The officer ignored him.

Memories of school detention flooded back to Cal. He looked at the young officer. Pearson was treating Cal like a kid in front of this guy probably not long out of school himself. It was downright degrading. Well if he thought he was going to force a confession out of Cal he was mistaken. Cal had nothing to hide. Well, nothing important.

Cal pulled his right foot onto the seat of the chair, crossed his arms over his knee, used them as a cushion for his head and stared unseeing at the wall. How could Katy have sent an email from the library? Where the hell was she? And why hadn't she called her father like she said?

He couldn't come up with any answers so his mind drifted to Lily. She'd been indifferent when they'd eventually spoken on the phone the previous day. He'd explained about the email, how elated he'd been when he'd first seen it, how crushed he'd felt when he discovered Katy still hadn't contacted her family. Lily's attitude said it all. He was losing her. That was the only thing that mattered at the moment. Pearson could make all the noise he wanted, threaten to lock him up, whatever, but nothing came close to the threat of losing your wife, not when you still loved her as much as Cal loved Lily.

The officer shuffled his feet and coughed. Cal glanced over at him.

The officer's cheeks flushed. "Um...Detective Pearson wanted you to write those descriptions."

Cal shrugged. "Not too good on memory games."

"You should try. He's got a reputation, this one. Never makes idle threats."

Cal raised his eyebrows. "Is that so?"

The officer nodded.

There was a long silence. The officer shuffled some more. Cal wondered how often the officer—Coyle according to his name badge—had seen Pearson in action. Or was he operating purely on hearsay? He pulled the paper towards him, wrote three words and tossed down the pen.

"Finished." He winked at Coyle. "You can tell Pearson to come back now."

Coyle was gone a long time. Cal watched the minutes tick by on his watch. Pearson's waiting games were becoming a real pain. Finally he decided he had better things to do than sit around in police stations all day. Seeing he had supposedly turned up under his own free will, he reckoned his own free will could tell him it was time to leave.

He opened the door. Coyle was standing outside.

"I have to go," Cal said.

"Pearson will be with you in a minute. Please go back and wait."

There was a hint of panic in Coyle's request, as if he knew he'd be in trouble from Pearson if he let Cal walk out of there. Cal reconsidered. Coyle was just a kid, probably new to the force, just trying to do his job. Pearson was a bully, using his reputation to scare his juniors. Cal didn't want to cause Coyle any trouble.

"A few more minutes," he said then went to sit back down. He was rewarded with an audible sigh of relief from Coyle.

Nine and a half minutes later Pearson sauntered back in. Without a word he picked up the pad of paper, read what Cal had written and tossed the pad back down.

"That's it, is it?" he said. "The best you can do? Man, woman, children?"

"What do you want, an essay?" Cal scowled at Pearson. "It's all irrelevant anyway, isn't it? You know, because that nice young lady in the library would have no doubt told you, that I was using the third computer." He could tell from the look on Pearson's face that he was right. "I didn't see anybody using the computer before I sat down and I sure as hell didn't see anyone using it after I left, so how could I possibly give you any help in determining who did send the message."

Pearson smiled.

Cal smiled back. It was an impasse. Pearson hadn't achieved anything by dragging him down to the station. He stood up.

Pearson stepped towards him. "You're under arrest for obstructing an investigation."

"What?" Cal looked from Pearson to Coyle to see if it was some kind of a joke.

"Book him," Pearson said to Coyle, "then let him call his lawyer."

"I don't have a lawyer," Cal said.

Impatience flickered across Pearson's face. "Help him find a lawyer. There should be a list out front. And don't forget to read him his rights." Coyle nodded. Pearson turned back to Cal. "Sit down, Mr. Miller. You aren't going anywhere."

"But..."

Before Cal could say another word, Pearson was out of the door.

Coyle consulted a card he'd pulled from his breast pocket and read Cal his rights. Then, in an infuriatingly slow manner, he wrote down Cal's personal details and took his fingerprints and photograph. He couldn't resist showing Cal the results of his work. Cal scowled out from the picture, his eyes glazed. It scared Cal to see how easy it would be to look at that photograph and decide the person in it was probably guilty of something.

And what if the press got their hands on it? The reports on the Katy Shore case had become a little predictable, boring even, in the last few days. There was only so much spin you could put on a police search that failed to turn up anything. The news hungry reporters would be all over this. If he wasn't already an unwilling celebrity in town, he would be by morning. He could kiss goodbye to the rest of his business.

He groaned. The office. He'd left the office thinking he'd only be away for an hour or so. The computer was on, the lights, even the coffee machine. He'd have to get somebody to go round and shut things down. He wondered how closely Leyton police officers followed the one telephone call rule.

Coyle gave him a list of local lawyers. He looked at the list in dismay. How was he supposed to know whether Archibald was his man or Vollaro? Just from their names? Why wasn't he one of those people who had a best buddy who was the hottest defense lawyer in town, who'd come charging in and put Pearson firmly in his place, or some stunningly beautiful female like in the movies?

"Take your time," Coyle said.

Cal looked up from the list. There was unmistakable sarcasm in Coyle's voice. Now that Cal was the official bad guy, Coyle knew who was in charge. So much for any thanks for Cal's earlier concerns on his behalf. He should have walked out when he had the chance.

He sighed. Yeah, walked out and given Pearson the

opportunity to arrest him in public. He looked back down at the list. "Just one call?"

Coyle nodded. "One call."

"Okay, I guess that settles it."

Coyle took him out into the main office. Thankfully it was deserted. Coyle pointed out a phone on a desk and then stood off to one side as if to give Cal some privacy. Cal turned his back on Coyle, took a deep breath, picked up the receiver and punched out the number. As the phone rang he closed his eyes, praying that he wouldn't get a voice mail.

The phone was picked up on the third ring. His luck had not deserted him completely.

"Hi."

Just hearing Kieran's voice made Cal feel better. "Kieran, it's Cal. I have a problem."

He cut to the point, outlining his position, asking Kieran to find him a decent lawyer, reading off a few of the names and numbers from the list to help him along. He could hear the shuffle of paper as Kieran made notes. Kieran made no comments until he was finished.

"Don't worry. I'm straight on to it. I'll make the phone calls, get someone down to the station as soon as possible and then I'll drive up myself. We'll have you out on bail before you know it. Then you can buy me dinner tonight, tell me all about it."

Cal looked across the room at the barred doorway. His spirits sank. Kieran could afford to be flippant. He wasn't the one who was going to be stuck in a cell waiting for other people to sort his life out. He remembered what it had been like the last time. He'd felt like a pawn in other people's games, helpless but desperate. He wished he could be so sure his stay here was going to be short.

"I have one more favor," he said.

"Ask away."

"Will you ring Lily? She's at her parents."

There was silence from the other end of the line.

"I was only allowed one call."

The silence continued.

"She needs to know."

"She's your wife."

Cal ignored the dig. "She needs to be told."

There was another silence. Then Kieran sighed. "As long as she doesn't shoot the messenger." He paused. "Sounds like one hell of a mess you've got yourself into."

The lump in Cal's throat threatened to choke him.

"Consider it done," Kieran said, probably sensing he was not going to get a reply. "Hang on in there, brother."

Cal still couldn't reply.

Coyle took him back into the interview room and made him empty his pockets and remove his tie, belt and watch. He itemized everything carefully before placing it in a large brown bag with Cal's name on it. Then he collected up the paperwork, glanced around as if to check he hadn't forgotten anything and left.

Cal heard the lock tumble. He shivered. He'd expected to be taken to a cell. This was better, just a small room, no bars in sight. He stood up and walked round the perimeter of the room. It was a short walk. He sat back down, changing position every few minutes as he tried to get comfortable on the hard wooden chair. Eventually he pulled the second chair up next to his and used it as a rest for his feet. Only then did he allow his mind to turn to his predicament.

One hell of a mess, indeed.

Chapter 22

Cal's stomach rumbled and his mouth felt dry. It was a long time since breakfast and nobody at the station house had even offered him a glass of water. He couldn't be sure how long it had been since Coyle locked the door on him, but it seemed like a lifetime. A lifetime of wondering whether Kieran had found him a lawyer or, more importantly, spoken to Lily.

He tried to imagine the conversation. The two had always gotten on well together, but would Lily's affection for Kieran be tainted by association? Or Kieran's for Lily by her defection? It was asking a lot of Kieran to make that call. He knew he should have called Lily and asked her to tell Kieran, but he'd been afraid that whatever she'd said might have made him cry.

There was a voice outside the door. Cal straightened out of his slouch. At last, his lawyer. But when the door opened it was Rigby who stepped into the room. He pushed the door closed again with his right shoulder and leant back against it, folded his arms across his chest and eyed Cal. Cal wasn't an expert on body language, but the crossed arms on Rigby looked anything but defensive. Then he realized that it wasn't Rigby's stance that was sending goose bumps down his spine. It was his expression. It was pure hate. He looked like he wanted to rip Cal limb from limb.

Cal gulped. Did Pearson know he was here? Or had Rigby come in unnoticed? It wouldn't be difficult, every time he had seen the outer office there had been nobody there. The timing was right too, for Rigby, before Cal met with his lawyer, so that the lawyer wouldn't have a before to compare with the after.

Cal pretended to look down at the floor, but he kept a sidelong fix on Rigby, waiting for his first move. Rigby remained immobile, silent. The tension in the room was palpable, increasing with every heartbeat, suggesting an imminent explosion.

Then Rigby stepped forward. Cal braced himself on the chair.

Rigby took another step forward.

Cal scraped his chair back with his legs.

There was a glint in Rigby's eye. He smiled, but it was a smile full of disgust. Then he shook his head as if he'd decided Cal wasn't worth bothering about and returned to the door. As he pulled it open he glanced back at Cal.

"Do us all a favor," he said, "tell the goddamn truth."

He slammed the door behind him, the noise blocking out Cal's audible gasp of relief. Then curiosity replaced Cal's fear. What truth?

There were loud voices from the outer office, loud enough for Cal to recognize Pearson and Rigby. He strained to listen. They might or might not be fighting over him, but at least they were disagreeing. It could only work to his advantage to have the two cops investigating his case arguing, couldn't it?

He thought of Pearson's attitude towards him, Rigby's look. He was trying to fool himself again. They both wanted to nail him. They were probably only arguing over minor details.

The shouting stopped and the station house went quiet.

Where was his lawyer? Surely he should have been here by now? Could Kieran have been distracted? What if one of the lawyers had turned out to be an attractive woman? But this was an emergency. Cal's emergency. Kieran wouldn't put a woman first, would he? He shouldn't think such thoughts about his brother, but if he ever found out that Kieran had been messing around while he was stuck in this place, there would be hell to pay. Damn, his mistake. One thing he could have guaranteed, Lily would have got him a lawyer, no messing.

The door opened again. Cal tensed.

A wizened white-haired man hobbled into the room. Cal

watched in stunned silence as the guy approached the table, opened his briefcase, took out a pad and pen, placed his briefcase next to the empty chair and straightened his tie before eventually looking across at Cal.

"Mr. Weinsteenberg." He held out his right hand, "your brother Kieran told me you needed a lawyer."

Dazed, Cal shook Weinsteenberg's hand. What was Kieran playing at? This guy was easily seventy, give or take a decade. Cal had imagined some snappy young defense lawyer, a little flashy maybe, but able to run rings round the police or prosecution. The only rings this guy looked capable of was round a walker.

Then it dawned on him that Kieran had chosen the guy over the phone and probably had no idea that he was a septuagenarian. "I think there's been a mistake."

"No mistake," Weinsteenberg said firmly. "Your brother called me direct." Weinsteenberg offered a conciliatory smile. "I'd already read a little about the case in the paper." He paused, giving Cal a quick once over. "From what I know, I'd say you definitely need a good lawyer."

"I'm not guilty of anything," Cal said.

Mr. Weinsteenberg nodded as he sat down. "I know. That's why you need a good lawyer."

"You know I'm innocent?" An inkling of optimism buoyed Cal. At last someone on his side. "How do you know that?"

"I'm a defense lawyer. I believe all my clients are innocent."

The optimism sank without trace. Cal wanted the personal belief of his innocence to be genuine, not a condition of employment.

"I'm innocent," he repeated. "I shouldn't need a lawyer."

Weinsteenberg glanced around the room, gestured towards the closed door. "You're here, you're under arrest. I'd say you need a lawyer. You even asked for a lawyer." He stretched his arms out. "Here I am."

Weinsteenberg reminded Cal of a grandfather welcoming a long lost grandchild. He looked away in despair. What the hell had Kieran been thinking about when he chose this guy?

"You think I'm too old." Weinsteenberg said.

"What? No, it's…"

"Please don't deny it. Let's not start off with you lying to me. It was written all over your face when I first walked in."

Cal blushed. Had he been that obvious?

"Besides, I'm not as old as you think. I know that, because I have to remind myself every morning when I look in the mirror. Let's just say it's the consequences of past decisions. I should be a poster boy for what happens if you don't lead a healthy life." He shuffled in his chair and grimaced. "And I should give up trying to thrash my sons at tennis." He massaged his lower back. "I'll concede that I'm probably getting a little too old for that."

"You play tennis?"

"As often as possible," Weinsteenberg said. "Keeps me sane. I imagine the ball is the prosecutor, or the judge, the latest witness, sometimes even my own client when they are being total idiots."

Cal warmed to the guy. Tennis was Cal's therapy of choice too. Not that he'd indulged in it much in the last few weeks, just when he most needed to work off some tension. The only problem with tennis as a therapy was that you needed a partner and the idea of finding out that his regular partners didn't want to know him at the moment was a bridge he didn't want to cross. He hadn't made the calls to set up a game. Neither had they. Maybe they were all very busy, or maybe silence could tell you a lot.

"Shall we proceed?" Weinsteenberg said, suddenly taking on a more serious demeanor.

Cal nodded. He couldn't see what choice he had really. He didn't exactly have the time or facilities to interview a series of lawyers and pick the one he liked best.

"I've spoken to Pearson. He filled me in on the situation from their perspective. Now, tell me yours."

Cal told him everything he had told the police.

Weinsteenberg took notes as Cal spoke. He didn't interrupt with questions and showed no reaction to what Cal said. Cal was disappointed. He wanted indignation, a mutual sense of outrage at the way he was being treated. Weinsteenberg looked more like a doctor listening to a patient's symptoms than someone who was going to go head on with the legal system and get Cal out of this mess.

"That's it?' Weinsteenberg said as Cal stopped speaking.

"Yes."

Weinsteenberg looked down at his notes, his pen tapping against the paper. "Okay, let me go talk to Pearson again." A look of pain flashed across his face as he stood. He waited a couple of minutes and then hobbled back out of the room.

Cal watched him go and then sank his forehead into his hands. If this was a nightmare, he wanted to wake up right now.

A few minutes later, Coyle reappeared with a large cup of coffee in a plastic cup bearing the local diner's logo.

"Compliments of your lawyer," he said as he put it down in front of Cal, his manner betraying the fact that he'd been the reluctant errand boy.

"Thanks." Cal ripped the top off, took a deep breath in of the fresh aroma and gulped down a mouthful. It could have been hotter, but his caffeine levels were well overdue for a boost. It would just have to do. Then he realized he couldn't be sure when the next cup was coming, so he slowed down and savored it.

Coyle stood and watched.

Cal shot him a look.

Coyle gave him a knowing smile in return.

Cal sighed. Okay, he knew who was in charge at the moment. At least he hoped it was just for the moment. Eventually, they would move him to the cells. He shuddered. Out here he still had some hope, however slim. Once behind bars that hope would seem like a joke. He swallowed the last of the coffee and popped the cup down on the table.

Coyle snatched it up as if it were a lethal weapon and disappeared out of the room. Had he really been instructed to watch Cal drink the coffee then confiscate the cup? What did they imagine he was going to do with it? Cal smiled at the stupidity of it all. He had to think of it as a huge joke. The alternative was too much to bear.

Somebody had sent that email from the library, somebody who wanted to make it look like he had sent it, who knew he was in the library, who knew it would cause him trouble. A frightening thought. But what was really scary was that he couldn't think of a single person who'd want to cause him that kind of problem.

How could you have enemies and not know about it?

Chapter 23

Weinsteenberg returned with good news. "They've agreed to drop the charges."

"Drop the charges? Why?" Cal almost didn't care, as long as he got out. But he was curious.

"I persuaded them that the email hadn't had any impact on their investigation. It wasn't as if they'd stopped their searches or gone off on a wild goose chase because of it. In fact I don't believe Pearson ever thought it was genuine."

"So they should never have arrested me in the first place?"

"I didn't say that. But I pointed out that they had other more important things to concentrate on and they weren't going to get a lot out of pushing this charge at this stage."

"So I'm free to go."

"As long as you agree to a couple of conditions."

Cal frowned. "Why should I agree to any conditions?"

"You want the charges dropped?"

"Of course. But if they don't have a case against me, why should I have to accept any conditions."

Weinsteenberg sighed. "I didn't say they didn't have a case. I said they were willing to drop the charges, if you agree to a couple of conditions."

"But isn't that a bit like admitting I'm guilty?'

"Don't you even want to know what the conditions are before you blow them off?"

"Go on, surprise me."

"No more red herrings."

Cal snorted. "I don't have any control over that. I didn't send that email. But if I get anymore you can be sure Pearson will be the last one to hear about it."

Weinsteenberg glared at him. "That's not a helpful attitude Mr. Miller."

"Well what do you expect? If he's going to threaten to lock me up for trying to help, I'm shutting up. So what are the other conditions?"

"Just one more. That you tell Pearson if you have any plans to leave town for more than a few hours."

Cal gulped. Pearson seemed determined to keep tabs on him one way or the other. "Can they insist on that?"

"Depends on how desperate you are to have the case dropped."

At this point, Cal would agree to almost anything if it kept him out of a cell, but he wasn't about to admit that to Weinsteenberg. Besides he wasn't about to mess with the investigation and he had no immediate plans to leave town. It was no big deal.

"Okay," he nodded. "I can live with those."

He was out of the police station within fifteen minutes. Weinsteenberg handed Cal his card and told him he'd send him his bill. Cal grimaced. Money was tight enough without expensive legal fees. Still he had to admit that the guy had earned his pay.

He sauntered back to his office. There was a slight fall chill in the air, but otherwise it was a picture book day—blue sky, fluffy white clouds, the foliage more lush and vibrant than he'd remembered from before his few hours in the gray room in the police station.

He stayed in the office only long enough to switch his equipment off and lock up. He just wanted to get home and relax, hang out with Kieran for a while, sink a few beers and try to work out what the hell was going on.

He drove home at a sedate pace, relieved he was going back to an empty house. The way things were between him and Lily at the moment, he could guarantee they'd rub each other up the wrong way. He needed some time alone to get his thoughts together, to come up with a plan. He was tired of it, tired of the whole goddamn business.

Reaching the cross street before his, Cal checked out the road ahead. The street was clear, no reporters. At least something was in his favor today.

He turned into his driveway and groaned. Two cars were already parked in front of the garage, Kieran's red convertible and Lily's blue Toyota. Lily must have driven straight back when she got Kieran's call. Cal knew he should be pleased, it showed she still cared enough about him to come back, but he wished she'd waited until the following day.

As he opened the front door a couple of small human cannonballs launched themselves at his legs.

"Daddy, Daddy, guess what?" Amanda yelled. "Grandma and Grandpa have a new dog and he is so cute."

"It's a baby." Sophie tugged at his trousers, determined to get her say. "He licked my toes. It tickled."

"She means a puppy." Amanda let go of Cal and held her hands out a few inches apart. "It's only about this big. It's so tiny and funny. Can we have one Daddy? Please? Can we have one?"

"Please," Sophie echoed, "please, please, please?"

Cal forced a smile. Damned puppies. All he wanted to think about was who was messing his life up and why.

"Say yes, Daddy, say yes." Amanda grabbed at his right hand and shook it, her excited eyes gleaming up at him.

"Not now!" He yanked his hand away.

Amanda and Sophie stepped back. There was a moment of silence as the girls swapped uncertain glances, then Amanda cast him a hurt look, took Sophie by the hand and pulled her towards the stairs. "Come on Sophie, I think Daddy wants some peace and quiet."

The tone of her words cut Cal to the core. He hadn't seen them for days, and within minutes he'd managed to upset them. What kind of father was he? He glanced up. Kieran stood in the kitchen doorway.

Cal grimaced. "Not my day."

Kieran shrugged. "Don't be too hard on yourself."

Cal looked up the stairs as his daughters disappeared round the corner. "They're three and five. I shouldn't be taking my problems out on them."

"Let it go, Cal," Kieran said. "They'll have forgotten about it in a few minutes. So should you. You've got plenty of other issues to deal with." He nodded towards the living room door. "You haven't changed, have you? Still as much a slob as ever."

Cal groaned. The mess, he'd forgotten about the mess. He could imagine Lily's reaction when she'd walked in. No wonder she hadn't rushed out to greet him. He took a deep breath and pushed open the living room door. Lily was piling debris onto a large tray. "I'll do that," he said.

Lily looked up. She had an empty beer can in her hand. For a brief second Cal thought she was going to throw it at him, but she settled for squashing it and dropping it onto the tray. Her face and eyes were red and puffy. The crying session must have been a major one. Cal glanced over his shoulder at Kieran, who looked as if he'd borne the full brunt of her outburst. This was serious. Lily usually kept her feelings bottled up, she wasn't a great believer in talk therapy, but in the space of a few days she'd unloaded first to her parents and then to his brother. She was talking to everyone but him.

Kieran made a patting gesture with his left hand. Two slight strokes downward. An old boyhood signal meaning, *beware they're mad.*

Cal turned back to Lily. "I'm sorry. I meant to do it before you got back."

"I should hope so." She picked up an old newspaper and slammed it down on top of the tray, causing an avalanche of smaller items to slide off the side and back onto the coffee table.

"Thanks for coming back so quickly." Cal stepped forward, reaching out to embrace her.

She sidestepped away.

He let his arms drop back to his side. "I missed you. And the girls. I'm glad you're back."

Lily swung round on him. "I came back because Kieran told me you might be spending the night behind bars. Seeing you didn't call me, I had no idea what state you'd left the house in."

Cal glared at Kieran.

"I just said it was a possibility." Kieran looked aghast. "I offered to come over to the house, but she said she wanted to come back."

Cal sank down in the nearest armchair and covered his face with his hands. He'd spent the best part of the day locked up in a police station, and now he was free all his wife was worried about was the state of the house. She hadn't uttered one single word of consolation or compassion.

"I would have called you first if I could have been sure you'd answer the phone." Cal spat the words at her. "I had one phone call, what was I supposed to do, leave a message, *Hi Lily, I'm in jail, get me a lawyer quick?*"

"I think I'd better leave now," Kieran said.

"No! You've driven all this way, stay for dinner."

Lily slammed another can onto the tray. "There is no dinner."

"I think I'd better go." Kieran backed into the hall.

"No. Please." Cal prayed that Kieran would pick up the plea in his request. "You should stay. Lily's right, but we can order in. Chinese, pizza, you pick. You came all this way, you helped me out, at least stay for dinner."

Kieran hesitated. It was obvious that he really wanted to get the hell out of the house, away from the two of them and their marital problems. He looked from Cal to Lily and then back to Cal. Caught Cal's glance and held it, held it for a long time and then relented. "Okay Chinese it is, but I'm going to have to camp out in your spare room overnight. I'm going to need a few beers with my food."

Cal could have hugged him on the spot. To his consternation even Lily looked relieved.

Chapter 24

"And in recent developments in the Katy Shore case…"

The news anchor's words caught Cal unawares. He froze with his beer can raised half way to his mouth.

"Sources say that her former employer, Cal Miller, spent several hours at Leyton police station today…"

Cal lowered his hand, his mouth agape. He looked from the screen to Lily, then Kieran in turn. Both seemed equally stunned.

"Police refused to comment on Mr. Miller's presence at the station, but he was seen leaving in the company of Joseph Weinsteenberg, a well known local defense lawyer…"

"Why are they doing this?" Cal's words were a mere whisper. "Why do they want to convict me of a crime that hasn't even happened?"

The screen went blank as Kieran hit the remote control.

"Why did you do that?" Cal grabbed for the remote.

Kieran snatched it away. "You don't want to watch,"

"Of course I do, I want to see what lies my neighbors are hearing about me."

"Why? What good will it do you?"

"Don't I have a right to know what people are saying behind my back, my neighbors, my friends?" Cal glared at Lily. "My family."

Lily leapt up out of her chair. "You want to know what I think?"

The venom in her voice startled them both. Kieran stood in

front of her, blocking her view of Cal. "Not now Lily, please, just leave this to me." He patted her on the shoulder. "You must be tired. Why don't you…"

Lily shook his hand off. "Who are you to tell me what to do?"

"Please Lily." Kieran lowered his voice. "You're both going to say things you'll regret in the morning. Just leave it for tonight. Please."

"What about all this?" Lily waved her hand at the remains of the Chinese take-out spread over the coffee table.

"I'll sort it out, I promise." He started picking up empty cartons and squashing them into a paper bag. "Just, please, go to bed."

Lily deliberated for a moment. "Okay. Because you asked nicely. Can't see that it's going to do much good myself. We're going to have to have this conversation sometime."

"Tomorrow," Kieran said. "Tomorrow."

"Okay, okay." Lily peered round at Cal. "But in the meantime, you…you can sleep down here tonight."

"What's wrong? Afraid to share a bed with me now, are you? Who knows what I might have done?"

Kieran swung round to face Cal. "Shut it, Cal."

Lily slammed the living room door behind her.

"I thought you were going to be the peacekeeper." Cal said. "Over a week she's been away and she won't even let me share her bed tonight. Ha! Share a bed? Do you realize she hasn't even let me touch her yet?"

"Of course I realize. There's so much tension between the two of you, if you did touch you'd explode."

"No welcoming kiss, no supportive hug. I'm facing all this crap, and all she's worried about is the state of the house."

"You're wrong," Kieran said. "She's scared. The mess was just the catalyst for her anger. She feels threatened, her whole way of life is at risk and the very person who should be her rock is the person who started it all."

"I didn't start anything. I didn't do this."

"Of course not. But you've got to face it, you've given her reason to doubt you in the past and no matter how much she might want to, she can't wipe that away. It's there, niggling, is he telling

124

me the whole truth now?"

"Well, it sounds as if you two certainly had a real heart to heart this afternoon. An expert on my wife's feelings now, are we? Tell me, did she let you touch her while she was pouring out her thoughts? Did you hold her while she cried?"

Kieran stared hard at Cal and then turned away shaking his head.

Cal jumped to his feet. "Who the hell is she ordering around? If I want to sleep in my bed, I will."

Kieran shoved him back down into the chair.

Cal blinked. He made to stand up again. Kieran's second push was more forceful. Cal tried to propel himself forward, head bent, aiming for Kieran's stomach. Kieran grabbed him by the shoulders before he could make contact, cutting off the force of the impact, but still allowing Cal's head to nestle against his body.

For a moment there was only the sound of their breathing and then Cal let out a strangled gasp.

He sank to the floor on his knees, pulling Kieran down with him. He kept his head low and sobbed silently. He didn't want Kieran to see his pain. He knew he was fooling himself, the shudder of his body betrayed his cries.

But Kieran still didn't say a word. He just pulled Cal closer and held him tight.

Chapter 25

Cal staggered across the street hunching his shoulders against the biting chill that had settled over Leyton during the evening. It was going to be a cold walk home. He toyed with the idea of going back to the bar, calling Lily and asking her to come and get him. It would take her all of ten minutes. Ten thirty at night, the kids would be asleep; they'd never know she'd gone.

He swayed on the spot as he considered her reaction. Who was he kidding? They'd barely exchanged a civil word since Tuesday, which is why, once again, he chose to spend Friday evening in the bar rather than face the frosty atmosphere at home. He pushed his hands deep into his jacket pockets, hugged his arms to his body and trudged off along the deserted street.

As he crossed the alley between the bank and the pharmacy he tripped, tumbling forward with no chance to break his fall. But before he hit the ground he was grabbed and hoisted back to his feet. Gasping with relief, he turned to thank his rescuers.

A fist smashed into his face.

Pain ripped along his jaw. He took an instinctive step back, only to be hauled forward.

A second fist slammed into his stomach.

His legs buckled with the force, but the grips on his arms just dug harder into the skin. He was dragged into the alleyway and slammed up against the concrete siding of the bank. Two of his attackers pinned his shoulders against the wall. A heavy solid object whacked across his shins. He blinked away tears of pain just before another fist caught the corner of his right eye and knocked his head back against the wall.

After that, he lost count of the number of times they hit him. There was almost a pattern to it—one to the head, then one on the lower body, then back to the head. His mind reeled from the blows, but he still realized he was in serious trouble. It wasn't his wallet they were after. Or information. There was no time between punches to form words, to plead with his attackers or answer questions. And they weren't asking any. The only sounds were the shuffle of feet, the thwack of blows and his involuntary uttered noises in response. These guys were intent on hurting him. Or possibly killing him.

Without warning the weight was removed from Cal's arms. He slid down the wall onto his knees, spears of pain shooting up his body, then flopped forward onto his stomach. His face was in the grime, something warm and sticky trickled across his cheek, but all he could think of was that they had at last stopped hitting him.

They hadn't. Feet kicked into his ribs. Then someone crouched down beside him and pushed him onto his side while a second figure swung a long object towards his back. A searing pain tore through his body. Then another. And another. He felt himself slipping into darkness. He tried to focus on the figure beside him. Who could want to hurt him this badly?

For a second they faced each other then realization struck. A ski mask covered the face but he knew those eyes.

That's enough," a voice said.

The figure stood up. Cal tried to lift his head up, to double-check what he'd seen. The effort was too much. Blackness engulfed him just as the answer came to him.

He'd been staring into Katy's eyes.

The doctor recited the long list of Cal's injuries as if he were reading from a medical dictionary. Cal had no idea what half the terms meant. He understood only that each one was responsible for a fraction of the pain that radiated through his body.

He closed his eyes to block out the doctor's droning voice and find a pain free spot to focus on. He wiggled the fingers of his right hand. They were encased in some kind of bandage even though they hadn't yet appeared on the doctor's list. It felt like he still had five fingers on that hand, though it was hard to tell whether the pain came from the fingers or from his finger-wiggling muscles. What did it matter? Pain was pain was pain, and he had a lot of it.

He tuned back in to the doctor's monologue in time to hear him say that he was lucky most of the injuries were superficial.

"Superficial!" His attempt to yell was muffled by the swollen, sponge-like mass of his lips and came out as an indecipherable mumble accompanied by drool. The doctor responded with a smile.

Cal just wished the doctor would go away so he could slip back to the black painless world he'd inhabited a short time ago. Instead he remained by the bedside plying Cal with information that Cal couldn't give a damn about.

At last the doctor got bored with him and left. A pretty little nurse replaced him. She smiled at Cal and asked was he comfortable? Did he need something for pain? Was she kidding? Like he was going to say no?

"Everything you've got."

Of course she didn't understand a word and continued to stand by the bed offering him nothing more than a cheery grin. He nodded his head in an emphatic way, causing needle like stabbing sensations to shoot through his skull so that his response ended in a moan.

The nurse's grin gave way to a sympathetic smile. She patted him on the back of the hand then injected something into an IV line.

He contorted his mouth into what he hoped was a return smile as he was whisked into darkness.

He had an audience the next time he woke. At least half a dozen faces peered down at him displaying various degrees of consternation. He scanned each face, looking for one he recognized. Panic flared inside. Was he supposed to know these people? Had he lost his memory? He focused on the young woman at the end of the bed. She looked nauseous herself. A doctor appeared at her side, whispered something into her ear and the woman turned and fled out of the room. As she left Cal realized she was wearing a white coat just like the doctor. Of course, they were all doctors. He was the show and tell specimen for the day.

With his mouth the way it was he wasn't about to try and tell them what he thought about that. But he did wonder about the expression on the young woman's face. Did he look that bad? Engorged black and blue lips probably weren't an immediate turn on to the opposite sex, but judging from her reaction there was a lot worse to consider. He glanced round the room. There wasn't a single thing there in which he could see even a snippet of his reflection.

He sighed. The remaining doctors all gave him compassionate glances back. It was that bad. He wished that silly nurse would come back and pat him on the hand again. Maybe he'd misjudged her. She hadn't seemed at all put out by his looks.

He dreamed he woke to find Lily sitting by the bed. She was sobbing quietly, looking down at the floor, unaware that he was listening. In between the sobs she was talking to him, telling him how much she loved him, how she couldn't bear to live without him. How all she wanted was for everything to go back to how it had been a few weeks earlier.

It was all he wanted too.

It was a wonderful dream. He wished he could tell her about it.

His periods of consciousness increased. The slightest movement hurt so he just lay there, staring up at the white ceiling or, for a change of view, the pale yellow wall opposite his bed. The only visitors he had were hospital staff. At first he couldn't understand that. Where were his family and friends? Then he remembered that he wasn't too high in the popularity stakes at the moment, so he could forget the get well cards and flowers. He was on his own.

He learnt from snippets of one-sided conversations that he'd been found in an alley, battered, bruised and cold.

Identification wasn't a problem since his wallet was still in his pocket. He'd arrived at the hospital with a police escort befitting his small town celebrity status. The police had ordered no visitors, except for his wife, until after they'd had a chance to interview him. They didn't have to worry on that score. Even Lily hadn't bothered.

He had bruising over seventy-five percent of his body, though they didn't mention which areas had escaped a beating, and he couldn't figure it out for himself. Surprisingly the only thing broken was his cheekbone, but he had hairline fractures on his shins, several ribs and his right collarbone. Two deep gashes on the right side of his head had needed extensive stitching, but the doctors were mostly concerned about his kidneys, given the amount of blood in his urine. That puzzled him, since he hadn't been anywhere near a bathroom yet, until he discovered that one of the many tubes snaking into his body was a catheter.

The tubes required constant adjustment and attention by the nurses. Sometimes he felt like screaming at them to leave him alone, but what was the point? They wouldn't understand his ranting. The silly nurse turned out to be the best of them all. He liked the way she patted his hand, giving him entry to a pain free existence—until he noticed the pats on the hand were becoming less frequent, she was making him wait longer for respite, and he decided she was really no better than the rest of them.

Chapter 26

"Did you get a good look at any of your attackers?"

Cal squinted at Pearson through his half-opened eyes. His head was throbbing and his body ached, but the swelling on his lips had gone down enough to enable him to talk. He'd shown this off to the doctor only to have the doctor decide he was well enough to be interviewed by the police.

Pearson had been all solicitous at first, acting as if Cal's physical condition really mattered to him, but the banality of the questions was beginning to grate on Cal's nerves.

"Yeah, while I was being punched repeatedly on the face…"

Pearson cut him off with an impatient sigh. "Cal, let's be productive here, shall we? Do you remember how many there were?"

He was Cal now. When he was the suspect he was Mr. Miller. "Cal" was more personal, helped create the impression that everyone was on your side, rooting for you, except they'd made a huge mistake. If they wanted to get close to him they should have assigned another police officer. There was only one reason Pearson was here and it had nothing to do with nabbing the people who had bruised and battered him. Catch him when he's down and out and maybe they'd get a confession. That was more likely Pearson's way of thinking.

"Did you manage to hit back at all? Could you have hurt

any of them?"

Cal closed his eyes and pretended to drift off. It was difficult to admit someone had used you as a punching bag, especially when there was a cocky young detective, Docherty, sitting next to Pearson eagerly writing down every word Cal said. He could imagine him retelling the story in the locker room at the station house, the appropriate level of disgust in his voice. "Imagine. The guy didn't even put up a fight." Damn it, he wasn't going to let them think that's the way it was.

"Four, five," he said, opening his eyes to check that Docherty was still writing. "Two held me down." He paused for effect. "One guy, maybe two punched me, and there was at least one with a bat or a piece of wood of some kind."

Docherty flinched at his words. Good. Cal held back on saying that one of them was Katy. After the e-mail, they'd never believe him. Hell, he didn't even believe it himself. What possible motive could Katy have for being involved in the attack on him? He had to work that one out for himself before he as much as mentioned his suspicions to the police, but the combination of pain and sedatives was making it hard to think.

"I think they wanted me dead," Cal said.

Pearson shook his head. "No, they didn't."

Cal groaned. "Certainly felt like it at the time."

Pearson leant forward, a suitably serious expression on his face. "If they'd wanted you dead, you'd be dead. There was nothing to stop them. You already said you were outnumbered, held down, and they were armed." He sat back as if he'd proved his point. "They wanted you to live."

"Well, I'll sleep better knowing that," Cal said.

"Any thoughts on who might have done it?"

Cal rolled his eyes before realizing that Pearson could barely see them beneath their swollen lids. "Are you going to catch them for me, bring them to justice?"

"We'll do our best to find whoever was responsible."

"Won't let it just slide into a…*well he deserved it anyway* category?"

"Did you deserve it?"

"Want a sick bed confession?" Cal attempted a smile. "You're out of luck. I've nothing to confess. But they're related, aren't they, my beating, your investigation?"

"We certainly have to look at all angles," Pearson said.

"All angles, bullshit! Someone out there decided you were being a little slow and that they were going to deliver their own justice."

"We're looking into all possibilities."

"Right. Considered it might have been one of your own?"

"All reasonable possibilities."

Cal noticed Docherty's reaction. He'd paused in his writing and looked from Cal to Pearson, a glint of interest in his eyes.

"Where's Rigby?" Cal said. "Didn't he want to come and pass on his condolences?"

"Detective Rigby is not working on the Shore case anymore," Pearson said.

"Why would that be I wonder?'

"He asked to be reassigned."

"I'd laugh but it hurts," Cal said. "Asked to be reassigned, bullshit. You had to pull him off the case. He was like a ticking bomb. Well, I think he went off."

"Are you quite finished?"

"Have you asked him where he was at the time? Out with a few friends perhaps?"

"That's a serious accusation, Mr. Miller."

"I'm in serious pain." Cal nodded at Docherty. "Go on, you're supposed to write this down."

Pearson shook his head. Docherty sat still, obviously unsure what that meant.

"Write it down!" Cal said. "You asked if I had any idea who might have done this, well this is my answer."

"You have no grounds to say that."

"Don't I? He sure looked as if he wanted to wipe the floor with me on Tuesday."

"Tuesday?"

"At the station house, when I was waiting for my lawyer. Remember..." And then it dawned. "You didn't even know he'd paid me an unofficial visit, did you?"

"Are you saying he threatened you?" Pearson said, a little too quickly.

"Not in words, but you should have seen his expression."

"So what exactly did he say to you?"

Cal sighed. Why had he ever gone down this avenue? "Why don't you tell the truth?"

"That's all?" Pearson made an incredulous face at Docherty. "Don't know about you but it doesn't sound much of a threat to me."

"So ask him where he was," Cal said. "If he's innocent, he has nothing to hide. Or so you've told me often enough."

The more Cal thought about it, the more he convinced himself it was Rigby behind the attack. True, most of the townsfolk thought ill of him at the moment. It wasn't too much of a stretch to think that one of them had suggested that the wheels of justice were far to slow and rounded up a posse. Maybe Pearson was right about their not wanting him dead, though. He remembered the voice saying, "enough". The voice.

And Katy's eyes. That was the confusing part. If it was a revenge attack for Katy's disappearance, why would Katy be there? And if it wasn't revenge, what was it? Certainly no mugging.

"Jeez, Cal, is that you?"

The voice cut through his attempts to connect the dots. He inched his head around on the pillow to greet Kieran. Kieran turned pale in front of him, his bobbing Adams apple betraying his struggle to keep his emotions in.

"That bad?" Cal said, afraid to smile in case it made him look worse.

Kieran took a couple of deep breaths and stepped towards the bed. "Honest? You look like shit."

"According to the doctors, there's twenty five percent of me that looks okay," Cal said, "though I can only guess where it is."

He managed to get a smile out of Kieran.

"Lily warned me that you looked awful." Kieran blushed. "I thought she was exaggerating."

"How would Lily know?"

Kieran frowned. "Because she's been sitting by your bedside almost since they brought you in."

"She has?" Cal remembered his dream—or what he'd thought was a dream. If he'd spoken, or at least tried to, would he have attracted her attention? He glanced around the room. "So where is she now?"

"A couple of rooms down, sleeping. The nurses finally persuaded her that she needed to get some rest too and that you would be sedated for quite some time." He made a face. "She's going to be mad when she wakes up. She wanted to be here for you."

The words were music to Cal's ears. She wanted to be there. She did still care. "Where are the kids?"

"They're at home with Mom and Dad."

"Mom and Dad know?"

"Of course. What do you expect?"

Cal looked away. "I hadn't told them."

"As I discovered," Kieran said. "They were really shook up. First they're told their son's been viciously attacked. Then they learn that he's at the center of a serious police investigation. Who wouldn't be upset?" Kieran paused until Cal looked back at him. "Damn it Cal, why didn't you mention the investigation to them?"

"I didn't want to worry them."

"Well, they're worried now. They would have been here if it weren't for the girls. I'm going back to the house later so they can come to see you."

"No! Tell them not to come."

"I can't do that. Why would you even want to say that?"

"I don't want them to see me like this. It'll only upset them even more."

Kieran glared at him. "You mean you don't want to face up to them, or admit the truth, whatever that is."

"Give me a break, Kieran, I'm hurting enough."

"You're beginning to sound as if you do have something to hide. Why wouldn't you want to tell Mom and Dad what's going on? Even see them?"

"Like you tell them everything? When did you last speak to them before today?"

"This isn't about me. I know I don't call as much as I should, but that's just the way I am, it's not because there's something I don't want to tell them."

"So, that's just the way I am."

"Look I didn't come here to argue with you."

"Why did you come?"

Kieran shot him a glance of total contempt. "My brother's beaten within an inch of his life; you think I'm not going to care? Make sure he's okay? You don't think I want to know who did this to you."

"So you can do what? Exact revenge on my behalf. Then Mom and Dad will have two sons to worry about. That's really going to help them."

"The people who did this deserve to end up behind bars."

"They probably think I'm the one who belongs behind bars."

"Of course they do. You've given them plenty of reason."

For a moment, Cal stopped breathing. When he could make his lungs move again, he said, "You think…"

"That you killed Katy? Of course not. But you've been lying to the police from the start, and you're a lousy liar, Cal. But instead of just admitting you've lied, you get almighty pissed at everyone for suspecting you. Keep on like this and you're going to alienate everyone, the police, Lily, Mom and Dad—"

"What the hell do you know about alienation?" Cal yelled.

His nurse stepped into the room. She made no attempt to hide her anger. "I'm going to have to ask you to leave. You're upsetting your brother."

Cal thought Kieran was about to start arguing with her too, but suddenly his shoulders slumped and he turned back to Cal, his face like stone. "I'm not going to be the one to tell them they can't visit." He was out of the door before Cal could reply.

Without further comment the nurse fiddled with the tubes around Cal's bed. Cal wondered how often she'd seen scenes like this played out. Where family tensions got the better of people at the very time they were trying to reunite in their concern.

"My wife," Cal said. "She's down the corridor?"

The nurse gave a slight nod.

"I'd like to see her. Would you tell her I'm awake?"

"I think you've had quite enough of visitors for the moment. You need some rest."

"I want to see my wife. I have to tell her something."

"It can wait." The nurse took hold of his wrist.

"No." He tried to pull his hand away. "I don't need to sleep." But she patted the back of his hand and he drifted into blackness.

Chapter 27

Lily was by his bedside when Cal woke. He tried to smile then stopped as he remembered the state his face was in.

She smiled back. It was a look of such love, such tenderness, that he thought it would break his heart. He wanted to capture it and hold it forever.

"Hi." Her voice was low and gentle as if afraid she would hurt him if she spoke too loud. "How you doing?"

"A lot better now that you're here."

Cal gazed at her. She was so unassuming, so unaware of her beauty and graciousness. When he'd asked her to marry him, he'd vowed to himself to cherish her, show her how lovable she was. To date he'd failed miserably. But if she gave him a second chance, he would do anything to prove how much she meant to him.

But where to start? He couldn't reach out to her physically, not even to kiss her, and words weren't enough, even if he could speak them clearly. He'd told her he was sorry so many times in the past few weeks that he'd worn the word out. A real sorry required amends. His had been no more than delaying tactics, while he hoped for a reprieve. Why would she want to give him a second chance?

He searched her face for reassurance that his first instincts had been right, that she was here out of love rather than a misguided sense of marital duty. Her eyes held his, even as she studied the revised outline of his features. She was stoic about his looks. There were no indications of distaste or repulsion. Maybe she'd had enough time to adjust during her earlier sessions by his bed while he slept. Hopefully she was seeing beyond the surface, beyond the puffy eyes, swollen cheeks and engorged lips, to the man she loved, and that softness in her look was not just pity.

Lily stood up and leant over him, touching her lips to the left side of his forehead. A small wordless gesture, but Cal was prepared to read a lot into it. As she pulled back he touched her cheek with his left hand. She nuzzled her face against the loose padded wrapping and then, taking his hand in hers, sat back down. She kissed the back of his fingers, the real sensation getting lost in the layers of gauze, but soaring in Cal's imagination.

"I can't remember what they said was wrong with my fingers," he said.

"Nothing."

"But the bandages?"

"To stop you scratching your head. You've got a lot of stitches on your scalp. The doctors said it would heal quicker uncovered but even while you were sedated you were trying to claw at them with your fingers. Instead of covering the wound, they immobilized your fingers." Lily smiled. "It worked."

"So now I'm awake I don't need them."

Lily looked doubtful.

"I won't touch my head, I promise."

"That's up to the doctors."

"Come on, unwrap it now, I want to feel your hand in mine."

Lily hesitated.

"Hey, if you hold my hand I can't scratch my head with it, can I?"

Lily laughed. "Okay, but just one." She started unraveling the bandage on his left hand. "If I get asked to leave because of this, it'll be your fault." But there was a slight sparkle in her eyes as she spoke. A sparkle that Cal hadn't seen for many weeks.

He smiled. "I'll cause such a fuss they wouldn't be able to let you leave."

Lily scrunched her nose up. "This is a hospital Cal. They've got ways of shutting you up faster than you'd know, and then who'd defend me?"

She dropped the bandage onto the bed. Cal flexed his fingers, then his hand. Lily was right. His hand appeared intact, no cuts or bruises—proof if he needed it that he hadn't had a chance to throw any punches back at his attackers.

Lily placed his hand in hers and started stroking over his knuckles with her thumbs. The gentle touch was an odd companion to the constant aches elsewhere in his body.

"What time is it?" he said.

"Almost four."

"Um… Morning or afternoon."

"Afternoon." Lily kissed his knuckles before resuming her stroking. "Sunday afternoon."

"Sunday!"

"You were in a bad way." Tears glistened in Lily's eyes. "They had to sedate you for the pain."

"Kieran was here, Pearson too," Cal said, wanting to distract her.

"I know. Your nurse gave Kieran a good tongue lashing for agitating you. Said she'd had to sedate you again. He went off looking very sheepish."

"Good." Cal's memories of his conversation with Kieran were vague, but a definite bad feeling lingered.

Lily shook her head, then chuckled.

"I think what made it worse was that he was quite attracted to the nurse. While he was waiting for you to wake up he kept making excuses to go and talk to her. I'm sure he was building up to asking her out." Lily grinned again. "I think he may have changed his mind now."

"Even better," Cal said.

"Cal!" Lily stopped stroking his hand.

"Well, he's an asshole."

Lily burst out laughing.

"What's so funny?"

"Just you two. That's exactly what he said about you." Lily resumed the stroking. "He cares about you, you know."

Cal waited for the addendum, the 'I do too' or 'we all do'. He waited and waited. Lily kept on stroking, her eyes fixed on his. He recognized the look. This time he would have to give in.

"I know," he said. "I know."

A nurse interrupted their silent communion. Lily excused herself and left. Cal wanted to call her back, but he was afraid the nurse would take it as a sign of agitation, so he stayed silent. He could only hope the absence would be temporary.

This nurse was quiet and businesslike. She checked the tubes and adjusted his pillows before appearing to notice the pile of bandages on the bed. Cal prepared for the lecture.

"Would you like me to take the other bandage off?" She stepped forward to examine his scalp. "We can always put them back on if you need them."

"Thank you." At last they were giving him some input into what happened to him.

The right hand was just like the left, unmarked and undamaged. He flexed the fingers in both hands. Whatever the rest of his body felt like, he had two good hands. He had to concentrate on that. He could touch things, feel them and hold them, a book, a hand, Lily. He looked across at the door, willing Lily to come back.

The nurse changed his catheter bag. Cal blanched as she held up a clear bag of pale red fluid. There was more blood than he'd imagined. Was he slowly bleeding to death?

"Don't worry," the nurse said. "It looks worse than it is. A little blood goes a long way mixed with urine."

"Shouldn't it have stopped by now?"

"They were serious blows. It will take a while before we can tell if there's any permanent damage."

"Permanent damage? I thought the doctor said my injuries were superficial?"

"Most of them will clear up and you'll never know the difference. Probably the kidneys will too. But there's a slight possibility of more long term damage there. We'll just have to wait and see."

"Is that the only thing? Or are there other possibilities you're keeping back?"

The nurse grinned. "No, that's it. Don't worry. The rest will mend in time." Her grin broadened. "Just as sure as your hair will grow back in."

"My hair!"

"We had to shave the right side of your head. For the

141

stitches."

The nurse didn't look as if she was kidding. "You're telling me I have hair on only one side of my head."

The nurse nodded.

"Okay, that explains some of the looks I've been getting. Why didn't you shave the whole head?"

"We did what we needed to in order to treat you. If you want the rest of your head shaved, we can arrange that."

Cal could only imagine what he looked like. He'd put the strange sensation in his head down to the stitching, but now he could feel the difference between the right and left sides against the pillow. He must look like a freak. No wonder Kieran had reacted as he did. There was no way his parents could see him like this.

Lily came back as soon as the nurse had left. It struck Cal that perhaps she hadn't wanted to stick around while the nurse was there in case she got any further glimpses of how battered he was. He couldn't blame her. He wouldn't like to say with certainty that if the positions were reversed he would be able to look at her and stay calm. And yet, when it came down to loved ones, what choice was there?

"I've just been checking on the girls," she said as she sat back down.

"Are they okay?"

"Yes, they said to say hello and get well soon."

"What did you tell them?"

Lily sighed, taking hold of his hand again, this time tracing one finger lazily back and forward across his fingers.

"I said you'd had an accident and that you were going to stay in the hospital for a few days to get better. I said that I needed to spend some time with you so they had to stay at home with Nana and Grandpa. That they were too young to come to the hospital. Not quite the truth, but I didn't want to scare them by telling them what really happened and we can't let them see you like this. I'd hate to think how they'd react."

"Yeah. Why didn't you tell me I only had half a head of hair?"

"I didn't know you didn't know."

"Would you bring me a mirror?'

142

"No."

"It would save me wondering what I look like."

"You don't want to know." Lily's words were gently spoken, but the statement still hurt. "There's no point Cal. In a few days you'll look a lot better, so why upset yourself now?"

"It's my face."

Lily swallowed hard. "No, it's not Cal. It's nothing like your face."

Chapter 28

Cal's mother burst into tears as soon as she saw him. The action was so uncharacteristic it unnerved him. Luckily, Lily took charge, ushering her mother-in-law into the corridor to comfort her.

His father watched them go and then turned back to Cal, a pained expression on his face. "She's been like that since she heard about the investigation."

Cal wondered how his father had been. His father was not one to show his feelings. If he had a problem, he dealt with it as best he could and moved on. Growing up, Cal had admired him for his stoicism, never quite being able to manage it himself. Right now he could do with a large dose of it, but tonight even his father appeared on edge and nervous.

"I'm sorry." Cal said. "I should have told you earlier."

His father held up his hand. "There'll be time for that later." He surveyed Cal's face and head. "Are they taking good care of you?"

The question puzzled Cal. "Yes, I guess."

"They're giving you all the pain medication you need?"

"What's this about?"

His father looked back towards the door as if he thought someone might be listening. "It's just, with the circumstances. People have opinions. Perhaps some of them feel you deserve to suffer."

"Dad, you're not making sense."

His father looked even more uncomfortable. "The staff here, they know who you are, they must with the police presence and all. I just want to be sure they're not prejudging this, letting it affect their behavior."

"Dad, they're professionals. They're not going to..." He frowned. "What do you mean, police presence?"

"They've got a cop down the corridor. He's got a very short list of people who are allowed into your room. It took a while even to get him to add your mother and me to the list."

A cop outside his room? That was something Pearson had failed to mention. Question was, was the cop there to protect Cal or to keep an eye on him? If the former, who did they feel he needed protecting from?

Cal looked at the concern on his father's face. Neither suggestion was going to offer him much relief. "I'm sure it's just normal procedure." he said.

His father was unconvinced. "Maybe we should get you transferred to another hospital, out of the area, up near our place perhaps. We haven't heard anything about this girl's disappearance. Nobody would know who you were."

It was a tempting thought, a chance to be a regular guy for a while, but... Hell, he'd have to clear the move with Pearson, and chances were that Pearson would inform the new hospital and the local police of the situation. Before he knew it, the story would be spreading round his parent's hometown. It was tough enough for him and Lily to live with the fallout of the investigation. There was no way he was going to put his parents through it too, at least not if he could help it.

"They're treating me okay," he said. "Besides the police may need more help in trying to track down my attackers."

"You can identify them?'

"No, but my thinking is all hazy at the moment, what with the sedatives and such. I might remember something useful later."

"You could remember just as well upstate. Lily and the girls could stay with us, so Lily could spend as much time as she liked at the hospital with you."

Cal remained silent. He wished his father would shut up.

"Your mother would be happier, knowing you were away from this place."

145

"Just leave it, Dad! I'm staying and that's final."

His father seemed stunned by his anger. "We're just trying to help you son. You've taken one hell of a beating from someone and maybe they're not finished with you yet. We don't want to see you get hurt anymore, that's all."

Cal turned his head away. He was doing it again, just like Kieran said. "I'll be careful."

"Whatever people here think, your mom and me, we know you couldn't do anything like what they're suggesting."

A lump started to build in Cal's throat. Maybe things weren't as bad as he'd thought. Lily was back, his parents were behind him, even Kieran, once he got over being mad at him, would be on his side.

"I'll be fine, Dad," he said. "I'll be fine."

The following day all the tubes were disconnected except for the catheter. Blood still colored his urine. The nurse's blasé attitude suggested it was one of the most natural things in the world, but it wasn't her blood.

Any movement still caused pain, so he resisted all attempts to get him out of bed. Besides, being in hospital, in bed, was like a haven. He felt safe here, as if the problems didn't exist. Once he got up, he knew they would come back with resounding force. He wanted to extend the hiatus as long as he could.

Lily sat for hours by his bed. They didn't talk much, just held hands, but it was enough. She left only when the doctors or nurses came to attend him and when Pearson and Docherty came back. The police hadn't made any progress with the case and Cal couldn't remember anything else that might help them—he still couldn't tell them about Katy—making the visit a waste of time. But at least they were still being conciliatory rather than accusatory.

Later that evening Cal dozed, his desire to sleep tempered by his enjoyment of the soft touch of Lily's fingers on the back of his hand. He was a lucky man to have Lily. A very lucky man. When this was all over he'd have to think of someway to repay her for her loyalty and...

He sensed someone watching them. He opened one eye,

sneaked a glance towards the door and jolted awake. Lily turned to see what had upset him. Her fingers tightened round his.

Rigby was standing in the doorway.

For a second Cal thought there was a hint of sadness in the detective's face, but his expression changed to a mask of indifference as he realized they'd noticed him.

Cal made no attempt to be polite. "What do you want?"

Rigby didn't answer. Lily turned her back on him and squeezed Cal's hand.

Cal watched Rigby. Was Rigby feeling self-satisfied at the sight of his handiwork? Or sorry that he hadn't finished the job? Had he come to taunt him—I know that you know I did this but you're never going to be able to prove it? "I said what do you want?"

"I heard you think I might have had something to do with this."

"You heard right."

Rigby just stared at Cal's face.

"Not very pretty, is it?" Cal said.

Rigby's expression didn't change. Cal stared back until Rigby looked away, a small sense of satisfaction setting in at Rigby's obvious discomfort. The callous bastard, coming here to gloat.

Rigby glanced around the room, finally looking at Lily. "I just wanted you to know that I had nothing to do with it."

"And why should I believe you?" Cal said.

Anger flickered across Rigby's face. "If I have any issues with you I can resolve them legally, I don't need to resort to this kind of retaliation."

Cal gaped at him. "You're telling me you're all calm and rational. You remember the visit you paid me at the station? You didn't look calm then."

"You shouldn't make accusations that you can't back up," Rigby said.

"You're a fine one to talk."

Rigby took a sidelong glance at Lily before continuing. "I never accused you of anything. I asked a question, that was all. It was you who turned it into a drama."

"Oh, bullshit. You think I'm guilty, and have from the start.

You hate me, Rigby. Why shouldn't you work me over?"

Is this what this is about? You lied to us, and I didn't like it, and now you're making accusations that put my career on the line."

"Your career! Do you know how many clients I've lost…?"

Wait a minute. His career on the line? Pearson must have come down hard on him. Did that mean Pearson did think there was some truth in the idea? That Rigby had something to do with it after all?

"Does Pearson know you're here?" Cal asked.

Rigby shrugged and looked away.

"I'll take that as a no," Cal said. "I'll be sure to mention your visit to Pearson the next time I see him. I'll be interested to hear what he has to say on the matter."

"Pearson advised me to stay away from you."

"You should have taken his advice."

"What? And let you continue to bad mouth me? That's not going to help solve this case, or Katy's, for that matter."

"What do you care about the case? You don't give a damn about me, and they took you off Katy's case, remember? I guess someone else felt you couldn't be trusted."

Rigby's jaw clenched. "I had nothing to do with this."

"Yeah, that's what I keep saying," Cal said. "Now you know how it feels."

Lily stood up. "Detective Rigby I'm sure you're not supposed to be here, and your presence is upsetting my husband. You've made your point, now please leave."

"Okay," Rigby lifted both hands in a gesture of surrender. "I'm sorry. I didn't intend to upset anyone." He paused. "Could I speak to you for a moment Mrs. Miller?"

Lily looked back at Cal. Cal shook his head. He didn't want Rigby having a chance to plant any more seeds of doubt in her mind.

"Please," Rigby said, "just a moment of your time."

Lily sighed. "If it gets you out of this room, okay. But just five minutes and then you're gone."

As he turned to leave, Rigby flashed Cal an almost sympathetic glance. "I hope you feel better soon, Mr. Miller."

"Get lost." Cal clenched his fists and thumped on the

mattress. He was so damned helpless at the moment he wanted to scream.

Cal watched the door swing closed behind them. He pushed the bedclothes away, rolled onto his left side and eased himself up into a sitting position on the edge of the bed. Arrows of pain rippled through his back and he flinched at the sight of the black and red bruises that covered his legs below the hospital gown. The doctor hadn't exaggerated. The unblemished areas of skin were mere frames for the angry abstract patterns on his legs. He shuddered and battled to shut out images from the beating that replayed in his mind.

Taking a deep breath, he clenched his teeth and lowered his feet to the floor. The soles of his feet were unscathed, but his shins rebelled, sending nauseous waves up his body, telling him to lie back down. He reached down for the urine bag then shuffled alongside the bed, reducing to a minimum the distance he would have to walk unsupported.

He staggered to the door and looked out into the corridor. There was no sign of Rigby or Lily, or of the supposed police guard. His room was the last one on a short, dead-end corridor. There appeared to be a nurses' station at the other end, but the effort involved in getting there was beyond him. He sagged back against the wall for a moment to regain his equilibrium. He didn't want a nurse. He wanted Lily. What lies was Rigby feeding her?

When no-one appeared he shuffled back into the room and slowly made his way to the bathroom. Now was as good a time as any to see what state his face was in. It was hard to imagine he could feel more wretched than he already did.

He was wrong. He stifled a gasp as he glanced up at the mirror. Lily was right. It was no longer his face. His well-defined cheeks and jaw line were hidden under mounds of sickly colored skin, the right side swollen to almost twice the size of the left, his eyes mere slits in the folds. A cut snaked its way across his temple from the corner of his right eye, which was bloodshot and teary. His lips were misshapen and split. A vivid scar stood out in sharp contrast against the pallor of the shaved side of his head. The remaining hair just added a touch of surrealism to the whole picture.

As the initial shock wore off, he peered fascinated at the reflection. He was amazed that anyone could bear to look at him. No wonder his mother had cried or that Kieran had looked repulsed. How had Lily coped? Sitting by his bedside for hours, looking at that? He had to believe that time would heal him, but in his current frame of mind it required an immense stretch of the imagination. He shuddered. It was his face and yet he couldn't bear to look at it.

He swung away from the mirror. His mother stood in the doorway. He turned his head away. She didn't speak, just stepped forward and held out her arms. He needed no more encouragement. He leant into her embrace, resting his chin on her shoulder, willing himself to ignore the discomfort as she wrapped her arms around him in a tight hug before caressing his back with her right hand. Thirty years slipped away in seconds. He was six years old again, safe in the arms of his mother.

His mother pulled him closer. Cal didn't resist.

Chapter 29

It was five more days before the bleeding from his kidneys stopped and he was allowed to go home. Five days of veering between relief at being able to hide away from the real world and fear at what waited for him on his return. Katy was still missing. Some days he wished he could stay in hospital until they found her. Here, he was a victim not a suspect. Here, Lily was by his side, caring, compassionate. Here, he could let his concerns about his health obliterate the worries of whether his business was about to go down the drain and his marriage on the rocks, not to mention the little matter of losing his freedom altogether. He knew the worries were still there, but without his health they seemed less important.

Pearson had paid him one more visit the previous day. Cal told him about Rigby's unexpected appearance. Pearson shrugged it off, but Cal saw a look of irritation flash across his face. Cal hoped Pearson would give Rigby hell. He deserved it. Lily had insisted that Rigby had only continued to press his innocence in the matter of Cal's beating. Cal didn't believe that was all. He was sure Rigby had tried to plant further suspicions of Cal's infidelity in her mind. He was only grateful that Lily had chosen to ignore them.

He sat on the side of the bed as the nurse gave him one last checking over.

"The scar's healing beautifully," she said, dusting her

fingertips over his bald head.

Cal snorted. "Why do you say things like that? It's a scar. Scars aren't beautiful."

She made a face at him. "My, my, you are grumpy this morning. What's the matter? You should be overjoyed at the thought of leaving this place."

"From the frying pan to the fire."

"What?" The nurse looked puzzled for a moment. "Oh, you mean the business about the missing girl?"

Cal nodded.

"It can't be easy, living with that."

"It's not." Cal sighed. "The problem is I don't know how to get people to believe that I haven't done anything wrong."

The nurse gave him a sympathetic glance. "Tell the truth, I guess, that's all you can do." She picked up a clip chart and started writing. "What do they say? The truth will set you free."

"I hope to God you're right," Cal said. "And I wish it would hurry up."

The nurse laughed and held the clipboard out to him. "Sign here and here and you're on your way." She signaled to a porter who had appeared at the door with a wheelchair. "Mr. Miller's wife will be waiting at the staff entrance." The porter nodded and then helped Cal into the chair. The nurse planted a kiss on Cal's bald head. "Goodbye Mr. Miller. And good luck. And remember, have faith. The truth will set you free."

As the porter pushed him away, Cal remembered his manners. He looked back and gave her a small wave. "Thanks for everything."

She waved back. "You're welcome."

He forced a smile for her. As the porter pushed him round a corner, the smile disappeared. Both Rigby and Kieran had said the same thing. That he'd gotten himself in trouble by lying. And maybe they were right. But what if it were too late for the truth?

Lily was waiting in the car for him. It had been Pearson's suggestion that they leave by the back exit. The press had been fed the story of the beating but not allowed access to him in the hospital. There could be no guarantee that somebody wasn't waiting out front for his departure. Cal was impressed by Pearson's concern for his privacy, nervous of his ulterior motives.

"Did my parents and the girls get away okay?" he asked as Lily started the car.

"Left about half an hour ago. The girls were rather tearful. Asked why they couldn't at least wait until you got home. I told them the doctors said you could only come home if there was lots of peace and quiet."

Cal grinned. "I bet they were out of the door like a shot on hearing that."

"On the contrary," Lily said. "Amanda promised they would walk on their tiptoes and only speak in a whisper if they could stay. It was quite a struggle to get them to go." As she pulled up at a red light she looked over at Cal. "Your parents were wonderful, you know. They really did their best to try and distract the girls. They have all sorts of exciting trips planned for them."

"That's my mother. Any excuse for being around children. I'm not sure she's forgiven us all for growing up."

"I don't think she wanted to leave either. I'm sure she'd rather stay here with you. She wants to help."

"She is helping by taking the children. I don't want them to see me like this. They'll think Halloween has come early. Admit it. I look scary enough without a mask."

"It's getting better."

"Yeah, if you think purple and yellow suit me better than red and black."

"The doctors said the bruising could take two to three weeks to disappear, but the swelling is already going down."

"Great. So I'll only look like something out of the Zombie from Hell movie for another two weeks or so."

"You don't look that bad."

"Yes I do. Admit it. It makes you sick to look at me."

"No!"

"Why not? It's my face and it makes me feel sick. I saw the looks Kieran gave me, and my parents. And Kieran and my father haven't exactly been rushing back to the hospital to see me."

"If you remember, you upset Kieran. Besides you know Dad hates hospitals and your mother more than made up for him."

"True."

"I think women are just better at handling this kind of thing. In our genes I guess. Somehow we seem more immune to the messes life can throw at us occasionally, whether it's the disgusting diaper, the bed full of vomit or the battered face."

"Charming."

"Well it's true. You have to look beyond the mess and see the person behind it. That might be why your mother is desperate to help. She looks at your face, she knows you're a grown-up, as capable as her of solving your own problems, but her heart tells her you're still her baby."

"And rues the day she had me."

Lily gave him a sharp glance. "That's not true Cal, and you know it."

"Oh no, I suppose you're saying you've never rued the day you met me? Not even now, when you're living with a murder suspect."

There was a sudden silence in the car. Lily focused on the traffic but a noticeable flush appeared on her cheeks. Cal wished he'd kept his mouth shut. What was he hoping to get from her anyhow? A declaration of everlasting devotion? Damn it, Kieran was right, he didn't deserve one. She was here now; he should be satisfied with that. But this whole business made him feel insecure, isolated. He had to get round it somehow. It was affecting his judgment.

Lily pulled up at another red light. She reached out to touch his left knee. "I'm here. Your parents are helping. Doesn't that tell you anything?" The light changed. She started the car up again. "When it comes to Katy's disappearance, we believe you're telling the truth."

Cal looked out of the side window as they drove through town, a town where most people thought he was a liar. The truth. It all came back to the truth.

But did anyone tell the truth anymore?

Chapter 30

The house had an unaccustomed quietness to it without the girls. They lay in bed until well into mid-morning with nobody demanding they get up. They passed the days watching television or DVD's and reading, their sole commitment the early evening phone call to say goodnight to the girls. Lily left the house only to get more groceries or restock their reading supplies. Cal never left the house. Until he could face himself in the mirror he didn't want to be seen.

At first Lily insisted he was being ridiculous, but eventually she gave up. She knew not to answer the door unless Cal was out of sight; knew to turn all visitors away. Not that there was many of them. Letters to the local editor expressed shock at such savagery occurring on their doorsteps, two serious crimes in a matter of weeks, what were the local police doing to control this crime wave? Few extended their condolences to Cal himself.

There were flowers and a card from Jim and Peggy, a card and hefty bestseller from Marc Coulson, and that was about it. Cal knew it was wrong. He didn't want people knocking on his door at all hours, but this was a small town and there should have been plates of cookies or pots of stew, people rallying round to help a family in distress. Instead there was silence.

It enraged Cal. Not for himself, but because of the effect it had on Lily. His alleged guilt was one thing, but her innocence was beyond doubt. She shouldn't have to suffer because of him. Sometimes he almost wished she would leave just so that he could be rid of the guilt. He loved her. He should be protecting her, not hurting her.

As the days passed, the bruises on his body changed color and slowly started to fade. He assumed the same was true of those on his face—he'd asked Lily to cover all the mirrors in the house so he wouldn't be constantly confronted by his disfigurement. By touch he could tell that the swelling on his face was going down and his mouth was almost back to normal apart from the occasional dribble if he spoke too quickly. Still, he waited.

From the local news he learned that the search for Katy had been called off. Pearson made the announcement then insisted that, though the search had been abandoned, the investigation into Katy's whereabouts would continue until such time as it was brought to a satisfactory conclusion. Cal wondered whether he was equally determined to catch Cal's attackers. He didn't mention it, despite the obvious connection.

Cal toyed with the idea of calling Pearson to tell him that he thought he'd seen Katy, but each time he went to the phone he chickened out. It would just sound too outrageous. There was the question of motive for a start. If he believed the attack was in revenge for his involvement in Katy's disappearance, how could he explain Katy's presence? That left only the idea that Katy was trying to get back at him because he'd somehow rebuffed her imaginary advances. But that would be… psychotic and Pearson wasn't about to buy that. Besides how could she have managed to stay invisible all this time?

He gave no thought to working, even though he knew that every bill that arrived was eating up their savings. Lily had offered to go and collect his computer and files from the office, but he told her not to bother, claiming that he wasn't up to working yet. How could he add to her worries by telling her that there was little or no work? He knew he should do something about that. Instead he sat in front of the television.

Lily suggested he should talk to someone, a therapist or at least a doctor. She said it was natural for him to feel depressed given everything that had happened. He told her he wasn't depressed; just living a nightmare that only Katy's return could end. Telling his problems to a shrink wouldn't solve them. He didn't mention the other reason. He couldn't afford the bills.

"Cal, this has got to stop!"

Cal glanced up from his paper. Lily's pale face glared at him across the breakfast table. She'd been looking off color for several days now. He'd put it down to stress. Maybe he should insist she see a doctor.

"We can't go on hiding away like this," Lily said. "It's been over two weeks. We've got to get our life back together, bring the girls home. You've got to think about going back to work, at least part time."

"I'm still recovering."

"You're not recovering, you're stagnating. Sitting in front of the television watching reruns isn't going to help you get better one bit. What about the exercises the doctor gave you? And you're supposed to be walking every day. I don't think the distance between the bed and sofa counts."

"I'm not going out looking like this."

"Looking like what? You haven't looked in a mirror since you left the hospital. You don't know what you look like."

"I know that people are going to stare at me."

"So? Ignore them."

Cal snorted. "That's easy for you to say. I've had enough of people staring at me already, whispering behind my back, pretending they haven't noticed me so they can walk straight past without speaking." He pointed to his face. "This would just give them more to talk about. You don't know what it's like."

"The hell I don't."

"What?"

"Cal, what do you think they say about me?"

Cal shook his head. Somehow, he'd never thought about it. "I would think they admire your loyalty. I know I do."

Lily laughed a high pitched nervous screech. "Admire my loyalty! Tell me you're kidding. They doubt my judgment. 'How can she stay with him knowing what he's done?' That's what they're thinking as they stare at me, whisper about me and pass me in the street without speaking." Tears spilled into her eyes. "Don't tell me that I don't know what I'm talking about." She sank her face into her hands.

Cal eased himself to his feet, crossed to Lily and caressed her shoulders. "I'm sorry, I've been selfish. I didn't think."

"We can't hide Cal. We're innocent. We have to stand up for ourselves. We have to take back our lives."

The idea filled Cal with dread. What would Lily say when she knew the truth? But he owed her this much at least. He forced a smile. "Where do you suggest we start?"

"I'm going to go and fetch the girls. I'll drive up today, bring them back tomorrow. You want to come? It'll do you good to get away for a while."

It was a tempting offer. Then Cal thought about having to get Pearson's permission for the trip.

"No, I'm not sure I could sit for that long in the car yet. I'll stay here."

He slid his arms down over Lily's shoulders, crossing them over her breasts as he leant forward and pulled her towards him. She tilted her head back so she could see him. He kissed her on the forehead. How had he not noticed how sickly she was looking? Had he been that self-absorbed? He kissed her again.

"I promise you that before you come back I'll look in the mirror."

"It's a deal," she said.

Chapter 31

Keeping his side of the deal was harder than he'd bargained for. Twice after Lily left, he stood in the bathroom and braced himself to pull down the towel hiding the mirror. Twice he walked away, kicking himself for his cowardice. He wasn't a vain man. He liked to think he judged people on their personalities, not their looks, so he should have faith that others did too. It shouldn't matter so much. But memories of the repugnance he'd felt on first seeing his face in the hospital kept coming back. If he felt that way, how could he expect others to feel different?

True, the doctors expected that his features would return to normal over time, but maybe they were wrong. How often would they have to deal with people whose faces had been beaten so methodically?

He returned to the kitchen and poured himself a large glass of whiskey, ignoring the doctor's advice not to drink while he was on pain medication. He needed something to calm his nerves. As he swallowed the last drop he looked at the refrigerator magnets containing pictures of Amanda and Sophie. His beautiful little girls. How would he cope if they screamed when they saw him? Ran from him rather than to him? What if seeing him caused them irreparable damage? It was a stupid idea to bring them back now. He grabbed the telephone, started to punch in the numbers. Then he slammed the receiver down. Lily wanted this, needed it. And he owed her.

He paced the kitchen, his stomach churning. He had to get

this over with. He took three huge gulps of air, marched into the downstairs cloakroom and yanked the towel from the mirror.

The whiskey came back up in a heaving hot gush, leaving him shaking and shivering. Turning a tap on to wash away the remnants, he looked up slowly from the sink.

His own face looked back. The skin was mostly yellow, with patches of fading red and black and there was still some puffiness around the eyes. And his right cheekbone had definitely been rearranged. But he was himself. He let out a huge chortle of relief. His daughters might be shocked, but at least they would know it was Daddy.

He ran his hand over his head. A fine fuzzy covering of new hair hid the baldness and the scar. He would never have dreamt of having his hair cut this short, but as he surveyed it from several angles, he had to admit it looked pretty good. He'd ask Lily what she thought. Maybe from now on he would keep it short.

Lily was right, as usual. He had to pull himself together. He found a notepad and pencil and sat down at the kitchen table to make a list of things he needed to do. First, he had to call Kieran and apologize. He hadn't seen him since that day in the hospital, but he knew Kieran had kept in constant touch with Lily, making sure they were all okay. He also had to get back to the office, get up to date with the existing work, see where he stood with his clients and figure out how bad things really were. He sighed. And then…

Then he had to come clean with Lily and his parents. About the journal, about everything.

He chewed at the pencil as he considered the list. He'd always considered himself an honest man. Until the affair, he'd never lied to Lily, not deliberately. Yet, now he had this whole web of deceit he had to undo before it destroyed him. When had he started leading such a secretive life?

He still hadn't been totally honest with Pearson about what he knew about Katy's disappearance. He'd meant to be, but at first he'd thought the information was irrelevant, then that damned journal appeared and he'd panicked about his marriage. And once he'd started lying, Pearson had been suspicious and Rigby had been out for blood. The information he had was innocent enough, but the way the case blew up against him it was bound to make a bad situation worse. And he knew firsthand how the police could get.

Besides, Pearson had never asked him the question. That was beginning to worry him a little. It seemed like an obvious question, even if it was quite possible Cal didn't know the answer. If he'd been in Pearson's shoes, he was sure he would have asked it.

He drummed the pencil on the table. Was Pearson laying some kind of trap? Had he fallen into it? He added one more item to the list. *Come clean with Pearson.*

Still it was odd. He'd insisted all along that Katy had left town. Why had nobody asked him if he knew how she planned to do so?

Chapter 32

The following morning, Cal was on edge. He couldn't wait to see the girls again. He'd been far too distant before the attack, leaving Lily to deal with them. He was determined to make up for it.

And his resolve to finally come clean was holding. It terrified him... he could lose his marriage, his freedom, everything. But he could see that, if he kept living the lies, he was going to lose everything anyway. And even if no one ever found out, he couldn't live with the suspicion and deception. Lily was more on his side than she'd ever been. Now was the time.

In fact, maybe *now* was the time. Lily wouldn't be back for hours, and he certainly had nothing else to do. Maybe he should pay a visit to Pearson, get that out of the way.

Then if he had enough time, he could drive down to the local mall outside Lewisville, buy the girls a gift and maybe one for Lily too. But when he locked the door behind him, he was surprised by how nervous he felt. He sat behind the wheel of his car, checking out his mobility. His reactions were slower than normal, he'd have to be careful, but he was sure he'd manage.

Passing the garage on the way to the police station, he realized the car was running low on gas. He turned round and pulled in, pleased to see that the owner, Billy Thorpe, was behind the counter again. As he stopped by the full service pump, Billy hobbled out. His walk was even more labored than Cal's, but that didn't stop him having an almost permanent smile on his chubby

Silent Lies

face.

"Hey Cal, how you doing?" Billy said as Cal wound down his window. "Whoa, that looks painful."

"Yeah, well…" Cal shrugged, not really knowing what to say. He was going to have to get used to this.

"Sorry to hear about your troubles," Billy said as he unscrewed the gas cap and linked up the nozzle. "I only heard about it yesterday. Just got back from Florida, been down there a few weeks, the youngest daughter's just given us our tenth grandchild. Can you imagine? Ten!"

Cal smiled. "Congratulations."

"Not all hers of course." Billy laughed. "In fact it's her first, but as I was saying, that's how the wife and I didn't know anything about the Shore girl being missing. I told the police I would've contacted them sooner if I'd known. I called as soon as I heard."

"You know something about Katy?" Cal's heart started to pound. Maybe at last there was going to be another link to Katy's running away.

"Only that I saw her that Friday evening."

Cal blinked. "You saw her? Where?"

"With you. Heading off towards Route 82."

Cal felt the blood drain from his face.

"You were at the red light." Billy pointed to the traffic lights just outside the garage. "I told the police it was definitely just after ten, because I'd just closed up and was getting ready to go home when I saw your car pull up." He laughed. "They asked if I could be sure, with it being dark and all, but as I told them, I reckon I know every car in town, hell, we service most of them. Besides I could see you and Katy in the front."

Cal stared at Billy, his mind blank.

"I told them you would have been giving her a lift somewhere. I know she doesn't have her own car. All this business with the searches, the investigation, whatever, they're wasting their time and I told them so. If anybody was going to run away from this town it would be Katy." He paused, looking thoughtful for a moment. "After all her mother did too. And who can blame her, Katy I mean, her father's never been the same since his wife left and those brothers well…" He shook his head,

163

"especially the two younger ones, I tell you, most people would want to run away."

Cal found his voice. "Who did you speak to?"

"When?"

"At the police station."

"Oh, a real friendly guy, not one of the locals. From Lewisville I believe." He laughed again. "The name escapes me. That's what happens as you age. You remember the old names but not the new ones."

"Pearson?" Cal said, "Was it Pearson?"

Pray it wasn't. Pray it was someone else who took Billy for a rambling old man and didn't appreciate the implications of what he had to say. Please God, be kind. He was finally going to tell the truth, damn it, he didn't deserve this.

"Yes, that's it. Dreadful isn't it, the way it happens? I only just met the guy and I've forgotten his name already."

The gas nozzle clicked off. Billy removed it, replaced it on the pump and screwed the gas cap back on. "You okay?" he said as he came back to the car window, "you look a bit pale. Maybe it's too early for you to be out driving. I hear they worked you over pretty good."

"Yes... No... I mean I'm fine..."

His brain finally started to work. Damn, he hadn't for a moment considered that anyone might have seen them. The streets had been deserted. He even remembered pulling up at that light, noting the pumps were dark, satisfied that Billy had gone home and wouldn't be wondering why he was driving Katy Shore through town at ten o'clock at night.

As he paid for the gas Cal tried to make his voice as normal as possible. "So you spoke to Pearson yesterday."

"First thing this morning. I didn't want to bother them late last night. It's not as if it's going to make a big difference to their investigation, not now. They already knew you were the last person to see her. I just thought it would help verify things if I told them I'd seen you driving her out of town."

Cal suppressed an urge to scream. It wasn't Billy's fault. If he'd told Pearson the truth in the first place he would have been grateful for Billy's confirmation.

"You sure you're all right?" Billy's voice was full of

concern. "Maybe you shouldn't be driving in your condition."

"Yes... No... I mean you're right. I think I'll go straight home."

Cal put the car into drive.

"Thanks Billy." He forced the words out. "And congratulations again, ten grandkids, that's really something."

He wound the window up before Billy could say anything else and pulled away.

He had to think fast. Even now, Pearson could be at his house, waiting to question him, wanting to know why Cal hadn't volunteered the information himself. The information just led to a dead end, but would Pearson believe that? He'd see it as just another inconsistency in Cal's stories. Never mind that he hadn't asked the question that might have prompted Cal to be up front. Cal's silence on the matter would be incriminating enough.

As soon as he was out of sight of the garage he pulled the car over to the side of the road. He was trembling now, panic overriding his reason. Could he be arrested? There wasn't even a crime, but try telling the police or the townspeople that. They were all convinced something dreadful had happened to Katy and the conviction just grew the longer she remained missing. So how could he stand up now and say he'd neglected to tell the police that he'd driven Katy out of town? He'd set her off on the first leg of her escape, but that it didn't make any difference and he'd been afraid to mention it because of how it would look and he didn't want her family to know he was involved. He thumped the steering wheel. There were so many reasons that had all seemed so damned sensible at the time, but now appeared for what they were—lame excuses of the weak and cowardly.

He still was. Weak, cowardly and paranoid too. And with good reason. He was sure Pearson was out to get him for Katy's disappearance. Forget all the niceties, the concern since the beating. When it came down to it, Pearson wanted to close this case and the only suspect he had was Cal. Pearson was a determined man, everybody said so. He wouldn't give up until Katy came back or Cal was behind bars.

Cal exhaled heavily. There was only one thing to do. He had to find Katy. He had no idea where to start looking, but it was the only thing that was going to clear his name. To do so though, he had to stay out of Pearson's clutches and there was only one way to ensure that. Leave town himself.

He looked at the road ahead. Maybe some hand of fate had brought him out this morning, made him pull in at Billy's garage. If he hadn't, he would have no idea of this latest development. It was giving him a chance, a chance he couldn't waste. Ideally he would go home, collect a few belongings and leave a note for Lily, but the police might be there, waiting for him. Hell, they might already be driving through the streets looking for him, checking out his office. No, if he was going, he had to go now.

He checked his wallet. He had his credit cards and driver's license with him. He'd draw out a chunk of money on his card. It would cost him, but what price his freedom? And he couldn't keep using his cards or the police would track him down in no time.

He pulled the car out into the traffic and turned right onto Route 82. The county airport was only ten miles away. He'd go there, take a flight to any of the major out-of-state hubs then consider his next move.

He let himself relax a little. He was doing fine. Thinking straight. That was it, get out of state. Hopefully then he'd be more difficult to track.

The airport terminal was a long thin building, arrivals to the right, departures to the left, separated by an information counter and a ticket sales office. Mid-morning, it was busy without being frantic. Cal checked out the departure board. There was a flight to Chicago in less than an hour. That would be ideal. He hurried over to the sales counter grateful to see that there was only a short line.

The sole ticketing agent dealt with the passengers in front of Cal efficiently and politely. Several more people joined the line. Cal was pleased. He would just be one more ticket sale in a busy day, nothing out of the ordinary. He stepped up to the counter. "Round trip to Chicago please. The twelve o'clock flight."

The agent tapped away at her keyboard, barely looking at him. "Identification please, sir."

Cal pulled out his driver's license and handed it over the counter.

The agent glanced at Cal, then his license and back to the computer, a hint of a frown in her expression.

Cal held his breath. Did she suspect something? It wasn't

possible.

She continued typing, her fingers flying over the keys.

Suddenly he realized what the problem was. "I'm afraid it doesn't look much like me at the moment, with the bruises and…"

"That's okay." She gave him a forced smile. "I can see the similarities."

Cal smiled back.

"I'm afraid the twelve o'clock flight looks as if it's full, but let me go and ring through to the gate. Sometimes they have a last minute cancellation." She slipped off her stool and disappeared through a back door before Cal had a chance to reply.

Cal looked at his watch. Forty-five minutes until take off. He still had time, no need to panic. He looked at the name card on the desk. Christine O'Leary, Ticketing sales agent. He hoped Christine was working some magic, getting him onto the flight.

She returned in less than five minutes, her expression grim. As she sat back down she forced another smile. "Mr. Miller, it does look as if that flight is full. However they're boarding it now, and if you'd care to wait here the stewardesses will ring through and let me know if anything does come available before they close the flight."

Cal hesitated. It wasn't what he wanted to hear. He looked at his watch again.

"If we can't get you on that flight I'm sure we can get you on the next one at two o'clock."

Cal forced himself to remain calm, no point in raising suspicions. "Okay. Thank you."

"If you just step to one side while we're waiting to hear from the gate, I can serve the next person."

Cal took a couple of steps to the right, waving the next person in line forward. He watched Christine issue tickets for JFK, Newark and Boston. Trust him to have picked the most popular destination that day. He kept his eye on his watch as the minutes ticked slowly by.

Christine seemed to sense his anxiety. "Don't worry, if there's room they won't go without you."

Cal did worry. The idea of hanging around for another two hours made him nervous. He'd feel a lot happier once he was in the air. To take his mind off his wait he read all the notices behind the counter; lists of disallowed baggage, new security regulations, even a complicated statement of when and where you were entitled to a refund.

Fifteen minutes passed. He was testing his eyesight by trying to read the small print about the refunds—the part which told you how much it was going to cost—when he felt a tap on his shoulder. Startled, he spun round.

"Planning to stay in Chicago long?" Pearson asked. Docherty stood off to the side flanked by two uniformed officers.

Cal looked from Pearson to Christine.

"Don't blame her," Pearson said, "she was just doing her job. Your name was already flagged in the computer so that if you tried to buy a ticket we'd be notified." Pearson paused. Then when Cal didn't speak added, "So. Here we are."

Cal stayed silent. A small crowd of people began to gather. He could sense them all staring at him, hoping to see some action to relieve the airport boredom and give them a story to tell at the dinner table that night.

"Mr. Miller, you are under arrest on a charge of obstruction of justice." Pearson recited Cal's rights, the words tripping easily from his tongue. "Please turn around and put your hands on the counter."

Cal turned slowly, trying to avoid eye contact with Christine. She stopped typing and watched as Pearson patted him down and then cuffed his hands behind his back. It felt like the whole damned airport was watching.

Pearson surveyed the floor around Cal's feet. "Where are your bags?"

"I don't have any."

"My, my, you do travel light."

He took hold of Cal's arm and guided him towards the exit. Docherty stepped around to Cal's other side. One officer walked in front, the other behind. Cal kept his eyes down as he was led through the growing crowd of spectators.

An unmarked car stood at the curb in an emergency parking zone, a black and white patrol car squeezed in tight behind it, its lights flashing. Another group of onlookers had gathered. The officer in front moved them to one side and opened the rear door.

Pearson nudged Cal towards the car then stopped. "You

drove here?"

Cal nodded.

"Where's the car?"

"Long term car park, Sector J2."

"The keys?"

"You should know. You've just patted me down."

Pearson grinned, reached into the right hand pocket of Cal's jacket and pulled out a set of keys and a parking ticket. He tossed them to Docherty. "A white Acura, LAS 63, Correct?" He looked at Cal for confirmation.

Cal just nodded.

"Bring it down to the station house for Mr. Miller."

Docherty started to walk away.

"Drive carefully," Pearson called after him. "Remember it's not your car." He turned back to Cal and gestured towards the open door of the patrol car. "Get in. I'll see you back at the station."

Cal eased himself into the car. The door was slammed shut. Both officers got into the front. There was a loud click as the automatic door locks were operated. They weren't taking any chances. They waited until Pearson had pulled out into traffic in the unmarked car and edged out behind him.

Cal tried to get comfortable, not easy with his hands behind his back. He looked out of the window as miles of countryside sped by on the way to Leyton. A cloudless blue sky accompanied by weak sunshine belied the chill of autumn. It was a day for raking leaves or an invigorating walk through the newly bare woods, their former glory scattered on the ground like a comforter to protect the earth from the forthcoming cold. It was a tease because he hadn't noticed it when he left home. It took the prospect of a windowless room to bring it to his attention.

He wondered if Lily, heading towards Leyton too, had noticed it. How would she and the girls react to arriving home to an empty house with no indication of where he was? Or to his phone call?

He sighed.

"What now?" he whispered softly to himself. "What the hell have I done?"

169

Chapter 33

The police car pulled up in front of the station house while Pearson's car continued on around the side of the building. Both officers got out, waited patiently for Cal to swing his legs out of the car before helping him to his feet, and escorted him into the building.

The same boyish officer sat behind the desk, this time in an animated conversation with a smartly dressed man who appeared to be taking notes. The officer glanced up at Cal's entrance and his companion turned to see what the distraction was. Cal tried to keep his face hidden as he was hustled across the reception area and into the back office, but he still caught the look of glee on the stranger's face.

"Isn't that the Miller guy?" he heard as the office doors closed behind him.

Great. Talk about lousy timing. A reporter from the local paper, no doubt, there to check up on the day's happenings. A dull routine assignment in a town like Leyton, until today. Today the guy had netted himself a scoop.

Two more officers sat in the back room deep in discussion. They too broke off and looked up as Cal was taken towards the interview room. One of them was the guy who had been with Rigby in the bar; the one he thought looked familiar. He still couldn't place him, but at least now he knew he had been right in his assumption that the guy was a police officer.

The guy sneered at him in an evil penetrating way that Cal could sense even after the interview room door was closed. A shiver went through him. One of Rigby's accomplices? If he worked here, Cal needed to get bail as quickly as possible.

"I want to call my lawyer," Cal said as one of his escorts, Benson, indicated for him to sit down.

"You will." The other guy, Stockman, sat down opposite him and began filling out a form, asking all the same questions as the last time. Cal was tempted to tell him just to dig out his file, but he kept quiet, embarrassed by the fact that he had a police file.

They were just finishing up when Pearson burst into the room. He took one look at Cal and turned in fury on Stockman. "Why is Mr. Miller still in cuffs?"

Stockman's cheeks turned deep red. "I thought that, as he was a flight risk…"

"A flight risk? The guy can hardly walk! Even you could stop him getting out the door. Now get those cuffs off immediately."

Benson practically dove at the cuffs. Cal heaved a loud sigh as his wrists were released and made a show of rubbing his shoulders and upper arms.

"I want to call my lawyer," he said to Pearson.

"When I say so." Pearson turned back to Stockman. "Whose stupid idea was it to bring him in, in front of that reporter?"

"But you said—"

"I said bring him here, not turn the place into a media circus." He looked at his watch. "Within the hour the whole place will be swarming with reporters, all hoping to get something to spice up the evening news."

Stockman remained silent.

"Fine. When you finish up here you're on crowd control. Get outside and make sure you keep the entranceway clear. And I mean clear, understand?"

"I'm off duty at three," Stockman said.

"Not any more." Pearson turned to Benson. "You go and find… find whoever else is on duty and tell them to get over to the Miller house and make sure there aren't any reporters making a fuss there."

Cal stood up. "I need to call my wife. She doesn't know about this."

"You sit down," Pearson said. "Tell them to notify Mr. Miller's wife that Mr. Miller is here."

"I need to speak to her," Cal said. "To explain."

"Sit down! We'll tell her you're here, not in Chicago."

"She doesn't know I was going to Chicago."

There was a sudden silence in the room.

"Ah." Pearson grimaced. "Don't know about yours, but my wife would give me hell if I didn't tell her I was going away."

Cal tried to look impassive. Inside he was raging at his own stupidity. He should have gone home first, left a note. And he should never have gone to the airport. He should have got on a bus or a train, anything where he wouldn't be required to show ID. Damn Pearson. He hadn't thought for a moment that he would put his name on a watch list. Lily wouldn't give him hell. She'd walk out. And he couldn't blame her.

"I'd like to make my phone call now," he said. Maybe he could contain the damage somehow if he spoke to Lily before the police turned up on the doorstep again.

"On second thoughts," Pearson said, "I'll go too. I'll speak to Mrs. Miller."

"No!"

"Pardon me, was that an order?" Pearson leant across the table until his face was only inches from Cal's. "I think you misunderstand the situation. You don't get a say in what happens next. You just do as you're told."

The words were like a slap in the face. Cal eased back in his seat so that Pearson wasn't breathing over him. "I have a right to make a phone call."

"And you will. Later." Pearson straightened up. "But let me give you a piece of advice, use it to call your lawyer. You're going to need him."

He made for the door. Benson followed.

"After you've spoken with the others," Pearson said, "you stay with Mr. Miller. Get his lawyer on the phone. Oh and give him a cup of coffee or something." He flashed a grin at Cal over his shoulder. "I don't want him saying that we mistreated him."

He disappeared out of the door, leaving Benson shaking his head. When he was sure Pearson was out of sight, Benson turned back to Stockman and rolled his eyes. "Good thing it's one of his better days."

They both laughed.

Cal couldn't see the joke.

Once again Cal was photographed, fingerprinted and made to turn out his pockets. The latter seemed a futile exercise when they were going to have to give it all back to him in a few hours when he made bail, but he went along with their demands.

All he could think of was Lily. How she would react to the news that he'd tried to leave town. His arrest wasn't much more than an inconvenience caused by panic, his panic. Pearson still didn't have anything serious on him, hence the resurrection of the obstruction of justice charges as a way to keep the pressure on, hope that he'd trip up and give them a lead. At least he didn't have to worry about that. He was innocent and all the secrets were out, so there was nothing to trip over. If Pearson insisted on pressing charges for obstruction of justice, so be it, he'd just have to face the consequences.

But Lily. Life without her would be like a life sentence.

Pearson was gone a long time. How long could it take him to tell Lily that Cal had been arrested and why? Even if she did react badly to the news. He imagined them sitting together in the living room, Pearson putting on his nice guy act, being sympathetic, conciliatory, hoping to get something out of Lily. Well he was wasting his time. Lily knew zilch. That was both Cal's saving and his downfall. Lily couldn't say anything she shouldn't to the police, but Pearson could definitely tell her a thing or two she wouldn't want to know.

Weinsteenberg hadn't showed up yet, which was another worry. Benson had finally volunteered that they couldn't reach anyone at his office. All they could do was to leave a message on his cell phone. The minutes dragged by, wasted minutes that should have been spent conferring with his lawyer before Pearson returned. Cal was banking on Weinsteenberg getting him out as quickly as last time. He passed the time drumming his fingers on the table while Benson hovered near the door, silent except to report on the attempts to contact Weinsteenberg.

Cal considered protesting against the wait. His muscles were certainly doing so, stiff and weary after the spell on the hard wooden chair. The last pain medication was beginning to wear off. He was tired and grouchy. It was no way to face a police interview. But maybe that was the point, to wear him down before they even started with the questioning. Cal rolled his head from side to side, trying to relieve the tension on his neck and shoulders. He looked across at Benson hoping for some sympathy. Benson ignored him.

Suddenly the door opened. The young officer from the front desk peered round at his colleague.

"Pearson just called in. He's had to go over to HQ. He said to tell you to put Mr. Miller in the cells until his lawyer turns up. Mrs. Miller will be dropping by to deliver some medication that Mr. Miller needs, but he's not to have any visitors apart from his lawyer until Pearson's spoken to him. He's already told her she will probably have to wait until tomorrow to see her husband."

"Tomorrow!" Cal gaped at the officer. "I want to make bail today."

"That's up to Pearson sir, but I know there's one catch already."

"Oh yeah?" Cal said cautiously. Surely Pearson wasn't going to object to bail. "What's that?"

"Justice Barnes was called out of town on an emergency this afternoon. There's nobody to cover for him. Everything will have to be held over until Monday."

"Monday! I could be stuck here until Monday?"

"Afraid so." The officer sounded genuinely sympathetic. "You've picked the wrong weekend to be arrested."

Cal slumped back in his chair and gazed up at the ceiling. "This can't be happening."

"Look at it this way sir, better here than in County Jail."

"Is that supposed to be a consolation?"

The sympathy quickly disappeared from the officer's demeanor. He turned to Benson, who dismissed him with a flick of his head. "Just passing on the message," he said sullenly as he disappeared from sight.

Cal lowered his head to hide his anxiety. Where the hell was Weinsteenberg? The lawyer had to persuade Pearson to drop the charges again. It was his only chance.

Benson led Cal into the outer office, clutching Cal's elbow as if he thought he was likely to make a dash for it.

"Got a guest for a couple of nights," he said to the office at large. Four new faces turned to look at Cal with interest. "Mr. Miller here tried to make an unauthorized trip out of town, thereby incurring the wrath of a certain police chief."

The officers laughed. "Tut, tut," one of them said, "somebody should have warned you, you don't mess with Pearson." He smiled broadly at Cal. "Say, what happened to the last guy who did that?"

"Twenty five to life," another called out.

They all laughed again.

Cal tried to block out their voices. It was the same as the last time. The taunts, the jokes at his expense, they were having fun while he was scared shitless. But last time he'd been young. The older officers intimidated him. This time he was the older one. These officers were kids, barely out of college to look at some of them. But they were in the position of power. They could show their contempt, make him feel worthless, and all he could do was cringe.

"So who's on babysitting duty tonight?" Benson said.

"I guess that's me." A tall burly officer stood up, a look of resignation on his face. "Would you believe, I've even volunteered for a double shift?"

"Yeah, well, let's do it, Butler," Benson said. "Some of us have homes to go to."

The rattle of keys and click of the lock magnified in Cal's mind as Butler unlocked the barred doorway then stepped aside.

Cal remained rooted to the spot.

Benson nudged his elbow.

Cal exhaled heavily and stepped into a narrow corridor. Five cells lined the back wall. They were above ground, but the place still had a vault-like atmosphere. There were no windows, the only light coming from dim recessed bulbs in the ceiling. Cal hesitated before the first cell. Benson signaled him to keep walking, down to the last cell.

Benson swung open the cell door and motioned for Cal to step inside. Cal complied then turned to watch, helpless, as Benson locked him in and, without so much as a second glance, walked away.

"He's all yours." Benson tossed the key to Butler. "Take good care of him."

Cal moved forward to the bars in time to see Butler follow Benson out, his departure marked by the clang of the outer door. He stared into the empty corridor for several minutes, biting on his lip to keep it from trembling, unable to stop the shivers that were spreading through his body, despite the overheated cell.

To distract himself he looked round. A narrow bed, a small sink and a toilet. He closed his eyes, standing for several more minutes before forcing himself to accept that he really was locked up. Opening his eyes, he slipped off his shoes and lay down on the bed, stretching each limb in turn trying to ease the tension in his muscles. The pain was creeping back. It was way past the time for his medication. They would surely bring it to him when Lily delivered it. He just had to wait for Lily to turn up.

His frustration rocketed. Wait. That was all he could do. Wait for Lily to bring relief, for Pearson to return to ask him awkward questions, for Weinsteenberg to get him out of this place, for Katy to prove she was still alive. His whole goddamn future hung in the balance. And all he could do was wait.

The medication turned up first. Butler brought him a single dose with a paper cup of water, passing it through the bars as if he was doing Cal a favor. Cal swallowed it down, thinking of how Lily must have felt, coming to the station, being so close to him but not allowed to see him. Had she brought the girls with her? He hoped so. Maybe seeing his girls would soften the officers' hearts. How could any man who was the father of such beautiful girls commit brutality? They would see that, see that he shouldn't be kept away from his girls, locked up like a common criminal.

He crumpled the paper cup in his fist.

The police didn't care how many angelic children he had. Desperation was making him think idiotic thoughts, desperation from lying staring at the ceiling, with nothing to distract him from his situation.

Where the hell was Weinsteenberg?

Or Pearson for that matter?

He was dozing when Butler unlocked the cell and gestured for Cal to come out. "Your lawyer's on the phone." He led Cal back to the office.

Cal grabbed the phone. "Where are you? I've been trying to contact you all afternoon."

"I've spoken to the police," Weinsteenberg said, "I know the situation. I'm out of town at the moment, just picked up your message, but there's nothing we can do until Monday anyhow."

"Nothing we can do!" Cal couldn't believe what he was hearing. "Can't you speak to Pearson? Tell him I'll come back with you on Monday, but there's no point in keeping me locked up here for the weekend."

There was silence at the other end of the line.

"Can't you do something?"

"Mr. Miller, you were on your way to Chicago. How can you expect Pearson to trust you now? Besides, I understand there are other matters complicating the situation."

"Other matters?" Cal exhaled. "You mean the business about me being seen with Katy in my car?"

"Mr. Miller, I'd advise you not to say anything else in the presence of the police, at least until we've spoken."

"Oh yeah, and how guilty is that going to make me look?"

"Nothing, Mr. Miller, that's my advice to you. I will call Pearson, see if I can do anything, but to be honest I doubt it. In the meantime, say nothing."

The phone went dead before Cal could reply.

To hell with you, he'd wanted to say. Weinsteenberg was probably anticipating a pleasant dinner with family or friends, a game or two of tennis over the weekend maybe. He wasn't the one locked in a goddamn cell. Cal slammed the receiver back down onto the handset.

Butler jumped up from his chair, his posture tensed, ready for action.

Cal glanced around the office. Two other officers were

watching him now. One pushed his chair back.

The temptation to lash out at something or even somebody was enormous. He was hemmed in by either men or walls, with no way to vent his fury at the injustice of his situation or his own stupidity. The rage trembled through him. He clutched at the edge of the desk behind him in an attempt to keep from taking a swipe.

Butler took a step towards him. He was almost within striking distance.

Cal wanted to tell Butler to stop, to give him a few minutes to calm down on his own, but Butler didn't look as if he was in an understanding mood. His gaze was fixed on Cal, a small smile playing at the corners of his eyes. Clearly, he wouldn't mind if Cal had a go. He reminded Cal of an animal tamer trying to corner a wild animal. Only this time instead of a wild animal, it was a potential killer, more than likely the only one Leyton had ever seen. Butler didn't know Cal from the next guy. He couldn't know that Cal felt more like a fox surrounded by baying hounds out for blood, his blood, closing in for the kill, his avenues for escape being cut off at every turn.

Cal took a step sideways to put some distance between himself and Butler.

The two other officers stood up. The atmosphere in the room suddenly became charged.

Don't move again, or they'll jump you. Just pull yourself together and go back to the cell. Wait for Pearson.

"Where the hell is Pearson?" he yelled at Butler.

"Behind you."

Cal spun round towards the voice. Pearson stood in the doorway, Docherty behind him.

Pearson turned on Butler. "What's going on here?"

"Not… Nothing, sir." Butler stammered. "Mr. Miller just took a call from his lawyer. We hadn't been able to contact him until now."

"So why is he still out of his cell?"

"I was… was just about to take him back sir, but Mr. Miller appeared a little… little upset by the outcome of his conversation."

"Did he now?" Pearson switched his gaze back to Cal. "I wonder why that should be? Disappointed perhaps that Weinsteenberg couldn't work any miracles for you today?"

"Weinsteenberg wants to speak with you," Cal said.

Pearson shrugged. "He can if he likes. But you're not leaving here until you've been before a judge, and that isn't happening until Monday. Nothing anybody can do about that." He gripped Cal by the elbow and led him across the office towards one of the interview rooms. "But that does give us lots of time to get to know each other better. I have quite a story to tell you, heard it only today."

Pearson paused just outside of the door, shook his head and then frowned at Cal. "But I'm forgetting. You already know it."

Chapter 34

Cal leant back in his chair, crossed his arms and gave Pearson a defiant stare. "I'm not going to say anything without my lawyer present."

Pearson turned to Docherty. "You hear that?"

Docherty nodded.

Pearson sighed. He looked at his watch before picking up a pen. "Four forty-five," he muttered as he wrote, "subject declined to speak without lawyer present." He signed the sheet with a flourish before sliding it across to Docherty to sign.

"Shame really," Pearson said, "now we can't swap stories." He put his pen in his jacket pocket. "I was looking forward to seeing which version I liked best." He looked across at Docherty. "Make sure whoever is on duty knows that Mr. Miller is not to have any visitors." He glanced back at Cal. "No chat, no visitors. Those are the rules, I'm sure your wife will understand."

He scraped back his chair as he stood up. "I'll be around for about another hour, in case you change your mind, about the chat. After that you'll just have to hold it in until tomorrow."

No, Monday. Cal was holding it until Monday.

Pearson looked back over his shoulder, "By the way, I met your daughters this afternoon. Delightful little girls, remind me of mine when they were that age." He smiled. "A wonderful age, seem to change right in front of your eyes, don't you think? You must be very proud of them."

His words hit Cal like a knife through the heart.

Bastard.

Weekends were a precious commodity to Cal. Time to spend with the family and indulge in his passion for tennis. They were always too short.

Not this one. It stretched into an eternity of isolation, silence and wretchedness. Even his meals—takeouts from the diner—were handed to him without comment. Maybe Pearson had given the order that he wasn't to be spoken to. But then again, why would they want to speak to him? They thought he'd killed a young woman he was having an affair with. At least this time they left him alone. Not like last time, when they'd kept appearing outside of his cell, to tell him what happened to pretty young boys like him who went to prison.

He slept in fitful dozes, interspersed with periods of imagining what Lily was doing. She'd try to maintain a semblance of normalcy for the girls, who probably had no idea that their daddy was in jail. He wondered who else she might have told. Kieran? Her parents? His parents? They would all have to know at some point, though there was nothing any of them could do. They'd all be worried, but would go about their daily life like the rest of the world out there. While he sat in a stinking cell, his life brought to a standstill.

He glanced round the cell. Actually, it didn't stink. It was in pristine condition. Leyton obviously didn't have a lot of lawbreakers. Two nights had passed without the addition of even a drunk to keep him company in the block.

By Sunday morning he was desperate for distraction. He asked the officer who brought his breakfast for a newspaper. To his surprise the officer agreed, but returned with yesterday's edition with so many missing pages it was barely worth it.

There wasn't a single mention of the arrest at the airport. He guessed it had made the front page, with linked stories on all the other missing pages. Leyton hadn't had an incident like this in years and they were making the most of it. By now everyone would know the latest gossip. Everyone but him.

Once he was released he wouldn't be able to set foot outside of the house for embarrassment. Or fear of retaliation. His attempt to flee would be seen as a sign of guilt. Even those who'd entertained doubts were now probably shaking their heads and saying how you never could tell, he seemed such a nice man, and what about his poor wife and daughters?

Cal gave up on the paper and lay back down. The irony was that, just when he'd decided to come clean with Pearson, his lawyer had ordered him to be quiet. He didn't want to stay quiet. It only antagonized Pearson, which kept him in isolation and away from Lily. Lawyers always instructed their clients to remain silent, they were afraid the clients would say something incriminating. But how could you incriminate yourself if you were innocent? What Weinsteenberg didn't realize was that it was silence that had got Cal into this mess in the first place, now his continued silence only compounded the problem.

To hell with Weinsteenberg. If he could make Pearson see he was telling the truth, maybe he could get him to understand there had been a terrible mistake here. His only crime, if it was one, was stupidity. He wanted to work with Pearson to sort this out, and his lawyer was just causing interference. Cal smiled. He could also save on legal fees if he spoke to Pearson himself. And, if he was seen to be helping the police, then surely people would realize he couldn't be guilty.

He eased himself up into a sitting position, listening for sounds of life drifting through from the main office. There was nothing. He picked up his shoe and, holding it by the toe, began slapping the heel against a bar. The noise reverberated in the corridor. He tapped out a rhythm, repeated it over and over, making it louder each time, until he heard the corridor door being opened.

Butler appeared outside his cell, looking no happier than he had on Friday. "What the hell do you think you're doing?"

"Trying to break out, what do you think?"

Butler scowled and turned away.

"I need to speak to Pearson," Cal called after him.

"It's Sunday," Butler said without looking back, "Pearson's not here." He slammed the door behind him.

Cal waited a few minutes then started hitting the bars again. There was no response. He picked up his other shoe, adding a second beat to his rhythm, beginning to enjoy the racket he was making.

Butler arrived back with reinforcements. The familiar looking officer stood behind him, giving Cal the same evil look that he had earlier.

Cal stopped banging.

"Tell Pearson I want to speak to him," he said.

Butler held out a hand. "Pass those shoes through the bars."

"Tell Pearson I want to speak to him."

"I told you Pearson isn't here, now put the shoes down and move to the back of the cell."

Cal sniggered. "What's wrong, don't you like the tune? Tell Pearson I want to…"

Butler put the key in the lock as his colleague stepped forward. Cal looked from one to the other, sensing the threat in the atmosphere and then froze as he spotted the name badge on the officer's chest. Before Butler could open the door he flung the shoes through the bars. "Here, take the damn things."

To his relief, Butler picked up the shoes, gave a victory smile to his companion and followed him out of the corridor.

Cal sank back down on the bed. No wonder the guy had looked familiar. He didn't actually know him, but the resemblance was strong enough to make it seem that he did. There was no way that Cal wanted to be in an enclosed space with him. He'd worried earlier about the guy being Rigby's friend, but that connection didn't matter a bit.

He was Katy's brother, Dennis.

Chapter 35

"I drove Katy out of town that Friday night."

Pearson appeared unimpressed at Cal's confession. "Where to?"

"To a house just off route 82, a couple of miles away."

"You're saying that's where she is now?"

Cal shook his head. "No, that was just the first stage of her journey. The house belonged to friends. They only used it in the summer. The place has a detached garage that's empty most of the time so it's never locked. Katy bought a car. She hid it there so her family wouldn't know about it. That's why I had to give her a lift. She couldn't walk there in the dark."

"Why'd she wait until ten?"

"She thought there would be less chance of being seen then. Remember she was supposed to be staying…" Cal exhaled with a sigh. "She was supposed to have told her family she was staying with a friend so she didn't want to risk being seen with me."

"But you were."

Cal looked away, trying to hide his discomfort. He was only sitting in this room now because someone had seen them. If Billy hadn't mentioned it to him, he would have come in and volunteered the information and he'd be at home with Lily watching television rather than having this late evening chat with Pearson.

Butler must have passed the message on. Cal had thought

he hadn't as the day passed uninterrupted. Then just when he'd resigned himself to the fact that he wasn't going to get to talk to Pearson, Pearson appeared. A glimpse of the office clock on his way to the interview room told him it was after nine, but he wasn't about to object. Despite the fatigue washing over him from two virtually sleepless nights, he knew he wouldn't sleep tonight, so he might as well spend some of the time until his court appearance talking.

"Why didn't you tell us this that first day we interviewed you."

Why indeed. Cal looked down at his feet. "I wish I had."

Pearson flipped through some papers in a file in front of him. "You told us you left the office at midnight. Why did you lie?"

"I didn't, that's what time I finally left, I went back to the office after dropping Katy off."

"Okay, so why didn't you tell us about the side trip?"

"You didn't ask."

"Try again," Pearson said, his tone harsh. "Why didn't you tell us?"

"Look Pearson, put yourself in my place. I thought her letter would show up in a day or two. I didn't think it mattered."

"And now?"

Cal shook his head. "It still doesn't matter."

"So why not let us decide if it's relevant or not? How many times have we spoken since that first morning?"

"Too many."

"So why not throw it in." Pearson's tone dripped sarcasm. "Oh, I think it's relevant, it's got relevant written all over it."

Cal leant forward resting his elbows on the table and his head in his hands. He didn't look at Pearson. "Look I could've shown you the house, but what would have been the point? She wouldn't have been there that Sunday morning. She would've been long gone."

"Corroboration. If she'd been there, there would be finger prints on the garage door, other evidence of her presence." Pearson paused until Cal was forced to look up at him. "Unless you're going to tell me you opened all the doors for her so the only prints would be yours, or that you were wearing gloves so there would be no prints at all."

"I wasn't wearing gloves." Cal snapped. "I dropped Katy at the gate. She went to the garage on her own. I went straight back to the office."

"You left her in the dark."

"She had a flashlight."

"Of course. So you just left her there."

"It was what she wanted. She didn't want me to be any more involved in her plans than I had to be."

"Right," Pearson said.

"All right, look, it wasn't just that I thought it was irrelevant. When the investigation became an assumed murder, I thought that if I mentioned driving Katy anywhere that night people would assume the worst of me."

Pearson was silent.

"Especially you."

Pearson still didn't speak.

Cal wiped his face with his hands. "What the hell, they assumed the worst anyway."

"So then you could have mentioned it. You had nothing to lose."

Cal slumped back in his chair. "Except maybe my freedom."

"I see. But having lost that you're prepared to tell us everything?"

Cal didn't answer.

"Yet originally you refused to speak to me without your lawyer. Why the change of heart?"

Cal looked away.

"Didn't you like your accommodation here? Did you think if you offered me a tidbit or two of information, I might let you go? Drop the charges? Are you telling me that if I'd locked you up last time you would have told me this then?"

"My lawyer told me to remain silent."

Pearson grimaced. "They have a habit of doing that."

"But I haven't got anything to hide now, so what's the point?'

Pearson flashed a glance at Stockman by the door. "You hear that?"

"Yes sir," Stockman said.

"Nothing to hide."

"What make of car was it?" Pearson said.

"I don't know," Cal said.

"Color?"

"I don't know."

"She told you she bought a car and you didn't ask what kind?'

Cal shrugged. "I never thought to ask."

Pearson looked disbelieving. "Where did she get it from?"

"I don't know."

"A dealer. A newspaper ad?'

"Still don't know."

"Did she tell you how she paid for it?"

Cal hesitated. "Cash."

Pearson grinned. "Might have known you'd have the answer to that one." He flipped through some more papers on the desk. "When did she buy the car?"

"A few days before she left."

"There's no sign of any large withdrawals from her bank account at that time. Do you know where she got the cash from?"

"Under the mattress?"

A flicker of irritation crossed Pearson's face. "Answer the question."

"I just did." Cal hesitated. "Katy asked me to pay her overtime in cash so she could save for the car."

"And of course you did?"

Cal shrugged. "Didn't make much difference to me. She was the one who did the banking each day anyhow."

"So how much cash did you give her?"

Cal ran the figures quickly in his head. "A couple of thousand, total."

Pearson pursed his lips. "A lot of overtime."

"Over a few months, it's not so much."

"And it was all for overtime? No special bonus or payments for other services she might have provided?"

Cal froze. "I don't like what you're suggesting."

"You don't have to like it. You just have to answer the question."

"It was overtime. It's all there in the payroll records, properly accounted for."

Pearson grinned again. "I'm sure. I'm sure you'd be willing to show us if necessary."

"Of course."

"Or even let one of our guys take a look for himself."

Cal narrowed his eyes. "Okay, what do you expect to find?"

"Just to confirm what you've told me." Pearson made a note on the file. "I'll add your office to the search warrant."

Cal sat bolt upright. "What search warrant?"

"The one for your car." Pearson gestured with his hands. "It's just routine. Last place Katy was, apart from this alleged house of course. Rather convenient that it's already parked outside, isn't it?"

"Search away, you won't find anything."

Pearson nodded again. "As I said, it's just routine."

"There's nothing routine about search warrants, not in my world at least."

"We'll expect you to show us exactly where the house is too."

Cal replayed the drive in his mind. "I think I can find it again."

"You'd better."

"Hey, I'm trying to help you here."

"Of course," Pearson said, "now you've got nothing left to lose."

Pearson grilled Cal for over two more hours.

The detective was a definite schizophrenic, one minute conciliatory and friendly, the next adversarial and threatening. Maybe it was tiredness, but Cal began to get confused by the sudden shifts in attitude and the constant repetition of questions.

And repetition of the answers. No, he hadn't had an affair with Katy. No, he didn't know where she was headed. No, he didn't know what kind of car. No, he hadn't sent the hoax email.

No, he hadn't seen where she went after he dropped her off. No, he had no idea why she'd lied to him about sending a letter to her father. Over and over again. No. No. No. All negatives.

Cal could tell that Pearson wanted a positive, something to work with, even if it incriminated Cal himself. But as the session wore on Cal began to realize how little he had to offer Pearson. Still Pearson kept digging, like a miner searching for the elusive gold nugget, until Cal wished he'd followed Weinsteenberg's advice and stayed silent.

Cal was relieved when Pearson suddenly called it quits, more so because it came during one of the conciliatory stages. Pearson had just commiserated with him about the effect the whole affair must be having on his family, sounding as if he really did care. Cal didn't believe him for a second, but it was better than being made to feel as if you were the worst kind of scum to crawl out of the earth, a reaction Pearson could raise with just the tone of his voice.

"By the way, I owe you an apology," Pearson said as Cal stood up to leave.

For a moment Cal thought he had finally convinced Pearson of his innocence. "Oh?"

"I had no idea your wife didn't know about your earlier arrest."

Cal frowned. "Of course she did. How could she possibly not? She was waiting for me when I got home."

"Not that business a few weeks ago. I meant the one when you were in college."

The blood rushed from Cal's face.

"For attempted rape, right?" Pearson said. "I think it came as quite a shock."

Chapter 36

There was no way Cal could miss the envelope. It was propped on the hall table against the silver dish in which he kept his car keys. Habit made him go towards it on entering the house, even though he had no car keys to deposit there, with his car still in the impound lot.

He fingered the embossed paper with his name written in Lily's neat script and then tossed it into the garbage. There was no need to read it. The silence in the house told him what it said.

He strolled into the living room. The cushions were plumped, the newspapers straightened, the coffee table spotless. The kitchen was the same. Not a thing out of place, not even a cup in the sink. He opened the refrigerator and felt a glimmer of hope. There were cartons of milk and orange juice, unopened boxes of cold cuts and eggs. He checked the pantry. A loaf of fresh bread sat on an otherwise empty shelf. His spirits sank again. Old habits died hard for Lily. She'd stocked up for him before leaving. The absence of juice boxes and cookies for the girls were proof of that.

He trudged up the stairs, telling himself he needed to shower and change. Three days in the same clothes had left him disheveled, sweaty and in need of a shave. He paused outside Amanda's room, took a deep breath, and pushed open the door.

The beds had been stripped of their colorful quilts and pillows, the soft toys had gone and there were empty spaces on the shelves where favorite games and books had once stood. He slid open the closet door. Wherever Amanda had gone she had enough clothes for a long stay. No doubt the same for Sophie and Lily too.

He bypassed his bedroom, entering the bathroom from the hallway. He would feel better when he'd cleaned up, more able to cope. He turned the hot water on full while he stripped, adding a little cold before he stepped in. He lifted his face up into the stream of water, letting it cascade over him and the steam envelope him. The day could only get better.

Weinsteenberg had all but resigned on him for talking to Pearson and then charged off to berate Pearson for allowing Cal to do so. Cal could hear the raised voices in the outer office. He hoped that Weinsteenberg was giving Pearson hell.

The lawyer returned with a grim expression on his face. "Did Pearson tell you he was going to object to bail?'

Cal's mouth dropped open. "On what grounds?"

"Try being re-arrested at the airport."

"Can they do that," Cal said, "for charges of obstruction?"

"Pearson's argument is that you're a material witness to an ongoing investigation, a reluctant one, and a flight risk."

"Would a judge go along with that?"

"Justice Barnes has a lot of respect for Pearson. Pearson is known to be fair."

Cal made a face.

"Tough but fair," Weinsteenberg said. "And it's true. He's not doing this for spite. Barnes will certainly listen to him."

Cal sank his face into his hands and groaned. The idea of another night in a cell—let alone weeks—filled him with dread.

"Is there anything we can do?"

"Start thinking with your brains rather than your feet."

Cal looked up. "What's that supposed to mean?"

"Your actions aren't exactly helping the situation."

Cal almost exploded with anger. How fucking easy it was for the guy to be on the other side of the table, to see things in hindsight, not to have his future life hanging over his decisions. This was just a job to him. Whether Cal ended up in prison or free, he'd move on to the next case. Try turning the tables, put Weinsteenberg in Cal's situation, where the odds were not only stacked against you but increasing, and see how clearly he thought then.

"No point in getting pissed off with me. I know what

you're thinking." Weinsteenberg leant across the table, jabbing his finger towards Cal. "A couple of weeks ago I'd never heard of you, right? So why should I suddenly care whether you walk out of here a free man or spend the rest of your life in prison? Long as you can pay the bills. That's all that matters, right?"

Cal looked away, embarrassed that his thoughts had been that obvious.

"Look at me!" The force of Weinsteenberg's voice made Cal snap his head back round in the lawyer's direction. "If I'm taking your money, I expect you to pay attention to me."

"I'm not paying you to lecture me."

"It's an all inclusive package. You want my advice. You have to put up with my lectures."

Cal stood. "No I don't. I'll find someone else to get my advice from."

Weinsteenberg didn't reply. Cal stormed across the room and opened the door. Stockman blocked his exit.

"I want a new lawyer," Cal shouted over Stockman's shoulder.

Pearson looked up from one of the desks. "Bit late now, you're due in front of the judge in fifteen minutes."

"In that case I'll represent myself."

Pearson grimaced. "I wouldn't do that if I were you."

"What difference does it make, you've got this all sewn up by the sound of it."

"I'd have to reconsider my deal."

"Deal?" Cal looked back at Weinsteenberg. "What deal?"

"The deal that you didn't give me a chance to tell you about," Weinsteenberg said.

Cal pushed the door shut in Stockman's face and slouched back to his seat. "Okay, so you have my attention."

Weinsteenberg gazed at Cal with such disdain that Cal shrank back into his seat, mortified by his own behavior.

"Pearson will agree to bail of $100,000 with conditions."

Cal snorted. "I don't have that kind of money."

"You own your house?"

"Yes, but—"

"They'll accept the deeds as security."

"I can't—"

"It's risk free as long as you turn up in court at the appointed time." Weinsteenberg smiled. "I assume you have no intention of making another run for it."

"At that price, I can't afford to."

Weinsteenberg's smile widened. "That's the point."

Cal scowled. "And the conditions?"

"You surrender your passport and your driver's license."

"My driver's license! What the hell for?"

Weinsteenberg ignored the interruption. "Your car is to remain impounded. You'll report here to the police station twice a day at pre-determined times and you can't leave the town limits without clearing it with Pearson first."

"Forget it," Cal said, "with conditions like those I might as well be in jail."

"It's your choice." Weinsteenberg leant back in his chair, stretching his arms into the air before clasping his hands behind his head and waiting for Cal's answer.

The silence filled with tension until Cal allowed the futility of his defiance to penetrate. His shoulders slumped. "He knows I've got no choice." His eyes narrowed. "Why would he want to make a deal in the first place? He's got me where he wants me."

"You just don't get it, do you?" Weinsteenberg sighed. "You're here because of you, not Pearson. Maybe he's offered you this deal because he thinks you belong at home with your kids rather than locked up in a cell, but he can't trust you to act rationally on your own behalf."

Cal said nothing. He was too angry. But he realized the anger was at himself.

It was finally sinking in. Pearson had a point.

He accepted Pearson's deal. At the end of the day what choice did he have? But Pearson's plan, if it was one, had a serious flaw. Pearson hadn't allowed for Lily leaving town again and taking the girls with her.

There was probably some court order he could get, he thought as he rubbed himself dry after his shower, to make Lily bring the girls back. Weinsteenberg would know, but Cal had had enough already with lawyers and courts. The last thing he wanted to do was embroil his family in litigation too.

Besides Lily had only done what she thought best. What kind of father was he turning out to be? In the space of a day Lily had learned that he'd been arrested while trying to leave town, without so much as a whisper to her about it, and that this wasn't the first time he'd been implicated in a crime. What did he expect? If it had been some other family and she'd stayed, he would have doubted her fitness as a mother.

But it wasn't some other family, it was his. He was innocent, and she should know that. And she'd left him. And he hated her.

Whatever happened to loyalty?

The phone rang at the exact moment that Pearson knocked on the door. Cal yelled "Coming" in the direction of the door and grabbed the phone.

"I'm on my way," Kieran said. "Sounds like you need some moral support. I'll be there in about half an hour."

"I have to show Pearson the house where I dropped Katy off," Cal said, grateful to hear a friendly voice. "I'm not sure how long I'll be."

"No problem. I'll let myself in, be waiting for you when you get back. You can explain it all to me over a beer."

Cal laughed. In Kieran's world, problems could still be solved by a beer. Cal had lived in that world once, where innocence was taken for granted and guilt belonged to people in newspapers, books and movies.

There was another sharp rap on the door.

"Got to go." Cal started to hang up the phone then hesitated. "Thanks, Kieran. I appreciate this."

Pearson stood on the step. By the look on his face he was in one of his pricklier moods. Cal sauntered past him and down the drive towards the police cars parked in the road. Docherty opened the passenger door of an unmarked car, motioned for Cal to get in then slammed the door and slid into the back seat.

Pearson drove. A patrol car followed.

Nobody spoke.

Cal leant his head back against the seat rest and closed his eyes. All this fuss over a dead-end lead. Fatigue washed over him. Once he'd got this little charade over he wanted to crawl into bed, his own bed, until morning. Everything else would have to wait: Kieran, Lily, his future. It would all seem clearer after a good sleep.

"Route 82," Pearson said suddenly, "which way?"

Cal opened his eyes. "Left for about a mile, then a sharp right."

"You tell me when." Pearson turned the car onto the highway.

Cal stared out the window. It all looked different now. Houses that had been hidden behind the foliage of spring and summer were now revealed in the bare countryside. Narrow leafy roads and drives were replaced by flat vistas, the tree trunks like sentries in the gloom. He almost missed the turn, the side road indistinguishable from the surroundings without its panoply of leaves.

"There." Cal pointed right as they came upon it.

Pearson made the turn without touching the brakes. Behind them, the patrol car was taken by surprise. They overshot the junction, braked suddenly, backed up and followed them round the corner. Cal smiled. He could imagine the comments being made about Pearson's driving.

There were few properties along this road. Cal scanned each driveway looking for the split-rail fence that marked the beginning of the one they were looking for. It was all he could remember. The house and garage had been set way back off the road, invisible in the darkness that Friday night. That's why he'd wanted to take Katy to the garage, but she was insistent, only allowing him to walk with her to the mailbox before giving him a huge hug and sending him back to his car. He'd lingered to watch the small pool of light from her flashlight progress along the winding drive, until finally it disappeared amongst the trees.

Good luck, he'd whispered after her. B*e happy.*

"This one." A wave of relief washed over him as he spotted the fence. The one uncertainty in his get-out-of-jail deal was now removed.

In the afternoon light, the aged colonial with its detached garage was clearly visible. It had a deserted look, but then, that's because it was. Cal could never understand why someone would want to own a house that stood empty for most of the year.

Pearson stopped the car.

Cal got out and looked down the drive, trying to imagine it in full foliage, figuring out the point at which Katy would have disappeared from view, starting this whole nightmare. He turned to Pearson and Docherty who had joined him on the roadside. "Yes, this is it."

"760 Rainers Lane," Docherty said, "I'll find out who the owners are."

Pearson nodded. "Certainly looks deserted." He turned to Benson and Stockman, who were waiting in the patrol car. "You can take Mr. Miller back now. Docherty and I will make sure there's nobody home, maybe walk round the neighborhood and see if anyone remembers seeing anything that night." He turned a full circle. "Not that it looks as if there are many neighbors around here."

He set off towards the house, issuing a stream of instructions to Docherty as he walked.

"Since when did we become a taxi service?" Benson said to Stockman before gesturing across at Cal. "Well, get in then. Some of us have work to do."

Chapter 37

"I met Sally at a party in my last year at college." Cal took a swig of beer. "She was a local girl, taking time out to work for her father. She was quite a looker; long blonde hair, blue eyes, an amazing figure. I was surprised she paid me any attention." He nestled back into the chair and took another long sip of beer. "I wish to God she hadn't."

He and Kieran were ensconced in the living room in front of a log fire that Kieran had built for his return. They sat in overstuffed armchairs pulled up close to the hearth, their feet propped up on the coffee table, a newly opened case of beer stashed into a cooler between them, an indication that Kieran at least was settled in for a long afternoon of soul-baring. Cal wasn't so sure he could last that long. The beer was adding to his fatigue, leaving him disjointed and confused. But he owed Kieran some explanation, at the very least.

His story was one that he'd never imagined having to tell, especially after all this time. Sometimes when he thought back on it—usually in the middle of a sleepless night when his mind liked to torture him with 'what if' games—he could eventually make himself believe it had happened to someone else. That it was just a story he'd been told or a movie he'd seen. But telling it to another person? That threatened to make it real and he wasn't sure he could face that.

Kieran waited in silence for him to continue, seeming to understand that this was a story that couldn't be rushed.

"We hit it off straight away," Cal said, "so I asked her if she wanted to go out the next evening. We agreed to meet in a bar in town. I couldn't believe my luck. As soon as we met she told me her parents were out of town for the weekend and that her brother was always out until the early hours of the morning." Cal paused, twisting the beer bottle round in his fingers. "That was all she said, but it sounded to me like an invitation, or why would she have told me?"

Kieran nodded.

"We had a couple of drinks and then went for Chinese. It was only just after eleven by the time we'd finished, so I offered to walk her home. She lived in a big house on the smart side of town. It took about half an hour to walk, up quite a hill, I remember." Cal paused again, jiggling the bottle in his hands. "We laughed a lot, seemed to be getting on really well."

Kieran put down his empty, reached into the cooler, pulled out a fresh one and held it out towards Cal. Cal shook his head, lifting his own bottle to show it was still half full. Kieran sank back into his chair and looked expectantly at Cal.

Cal took a deep breath. "She asked me in for a coffee. From the look on her face I knew she meant more than coffee. When we got indoors I kissed her, just kissed her on the lips. It was dark in the hallway so she turned on a table lamp and then she kissed me back. She kissed me."

Cal took another long swig of beer.

"Instead of going into the kitchen, she started leading me up the stairs." He sighed. "I didn't argue. Every couple of steps we'd stop and kiss again. I thought she was going to take me to her bedroom, but by the time we got to the first landing we couldn't keep our hands off each other. We started undressing each other then and there. Or at least she unzipped my jeans while I fumbled with her blouse. She was a hell of a lot more adept at it than me. She was giggling into my chest as I tried to get her bra unhooked and all the while, I swear to God, she was stroking me until I felt I was going to burst. I knew I was running out of time so I gave up on her bra and hitched up her skirt."

Cal broke off. Tightness constricted his throat and chest forcing him to gulp for breath. He really didn't want to do this.

Kieran leant forward. "You okay?"

Cal ignored him. He had to finish the story now, whatever it cost. "The next thing I knew I was lying on my back with a two hundred pound guy on my chest, and Sally was screaming rape."

Kieran gasped.

"I tried to reason with him, but Sally was freaking out. She wouldn't stop crying and yelling, all this crap about how she'd told me to wait downstairs, but I'd followed her up and jumped her. Eventually she calmed down enough to bring her brother...that's who the guy was...brought him a phone and he called the police." Cal shivered. The memories of his shock and fear surged back. "He sat on me until the police came. It was just as well, because while he was doing that he couldn't do me any other damage. He certainly looked as if he wanted to. It was probably only ten minutes, but it felt like forever. I pleaded with Sally to tell her brother the truth, but they just gagged me with a wash cloth.

"The police turned up in force. There must have been at least six of them, including a couple of women. Six! All looking at me as if I was a piece of shit, not caring that I was lying there with my pants around my knees.

"They handcuffed me, made me stay on the floor while they interviewed Sally and her brother and until some photographer had taken pictures of the alleged crime scene. I was so embarrassed. I tried to roll over onto my side, but they pushed me back. All I wanted at that point was for them to let me cover myself up.

"By the time the photographer had done his work they'd charged me with attempted rape and read me my rights. Nobody listened to my side of the story. As far as they were concerned, I was caught in the act. It was well after midnight by the time we got to the police station. I was locked up in a cell and told I'd have to wait until morning to see a lawyer."

"They didn't let you make a phone call?"

"Who was I going to call at that time of night?"

"Mom or Dad?"

Cal shook his head. "They were miles away, what were they going to do? More to the point, how was I supposed to tell them?"

"You should have called them," Kieran said.

"We were talking about rape," Cal said, his voice louder

199

than he'd intended. "Or at least attempted rape. How was I supposed to explain that?"

"They would have believed you."

"I was terrified, for God's sake. I was only twenty-one-years-old and surrounded by people who thought it was a slam dunk case. One officer stopped by my cell to tell me that other local police stations were being contacted in case they had any unsolved rape cases they might be able to link to me. There I was, an innocent student, and the powers that be were trying to prove I was a serial rapist."

"Jeez Cal, you should have told someone."

"I didn't know how. I thought I was finished. The cops had already told me I wouldn't get bail, that I was headed straight for prison." Cal swallowed the last of his beer. "I would have eventually, but then the charges were suddenly dropped. I guess Sally refused to testify, or her parents didn't want her going through a court ordeal, I never found out. Monday morning, just before I went before the judge, they told me the case was dropped and I was free to go. It was obvious the police didn't like it, but they had no choice. Needless to say, I never saw Sally again."

"And you never told anyone about it?"

"What was the point? It was all over. I was free to go back to college. Who needed to know?"

"Cal, you'd gone through a terrible ordeal. You've got to talk about that stuff. I'm surprised you ever looked at another girl again."

Cal snorted. "I almost didn't. Not until Lily, anyway. My dates were strictly platonic for a long time. Didn't make me very popular with the girls, I can tell you."

"And I thought you'd just grown old and serious." Kieran sighed. "All that time. You never told anyone. This is why you lied to the cops, isn't it?"

"Not at first. At first I thought Katy wanted to get away, and I was helping her. But after I saw the journal... well I just couldn't give them anything they could twist around and use against me. I just couldn't."

"Sure." Kieran shook his head. "Still, I would have had to tell someone. I would have told you at the very least."

Cal fiddled with the empty bottle in his hand. "Thanks to

Pearson I think everyone knows now, especially Lily." He glanced away. "Knows that I was accused, but never proven innocent." He let the bottle slip out of his fingers. "I've lost her this time."

Kieran didn't even try to disagree.

Chapter 38

He woke to Kieran's voice, rising loud and indignant from the hallway, followed by heavy footsteps on the stairs. Cal pulled the blankets over his head. Whatever was happening, Kieran would have to deal with it. He was too tired to care. The emotion of admitting his past to Kieran all but finished him off. He'd no idea how long it was since he'd crawled into bed, but he knew it wasn't long enough.

The bedroom door burst open.

Suppressing an urge to yell, he squinted out from under the blankets. His heart skipped a beat as the light from the hall revealed Pearson and Docherty standing in the doorway. Pearson scanned the room, his face a mask of anger and contempt. Beside him, Docherty looked unusually pale, almost nauseous.

The guns in their hands were trained on the bed.

There was a moment of silence. Cal clutched the blankets around him, unsure of what to do.

"Mr. Miller, you're under arrest for the murder of Katy Shore." Pearson stepped towards the bed, holstered his gun and pulled out a pair of handcuffs.

Cal eased himself up away from Pearson, pulling the blanket with him. He was dreaming. He had to be. This was a nightmare, and he would wake up any moment.

"It's over Mr. Miller." Pearson said. "We found her."

In stunned silence Cal glanced back and forth between Pearson and the gun in Docherty's hands.

"Slowly move your hands from under the sheet and put them on your head," Pearson said.

Cal didn't move. Found? Katy?

"Mr. Miller, put your hands on your head and stand up."

Cal looked down beside the bed then back up at Pearson.

"Mr. Miller—"

"I'm naked," Cal said. "My clothes, they're in the closet."

Pearson sidestepped to the closet. His gaze never left Cal until he'd opened the door. He glanced in, grabbed a pair of jeans and navy sweatshirt and tossed them onto the bed, then rummaged in a drawer adding boxer shorts and socks to the pile.

"Get dressed Mr. Miller."

Cal still didn't move. Katy had been found.

"Now, Mr. Miller, or we'll have to take you as you are."

Cal let go of the blanket. Moving as if in slow motion, he reached down the bed for the clothes and drew them back towards his end. He slid sideways, turned his back on the officers, eased up off the bed and started to dress. His fingers shook, as he tried to pull on his pants.

Murder.

Found.

The words spun in his mind. Two separate words, so far apart in meaning. But together....

At last he managed to force the words out. "Katy's dead?"

"We found her body," Pearson said.

"No!" Cal sat back down on the bed, afraid his legs would give out. "It's not possible. She ran away."

"She was right where you left her," Pearson said.

Cal gasped for air. "You're lying." He pulled the sweatshirt over his head.

"Hell of a state after all this time," Docherty added.

Cal froze on the spot. "What do you mean?"

"What we mean, Mr. Miller," Pearson said, stepping around the bed and taking hold of Cal by his left elbow, "is that you're in deep shit." He snapped the cuffs onto Cal's wrists. "Very deep shit. Now let's go."

Kieran stood at the bottom of the stairs, his face devoid of color, confusion written all over his expression. Benson blocked his access to Cal as Pearson led Cal down the stairs and out of the front door.

"I don't know what's going on here Kieran," Cal called as he passed. "You have to believe me."

"Katy is dead." Kieran's reply was an incredulous whisper. "Somebody… somebody did kill her."

Cal bit on his lip, emotion threatening to choke him. He could hear Kieran's unasked question as surely as if he'd spoken it.

Was it you Cal? Were you that somebody?

Chapter 39

Five hours and forty-five minutes, give or take. That was all it had been. Time to freshen up, go for a quick enforced drive in the countryside and have a couple of beers with his brother, and wham—he was back in the same cell, staring out at the same narrow corridor.

The charges weren't the same though. Obstruction of justice was no comparison to murder. Even the fear of being charged with murder didn't match up to the reality. The fear had been tempered by the knowledge there had been no crime, let alone any evidence. Now they had a body, a body which, by the sounds of it, Cal had led them straight to. In his eagerness to confirm his innocence, he'd proved the police right in their suspicions of foul play. And given them evidence to use against him.

Murdered! Katy was dead. Not off making a new life or even here in Leyton making his life hell. Dead. If she hadn't tried to leave Leyton she would still be alive. If he hadn't helped her try to leave she might still be alive.

How did he know that?

All right, he didn't. It was a gut instinct. But her death had to be related to her leaving, didn't it? Was it possible she'd lied to Cal? That she'd been running from a danger greater than her family? That would explain the absence of any mention of family problems in her journal. But what kind of danger could a young woman in a small town like Leyton get into? It was hard to imagine she could be involved in anything too illegal. Besides,

Pearson would have checked out all these angles, and if he'd found evidence of it he wouldn't be hounding Cal.

Of course, Pearson said he'd checked out the family too, but how much? Some of them were cops. Maybe he hadn't been too thorough. What about the boyfriend? Lily had said he was a policeman. How closely had Pearson looked at him? It had to be someone, and it sure as hell wasn't Cal.

Cal stood. These thoughts weren't getting him anywhere, just making him feel sick, sick with a deep-seated fear that he was on a one way path to hell.

If only he had some idea of what was going on. Nobody had spoken to him since Pearson had handed him over for transportation to the station house. There'd been no formalities, no fingerprints or photographs, just a rush through to the cell, the handcuffs removed and the bars slammed shut.

He'd been too shocked to protest, first from the arrest and then from the look on Kieran's face as the police led him away. By the time he'd come to his senses, the officers were gone, leaving him to his thoughts. He could hear a general hum of activity drifting down the corridor from the back office, an air of excitement not noticeable on his previous stays. They'd cracked the big case, or so they thought, and there was a lot to talk about. Pearson would be basking in the glory from the younger officers, their earlier lack of respect abandoned in the face of a job well done, a job that they would probably all try and claim some credit for.

How had Katy died? Shot? Stabbed? Strangled? Cal shuddered. It was too unbearable to think of. He could remember the feel of her body against his when she hugged him, warm, embracing. She couldn't be dead. Could Pearson be conning him? Hoping that Cal would blurt out the truth in an effort to prove his innocence? Again? Could Pearson do that? Was that entrapment?

He sank back down on the bed. He had no idea. No idea at all. Where the hell was Weinsteenberg?

Weinsteenberg was out of town again. Not expected back until the following day at the earliest. How could he do that?

"Where does that leave me?" Cal asked.

"Right here, I guess," Benson said, a little too glibly.

"You expect me to wait until tomorrow night to see my lawyer?"

"Or Wednesday morning. He did say tomorrow at the earliest, sounded like it might be a bit of a push."

"A bit of a push! What about me? Stuck here!"

"Wouldn't worry about that too much. You're going to be stuck somewhere for a long time. If not here, at County." Benson glanced round the cell. "I wouldn't be in any hurry to get there. If you ask me, you're better off here."

"I'm not asking you," Cal muttered under his breath. This could not be happening. "There has to be something I can do."

"Start talking." Pearson stepped into the corridor. "Save us all a lot of time and energy."

"I'm innocent! How many times do I have to tell you?"

"As many times as it takes."

Cal glared at Pearson.

"Takes to what?"

"To get at the truth."

"I'm telling you the truth."

"You're not very good at it, are you?"

Cal frowned. Where was Pearson heading? It was an outright taunt, but he wasn't going to fall for it. He stayed silent.

"Not at telling it or facing up to it by all accounts." Pearson pulled an envelope from his jacket pocket, held it out towards Cal. "We found this in your garbage. Seems like you forgot to open it. Thought you might like to now, seeing you've got some time on your hands."

Cal looked down at the embossed paper, Lily's writing. He made no effort to take it.

Pearson tossed it through the bars onto the bed. "You might change your mind later. It can get rather tedious in here, as you know." He left without waiting for a response. Benson followed.

"Don't you even want to question me?" Cal called after them.

His offer was met with silence.

They made Cal wait a long time, but finally he was taken

207

back to the interview room. Pearson and Docherty were already there.

As Cal sat down, Pearson dropped an evidence bag onto the table. "Recognize this?"

Cal made no attempt to pick the bag up. He didn't have to. He could see the blood encrusted white cloth that it contained. He swallowed hard. Katy was dead and the death had been bloody.

Several silent minutes passed. Cal knew that the cops were gauging his reaction, but there was nothing to worry about on that score. His reaction was pure honest horror, the only one he had to offer. He had nothing more to conceal. He had no idea either what the cloth was or where it had come from. If it was valuable evidence it was going to help clear him.

Pearson shuffled in his seat. "Well?"

"What?"

"Do you recognize it?'

"No."

Pearson picked up the bag, turned it over and pushed it closer to Cal. "It's a handkerchief." He sat back, his eyes never leaving Cal's.

The cloth was not so bloody on this side. Cal could see a neat hem edging and what looked like some embroidery in the corner. He peered forward to get a better look. It was a blue fancy C.

He blinked. Opened his mouth to speak and then closed it without a word. He had to remain calm.

"I don't use cloth handkerchiefs." He straightened in his chair and returned Pearson's stare. "Where did you get it?"

"You do have some just like it though, don't you?" Pearson said.

"I don't think…" Cal stopped abruptly when he saw the expression on Pearson's face.

"We found some identical ones in your house," Docherty said.

"You searched my house?"

"Your wife confirmed they were yours."

"Lily… she's not… What are you talking about?"

"After we searched your car we got a warrant for your house," Pearson said. "Your wife was there, with your brother.

They were both very helpful."

"Helpful? How could they have been helpful? They don't know anything."

"Your wife knew that the handkerchiefs we found were yours."

Cal grinned as he finally remembered. "Of course she did. It was her Aunt Sophia who used to buy them for me, every Christmas. Lily tried telling her I was more the tissue type of guy, but she didn't pay any attention. Every year, the same present. But she died about three years ago. I thought we'd chucked them all out."

"No, they're all in the bottom drawer of your closet." Pearson gave him a false smile. "Or at least the ones that haven't been used."

Cal nodded towards the evidence bag. "You didn't find that one in my house did you?"

"No, I'll give you that, we didn't."

"Pearson, these things are mass marketed at Christmas. There must be millions of them around. Every man in Leyton whose name begins with C could have some, for all you know. So don't try and implicate me in a crime just because you've found a handkerchief with my initial on it."

Pearson looked genuinely shocked. "I wouldn't dream of it."

Pearson's response was devoid of sarcasm. What he was up to? And how had Lily reacted to the police turning up and searching the house, going through their private belongings, no doubt messing the place up? It spooked him to think of it and he wasn't the least bit concerned about mess.

"You didn't upset my wife, did you?" Cal said. "When you searched the house?"

"No, I don't think *we* upset her," Pearson said. "We tried to keep any disruption to a minimum."

"Bastard." Cal looked away quickly.

He should have been with Lily when she went through an ordeal like that. That was what marriage was all about, standing together through thick and thin. Never mind that Lily seemed incapable of keeping her side of the bargain, he wanted to stand by her no matter what. Pearson could have arranged for Cal to be there, if he'd really wanted.

"She shouldn't have to deal with this on her own," Cal said.

"She didn't. I told you, your brother was there."

"I'm her husband. I'm the one accused of committing a crime. I could have reassured her."

"Reassured her? You didn't think of that before you left for the airport and got yourself arrested."

"On false charges, damn it."

"In your eyes."

"In anybody's eyes. What evidence can you possibly have?" Cal stood up and kicked his chair away. "None. And you know why? Because I didn't do it!" He pointed to the bag on the table. "For God's sake, Pearson, that's not my handkerchief, it's not my blood, and there's nothing that can tie me to it. You have nothing. Zilch!" He turned towards the door. "You're harassing me, plain and simple. Maybe I didn't speak up when I should have, but that does not make me a murderer."

"You finished?" Pearson asked.

"Yes." Cal spun round to face Pearson again. "And I'm finished talking to you without my lawyer. If you want to go on wasting your time chasing dead end leads until he turns up, then that's your problem, but I'm done."

Pearson shrugged. "Your call." He reached for the evidence bag. "Would you like to know where we did find this?"

Cal remained silent, not wanting to admit his curiosity.

Pearson held the bag out, twirled it round in his fingers as if it was an object of rare value, and then glanced up at Cal.

"Under the driver's seat of your car."

Chapter 40

Cal spent the night and most of the next morning staring at the ceiling of his cell. He was being framed.

The bloody handkerchief wasn't his, so where had it come from? His first instinct was that Pearson was lying. They hadn't found it in his car at all; they were just saying that to scare him. But if he was right, it was a hell of a scare tactic, surely one that could get Pearson into big trouble.

But what was the alternative? That the police were framing him? It didn't make sense. Why would they do that? Docherty did have ample opportunity to plant it while he was driving Cal's car back from the airport, but the worrying aspect of that argument was that it was so obvious a defense it made the idea almost laughable.

It was difficult enough accepting that Katy was dead. That he was being charged with the murder was beyond comprehension. He needed to talk to Weinsteenberg. He would know what was worth worrying over and what could be dismissed. With luck he would say that Pearson didn't have anything worth pursuing.

Cal swung himself up into a sitting position. Of course. Weinsteenberg would clear it up in no time.

Once he got there.

Cal slumped back onto the mattress. Once he got there! It could be hours. It might not be until tomorrow. Damn it, this was supposed to be a serious crime, but nobody was treating it with any urgency. Even Pearson wasn't in a hurry to get him before the judge. All he was interested in was dropping ever larger bombshells on Cal and seeing how he reacted, like some sadistic game to keep Cal on his toes.

Cal reached into the back pocket of his pants and fingered Lily's envelope. He was afraid to open it now. Not just because of what Lily might have to say, but because the police could confiscate it later and read it for themselves. Whatever Lily had to say was personal. Like the email he had sent her from the library, it wasn't something he wanted to become public knowledge.

But… Lily had come back to the house after hearing of his arrest. What was that about? Was it a show of support that she wanted to be near him, or was it just she didn't want to leave the house empty? What would she be thinking of it all? How would she cope?

Cal rolled over onto his stomach, pressing his face against the pillow. He had to stop these thoughts. Trying to fix Lily's life in his mind, trying to ease the guilt he felt at the mess he'd got her into. All it was doing was driving him mad; insane with jealousy of her freedom and her choices. He loved her so much, missed her so intently that he thought he would burst.

"Mr. Miller."

Stockman's voice cut through the silence. For a second Cal thought of pretending he was asleep.

"Mr. Miller, you okay?"

Cal turned slowly onto his back. Stockman stood outside the bars with a foil container in his hands and a look of concern on his face.

"You were moaning," Stockman said. "Yeah, real low, I thought you might be in pain."

"No." Cal blinked hard. "Must have been in my sleep."

"Oh." Stockman shuffled his feet for a moment then seemed to remember why he was there. He put the container down onto the small food shelf cut into the bars and removed the lid. As he stepped back a familiar aroma of garlic and cheese wafted across to Cal. Lily's take on Macaroni and cheese, heavy on the onions and garlic, a far cry from the children's version. And his first choice in comfort food.

Cal leant forward to retrieve the dish. "My wife?"

"She asked Pearson whether she could send in some food,"

Stockman said. "Pearson didn't mind, saves one of us going to the diner." He sniffed as he walked away. "Smells good."

A couple of warm rolls, a piece of frosted brownie, a carton of orange juice, and a plastic fork and napkin—Lily had thought of everything. Kieran must have told her about the weekend diet of hamburgers and muffins, as far as the officers' imagination seemed to stretch when it came to food.

Cal savored the meal, his enjoyment enhanced by the fact that Lily had taken the trouble to make it for him: surely a sign that she hadn't given up on him completely yet.

Afterwards he lay back, more than ready for an afternoon nap. He closed his eyes and offered a silent thank you to Lily for being so thoughtful. Then he remembered the letter.

Sleep now and read the letter later, or read the letter now and then sleep? His choice. He debated the options in his mind until he realized that he wouldn't sleep until he had read the letter.

He noticed a slight tremor in his hand as he opened the envelope. It could still prove to be a farewell note, and he braced himself for the worst.

Saturday

Dear Cal,

I don't know where to begin. Pearson came by yesterday and told me that you'd been arrested trying to leave town without his permission. You can imagine my shock. I don't understand, why didn't you tell me that you were going? How did you plan to tell us? Ever since this began, you've been so secretive. Why, unless you really have something to hide?

I've told you that I love you, but what's going on at the moment frightens me. Pearson warned me that I might find the press hounding us again. I don't want to put the girls through that. It would raise too many awkward questions, questions which I'm not up to answering at the moment. So I'm taking them to stay with my parents until this all blows over.

Pearson said that you'd probably be out on bail on Monday but please don't call me. I need some time to think and work out how I really feel. If I speak to you now I know it will just confuse the issue even more.

Take care of yourself. Lily.

Cal let the letter drop onto his chest. Without speaking to Lily he wouldn't be able to explain what had happened on Friday. She was preparing to make a life defining decision, for him as well as her, with only half the facts. He could see how it must look to her, he knew he'd behaved appallingly, but he should be allowed to tell her his side of the story. He couldn't let his marriage fall apart over one rash act.

He let out a sudden gasp. He couldn't stop it falling apart now. His arrest for murder would be the final straw. He looked round the cell, at the bare walls, the metal sink and toilet, the solid bars. He'd better get used to it. Short of a miracle this was going to be his future.

Lily knew it too. That explained the lunch. It soothed her guilt, because Lily was the type who felt guilty about making decisions that affected others, even when she had no choice.

She was standing by him in the knowledge that soon she wouldn't have to.

Cal was too indignant to respond. Had Lily told the detective about his affair with Sheila?

"I think that's a bit too simple, though," Pearson said. "So say, you and Katy had an affair. You try to stop, marital guilt and all that, so Katy blackmails you. That would explain the cash payments, all recorded in the books to make them look bona fide. But then Katy gets greedy, wants more. Your business can't afford more. She threatens to tell Lily exactly what you've been paying her for, so you're in a no win situation... unless you eliminate Katy."

Cal froze. The bastard. Pearson only knew about the overtime payments because Cal had told him. And now he was trying to use them against him? So much for being honest. He should never have told Pearson about the overtime. About any of it. He should have kept his damned mouth shut.

He lowered his head. Yeah, like Weinsteenberg told him to. Why hadn't he listened?

He raised his eyes. Pearson looked expectantly at him.

Cal let the silence drag out. There was safety in silence.

Oh hell, he was going round in circles now. Hadn't he just decided that his silence was partly to blame for this mess? What was he supposed to do?

He felt his throat tighten. This was way beyond any game. There had to be a rebuttal for Pearson's accusations. He just had to think.

Think.

Think right. Hard enough without Pearson's unwavering glare.

But of course! Cal straightened up. The file of timesheets he and Katy kept of the work they'd done on various clients' accounts. Written proof in Katy's own hand writing of what she had been doing on those late evenings at work.

He made to speak then stopped. The police had their own trump card—Katy's journals, also in her own handwriting, with a different explanation of what she'd been up to in the office. Which would a judge or jury believe? Damn. The journal was his undoing.

"You don't have anything," Cal said finally. "It's all conjecture."

"It always is for us until we get a confession or a conviction. Part of the job. Trying to work out why people do the terrible things that they do. And there's usually one piece of the puzzle, a key piece. Once we have that the rest often falls into place."

"Not in this case."

"That's your opinion. Think of how others will see it."

Cal couldn't hide his contempt. "So you'd be prepared to make Katy out to be a blackmailer, knowing she can't defend herself. What is her family going to think of that?"

"If it helps put away her killer, I'm sure they'll understand."

"You don't care do you, so long as you get your conviction?"

The suggestion enraged Pearson. "Yes I do. But Katy's past is no secret, as I'm sure you're aware."

"Only because my wife told me a couple of weeks ago. Nobody thought to mention it when I took up references before she started working for me."

Pearson had the decency to look surprised then he shrugged. "She was only a child at the time. Most people thought of it as being in the past. By all accounts she turned into a straight living woman."

"Who was blackmailing her employer? You're just knocking down your own argument."

"I said, 'by all accounts'. Maybe her tendencies were just latent. You were the new guy in town. Who better to target?"

"I'm confused," Cal said, "now you're making me out to be the victim?"

"You might have been to start with, and if so Katy deserved to be punished."

"Where are you going with this?"

Pearson took a moment before replying.

"She deserved to be punished, but not to be killed."

Cal leapt up from his chair, sending it crashing to the ground.

"I did not kill her!"

Pearson looked across at Docherty. "Take Mr. Miller back to his cell. We're done here."

Chapter 42

Cal lay on the bed feeling the blood pound through his veins. The sense of injustice that had been simmering inside was almost at boiling point.

It didn't matter what he said, Pearson turned it around and used it against him. He hadn't shown the slightest interest in Cal's allegations about the attack although he was perfectly willing to make Katy look bad if it helped the case against Cal.

It was pointless talking to him any more. He'd given nothing away regarding Katy's death, apart from the bloodied handkerchief. The manner of Katy's death was as much a mystery to Cal as the identity of the killer.

Tomorrow he'd go before a judge and then he'd be transferred to County Jail. In the hierarchy of terrifying life events, others cited dentist appointments, exams, even the driving test. As a twenty-one-year-old, he'd learned the true meaning of terror. Now he was been given a second insight, but from an adult perspective. Scared didn't begin to describe it.

A guttural snore broke the silence.

Cal had forgotten about his companion in the cell block. Someone whose sense of guilt at what they'd done wrong was obviously not interfering with their capacity to sleep. On his way back from his interview, Cal had caught a glimpse of a prone figure under a blanket in the first cell. As far as he could tell, the guy was asleep then and had stayed so. Until now there had been no sounds, even when Cal's dinner, a rich beef stew sent in by Lily, had been delivered. Come to think of it, nobody had fed his neighbor.

Interesting. In the brief heated exchange earlier Pearson had not officially arrested the guy, but he'd locked him up anyhow. That had to be illegal. Was it a sign of Pearson's willingness to break the rules? Or maybe just an unofficial method of dealing with the occasional drunk? But instinct told Cal that this was no ordinary drunk. Pearson's anger at the sight of him had been too visible, too personal.

Cal toyed with the idea of trying to wake the guy up. Conversation would be tough with the cells separating them, but at least it would be a distraction.

He stood up close to the bars.

"Hey!" he called as loud as he dared. He didn't want to be heard in the outer office.

There was no response.

Cal raised his voice a little louder. "Hey."

He got a snore in reply.

"Hey!"

Cal flopped down on the bed as he listened to the keys in the lock, followed by the measured footsteps along the corridor.

"Well?" Butler said. "What do you want?"

"That guy," Cal said, "he's snoring, it's disturbing me."

Butler laughed. "Tough."

"Who is it anyway?"

"None of your business," Butler said as he walked away.

It was a long restless night, but at some point he must have fallen asleep. He was woken by the sound of Stockman delivering breakfast. This time the standard coffee and muffins.

He wiped the sleep from his eyes. Why was it that when he did manage to sleep, someone saw fit to disturb him? If it kept up like this much longer he was going to end up a basket case.

"How's my companion," he said through a half yawn as he took the coffee from Stockman.

It took Stockman a moment to realize whom he was talking about. "Oh him, he's gone, out of here first thing this morning."

It must have been a drunk after all.

Weinsteenberg finally put in an appearance.

As Cal was taken to the interview room, he noticed Rigby sprawled in a chair in the corner of the outer office, apparently asleep. He looked nothing like the well-groomed officer Cal had seen in the past. He was dressed in crumpled jeans and a sloppy blue T-shirt. His hair was ruffled and dark stubble covered his chin.

Undercover duty? In a town the size of Leyton? Whatever, it certainly couldn't have anything to do with Katy. Pearson seemed confident he'd got his man in Cal.

As Benson opened the interview room door, Rigby looked up. His eyes were red rimmed and bloodshot, a testimony to lack of sleep, but there was something else in the look too—an angst that stopped Cal in his tracks. Then he remembered his place. He'd been reduced to a pawn in a police investigation, shuffled from square room to square room while the major players plotted their strategy to kick him off the chessboard of life altogether and into prison.

With a final glance at Rigby, he allowed Benson to usher him into the interview room. One thing for certain, whatever was bugging Rigby couldn't compare with what he himself was facing.

Weinsteenberg was in a somber mood.

"Pearson's prepared to offer a deal if you confess," he said before Cal even had time to sit down.

"Confess! Are you crazy?"

"Calm down," Weinsteenberg said, "it's part of my job to inform you of any such offers the police make."

"He wasn't making any offers yesterday when we spoke, what's he up to?"

"He has to go through procedures with this or the confession could get thrown out later."

"I don't know why he's worried about technicalities like that." Cal paced back and forth trying to release the pent up tension inside. "But if he wants a confession, there's still one big hitch,"

"And that is?"

"I don't have the first idea how Katy died."

Weinsteenberg didn't reply.

Cal stopped pacing and gestured helplessly. "I don't."

"I believe you." Weinsteenberg nodded towards the empty chair. "Sit down. We need to work out how to make Pearson believe you too."

It wasn't going to be an easy job. Weinsteenberg cited the facts. Cal was the last one to have seen Katy. He'd driven her to the empty house where she'd met her death. He seemed to be the only one who knew about the house. He'd lied to the police, changed his story several times. The police had evidence of an affair, possible evidence that he'd tried to obstruct the investigation, not to mention the bloody handkerchief found in Cal's car. Cal had no alibi. The police thought they had a motive. There was a hint of possible violence against women in his past. In short, a multitude of factors, while all Cal had to offer in his defense was his word.

As his lawyer spoke, Cal stared down at the ground, not sure whether he was going to gag or sob. He'd read of innocent men being found guilty, wondered what had gone wrong. Now he was finding out first hand.

Weinsteenberg was all reassurance. Cal wished he could have a similar level of confidence. As Weinsteenberg worked through the ways of contradicting the police evidence, Cal found his thoughts drifting towards his impending trip to prison. These trials could take months to come to court and it was a near certainty that he was going to spend that time locked up. He'd have to ask Kieran to wind up what was left of his business. Lily would have enough on her hands with the girls and having to become the breadwinner too. There was no doubt about it. He'd failed Lily and his daughters. They depended on him and he hadn't come through.

And all because he'd lied to the police.

"Mr. Miller, are you paying attention?" Weinsteenberg's voice cut through Cal's thoughts. "I really need you to concentrate."

"What's the point?" Cal flopped back in his seat. "It's a lost cause."

Weinsteenberg looked disappointed. "If you're truly

innocent, and I think you are, you should never give up fighting."

Cal looked back down at his feet. A fine sentiment, but the odds against him were just too immense.

"Mr. Miller?" Weinsteenberg's voice was softer this time.

Cal looked up.

"Mr. Miller, have you ever played a game of tennis where you've been two sets down and it's four all in the third set?"

Cal nodded.

"And have you ever still managed to win?"

Cal nodded again.

"How did you win?"

"Luck?"

"You don't really believe that?"

"So... okay... you just keep fighting for every point."

"Despite the odds against you."

Cal scowled. "When I've been down that far, I've lost a lot more often than I've won. And we're talking about my future, not a goddamn game of tennis."

"If you think it's that bleak, what's the harm in treating it as a game of tennis? They may have games and sets in their favor, but the match is not over yet, not by a long shot."

Cal thought for a moment and then shrugged. "I get your point. I do. But I think they're about to take my racquet away."

"And you're prepared to stand by and let them?"

"Hell no, that's why I'm paying you to stop them."

Weinsteenberg studied Cal for a moment, his forehead furrowing in thought. Then he stood up and swept up the files in front of him. "If that's going to be your attitude, I don't think there's much I can do to help you." He headed for the door.

Cal gaped at him. "Where you going?"

Weinsteenberg turned as he opened the door. "To tell Pearson you need to find a new lawyer." He hesitated. "I make it a point to only represent clients I feel I can work with. It's a difficult enough job without having to battle with your client as well."

Cal leapt to his feet. "I'm due in court later this morning. You can't walk out on me now."

"It's my right to re-excuse myself if I see fit. In fact it's my duty if I don't believe I can provide adequate representation."

Panic overwhelmed Cal. Weinsteenberg was all he had at

the moment. He couldn't be allowed to walk away.

"I'll do whatever you tell me from now on."

The lawyer shook his head. "Believe it or not, that's not what I want to hear from you."

He was gone before Cal could work out what he meant.

"Have you always had a knack of annoying people," Pearson asked.

"Only since you arrived in my life."

"Shame. Weinsteenberg's a good lawyer, one of the best."

"Shouldn't you be pleased? Makes your job easier without him."

"It's always more satisfying when you pit yourself against the best."

Cal exhaled sharply. "What is it with you guys, that you treat my whole fucking future like a game? With Weinsteenberg, it's tennis. What do you think you're playing? Let me guess, football?"

Pearson didn't reply.

"Basketball? Going for the slam dunk, are you?"

Pearson still remained silent.

"Baseball? Think you're going to get a home run?"

Pearson slammed his palm against the table. "In this case I think soccer's more appropriate."

Cal jerked back in surprise. "What?"

Pearson leant across the table until his face was almost in Cal's. "Because you keep scoring own goals."

"So where does that leave us?" Cal said after sitting in tense silence for fifteen minutes watching Pearson ignore him in favor of his paperwork.

"It leaves *you*," Pearson said without looking up, "without a lawyer." He glanced at his watch. "And due before the judge in half an hour."

"I can't brief a lawyer in half an hour."

Pearson put his pen down and sat back. "You don't have to have one at this point. It's only a bail hearing. The judge isn't going to grant you bail anyway, so there's nothing a lawyer could do for you."

"Isn't that a bit of a premature assumption on your part?"

"It's a murder case. We've got enough to substantiate the charge. Don't kid yourself you're going to walk out of here today, lawyer or not."

"Sounds as if you've already got my room booked at County."

There was a slight pause before Pearson replied. "I'm asking the judge to remand you here for a few more days so that you can help us with the ongoing investigation into your beating."

"Bullshit. You don't give a damn about my attack, never did. What's the real reason?"

"Would you rather be in County?"

"I don't know, I've never been. So what's the reason?"

"Home cooking, privacy. If you behave yourself we'd let your wife visit."

Cal wasn't sure Lily would even want to. "And if I don't?"

"You're going to be rather lonely."

The offer was tempting. Cal had no desire to experience County Jail any sooner than he had to. He had to be better off here and he could deal with the quiet, might actually get some decent sleep. But why was Pearson dodging the question about the reason? Was it a trap? Damn, he could use Weinsteenberg's advice right now. He'd know what Pearson was up to.

"What about Dennis Shore?"

"What about him?"

"Doesn't exactly make me feel comfortable knowing that the brother of the girl I'm accused of murdering is in the same building."

"He's on compassionate leave now. You'll be gone before he comes back."

"You're very confident for someone who's so wrong."

Pearson grinned. "I can't lose. For you to prove I'm wrong, you're going to have to help me prove that someone else is guilty."

"And if I can't?"

"I think you know the answer to that one."

Chapter 43

Pearson got exactly what he wanted at the hearing. The judge granted bail, but set it so high there was no way Cal could afford it. He was remanded into Leyton police custody for another forty-eight hours. The judge also advised him to find a lawyer, as if that might have helped in this case. Cal tried to explain that he'd had one until Weinsteenberg had walked out on him, but the judge seemed more interested in the next case on his docket.

The courtroom was nothing more than a large modern room, devoid of grandeur or any sense of occasion. It was attached by a covered walkway to the police station. Unlike the last time, Cal had an audience for this appearance. Not only reporters but also some local residents attracted by a home grown murder case. There was no one he recognized, no one to offer him a smile of support. He'd told himself not to expect it, but he was still disappointed. He wasn't expecting Lily, that would be too much to hope for, but he'd thought Kieran might show his face.

He was the only one in handcuffs—his case coming between a reckless driving charge and an underage drinker. The cuffs embarrassed him. It was difficult to feel dignified with your hands chained behind your back and a policeman leading you around by the elbow.

He was grateful that the hearing was so short and he could return to the comparative safety of the police station without having to go through a barrage of reporters. At least there were some plus points to living in a small town.

As Cal waited for Butler to unlock the door to the cells, one of the office doors burst open. Rigby stormed through, still as disheveled as earlier. Oblivious to the other occupants, he marched across the office, grabbed a black jacket from the back of a chair and headed for the exit, all the while muttering under his breath. As he passed one of the desks he bumped against it then lashed out with his foot at the offending piece of furniture before disappearing into the reception area.

Cal stood frozen until Butler tugged at his arm. As he was led back to the cell, his mind replayed what he'd just seen.

"Trouble in the ranks?" he asked as Butler removed the handcuffs.

"I don't know what you're talking about," Butler said.

"Rigby." Cal figured he had nothing to lose by asking. "He was the one Pearson locked up last night, wasn't he?"

Butler walked away.

"Oh come on." Cal said, "I know it was him. How many other guys around here are wearing red and white sneakers?"

His words fell on deaf ears.

Cal spent the next hour or so dreaming up reasons why Rigby had ended up behind bars. It was easy enough to come up with some serious ones, including the possibility that he'd come intending further harm to Cal. If that was true, Cal was grateful to Pearson for heading him off, but pissed at the idea that Pearson may have somehow protected Rigby from the real consequences of his criminal intentions.

He was deep in thought when he heard the warning sounds from the corridor that his solitude was about to be interrupted again. He remained where he was, sitting at the top of the bed using the wall as a backrest. What would it be this time? A new lawyer? Or Pearson looking for another session of truth and lies?

"Last cell down, ma'am," a male voice said.

Cal straightened with anticipation. A female lawyer?

His mouth fell open as Lily appeared.

"Pearson called." She held up the foil tray in her hands. "He said I could deliver your lunch myself... if I wanted." The hesitancy in her speech suggested she wasn't comfortable with the idea. "He said you'd be staying here for a couple more days." Her eyes flickered as she tried to maintain eye contact with Cal and take in his surroundings at the same time. She flashed him an awkward smile. "So here I am."

Cal was shocked by how desperate she looked. Her face was devoid of color save for heavy dark shadows under her eyes. Her hair had been scraped back into a tight ponytail accentuating the gauntness of her features. He guessed she hadn't slept well either over the weekend.

He stood up, trying to conceal the pain it caused, and crossed to the door.

Lily waved the tray around in front of her. "How do I—?"

"Here." He pointed to the slot in the bars. "Put it here."

Lily slid the tray down then stepped back sharply as if afraid the bars might ensnare her too. Cal ignored the food, his desire to embrace her so great that he was at a loss for words.

"It's not hot," Lily said. "Only a sandwich and some pie."

"That's fine. Wonderful. Thank you."

"We didn't know what to expect..." Lily let her words trail away. "Where they would send you... they wouldn't tell us..."

"Us?"

Lily looked puzzled by the question.

"Kieran, myself..."

A sliver of jealousy pierced Cal into silence.

"He's been so supportive... I don't know what I'd have done without him."

Cal wanted to ask whether the support was in any way physical.

"He said he'd stay. For a few more days at least."

Cal hated him.

"He wanted to know if there's anything he can do for you."

Leave my wife alone. Cal started to speak but the words caught in his throat. He didn't mean it, it was just...

He turned away, trying to hide the emotions that he was sure were written all over his face.

He waited to hear Lily's footsteps indicating that she'd left, but there was only an uncomfortable silence. After a long pause she spoke again. "What does your lawyer think?"

Cal turned back to her. "Have they told you how Katy

died?"

Lily flinched. "No, the police only announced they'd found the body and that… that…" Lily swallowed hard, "that she'd been dead for several weeks."

Cal looked up at the ceiling.

"Cal." Lily's voice shook. "You told us she'd run away."

Cal clenched his lips together, afraid of what might come out if he tried to speak.

"So how can she be dead?" Her words ended in a gulp.

Cal looked away again, not wanting to see her tears. His chest and throat burned with anguish. Even the family was now having doubts about his innocence. There was only one person who was still willing to believe in him, and Cal had driven him away.

Lily let out a strangled sob. As Cal turned back to her, she wiped a tear from her cheek, raised her head and straightened her posture as if she'd made a definite decision.

"I have something to tell you." The words came out in a breathless rush.

Cal's throat closed up. He was already close to tears too. All he could think of was how, even distraught, she was still beautiful. And how he was losing her.

He waited.

Waited for her to finish.

Finish their marriage.

Tell him it was over.

"I'm pregnant," Lily said. "Almost three months pregnant."

Chapter 44

The flicker of excitement at the news was snuffed out in seconds–Cal's instinct to pick Lily up and swing her round thwarted by the metal bars between them. And the look on Lily's face. Joy was not the word that sprang to mind.

"Three months? Already three months? Why didn't you tell me earlier?"

"I only found out when you were in the hospital. At first I thought I was late because of all the stress. Then, with everything else going on, it never seemed like the right time to bring it up."

"We had all that time alone together after I left the hospital."

Lily's cheeks flushed. "I know, but your moods were so erratic. I was concerned about how you'd react." She paused. "Cal, I needed time to sort out how I felt about it."

"What do you mean?"

"What do I mean? I'm expecting a baby…and it's very possible its father is going to be in prison when it's born…if not for most of its childhood. Don't you think that gives me cause for concern?"

Lily used the third person, as if she were already trying to distance herself from him. Then her words registered.

"Prison? You mean even then you thought I was guilty? Even before they found Katy?"

"It didn't matter what I thought, I had no say in whether you would end up in prison. But the press, the talk on the street, it all seemed like it was only a matter of time." Lily twisted her ponytail round in her fingers. "And you were being so secretive. You never told me that you'd driven Katy to that house, that there were conditions attached to the charges being dropped the last time you were arrested." She tugged even harder at her hair. "I only found out because the police told me."

Cal waited for her to mention the earlier arrest. She didn't.

"Lily, I…"

"I was going to tell you after I brought the girls back on Friday, but you took off without a word, no thought for me or the girls. What were we supposed to do? When I first heard you'd been arrested at the airport I thought you must have been telling the truth, Katy was alive, and that you were going to join her, wherever she was. That you would have joined her earlier if it hadn't been for the beating. That you were just waiting for your chance to go, waiting for me to go to my parents."

Cal was dumbstruck. She was so far from the truth. Couldn't she see that?

"Then they discovered the body, and I didn't have a clue what to make of it. Cal, I don't understand what you're about."

"Lily, please!" He had to calm her down. As her fears tumbled out, one after the other, her voice grew shriller with every word. If she kept on like this she would attract attention.

But he had nothing to offer her. At least, nothing that would help. "Everything will be all right."

Lily stared open-mouthed at him. Then she sniggered. She clutched at a bar as if she needed support to stay upright. "All right!" The shrill turned to a shriek. "How can it be all right? You're already in jail."

"Lily, stop it!"

Her whole body shuddered as she wept. She let go of the bar, clutched her mouth to muffle her sobs and turned her back on him.

Cal slapped his hands hard against the wall. The stinging pain barely registered. How could they expect him to stand there, watch his wife in such distress and not be able to hug her? Console her. This wasn't her fault. She shouldn't have to suffer too.

He stumbled to the back of the cell, supported himself against the wall and covered his head with his arms. He wanted to scream at the insanity of it all. Rage, fear, heartbreak, all vied for his attention. Lily was going to have another baby. His third child. Perhaps a son this time. But what the hell difference would it make to him? Years from now he could be sitting in some prison visiting room while some polite kids tried to make conversation with a stranger they'd been told was their father. And why? Because of a few lies?

The sound of footsteps cut through his thoughts. He rushed back to the bars just in time to see Benson guide Lily out of the corridor. "Lily. Come back."

She didn't even look around.

"Lily."

As Lily disappeared from view, Benson shot Cal a warning look.

"Lily!"

The door slammed shut.

Cal stared into the empty corridor, then down at the food on the shelf. He raised his hand and whacked the container out into the corridor like a missile. The force burst the foil open, spewing tuna salad and apple pie all over the floor.

Tuna salad.

He sank to his knees.

Tuna salad. It had been Lily's craving when she was pregnant with Sophie. He'd learned the recipe, made huge bowls of the stuff so that she never went short, no matter what time of day or night the craving hit. He had memories of feeding it to her by the spoonful, joking that their second child would have fish-like attributes, but secretly reveling in the opportunity to help Lily nurture their unborn child. That second pregnancy had helped paper over the cracks in their marriage.

This one threatened to reveal the crevices.

He struggled to breathe. He wanted to scream and curse. Blow off the anger that coursed through his veins at the injustice of it all. He'd never been a violent man, never, but without some avenue of release he was in danger of becoming one. And he couldn't afford that. To lash out now would only give the police more ammunition against him. But the alternative could cost him his sanity.

He got to his feet, flung himself down on the bed and

pushed his face into the blanket. What the hell was he going to do? He'd had it all and now what did he have? Why had he been so goddamned stupid? Thinking he knew best. Thinking he could trust people... Katy... hadn't he learnt his lesson with Sally?

He scrunched his eyes shut. No, it wasn't other people who were the issue here. It was him. Thinking he could get away with secrecy. It hadn't worked the last time, but he'd been lucky, Lily had forgiven him. But this time? There was more than just Lily's forgiveness at stake.

Lily thought... no, feared, he'd done it. She didn't trust him now and he couldn't blame her. No one trusted him—except maybe the kids. But the girls would realize he had let them down, let them down in the worst possible way. What had he done to their future? It had been entrusted to him and look how he'd handled it. Not even they would trust him. Not now.

He clamped his hands across his face. He could not allow that to happen. Not to his girls. Or the new baby.

No matter how precarious it was, he had to look to the future. This third child was his future. Amanda and Sophie were his future. He would like Lily to be part of it too, despite all that had happened between them, but if she chose not to be he would have to accept it.

The children didn't have that choice. He was their father. They deserved the best he had to offer them. Weinsteenberg was right, he had a lot of ground to make up, but the least he could do for his children was to fight and fight like hell. He had no idea where to start, what ammunition was left to fight with, but even if he lost, he'd still have his dignity.

His children would see that. They would know he'd never meant to hurt them.

He had to believe that.

He yelled for Benson. It was time to give Weinsteenberg a call and make amends.

Chapter 45

"I hear you didn't like your lunch," Pearson said as Cal sat down in the interview room.

"It was an accident," Cal said.

"Was it? Was Katy's death an accident?"

"How would I know?"

"You're good. I have to admit it, very quick with your responses."

"It's easy when you're being honest."

"Now you've confused me. Are you talking about the lunch or Katy?"

Cal glared at him. Pearson seemed amused. Maybe it was the thought of Cal on his knees, forced to clean up his mess to Butler's satisfaction while Benson looked on.

"Can we just get on with this? Benson said you wanted to talk to me about the attack."

"I assume you're prepared to do that without a lawyer present."

"I've talked to Weinsteenberg, and he's okay with it. As long as you're not going to accuse me of self-mutilation."

Pearson laughed. "Just wanted you to have a look at some photographs."

"Photographs?"

"You said that Katy had distinctive eyes, you'd recognize them anywhere. That you saw her the night of the attack, despite being on the verge of blacking out."

"And you said she was murdered long before that."

Pearson held up his hand. "I'm trying to keep the two issues separate here. Your lawyer's not here. I don't want you to think I'm trying to violate your rights. Can we just stay on the subject of Katy's eyes?"

Cal hesitated. His rights? The stress must be getting to Pearson too. He'd never shown much concern about rights before. Or was this another of his games? "Okay."

Pearson passed a piece of paper across the table. There were six photographs on it. Six pairs of large brown eyes, no other features, just a small band of forehead above and the bridge of the nose below.

"What the...?"

"Just point out which one is Katy," Pearson said.

Cal took another look. Maybe his memory was hazy, or the photographs were poor quality, but he realized he couldn't tell. A knot formed in his stomach. He lingered over the fifth picture. The shape was similar, he was sure of it, but they still didn't look right. But if he couldn't tell...

No, it was long past time to start being honest.

Cal let the paper drop onto the table. "None of them." He hoped he sounded more confident than he felt.

Pearson raised his eyebrows. "You sure?"

"Yes," Cal said without looking at the photographs again.

"What about these?"

Pearson passed another sheet across. Six more pairs of brown eyes, all very different in shape.

Cal relaxed. "That one." He pointed to the third picture. "That's Katy."

"How about this one?" Pearson slid a third sheet over. Six more pairs of eyes, all quite similar this time.

Cal scanned the sheet. The answer was still clear. "Number five."

"And this one?"

The fourth sheet had only four photographs on it. For a second Cal thought they were identical, but one held his attention, the one with the deep sadness that was always there even when Katy laughed.

"Number one."

"Last one," Pearson said.

Cal looked at sheet five and sniggered. It was a duplicate of number four except that Katy's photograph had been moved to the other side.

"Number four." He pushed the pictures back towards Pearson. "Satisfied?"

"Impressive. Only one wrong."

"No way is Katy in that first set."

Pearson nodded. "That's right, but neither is she in the last." He handed a final piece of paper across to Cal. Full versions of the final four photographs: four males, all quite similar, but the last one the double of Katy in all but gender.

Cal's heart skipped a beat. He didn't know who the male Katy was, but he could have a good guess because there was no confusion over one of the other three—Officer Dennis Shore.

"Andrew Shore," Pearson said before Cal could ask. "The third of Katy's brothers."

It was another own goal, in Pearson's parlance. By identifying Andrew, Cal had scotched the argument that Katy had been alive to play a part in the attack.

The timing was lousy. He'd only just persuaded Weinsteenberg to take his case back, pledging that he was prepared to fight to the bitter end to prove his innocence, and now look what he'd done. Weinsteenberg would probably wash his hands of him once and for all.

He was wrong again. It was beginning to unnerve him. It happened so often. He wondered just when he'd become so stupid.

"Don't worry about it," Weinsteenberg said. "The coroner's findings about the time of Katy's death would have more sway in any jury's mind than anything you could say. Nothing's lost, and Pearson's happy, so relax."

Once more, Weinsteenberg proved his worth. He appealed the bail terms and got the judge to agree to drop the bail amount to a hundred thousand again on condition that Cal be put under house arrest. Hardly complete freedom, but it was a big step in the right direction. Cal had to spend one more night in jail while the electronic tagging was arranged, a night where, out of sheer relief at the idea of going home, he managed to get a few hours sleep.

Pearson stopped by Cal's cell before he left to tell him the police had picked up Andrew Shore the previous day, charged him and he'd been released on bail. He hadn't provided an alibi, but neither had he confessed which still raised the question of who his accomplices were.

Cal tried to put the news in perspective. Andrew knew Cal had identified him. Andrew was free. Cal would be at home, out of police protection. Should he be worried?

Pearson reassured him. There was also an injunction against Andrew. He had to stay away from Cal's house.

Cal almost laughed. As if the criminally intent worried about a small thing like that.

There was no injunction against the press. They were outside the station house when Cal was led out in handcuffs and they were outside his home when he was led in. Cal kept his chin down and his eyes focused on the ground, allowing the officers on either side to direct his path. He could hear Weinsteenberg fielding questions, his confident assertion that his client would be proved innocent of any involvement in this dreadful matter sounding more hollow each time Cal heard it.

Cal sighed with relief as the front door closed behind him, shutting out the jostling and shouting of the reporters in the street. Lily greeted him as she might a visitor, formal and distant, her eyes drawn to his handcuffs, a flicker of uncertainty in her eyes. But then, this was not a normal husband-returning-home scenario. Nobody knew how to react.

The electronics guy was already there, a jovial bulky man who extolled the virtue of modern technology while he rigged Cal's telephone in order to turn the house into a self-enforced prison. The police kept him handcuffed until the phones were set up and a bulky bracelet had been clipped round his ankle and tested to the installer's satisfaction. Did they really think he would try to run in front of his wife and with the county's entire press corps on his doorstep?

Then again, it was just the kind of thing that happened all the time in the movies, so maybe he had to allow for their caution.

These officers were dealing with a situation they'd probably never had to handle before—and more than likely would never handle again. They were fascinated by the gadgetry, asking nonstop questions about how it worked, like it was a new toy. Which in terms of incarceration, he supposed it was.

He sat in silence on the sofa, waiting for the ordeal to be over, barely listening to the instructions and regulations thrown his way by the installer. He tried to catch Lily's eye, but she avoided him to the point where he began to wonder whether she was pleased to have him home. He watched as she bustled round making coffee for the intruders, ever the perfect host. Because of the handcuffs he wasn't included. He'd been home less than an hour and already he was growing irritated with her.

At last Lily saw the lawmen out, leaving Weinsteenberg with Cal. They listened to the sound of the front door shut and then Lily's footsteps as she bypassed the living room and went into the kitchen.

Weinsteenberg gave Cal a sympathetic glance. "It'll take her a while to get used to the idea."

"Maybe she doesn't want to. Maybe it would be easier for her if I stayed in jail."

"I doubt it. She's had a couple of opportunities to walk away from this and she's still here. I think she's in this for the long haul."

Cal wished he could be so sure. His actions had ripped Lily's life apart in a way she could never have imagined. She was like a boat lost at sea, not knowing which way to sail. He could understand that. He was in a similar boat, struggling to survive the almost daily onslaughts of forces that were now beyond their control. But when the storm ended, as it would following his day in court, who was to say whether Lily would be prepared to sail into the same port as Cal?

Weinsteenberg looked at his watch and stood up. "I'll be in touch." He looked in the direction of the kitchen. "Good luck."

"Thanks. You know where to find me."

Weinsteenberg nodded. "A piece of advice." The lawyer moved towards the door. "Find yourself a hobby, anything, to take your mind off all this, or you're going to drive yourself crazy thinking about it."

Chapter 46

Cal strolled round the house enjoying the sense of space and the relative freedom of being able to go where he wanted, a luxury he'd taken for granted until now. He avoided the kitchen. He wanted to give Lily all the time she needed to get used to the idea of him being there. So when he'd completed his tour he slipped on a jacket and went through the living room onto the deck.

A weak sunshine flooded the area. Cal lifted his face to feel the rays, realizing that he'd barely been out of doors for the last month. He dragged an ornate white metal chair into the sunniest spot, sat down and surveyed the back yard. His new prison extended fifty feet beyond the house. Mentally he marked off the distance. Better than nothing. At least he had a good excuse for not doing any yard work this winter.

The door behind him clicked open. A second later a firm hand came down on his right shoulder.

"Okay, brother?"

Cal looked up. Kieran was dressed for action in sweat suit and sneakers, but his tousled hair and sleepy eyes said he'd just got out of bed.

Cal stood up and embraced Kieran tightly, the negative thoughts he'd harbored about him forgotten in the pleasure of the reunion.

"It's good to have you back," Kieran said.

"Thanks for sticking around. I hear you've been a tower of

241

strength." Cal grimaced at the little barb in his tone. Well, not forgotten completely. Kieran chose to ignore it.

"Least I could do," Kieran pulled another chair close to Cal's. "Boy, that was one unreal day. I thought I'd fallen into the plot of some TV show, the police barging in, rushing upstairs like they did."

"I'm sorry you had to be here for it."

Kieran shrugged. "No problem. I like to think I saved your front door. If I hadn't been there to open it, would they have broken it down?"

Cal shuddered. "Thank God the kids weren't in the house at the time."

"They almost took the place apart after you'd gone. By the time Lily turned up they were almost done. As soon as they finished with a room I tried to tidy it up a bit so it wouldn't look too bad. Unfortunately they saved your bedroom for last, so Lily arrived back to find four guys searching through your closets and drawers."

Cal groaned.

"Look on the bright side," Kieran said, "they didn't appear to find anything suspicious."

"Only some initialed handkerchiefs."

"Oh, yeah, what was that about? Lily said they seemed interested."

"They didn't tell you?"

"Tell us what?"

"They found a similar style handkerchief, only covered in blood... blood that matched Katy's... under the front seat of my car."

Kieran looked as if he was about to throw up.

"Why would anyone want to frame you?" Kieran asked after he regained his composure.

"You tell me. I haven't a clue."

"It's not as if you were a lawyer or a police officer, where someone might have a grudge against you." Kieran paused. "You haven't messed up someone's accounts, big time, have you? Ratted them out to the IRS? Discovered a huge fraud?"

"In Leyton? Come on Kieran, be serious. Most of my clients are either sole proprietors or retired couples." Cal sighed. "Or at least they were. By now I'll be lucky if I've got any left."

"First things first. If you don't sort this out you're not going to need any clients." Kieran lowered his voice. "And you swear you weren't having an affair?"

"I told you. No."

Kieran sprawled back in his chair. "What's your lawyer say?"

"He's trying to put an optimistic spin on it. Say's he's not sure the police could prove I was the murderer beyond reasonable doubt. But we don't know all the evidence they have yet. They're been fairly tight lipped about it. Makes me think they've got something conclusive, but if it's against me, how can that be?"

"The handkerchief in the car?"

Cal shook his head. "It's got to be more than that. That's potentially tainted. Pearson had one of his guys drive my car back from the airport before they found the evidence."

Kieran frowned. "But they didn't discover that Katy had been murdered until Monday, well after your car was in the pound."

Cal's face fell. "So either it was planted in the pound, which means it was an inside job, or it was put in the car much earlier."

"By someone who knew Katy was dead. The murderer. Who's had access to your car?"

"No one. It was locked in the garage the whole time I was in hospital. Lily drove it back from the office after the attack. Other than that…"

"What?"

"Damn. It could have happened earlier, outside the office. Sometimes I don't lock it."

"You park on Main Street right?"

"Yes."

"So somebody would be taking quite a risk, trying to get into your car in daylight."

"Except sometimes I left it there overnight."

"Great," Kieran said, "you mean it could be anyone."

The two sat in melancholy silence.

Eventually Cal stood and looked out across the yard. "One hell of a mess."

"You do realize," Kieran said, "that if you'd told the police the truth from the start that you might have saved yourself all this."

Cal didn't respond.

"For one, if you were guilty, why would you willingly lead them to the murder scene? And two, if they'd done a routine search of your car then, the real killer might not have had time to plant the evidence."

Cal hesitated. The beauty of hindsight. If only.

"You do realize," Cal said, "that I told that first lie thinking it would keep me out of trouble."

He bit down hard on his lip. "Biggest mistake of my life."

Cal drifted around for the rest of the morning at a loss what to do. Lily avoided him. From time to time he heard her talking to Kieran, once he even heard them laughing, which made him feel like a stranger in his own house. At intervals, he peered out the front window to see what the press was up to. Their numbers dwindled as the hours passed with nothing to report.

Lunch was an ordeal. They ate Lily's lentil soup and tomato baguettes in almost total silence. Kieran opened a bottle of wine, possibly hoping it would ease the atmosphere, but to Cal it only demonstrated once again how at home Kieran appeared to be around his house.

Lily didn't think it was a good idea to drink. Cal had no such qualms. He knocked it back as if it were beer. He knew Lily and Kieran were watching him, building up to say something about it. But they had no idea what he'd been through—the fear, the humiliation and the loneliness. He had a whole gamut of emotions to blow off and without recourse to the tennis court, sinking as much red wine as he could manage seemed the only alternative. Besides, he had some things to say and he needed the Dutch courage.

He emptied his third glass almost as soon as Kieran had topped it up. When Kieran made no effort to get a second bottle, Cal pushed away from the table, staggered across the kitchen and got one himself. Out of the corner of his eye he saw Lily start to stand up too, only to stop as Kieran put his hand on hers and shook his head, as if warning her off.

It was the final straw. He was in the shit and his brother was usurping his place. He slammed the wine bottle down in front of Kieran.

"Here, open this and then go and find yourself something useful to do. I need to talk to *my* wife."

Lily gasped, but Kieran merely opened the second bottle, filled Cal's glass, put the bottle down in front of Cal and headed for the door. All without a word.

"On second thought, stay," Cal said. "You might as well hear this. Save me repeating myself."

Kieran strolled back to the table and stood opposite Cal. His stance suggested he'd just about had enough. Cal edged the wine bottle towards him. Kieran ignored it.

Cal turned to Lily. She looked as if she wanted to throttle him, but instead twisted her napkin between her fingers.

Cal took a large gulp of air. "First off, I did not murder Katy Shore."

Lily didn't react.

"Nor was I having an affair with her."

Still silence.

"I did drive her to that house. I didn't tell the police in the beginning because I didn't want them or the Shore family to know I was involved in Katy's plans to run away. But only because I didn't want any unpleasant feelings between our families."

The silence continued.

"I dropped her off at the end of the drive. The last time I saw her she was still alive." His voice cracked on the words. "I swear to God she was."

"Cal," Lily said, "you don't..."

"Yes, I do. There's more. The police have Katy's journal." He closed his eyes. "In it she writes about us having an affair." He opened his eyes and looked at Lily. The increased tightness in his throat threatened to cut him off. "She mentioned my... my birthmark. That's why the police believed what she'd written. I have no idea how she knew about it. Believe me, she certainly never saw it."

Lily looked as if she was about to speak.

Cal put his hand up to stop her. He didn't feel so belligerent now, as if finally telling the truth was draining off his anger. "I need to finish."

Lily nodded.

Cal looked away. He hated to think how she would react. But he was finished with secrecy. It wasn't working out.

"The police have a bloodied handkerchief, Katy's blood type, which they claim to have found in my car on Monday. I have no idea how it got there. I think that's the principle piece of evidence at the moment. Except they're trying to tie in overtime payments I made to Katy as a sign that I was paying her off to keep quiet about the affair, or that she was blackmailing me. As far as they're concerned that provides a motive. That gave them enough to arrest me.

"In a couple of weeks I have to go back to court. If the judge decides the evidence is sufficient he'll send the case to county court. Weinsteenberg suggests he might be able to get the case dismissed, but I'm not so sure. Why insist on house arrest? They know I can't afford to run. We'd lose the house. Makes me think Pearson is confident of a conviction, although I can't think what else they can possibly have.

"When I…" He looked straight at Lily. "When I went to the airport on Friday it was out of sheer panic. It was stupid, I know. I…I thought I could be arrested again when they found out I hadn't told them the whole truth. And if I was arrested I had no chance of finding Katy."

He took a large swig of wine.

"Of course I had no idea that when they did find the house they would find her body." He bit on his lip and looked away. Tears welled in his eyes. He forced himself to look back at Lily. "I just knew I had to find her so that I could stop all the damage it was doing to our lives. I've lost most of my clients over this. Nobody trusts me, wants to have anything to do with me. I didn't know how to tell you. Tell you that I don't know how I'm going to support you and the girls." He lowered his gaze to Lily's stomach. "And now the baby.

"I've made such a mess. But I've told you everything now. In all likelihood twelve complete strangers are going to get to decide my future… yours too, to some extent." A tear rolled down his cheek, but he made no attempt to wipe it away. "I'm not sure how, but I want to fight this thing. You and the girls deserve that. But what I need to know from you is… is… is what you want to do?"

He bit his lip again. "I love you, and I need you. But I'll understand if this is all too much. I know I'm not offering much of a future, whichever way you look at it. But I need to know whether I have your support."

Lily didn't respond.

"I love you. That's all I know."

Lily wiped a tear from the side of her nose. She looked completely overwhelmed at what he'd told her. Damn. Had he messed up again? Should he have told her in stages? Given her a chance to get used to one idea at a time? No, there wasn't time. The relationship was already close to breaking point. He had to know now what she was going to do.

"I… I need to think about it," Lily said suddenly and fled from the room.

Cal stared blindly after her for several minutes. He'd expected some questions at least.

He turned to Kieran. Kieran looked away, embarrassed no doubt, but the sheen in his eyes said he too had been affected.

Cal slumped down into his chair, so far forward that his forehead touched the edge of the table. The linear design on the kitchen floor seemed to undulate before his eyes. He should have known. Did he really think he could make things better? His emotions threatened to choke him. He gasped for air. Then he gave into his nerves and threw up.

Chapter 47

Lily's immediate response to the truth was to lock herself in their bedroom. From the constant red light on the extension in the kitchen, Cal could tell she spent most of the time on the phone. Who was she talking to? More importantly, what was she saying? Was a jury of her friends hearing her one-sided evidence, helping her decide whether she should stay married to him? He hoped not. He didn't hold out much hope for their future together if she was. A significant number of her friends were already divorced, some still in the man-hating stage.

Keiran wasn't helping. He'd already scuppered Cal's plans to starve Lily out of the bedroom by delivering regular trays of coffee and snacks to her door.

"Don't force it," he kept telling Cal, "give her time."

Time for what? Time to ask everyone on the planet for an opinion? The only opinion Cal cared about was Lily's.

He was the lead story on the local news again that evening. His release on bail sparked a protest from local residents, irate at having a murderer on the loose in their neighborhood. Few of those interviewed bothered to include the word "possible" or "potential" in their arguments. What happened to the principle of innocent until proven guilty?

Pearson appeared on screen and explained that Mr. Miller was under house arrest and therefore should not be considered a threat.

"What's to stop him just walking out of his house?" one guy asked.

How about one hundred thousand dollars and prison?

After the early edition of the news, the last of the press outside the house packed up and left. Lily was still locked in the bedroom so Kieran volunteered to go and get Chinese take-out for dinner. Cal watched as his brother pocketed his car keys and strolled out the front door, a simple every day action. Until now.

He sprawled in an armchair and flicked through a few television channels, desperate for distraction. On one, a scantily dressed girl sang about being a prisoner of love. The song was rubbish, but the girl was worth watching. His admiration of her attributes was interrupted by a loud authoritative knock on the front door. He wasn't expecting any visitors, and Kieran had a key, so he stayed seated.

The knock came again.

Cal perked up. Perhaps this would entice Lily out of her room. He crossed to the living room door just in case.

The upstairs of the house remained silent.

The third knock was more insistent, demanding an answer.

"Go away," Cal yelled.

"Mr. Miller, open the door." A familiar voice.

Cal yanked the door open. "What do you want now?"

"Next time, answer a little quicker," Butler said. "We almost called in an alert."

"Next time?"

"Yeah, we'll be calling by a couple of times a day, just to check there's no problems. Make it a lot easier if you'd answer the door straight away."

Cal lifted his trouser leg so that the ankle bracelet was showing. "You've already got me tagged like a dog."

Stockman shrugged. "Just following orders. Pearson says he wants us checking on you and nobody's going to argue. You know Pearson."

It was all Cal could do to contain his rage. "Haven't you got anything better to do? Like find the real murderer."

"We won't disturb you any longer, Mr. Miller." Butler turned away. "Have a good evening."

Cal slammed the door on them. Was there no end to this

invasion of his life? He nudged the curtain at the hall window aside and looked out into his drive. The two officers sauntered back to the car and stopped at the roadside to talk to a passerby. Probably another nosy neighbor, pretending to walk the dog so that he could just happen by, eager to know why the police were once again outside number sixty-eight.

Cal hoped he was suitably disappointed.

After a night spent in Amanda's bed, Cal got up to find Lily had gone out. Kieran knew where but wasn't saying. His edginess worried Cal, made him feel that Lily was doing something he wouldn't like. Consulting a divorce lawyer, maybe?

By the time she came back, Cal was prepared for the worst. She found the two men in the kitchen amidst a sea of dirty breakfast dishes, eating being the only activity Cal could think of to keep busy.

She hooked her purse over the back of a chair and flopped down onto the seat. "I've been talking to Pearson."

Cal's mouth fell open. "What the hell for?"

"There was something I needed to tell him, something I think might help your case."

"You're not supposed to be talking to the police. If you had something to say you should have told my lawyer."

"You forget, I barely know your lawyer."

"And you're best buddies with Pearson now?"

Lily scowled at him. "I said, I told him something that will help your case."

"Oh yeah, and what would that be?'

"I can't tell you at the moment. Pearson said it would be best not to, for the time being."

"What?" Cal glanced across at Kieran. "Do you know what's she's talking about."

Kieran shook his head, and he looked like he meant it.

Cal looked back at Lily. "Whose side are you on here?"

"Yours, if you'll let me."

Did that mean what he thought? The anger was fading, but he was still confused. "So why not discuss this with me first?"

"I thought Pearson might take it more seriously if I could

persuade him you had no knowledge of what I had to say. That he'd know we weren't just making it up."

"Making what up for God's sake?" Cal raised his hands. "How can I use it in my defense if I don't know what it is?"

"You may not have to."

Cal shrugged. "I don't see Pearson rushing round to tell me he's dropping the charges."

There was a loud knock at the door.

Cal gaped at Lily, his eyes widening into a smile. He jumped up from his seat.

Lily started to say something.

He ignored her and rushed into the hallway. As he opened the front door, his optimism plummeted.

"Just checking in," Benson said in a bored voice. "Any problems?"

"Yes," Cal said, "you guys keep bugging me."

He slammed the door on them. He may have to prove he was still there, but nobody said he had to be polite.

He hesitated.

Or an asshole. He had to admit his recent manners left a lot to be desired and these guys were just doing their job. Maybe it was time to rethink his attitude.

Lily and Kieran were talking in low voices when he walked back into the kitchen. The conversation stopped as soon as they spotted him.

He gave them both a petulant glance, poured a cup of coffee and leant back against the counter. "Please don't let me interrupt you."

"I'm trying to help you Cal," Lily said.

"By keeping secrets from me?"

"I told you I'd been to see Pearson. I didn't have to tell you that. Besides, until yesterday you didn't have a problem keeping secrets from me. It can work both ways you know."

The expression on Lily's face was so earnest that, even though he wanted to be annoyed, Cal felt himself softening. Lily might leave him yet, but she wouldn't deliberately hurt him.

"I'm asking you to trust me," she said.

And there it was, out in the open. The assumption that had been lying under the whole conversation. The one Cal hardly dared believe.

"Does that mean what I think it does?" he said.

Lily got up and walked over to him. She placed one hand on his shoulder and stroked his cheek with the other. It was enough to make him crumple.

"I'm not giving up yet, if that's what you're asking."

She leant forward and kissed him gently on the lips then pulled her head back and smiled at him. "You're allowed to kiss back, if you want." She slid her arm around his neck, brushed up against his chest and kissed him again.

This time, Cal responded.

Kieran made a dash for the door. "I'm out of here."

Chapter 48

For the next couple of days Cal pretended that everything was normal—that he stayed around the house out of choice. That the twice daily police patrols were short social visits—nothing to get upset about. He stopped looking out the front windows, so he had no idea whether the press was there or not. And he made a point of not watching the local news just in case.

At the same time, he found himself starting to appreciate what he had. He guessed the prospect of losing it sometime in the future would do that. The ability to open his back door and just stroll out now seemed precious. He appreciated the beauty of the home that Lily had created for them, the time she put into it, but most of all, he appreciated Lily. Barely an hour would go by without him finding some excuse to kiss or hug her.

They didn't make love. It was as if they had pushed their relationship to the extreme and that, while the desire was there, they needed a little more time to reconnect. Instead they spent hours in bed together, lying in each other's arms, caressing each other as they talked. Sometimes when Lily was asleep with her head on his chest, Cal would force himself to make a mental image, to memorize every detail, just in case that was all he was left with.

It had taken only those few nights in jail for him to realize what was important. His freedom wasn't at the top of the list. Being locked up would be devastating. But being denied daily contact with Lily and his daughters? Without that, what was the point?

He needed Lily, he knew that, better than ever, but he puzzled over why she'd decided to stick with him. What was it that she'd told Pearson that could make such a difference?

Trust me, she'd said. Trust. The very attribute that he had been in the process of tearing apart in their relationship. They were going to have to rebuild it, step by step.

Trust me. He did. But what if she was wrong? What if Pearson had tricked her? How would Lily live with herself if she thought she'd been part of his downfall?

Trust me. She meant not only her actions, but also her instincts. Well, his instincts were shot. He'd a litany of bad decisions to berate himself with. A child could have handled the matter better than he had.

He watched the rise and fall of Lily's chest as she slept. He caressed her stomach, marveling at the thought of the unborn child forming within. He would trust Lily. He would trust her with his life. And if that bastard Pearson was in any way plotting to betray Lily, Cal would see to it that somehow he paid.

Promising Weinsteenberg and Lily that he would fight to clear his name was one thing; actually doing it another. He didn't have a clue where to start. Groundless optimism was unlikely to prove a case winner and, at the moment, that was all he had. There were no last minute alibis or witnesses that could be found to save him and, much as he would like to, he was hardly in a position to track down the real murderer. His only hope was that Weinsteenberg would be able to cast doubt on the police's conclusions. Weinsteenberg had a good reputation. Even the police said so. Cal just wished like hell that it wasn't him who had to depend on it.

To Cal's amazement there was some good news amongst the gloom. Marc Coulson called, ebullient at having got approval for his business expansion loan, approval which he claimed was all due to Cal's business plan. Cal was pleased for Marc. He was a hard worker, dedicated and determined. He deserved success. And besides he was one of the few who hadn't jumped ship. But it was difficult to share someone else's joy with the sword of Damocles hanging over your own head.

Marc wanted to set up a meeting to discuss the installation of a new accounting system that could cope with his enlarging business. Cal broke the news gently that he was under house arrest.

"But you're allowed to have visitors at home?" Marc asked without missing a beat.

"Yes, but—"

"Then we can meet at your house. I guess that's where you're working from at the moment anyhow."

Cal didn't like to admit he wasn't working at all, and Marc had answers for all his objections, none more powerful than the monetary one. It was several weeks' worth of work, and he was in no position to refuse a source of income.

Cal rushed to tell Lily the good news. She had some of her own. Her father was bringing the girls back home later that day to save Lily another round trip.

Cal tried to return her smile. He couldn't wait to see his daughters. His father-in-law was another matter altogether. "I think I might be coming down with something." He wiped at his forehead. "I should go and lie down."

"Cal, don't be stupid." Lily said, but she kept her smile.

"Well I'm hardly on his list of favorite people at the moment, am I?"

"What do you mean?"

"Lily, he hates me. He always has. And now... well now... he thinks he's got a murderer for a son-in-law."

"I can't believe you said that. Daddy doesn't hate you."

"He hardly greets me with open arms, does he?'

Lily laughed. "You jackass, he's jealous of you. He's a typical doting Dad and you've stolen his daughter's heart." She paused. "He'd probably like to hate you, but he knows I love you and that you make me happy..."

"Made."

Lily rolled her eyes.

"Am I making you happy now Lily? Hardly."

"Where do you get off telling me what makes me happy?"

Cal recoiled at the ferocity of her tone.

"You might want to, but you can't tell me what to think," she said, a little calmer. "I reach my own conclusions, thank you."

"But you look so unhappy."

"So do you," Lily said, "are you saying it's me that makes you that way?"

Cal was speechless for a moment. "Um, of course not. It's all the other stuff that's going on at the moment."

"My point exactly," Lily said.

"But in all the lies I've told. And trying to run." He raised his pant leg and pointed to the anklet. "I did this to myself, to us."

"I know, and if you say it was stupid, I won't argue. But I've done a lot of talking with Kieran, about what happened to you in college, about what you told him after the affair. And I've tried to imagine how I'd have felt if a journal like Katy's showed up. I can see why you lied. It was stupid, but I understand it."

Cal stared at her. He could feel the weight peeling off his heart, feel the surge of a new hope, a new love.

"Besides," she said, "I never knew what you were hiding. But you're telling the truth now."

"I… yes, I am. But how can you tell?"

She laughed. "Cal, in case you hadn't noticed, you're a lousy liar."

"Could I have a word in private?"

Cal glanced up at the sound of his father-in-law's voice. He'd said a rushed hello to John Holmes on his arrival an hour earlier before focusing all his attention on Amanda and Sophie, both of whom were now curled up on his lap, snuggled against his chest. It was the most wonderful feeling in the world, and Cal was reluctant to give it up for what was bound to be a fruitless conversation.

"I don't…" He paused as he thought of Lily. Lily was supporting him. The least he could do was to be civil to her father for a few moments. He slid Sophie and then Amanda off his knees and onto the sofa.

The girls wailed in unison.

"Daddy just needs to talk to Grandpa for a few minutes," he said, "I'll be right back." He hoped the old man got the message that this was going to be a short conversation.

Cal led the way into the small study off the living room that he used as an office. He offered the only chair to John and perched on the corner of the desk.

He decided to take the offensive from the beginning. "What can I do for you?"

The question appeared to startle John. Cal eyed him with interest. Despite being well into his seventies, Cal had always regarded John as a force to be reckoned with, an upright, solid person who didn't suffer fools. Today he appeared ill at ease and frail. Was he sick? Cal hoped not. Lily had a heavy enough burden without having to cope with a sick parent as well.

"I was thinking more along the lines of what I could do for you." John reached into his shirt pocket, pulled out an envelope and held it out towards Cal. "I'd like you to have this."

The old man's discomfort was obvious. Cal took the envelope, held it at arm's length, afraid of what was inside. He turned it between his fingers.

"What is it?"

John didn't answer.

The envelope was closed but not sealed. Cal fumbled with the flap, his hands shaking as he removed a rectangular piece of paper and flipped it over.

It was a check. Made out to Cal from his father-in-law. For twenty thousand dollars.

Cal's fear turned to rage. He looked up at John. "You bastard."

John gasped.

Cal waved the check in John's face. "You think this is how much it will cost for me to walk away from your daughter?"

John, his face ashen, opened his mouth to speak, but Cal didn't give him a chance.

"Let me tell you something, you could add another zero to this figure and I still wouldn't accept it. I love Lily, she's my wife and I'm going to do whatever I can to make sure she stays my wife." He ripped the check in half, flinging the pieces at John. "Whether you like it or not."

John bent down and picked up the two pieces, holding them together as if he expected them to miraculously become one again.

Cal watched, surprised by his father-in-law's lack of response. He was about to walk out of the room when John glanced up, a puzzled expression on his face. "You thought I was offering you a bribe?"

Cal hesitated, the simplicity of the question rendering him speechless.

John held the torn check out to Cal. "All I wanted to do was help you with legal costs. Lily told me you'd lost some of your clients. Hardly surprising, under the circumstances, but you can't afford a good lawyer if you're not earning, and by the sounds of it, you need a damn good lawyer."

Cal closed his eyes. He deserved to be taken out and shot.

John was prepared to give away part of his life savings to help him and how had he responded? By throwing the offer back in John's face. And all because he was a hot headed, worthless shit who was so scared by the current turn of events that he could only respond with rage, pure fearful rage. And he expected people to be on his side? Hah!

He opened his eyes.

John was still standing there.

"I am so sorry." Cal said, unable to look John in the face. "I don't know what came over me."

"The truth, maybe? I could always tell you didn't feel comfortable in my presence, but I never dreamt that you thought I was against Lily and your marriage." He paused. "Lily loves you, that's all that matters, as long as you treat her right."

"Well… haven't had your doubts on that score recently?"

"I'd be lying if I said no. But if Lily is prepared to believe you're innocent, then so am I."

"And if she believed I was guilty?"

John was silent for a moment. "Lily loves you, she lives with you, deep inside she knows what you're capable of. She wouldn't still be here if she thought there was the remotest chance you'd hurt that girl."

Cal rubbed at the bridge of his nose. The temptation to flee the room was overwhelming. He was surprised John hadn't stormed out, he would have done so, but John stood waiting for Cal to reply, no rage, just hurt. And control. Like father like daughter. They thought before they acted, took the time to decide what was worth getting upset about instead of erupting on the spot like a volcano and then having to apologize for the mess afterwards.

"Thanks," Cal gestured towards the check, "but I can't take your money."

John looked at the torn check. "I'll send you another one when I get home."

"I can't accept it."

"Why not? Think you can do this by yourself?" John stepped towards Cal, for the first time a hint of anger in his face. "Take it, you can pay me back later if it makes you feel better, but at least I'll know that if you do end up in prison my daughter's not saddled with debt from your legal expenses."

Cal sighed. It was an offer he couldn't afford to refuse. "Okay, as a loan. I'll take it as a loan."

John smiled. "Good." He lowered his voice. "But do me a favor, don't mention it to Lily. I'd rather she didn't know."

Cal sniggered. How was he supposed to hide twenty grand from Lily? He'd just told her that they were running short of money, where was he supposed to say he'd got the unexpected windfall from? He stood and crossed to the window. An advance from Marc Coulson? No. Lily would know it was too big to be an advance.

Lily would know. Lily should know.

Cal turned back to his father-in-law. "Lily has to know about it. I'm done with keeping secrets from her."

John's smile widened. "Even better." He ripped the two pieces of check in half again and tossed them into a garbage basket. "You'll have the replacement in a couple of days."

Cal kicked at the carpet, unsure of what to say next. Thank you seemed insufficient.

"I think your daughters are waiting," John said. "They've missed you."

Chapter 49

Before it got dark, Cal took the girls out into the yard. He sat on the deck and watched as they rode their bicycles and pushed their dolls around in miniature strollers. They were so lost in the moment that it made him jealous. He wished he could find some activity that would take his mind off the future for even just a short time.

Exercise would do it. A few weeks of inactivity and his body was showing signs of flab, aggravated by his choice of food and drink as his main comfort since the attack. He enjoyed the pure pleasure that a taut, powerful body engendered. A fit body, a fit mind. If he got back his fitness maybe he wouldn't make so many half-assed decisions.

But where to start? Running and tennis were out. He could be stuck at home for months. He had a few small weights around the house, but unlike a lot of his pals he'd never invested in treadmills or stationery bicycles. He preferred the real motion of being on the road, the sense of freedom. Being cooped up on a machine was not his style.

He sighed. Being cooped up, that was the problem. Being at home was better than being in jail, no doubt about it, but by insisting on the tagging the law was still exacting a price for a crime he hadn't committed. He knew it was his own fault. If he'd never made that trip to the airport he might have been freed on bail alone.

Kieran came out of the house carrying two cans of beer. He

handed one to Cal then sat down next to him.

Cal considered the beer. It wouldn't help, but there was little he could do today to improve the situation. He listened to the click as he tore open the ring pull. There was a reassuring feel to the sound. Ordinary. Normal.

Tomorrow. Tomorrow he'd start getting back into shape.

"Cheers," he said to Kieran, before taking a large gulp. He watched as Amanda and Sophie, tiring of the bicycles, raced down towards the swing set at the back of the yard. It was the simple things in life that made you happy. Sitting out in silent communion with your brother, sipping beer and watching children play. Life was in the moment, not the future.

"Daddy! Look at me!" Amanda hooked her legs over a ladder on the climbing frame and allowed her body to flop backwards so that she was hanging upside down. Her face was aglow with a sense of achievement. She waved and then stretched her arms down, reaching for the ground with her fingertips, her ponytail swinging between her arms in the effort. She was several inches short of the ground.

Beside him, Kieran tensed. Cal grinned. Kieran thought Amanda was stuck, but Amanda had been working on this routine since they'd installed the swing set. It was a measure of how much she'd grown. Soon she'd get her fingers down on the ground, but for now she knew it was beyond her. Eventually she gave up and pulled herself back up.

Kieran let out a sigh of relief.

"We use to do that kind of thing all the time when we were kids." Cal said, "Remember?"

"Yeah, but it's different when you do it yourself, something else to watch, especially when it's family."

Cal thought of all the heart stopping moments Amanda and Sophie had caused him in their short lives. "You just have to get used to it."

"Daddy," Sophie yelled, "push me please."

Cal stood and put his beer down on the table. "Duty calls, back in a moment." He hesitated when he saw the expression on Kieran's face.

Kieran looked pointedly at Cal's ankle.

Cal looked down the long length of the yard and swore

under his breath. Fifty feet. He couldn't even push his own daughter on her own swing.

"Not now, sweetie," he called back as he sat down.

"I'll do it," Kieran said.

Cal watched with mounting jealousy as Kieran crossed the grass, repositioned Sophie on the swing and started to push, gently at first, building up in height and force in response to the little girl's commands.

"Look Daddy, look!" Sophie yelled. "Look at me. Wheee!"

Cal forced a big smile. He could hardly bear to watch. It would be better if Kieran left. Wasn't around to remind Cal what he'd lost. But... could he ask him to leave? After all Kieran had done for him? Kieran deserved better than that. And how would Lily react? He shouldn't do it... but the alternative...

He looked away. No, he couldn't let jealousy ruin everything. Not now. He reached for his beer as his words of advice to Kieran sprung to mind. He grimaced and forced himself to look back at Sophie and Kieran. "You just have to get used to it."

Kieran left that evening, saying he had to return to work, had already used up most of his annual leave. It was a reasonable excuse, but Cal knew it was just that. Kieran had sensed Cal's discomfort, knew he wasn't exactly a welcome presence. Despite Cal's good intentions, he hadn't been able to bring himself to persuade Kieran otherwise. He knew that somehow in the future he was going to have to make it up to Kieran, he owed him that much at least, but at the moment it was too much for him to cope with. He hoped Kieran would understand.

Without Kieran, Cal's boredom was more intense. Weinsteenberg had told him to find a hobby, but there was nothing Cal could think of that appealed. He'd never been a do-it-yourself fanatic, hardly knowing one end of a hammer from the other, and he had no musical ability whatsoever. He tried books, videos, even jigsaws, but fifteen minutes into the movie or the book or the puzzle and he would be thinking about Katy, the law, prison. The thoughts nagged at him constantly until he thought if it went on much longer he was going to go mad.

Even his sleep was full of unwanted images, leaving him tired and increasingly irritable. Why Lily wanted to stay with him at this point was beyond him. He knew he was turning into a nightmare to live with. She never left the girls with him when she went out, even to the supermarket. She wasn't afraid he'd hurt them physically, she knew he'd never do that, but that he would frighten them with his rage. Sometimes it infuriated him, but he couldn't blame her. He knew she was right. No matter how hard he tried there were times when his fear just got the better of him.

On Wednesday Lily took the girls to a friend's house for the afternoon. It was a glorious autumnal day, cloudless sky, no breeze, only a hint of a chill in the air. Cal prowled round the house looking for something to do. He ended up at the patio doors, watching the squirrels burrow for treasure beneath the layer of leaves littering the yard and the cardinals and robins seeking out berries on the bushes.

A scattering of leaves lay across the deck. Cal decided to go and sweep them up. It was a small job, but he made it last by sweeping until every single bit of leaf had been cleared away. It was definitely a day for being outside. When he'd finished, he leant on the broom and surveyed his work, then looked out at the leaf strewn grass. A regular service came and tidied the yard every month. They were probably due any day, to judge by the state of it, but there was no harm in him starting now.

He exchanged his broom for a rake, mentally marked off his fifty feet and set to work. He soon had large piles of leaves. He smiled at the thought of the fun the girls would have jumping in them. Who knew? He might even join them. With that in mind he started to rake the leaves into one huge pile, ignoring the aches and pains that suggested he might be overdoing it. It was a long time since he'd felt such a sense of purpose, trivial as it may be.

He heard the sirens in the distance. A relatively rare sound in Leyton. Usually it meant that some unlucky soul had been caught speeding. The sirens got closer. Who ever it was, they were headed in his direction. At almost full volume they stopped. If it wasn't for the press van parked out front, Cal would have been tempted to go and see who the unlucky neighbor was. Instead he kept on raking. His leaf pile was now so big that even he could hide in it. He couldn't wait to see the girls' expressions when they saw it. There was still more leaves to be raked so he continued on, his back to the house, his mind on Amanda and Sophie.

"Mr. Miller!"

Startled by the commanding voice, Cal spun round.

Butler and Coyle stood by the deck. Their expressions were grim, their stance aggressive.

Butler put his right hand on his holster. "Put down the rake and walk towards us."

Cal looked from one officer to the other. It was rather early for the evening check in. Then he remembered the siren. No wonder it had sounded loud. It had stopped outside his house.

"Put down the rake," Butler repeated.

Cal looked at the distance between himself and the officers. In his flurry of enthusiasm to build the world's largest leaf pile he'd forgotten about the fifty feet. Even the pile itself was now beyond the mark. He started to walk towards the deck.

"The rake, Mr. Miller, put it down."

"I was only raking my yard." Cal smiled to show it was a genuine error. "Guess I forgot where I was."

"The rake!" Butler flipped his holster open.

"Hey!" Cal let the rake fall at his feet. "No need for that." He stepped over the implement and continued walking, his hands raised slightly in front of him to show that he was being a good boy. Inside he was fuming. This was ridiculous. The police were threatening to pull a gun on him in his own home just because he'd overstepped some idiotic rule. What if the girls had been here? Would they have done the same thing?

Butler stayed by the deck, his hand still on his holster. Coyle pulled out his handcuffs and approached Cal.

Cal stopped walking. "You've got to be kidding."

Coyle had a handcuff on Cal's left wrist before Cal finished speaking.

"This is total over reaction." Cal looked from Coyle to Butler. "I was raking a few leaves, for God's sake, not trying to make a run for it."

"You breached the terms of your bail." Coyle clipped on the other cuff and nudged Cal towards the path round the side of the house. "We have to take you downtown."

Cal dug in his heels. "This is crazy! Haven't you got anything better to do than harass me?"

"You left the agreed perimeter." Coyle was calm and matter of fact. "The alert went out. We have to take you in."

"You're saying I broke my bail because I mistakenly wandered a few yards away from where I should have?"

Coyle shrugged. "That's the rules."

"That's not the rules. That's ridiculous."

Coyle grabbed him by the elbow. Cal stood firm. He reckoned he was back within the fifty feet mark again. He wasn't breaking any rules. Coyle tugged at him.

Cal still didn't move. "Did Pearson tell you to do this?"

"We're responding to an alert from the monitoring company. This has nothing to do with Pearson. You breach the rules—we take you in, simple as that."

"I want to speak to Pearson."

"You can do that at the station house," Coyle said.

"No. On the phone, now." Cal had no idea whether Pearson would back him up, but it had to be worth a try.

Coyle tugged again at Cal's arm. "At the station house."

"No. Call him from the house. Let me speak to him."

Butler stepped forward and took hold of Cal's other arm. "Strikes me you're resisting arrest. I'd be careful. You're in enough trouble as it is."

"I'm not resisting arrest." Cal stood stock still making no attempt to shake either officer's grip off. "I just want you to make that call. Look what harm can it do? You've got me here, in handcuffs. Just please call Pearson."

Coyle looked at Butler in a way that suggested it was okay with him. Butler deliberated in silence.

Cal willed himself to stay quiet.

"Okay," Butler said, "but if Pearson's not there, we're taking you in."

Pearson was there. Butler spent a few minutes outlining the situation then pressed the speaker phone and nodded to Cal that it was his turn. Cal hesitated. He would have preferred some privacy for his request for leniency, but he sensed he'd pushed Butler far enough for one day.

"I was out raking the lawn, that's all," Cal said into the phone. "I forgot to take my tape measure with me."

There was no response.

"I made a mistake. I'm sorry. It won't happen again." Short of begging, what else he could say?

"Okay." The abruptness of Pearson's response took him by surprise. "Butler, write it up as a warning. I'm sure Mr. Miller won't repeat the offense."

Cal grinned. He detected a hint of sarcasm in Pearson's comment. Butler appeared to spot it too. He scowled at Cal as Coyle released the cuffs.

"You can leave the way you came," Cal said, not wanting to show his face at the front door.

Butler and Coyle walked out into the back without so much as a goodbye. As soon as he was sure they were out of the house, Cal raced back to the front window and peered around the curtain to watch their departure. A bank of cameras were aimed at the house. Reporters sprang into action as the officers appeared from the side path.

Cal watched with relief as Butler and Coyle walked through the reporters and got into their cars without saying anything. Too proud to admit they'd come on a wild goose chase no doubt. He wondered what the press would make of it all. He sighed. If he put the evening news on, he could find out. It might be worth it for a laugh, see what fantastic stories they conjured up.

He sighed again. Problem was it was hardly a laughing matter.

The police car pulled away from the curb, made a wide U-turn in the road then stopped suddenly. Coyle got out.

Intrigued, Cal watched as the officer gestured for reporters to move back, a one-man crowd control unit. As he shepherded them to the side, Lily's car inched into the drive.

Cal let the curtain drop. More explaining to do. Still, at least the police visit had proved to be of some use after all.

Chapter 50

Thursday was Katy's funeral. Cal only knew about it because he caught a snippet on the local news—the casket being carried from the car into the church. He flicked the television off. Katy, or what was left of her, in a box. It was too much to bear.

For the rest of the day he clicked onto the news, watched for a few moments, then switched off. He wanted to know, and he didn't. He recognized the Shore brothers from Pearson's photographs, and an older man who had to be her father, being supported by the sons, his legs barely strong enough to carry him. The camera picked out Pearson and Docherty as the investigating detectives and briefly showed Rigby, whose presence startled Cal until he remembered that Rigby was a friend of Dennis Shore. Of course he would be at the funeral.

He drank even more than usual that day knowing that people at the funeral thought he was responsible for Katy's death. She was so young, so full of life, and now she was nothing. Just like that, at the whim of some maniac who was probably watching all this on television and smiling, secure in the knowledge that the police had got their man. The wrong man.

Lily tried to console him, but there was really nothing she could say. And he knew she needed comfort as much as he did, but that he was too far gone to help her. Eventually she saw she was making him worse and withdrew.

He watched from the window as Amanda and Sophie discovered his leaf pile—a spectator rather than a participant to their joy and excitement. Over and over they jumped into the leaves, their laughter growing by the moment. Amanda rolled onto her back, threshed her arms and legs around, causing a flurry of leaves to cascade into the air. Within seconds Sophie was copying her, her little limbs pumping like machines in an effort to keep up with her sister.

Cal turned from the window. It was pure torture. If he went to prison he'd miss all this. Even if down the line they discovered their mistake and freed him, they would have robbed him of weeks, months, years of his girls' childhoods. Nobody could give it back to him or compensate for the girls' loss of a father, or Lily's loss of a husband.

He sat down on the sofa and hugged his knees to his chest. His hand brushed against the ankle bracelet. The damned bracelet. Pearson knew what he was doing, because right now, if it wasn't for the tagging, Cal knew he'd be tempted to take Lily and the girls and run. Even if it did cost him the house.

The next evening Cal was alone again.

Lily had taken the girls to watch some animated thing at the local movie theater and Kieran, who was due back for the weekend, hadn't shown up yet. Cal was looking forward to Kieran's arrival. Not just for the company, but Kieran had managed to rustle up a treadmill from a friend who was only too keen to get the guilt-inducing piece of machinery out of his bedroom. If they set it up on the deck, Cal could at least pretend he was running outside.

He was in the kitchen, trying to decide what to have for dinner, when there was a loud knock at the front door. Cal hesitated. The police had already done their evening check. Lily and Kieran both had keys. He wasn't expecting anyone else.

The knocking persisted.

Cal crossed to the door and peered out through the spy hole into the early evening darkness. Rigby came into focus.

Rigby?

Cal stepped back from the door. What could Rigby possibly want? He took another look through the spy hole. He couldn't see anyone else; no partner or posse.

The next knock was more of a thump. Cal flung the door open. "What do you…?"

His voice failed him as he saw the gun in Rigby's hand.

Rigby took a step forward, Cal took a step back. Another step and Rigby was inside the house, slamming the door behind him, the gun angled towards Cal's stomach.

"Rigby. What… What are you…?"

The gun wavered in Rigby's hand. In fact Rigby's whole body was swaying slightly, but there was a look of such desperation in his eyes that Cal had second thoughts about tackling him. He appeared to be dressed in the same suit Cal had seen him in at the funeral, except now it was crumpled, the black tie loosened so the knot was in the middle of his chest, beneath the open neck of his stained white shirt.

"Put your hands on your head," Rigby said.

Cal did.

"Now, slowly, back into the living room."

For every step Cal took, Rigby moved one forward. As Cal stepped beyond the door, Rigby pushed up against it preventing any chance of Cal slamming the door in his face. Rigby glanced around the living room and then gestured to the overstuffed armchair.

"Keep your hands on your head. Sit down there."

Cal sat.

"No, no, no, get comfortable. Right back on the chair."

Cal wriggled back in the seat while Rigby pulled an ottoman in front of Cal's chair and perched on the edge. His gaze never left Cal's face.

Cal tried to hide his fear. Rigby was clearly operating beyond the law. He wasn't there to arrest Cal or read him his rights, which meant this meeting was not going to end happily. He glanced at the clock on the bookshelf. It was at least an hour before he could expect Kieran, even longer for Lily.

Rigby noticed his glance and smiled. "I don't expect to be interrupted. I saw your wife leave. I know the boys have already done their evening call. There's not even any reporters outside."

He didn't know about Kieran. He couldn't. He might have been sitting outside the house somewhere watching the comings and goings, but the only way he'd know about Kieran was if he'd tapped the phones. Cal felt a flicker of hope. If he could only string out whatever was going to happen until Kieran arrived. Rigby might have a gun, but it would still be two against one and they'd have the element of surprise.

"Don't you want to know why I'm here?" Rigby said.

"I'm sure you'll get around to telling me."

"Tough talk, but it's not going to do you much good here."

"How should I respond?" Banter. Keep him talking. That had to be the way.

"Why don't you try listening for once?"

"Listening? Listening to what?"

"The truth."

The tone of Rigby's words sent a shiver down Cal's spine. He knew the truth, as far as his role in Katy's death was concerned, so Rigby's so-called truth could only be wrong. Cal looked at the gun. Not necessarily the right time to point that out. Better humor him, at least for now.

"Okay, I'm listening."

There was a long silence. Rigby was still staring at Cal, though as if he was looking through him rather than at him.

Cal reconsidered. The gun was still aimed at his stomach, but if he lunged fast to his right he might just have a chance of avoiding a bullet. He tensed the muscles in his back and shoulders and braced his legs against the chair for extra support. Rigby's expression remained unchanged.

Cal launched himself out of the chair, brought his hands down from his head and threw himself towards Rigby's left.

Rigby toppled backwards. The gun fell out of his hands.

For a brief second Cal sprawled half on top of Rigby across the ottoman then Rigby jerked back up, flipped Cal face down onto the floor and dropped down on top of him. He used his knees to pin Cal's arms to the ground, his hands pressed down on Cal's shoulders and he leant forward until his face was almost against Cal's, his breath stale and reeking of alcohol.

Cal recoiled at the smell and tried to move his head away.

Rigby laughed. He straightened up again, the movement sending shooting pains through Cal's ribs. "How am I going to get you to listen?"

Cal kept quiet. Rigby was drunk. Drunk and armed. It was

a dangerous combination. At least for now the gun was still lying on the floor out of reach. Rigby was going to have to get up if he wanted to retrieve it, and if he got up Cal would be ready. He lay, figuring his options, uncertain any of them would work but knowing they might be his only chance.

Rigby stayed where he was, his full weight bearing down on Cal. Why? Then it dawned on Cal that Rigby didn't know what to do next either. It was a stalemate, but Rigby had to make the next move.

The heavy silence was broken by the telephone. As it rang, Rigby bore down more heavily, as if to emphasize that Cal was not going to answer it. Four rings and the machine cut in. Cal listened to himself say there was no one home.

"More lies." Rigby shifted his weight again, pulling Cal's right hand so that his arm was bent at the elbow, his hand up against his shoulder.

"Cal, it's Mom, pick up."

Rigby shifted again, this time moving Cal's left arm.

"Cal, I know you're there. Pick up please."

"Oh yes, Mom," Rigby said, "Cal's definitely here."

"Cal, please, I just want to know that you're okay."

"Sorry mom," Rigby snapped handcuffs onto Cal's wrists. "Cal's a little tied up right now."

"Cal... I... Call me back as soon as you can. We worry about you, you know."

"Touching," Rigby said, as the line went dead. "Someone cares." He stood up, straddling Cal. "You're a lucky guy." He nudged Cal's leg with his foot as he stepped aside. "Get up and don't try anything else stupid."

Cal rolled onto his side. His ribs pounded with pain. He slid his arms down his back into a more comfortable position and struggled to his feet.

Rigby bent down to retrieve the gun then turned to Cal. "Aren't you going to offer me a drink?"

Cal glared at Rigby. A drink? The guy had to be seriously disturbed.

"It's the polite thing to do when you've got visitors." Rigby smiled. "Even unexpected ones."

"Don't you think you've had enough?" Cal said.

271

"Enough for what? Enough to forget? Enough to forgive?" He aimed the gun at Cal's chest. "I don't think so. Not yet."

A cold tremor swept through Cal. He widened his stance to prevent his knees from buckling and uttered a silent prayer that the rush hour traffic would be light and Kieran would get there early. God only knew what Kieran would do about this, but it had to be better than being alone, with the options becoming scarier by the minute.

"There's beer in the refrigerator." Maybe Rigby would prove to be a slow drinker. Maybe he would pass out.

Rigby lowered the gun a fraction. "Lead the way."

Reluctantly, Cal walked through into the kitchen.

'Forget and forgive', Rigby had said. But what? And why was he taking his anger out on Cal? Had he been thrown off the force because of what Cal said about the beating? It was the only reason Cal could think of, but Andrew Shore had been arrested for that. Cal lived with the fear that Andrew might turn up on his doorstep, but Rigby? It just didn't make sense. And the state Rigby was in, there was little chance of getting much sense out of him.

"Stop there," Rigby said as Cal walked across the kitchen. Cal turned around. Rigby dragged a high stool into the center of the room. "Sit there."

Cal maneuvered himself up onto the stool. Even with his height, his feet were inches off the ground. There was a space of a couple of yards all around him. Rigby wasn't taking any chances this time.

Rigby opened the refrigerator and found a can of beer. "Shame you can't join me." He ripped off the ring pull and tossed it towards the sink where it landed with a ping. There was silence while he took several mouthfuls, then he lowered the can and let out a satisfactory sigh.

"They say it doesn't help." He held the can back up in the air. "They're wrong. It helps blur the edges, takes away the constant pain." He took another mouthful. "Of course they don't know what they're talking about, these doctors, these counselors. They only know what they've read. They don't know what it's like to have your life torn apart, to feel that your heart's been ripped out while you're still alive."

Rigby's smile had gone now. The look of despair that Cal

had noticed earlier was back, although this time accompanied by sheen in his eyes as if he was near to tears.

"What the hell do they know?" Rigby suddenly sounded quite sober.

Cal shifted uneasily on the stool. He'd heard of dedicated police officers, but Rigby was talking as if the job was the love of his life. No wonder he was mad at Cal. He was married to the job and Cal's allegations—which yes, may not have been true—had rendered him divorced. That didn't bode well for what might happen next.

Come on Kieran, before this turns nasty.

Rigby put his beer down on the counter and walked in a large slow circle round Cal.

Only the hum of the refrigerator broke the silence.

Cal ignored the temptation to twist around and watch Rigby, despite the fear he felt with him out of sight. His whole body shook and he couldn't do a damn thing to stop it. He bit down on his lip. Listened to the deliberate even pace of Rigby's footsteps on the wooden floor.

Several times round, then Rigby paused in front of Cal, the sheen still in his eyes.

"You and I are going to have a little chat. Or at least I'm going to tell you a few truths, and then we're going to take a drive, meet a few friends, hear a few more truths."

Cal thought fast. He couldn't let Rigby force him out of the house. If that happened he'd have no chance. He looked at the clock on the kitchen wall. It was only twenty minutes or so since he'd let Rigby in. It seemed like hours. How could he stall?

He stuck his leg out so that Rigby could see the bracelet. "You forget. I'm under house arrest."

Rigby shrugged. "You forget, I'm police."

"Are or were?"

Rigby frowned, reached inside his jacket and pulled out a badge. He waved the badge in one hand and the gun in the other. "Badge and gun. Guess that makes me a police officer."

Cal struggled to understand, his mind spinning into freefall. "But I thought—"

"Yeah, strictly speaking I shouldn't be here. Compassionate leave, conflict of interest, all those fancy terms."

"Compassionate leave?" Cal's breath stuck in his throat. He had to force the next words out. "What for?"

"You really don't know do you?" Rigby aimed the gun at Cal's chest again. "Pearson said you didn't, but I didn't believe him. You worked with Katy all those months, she must have said something."

Cal's mind reeled as the connection clicked.

Rigby. Detective Rigby. They were the only names Cal knew him by, although he'd come up with a few of his own privately. But he hadn't come up with Paul. The policeman Paul.

Whom Katy was set to marry.

Rigby gave him a tight lipped smile. "I think you're beginning to catch on."

Chapter 51

Rigby opened another beer and settled himself up on the kitchen counter facing Cal. The gun was still in his hand, resting on the top of his thigh. It would only take a second to raise it and aim, but from Cal's perspective that was a second longer than if it was pointed straight at him, a second where Rigby would have to think before pulling the trigger. At the rate Rigby was drinking, his thinking abilities were really starting to matter to Cal. The odds on him being shot on purpose looked high to start with. He didn't want there to be an accident.

"I first met Katy when she was only thirteen," Rigby said. "I was based at Leyton at that point with Brad and Dennis Shore. Katy was getting into all kinds of trouble and there was talk of sending her away. Her father was desperate, Katy was his only daughter, he'd already lost his wife, so he came up with a plan. He talked the station chief into keeping Katy locked up in Leyton for two weeks. He wanted to teach her a lesson, that if she kept on as she was, she was going to end up somewhere similar but for a much longer time."

Rigby's eyes were full of contempt. "She was only thirteen years old, a scared little girl. Yeah, her brothers would be around most of the time to keep an eye on her, but when it came down to it she was still a small girl locked up in a male environment.

"The first week she was there I was on the night shift, not exactly a demanding job in Leyton. That first night she cried herself to sleep." He took a gulp of beer. "It took a long time. I

275

didn't know what to do." He snorted. "Like there was something I could do.

"The next night I took a pack of cards to work with me. She was already crying when I got there. Hell, for all I knew she could have been crying all day. Her old man said she should only be allowed to have a Bible with her, no books, not even school work, anything that might distract her from thinking about what she was doing with her life." Rigby took another swig of beer. "Basically it was two weeks of solitary confinement. You can't do that to a thirteen-year old.

"That second night I persuaded her to play cards through the bars. I taught her gin rummy, pinochle, all the games I used to play with my kid sisters. We played for a couple of hours. We did the same the next night and the next. By the end of the week she was beginning to open up a little, tell me about her home life. When she found out that I wasn't going to be around at night in the second week she got all upset and panicky so I switched shifts so I could keep her company. I couldn't see that it would do any harm. In fact for the first time as a cop I felt as if I was doing some good."

"Yeah, I bet," Cal said. "Hitting on a thirteen-year-old. That must have made you feel real good."

Rigby's lips tightened into a thin line and his gun hand twitched against his leg. Cal wished he'd kept his mouth shut. Keeping Rigby talking was vital, but upsetting him was just plain stupid.

And why was he being told this story now? All he needed to know was that Katy and Rigby had been about to get married and Rigby thought Cal had murdered her. What did it matter that they had played cards together when she was thirteen?

Cal's stomach did a flip. Unless it was to show Cal that Rigby was capable of following his own sense of justice. That he didn't always prescribe to the laid down remedies and that was why he was sitting on Cal's counter, drinking Cal's beer and pointing a gun at him.

There were a few tense moments before Rigby spoke again.

"I had a couple of kid sisters who were about Katy's age. When Katy went back to school I got them all together. Mr. Shore approved because he knew me, thought my sisters would be a good influence, and I guess they were. Katy started hanging out at our house whenever she could. My mom took on the role of a surrogate mother. At last, Katy had another female she could relate to. Discuss all the girl stuff with. It would never have happened if I hadn't played cards with her."

"And the princess grew up and wanted to marry the prince who had saved her so they could all live happily ever after?"

Cal ducked as the beer can came hurtling in his direction. It missed his face by inches, bounced off the cabinets behind him and fell to the floor splattering its contents over Lily's pristine floor.

Rigby looked on the verge of tears. His jaw was clamped together. His strained neck muscles betrayed his attempt to hold back his emotions.

Cal knew his comment was callous. But dammit, why should he hold back? He was going to die. Rigby was probably going to kill him, no matter what he said, so why shouldn't he say what he wanted? Besides, who said he had to be compassionate towards his killer?

"Katy was eighteen when we began to realize there was more than just friendship between us. Both families were delighted. Her father wanted us to get married as soon as possible. I think he thought once she was married he could stop worrying about her. But Katy wanted to wait. Wait until I'd made detective and could get myself transferred to another city. At first she saw our marriage as her chance to get away from Leyton for good, away from her family. She blamed them all for driving her mother away in the first place and she hated her father for putting her through those two weeks in jail."

"So you did know she was unhappy at home," Cal said, "unhappy enough to run away."

Rigby shook his head. "After a while she realized if she was with me, she didn't need to run anywhere."

"But you were friends with her brothers."

"Only as far as they were going to be my in-laws." Rigby reconsidered. "Actually Brad Shore's okay, but I don't have much time for the other three. Dennis is a younger version of his father, domineering, arrogant and loud. Andrew is a thug at heart and as for the youngest boy, Chris, well, I guess he never got over his mother leaving like she did. He's a real loose cannon, you never know what he's going to do next. Though unlike Katy when she was a kid, he's managed to stay out of trouble up to now."

"No wonder she wanted to run away."

"She told you she was planning to go, didn't she? That's why you came up with that cock and bull story about her doing it that weekend. You were hoping it would ring true."

Cal shook his head. "She told me she was leaving that night." He looked at the clock. Forty minutes. Another twenty and Kieran might come to the rescue. He had to keep this going. "What I don't understand is why she worked for me for all that time and never mentioned you at all."

"You were having an affair."

"No, Rigby, we weren't."

"She wrote about it in her journal."

"But she didn't write about you in her journal. She didn't write about her horrible family. Doesn't that strike you as odd? Doesn't that make you think that maybe she made up what she did write?

"Katy didn't keep one journal. She had several, one for each element of her life." Rigby gave Cal a sad smile. "You rated one to yourself. That's why there's very little else in it apart from work and… and the sex."

Son of a bitch. He never would have guessed.

"The one about me was true enough," Rigby said, "why should I doubt the one about you?" He paused. "Even though I'd love to."

Damn, maybe it was time to try some kindness, to string this out.

"You're willing to accept that you're girlfriend was having an affair with her boss?"

"I don't see I have much choice, given the evidence."

"That must hurt." Cal took another sidelong glance at the clock.

Rigby was silent for a moment.

"Not as much as knowing she's been murdered." Rigby slid down from the counter, raised his gun and glanced at the clock. "Story time's over, time to go."

The telephone rang.

"Popular guy," Rigby said. "Shame you're not home." He

motioned with the gun for Cal to stand up.

A burst of static followed Cal's message then Kieran's distant voice filled the room. "Cal where the hell are you?" There was a long pause. "Cal!" Another pause. "Look I just wanted to let you know the traffic's backed up for miles, some kind of major accident, no chance I'm going to be there for six. More like seven." A weary sigh came down the line. "But don't worry okay, I'm on my way."

"Tut, Tut." Rigby wriggled the gun at Cal. "You never mentioned you were expecting visitors."

Chapter 52

Rigby may have been drunk, but he'd left nothing to chance. His Ford Explorer was backed up to the front door just out of sight range from the spy-hole. In the dark, a person would have to be coming up the drive to see anybody get in or out. Even so, he was cautious when he opened the front door, his gun pressed firmly against the small of Cal's back. When he was sure the coast was clear they walked to the car and Rigby opened the hatch.

The luggage compartment was empty save for a few sandy brown dog hairs and a small length of chain with a clasp welded to the lower lip of the opening, presumably to secure the dog.

"Get in," Rigby said.

Cal hesitated. The car had seven seats. What was the point in making him ride in the back?

Rigby poked him with the gun.

Cal perched on the edge of the car, swung his legs up and shuffled to the left side in a sitting position. Pain rippled through his ribs.

"No," Rigby said. "Lie down on your side, facing the seats."

Cal had to bring his knees up towards his chest to fit, but he managed to do as Rigby ordered. The sense of hopelessness increased as Rigby attached the clasp to the central links of his handcuffs and slammed the hatch door shut. He was stuck below the window line. He couldn't see out, nobody outside could see him. Any hope of attracting attention or even attempting an escape was gone.

There was a long silence. Wherever they were headed, there was no obvious hurry. Then the front door slammed and finally Rigby got into the driver's seat. As he started the engine, a slow sad melody filled the car. Cal thought he recognized it from some old movie, a haunting number that spoke of pain and grief.

For a brief moment Cal had a rush of compassion for Rigby. How must it feel to have lost the person you loved the most in such a cruel and unnecessary manner? He could almost understand the need to take the law into your own hands, to make sure the killer was brought to justice. If it were Lily, he might do the same. But, damn it, Rigby had the wrong man. If he did what Cal thought he was about to, he was just going to bring even more heartbreak and grief to Leyton.

Cal kicked in fury at the side of the car. "I didn't do it," he yelled at the top of his voice.

The volume of the music went up.

They turned right out of his drive, meaning they were heading into town. Cal tried to concentrate on the route. Not that it would do him much good, but it kept his mind off what lay ahead. They drove for a few minutes before Rigby brought the car to a stop and then made a left turn.

The center of town, early Friday evening. There'd be other traffic, pedestrians, plenty of potential witnesses to the green Ford Explorer with the solitary driver. Cal counted off the traffic lights as the car stopped and started along Main Street, then made a sharp left. Route 82, it had to be. They drove a little further then turned right. Cal's heart sank as he realized where they were headed.

The house where Katy was killed.

A few minutes later they made another right. The wheels crunched over gravel, the car bounced on the uneven drive, every bump agony to his ribs. The car pulled to a halt. The engine was switched off, but the music remained, that same tune over and over again. Cal heard Rigby get out of the car, the driver's door slam shut and then there was nothing save the music.

He thought of Lily and the girls sitting in the theater, laughing at silly cartoons, unaware of what was happening. He imagined them arriving home to an empty house, or finding the police there, following up on the silent monitoring system, putting out their arrest warrants for the murderer on the run. How long would it take for his body to found, for Lily and his family to be put out of their misery? He wondered whether Rigby would ever be brought to justice, or Katy's murderer for that matter.

With the engine off, the temperature in the car started to drop. Cal shivered, his thin sweatshirt offering little protection against the bitter cold. He tried to roll over on his back, take the pressure off his side, but Rigby had coiled the chain so tight that his wrists were almost pinned to the floor.

In the lulls in the music he thought he heard other sounds, cars, voices, but he couldn't be sure. Finally the hatch door opened and Rigby released the chain. Slowly he edged out of the car, taking in his surroundings as he allowed his circulation to recover before standing up.

They were parked outside the detached garage several yards from the main house. Both buildings had the slight ramshackle air of disuse; the yellow siding graying and chipped, the windows dirty and decorated with cobwebs. Cal focused on the garage, the garage where Katy had died, or at least where they had found her decomposed body. He shuddered.

The front of the garage had two double doors, the rust on the hinges suggesting they weren't used often. On the left of the building a small side entrance stood open, a rectangle of light from inside escaping into the gloom. Three more cars were parked round about. Rigby's friends no doubt.

Four against one. Hardly fair odds.

Rigby appeared in no hurry to go inside. He pulled a hip flask out of his jacket pocket, unscrewed the top and took a large swig.

Cal hoped he was having second thoughts. As he watched he realized Rigby seemed less drunk than before. The gun was aimed firm and steady towards Cal, none of the wavering of earlier. Maybe his frightened mind was playing tricks or maybe the excitement had sobered Rigby up. He looked up into Rigby's face. There was a strange expression in the detective's eyes, as if he were weighing Cal up.

Rigby made as if to speak then stopped.

There was no harm in trying.

"You've got the wrong man," Cal said. "Big mistake."

"Mistake?" Rigby pushed Cal towards the open door. "Next you'll be claiming it was an accident." He gave Cal one final push, sending him stumbling into the garage.

Cal staggered, only just managed to stay upright. He breathed shallow until the pain in his ribs had eased, then looked around. He had an audience.

He froze.

There were four more not three and he knew them all by sight.

Rigby stepped forward, a frighteningly inane grin on his face. "Let me do the introductions." He pointed towards Cal. "Gentlemen, Mr. Miller, or Cal as he's known to his friends."

He stepped to one side and looked at the guy nearest him, Katy's double. "I believe you two have met but never been introduced. Mr. Miller, this is Andrew Shore. Next to him are Chris, Brad and, of course, Dennis, who I think you met during your recent stay with us."

He laughed, so did Chris, but the other three seemed anything but amused.

Cal looked at each of them in turn, waiting for one of them to speak. They all looked more than capable of doing him some serious damage. His mind flicked back to the beating in the alley. What the four of them together could do was not even worth contemplating.

His knees began to shake. He knew he was a coward at heart. Normally he didn't have too much of a problem with that idea—not everyone could be a hero—but he prayed that if today was his day for squealing he wouldn't squeal for too long.

He took a quick glance round the garage. It was completely empty save for a few rusty gardening tools hanging on a rack to his right. Katy's car, assuming there had been one, must have been taken away as evidence. He realized he had no idea whether Katy had been murdered in her car or outside of it. There were various black splotches on the ground but no obvious signs of blood. In fact it was impossible to tell that any violent act had taken place here at all. He didn't know what he'd expected to find, but he'd thought there'd be some indications of Katy's death.

"Shall we get started gentlemen." Rigby's voice brought Cal's attention back to his companions. "I don't want this to drag out any longer than I have to." Rigby tossed something to Chris. "Here put these on, we don't want fingerprints."

Chris pulled on a pair of latex gloves.

Cal's stomach started to churn.

The Shore brothers strolled past him, much as they would an exhibit in a museum. Cal spun round to face them. They lined up next to Rigby, five men between him and the open door.

Rigby continued to point his gun at Cal, reached into his jacket pocket and pulled out a second pistol.

Chris snatched it from his hand and aimed the gun at Cal's head. His eyes were bright and excited, full of challenge.

Cal's stomach heaved.

"We've all been through a lot in the last few weeks," Rigby said, "worrying about Katy, fearing the worst, while this guy messed us around, making up one story after another." He paused. When he spoke again there was a catch in his voice. "Then finding her body, coping with the grief and yesterday… yesterday…" He glanced away for a second. "But it's still not over because now Mr. Miller is going to drag this whole business through the courts in the hope that his lawyer might just be able to persuade twelve strangers that they can't be certain that he's the killer. We're going to have to listen to the testimony and the lies. Hear over and over how Katy died, and all because Mr. Miller won't admit the truth."

Cal started to protest but barely got his mouth open before Rigby fired. The shot hit the ground a few inches to Cal's left.

Cal jerked to his right.

Chris let out a hysterical cackle. His gun wavered. He looked dangerously close to pulling his trigger too.

"We'll tell you when it's your turn," Rigby said.

Terror muzzled Cal. Fear pounded round his body, tightened his chest muscles, closed his throat. He struggled to remain standing. He was either going to fall over or black out, but Rigby showed no concern for his discomfort.

"We've buried Katy," Rigby said. "We want this to be over."

There was a murmur of agreement from the Shore brothers.

Rigby pulled out his flask, took another swig then offered it to the brothers.

"Don't you think we should save that for after," Brad said.

Rigby fired another shot. This time into the wall behind Cal.

Brad held a hand up. "It's your show."

Chris laughed again.

Rigby slipped the hip flask back into his pocket and gave Cal an inebriated smile. "So we decided to make you an offer." The words came out in a slur. "But it's a one-time-only deal."

There was another murmur of agreement.

Cal looked from one face to another. There wasn't a hint of compassion in any of them. He guessed he wasn't going to like the offer.

"Confess now," Rigby said, "and we'll take you back down town, hand you over to Pearson, and hopefully you'll spend the rest of your life in prison."

Cal was taken aback. He'd assumed he was a dead man. Could Rigby be serious about letting him live? There had to be a catch.

"If you don't confess," Rigby said, "Chris here will shoot you."

Chris sniggered his agreement.

Cal gulped.

"So, quite simple." Rigby said. "Life or death? More of a choice than you gave Katy."

Chris lowered his arm so his gun was level with Cal's chest and eased his finger around the trigger. "So what's it to be?" he said. "Are you going to start talking or do I get to use this?"

Cal stared at the barrel of the gun. His mind was a complete void. He looked at Chris' finger curled round the trigger. How much more pressure would it take before the gun went off? A choice between death and prison? What kind of choice was that?

No choice at all. Dead, he'd be silenced for ever. But if he confessed? Confess now to save his life and he could recant later. He was sure there was a law disallowing confessions taken under duress. And if this wasn't coercion, what was? So maybe there'd been a lapse in judgment.

Or maybe the three police officers in this room knew exactly what they were doing and he would never see a courtroom, confession or no. If he confessed, they'd have the closure they were looking for. They'd be free to kill him. In their minds, justice would have been served.

Only Brad Shore looked at all uncomfortable. Cal noted how Brad kept glancing uneasily at Rigby. Was there any mileage in that? Cal almost laughed at the thought. His mind really was going. Brad Shore was fully implicated in what was about to happen. Appealing to his better nature, even assuming he had one, was out of the question.

"I'm innocent," Cal said, the words coming out as an unintended whisper.

Rigby whooped. He walked towards Cal, his gait unsteady. "What do you think?" he said to Chris as he pushed his gun up against Cal's right temple. "A right handed man, angle the gun slightly upwards like this," he moved the gun to demonstrate, "and boom! One neat suicide. Gun found near the body, only the deceased's fingerprints, open and shut case. The remorse was too great, or the shame, or the humiliation of a trial, or the fear of a lifetime in prison, all brought to an end by a single shot." Rigby lowered the gun. "Do you have life insurance?"

Cal nodded.

"Shame," Rigby said. "Such a waste. Won't do your family much good. Not after a suicide." He turned away, started to pocket his gun, then swung back. "But start talking and at least *you'll* have a roof over your head and hot meals for the rest of your life."

"Go to hell," Cal said.

Rigby suddenly grabbed Cal's right shoulder and swung at Cal's stomach with his right fist. Cal arched his body to try and soften the blow. But it hit without any weight behind it. Instead it was an almost simultaneous push on his shoulder that sent him stumbling until he lost his balance and fell backwards, the weight of his body on his arms digging the handcuffs into his wrists and making him gasp.

As Rigby walked towards him, Cal rolled onto his side, trying to catch his breath. What the hell had just happened?

Rigby leant over him, grabbed his chin and forced him to look up. There was a strange expression on Rigby's face. Not the murderous intent of earlier. And his mouth was moving. In the half-light Cal made out the words.

Be careful.

Rigby yanked on Cal's arm and pulled him to his knees. "Don't let me have to do that again."

Chris sniggered.

Rigby crouched down so that his face was level with Cal's. "Now why don't you save us all a lot of hassle and tell us exactly what happened." He pointed off towards Brad and Dennis. "Police officers. Just tell them how it happened."

Cal looked down at the ground. Was Rigby trying to get him out of this? Was this set up for the Shore brothers? What the hell was he supposed to say?

Rigby nudged him under the chin, forcing him to look back up. "Your choice." He gestured towards Chris. "My friend there is getting a little impatient."

"Friend! Not so long ago you described him as a loose cannon."

Rigby smacked Cal across the face. The impact was a mere pat compared to the force Rigby appeared to put into it.

"Be very careful what you say," Rigby said. But his voice was a whisper, as if only Cal was to hear it. And there was something about the tone. A warning within a warning? Dammit, was Rigby somehow on his side? But still wanted him to confess?

Chris took a few steps towards them; his gun still aimed at Cal. "Let's just do it, the guy's not going to confess."

"Not yet." Rigby almost sounded as if he was enjoying himself. "Let's give him time to reconsider. A confession for his life. It's a small price to pay, don't you think."

It was a very small price to pay, if you had something to confess. Under the circumstances it was a small price to pay even if you didn't have anything to confess. There was only one problem. How could he confess when he didn't know what he was confessing to? He knew Katy was dead, but how had she died? He had no idea. All he had to work with was a bloodstained handkerchief.

But Rigby would know. And probably the Shore brothers too. So he was going to have to get it right. Why the hell didn't Rigby give him a clue?

Wait, he could rule out a shooting. The subject of a gun would have come up. Either the police would have searched for one or, if it had been left at the scene, tried to track down the source. Cal didn't own a gun, never had, nor did he know anybody who did. He looked at the gun in Chris' hand. Or at least he hadn't until now.

"How much longer are we going to give him?" Chris said after a few minutes.

Rigby glanced at his watch. "We can afford to be generous. After all it's a serious issue. I'd hate him to make a mistake."

Cal glared at Rigby. What? Was that another message? How could he make a mistake over whether he confessed or not, when it was the only thing that was going to keep him alive longer than thirty seconds? Assuming Chris didn't shoot him anyway. The guy was getting so worked up at the prospect that he could barely keep his gun hand steady and his finger never left the trigger. How ironic if he were to die by accident. Although he guessed for the Shores the outcome would be the same. They'd be rid of him.

Rigby had stood back up and was taking yet another mouthful from his hip flask. What was he playing at? He thought Cal had killed Katy, he'd dragged him here to face the Shore brothers and now he was trying to help him? Why should he trust Rigby? Cal tried to signal with his eyes. He needed some other sign, some guidance.

Rigby stepped back in front of Cal, grabbed him by his collar and gave him another of those half slaps.

"What the f...?"

Rigby slapped him again. "Just confess."

"I didn't..."

Rigby slapped him again. This time with a little more force.

Cal sank back onto his heels. Rigby still had that strange expression on his face, his eyes like drills, as if he were trying to put the right words into Cal's mouth.

He had to focus. How could Katy have died? If not a shooting, what? A stabbing? Would explain the blood, but there'd have to be a weapon and Cal hadn't been asked anything about a knife or any other sharp implement. He shuddered again at the thought of Katy being confronted by a knife wielding killer. Had she had a few minutes of sheer terror knowing she was going to die?

He looked back at Rigby. Rigby was still holding his collar, glaring at him.

Giving him time.

Strangulation? No not strangulation, he'd already ruled that out. No blood. There was blood. Blood from where? The chest? The head? A blood spill that killed, not wounded.

Wounded!

Cal looked from Rigby to Chris, to Andrew, to Dennis, to Brad. Oh God, had she been left to die? Too injured to seek help, left to waste away? How long did it take? Minutes? Hours? Days? Friday night, Friday night he'd dropped her off. Sunday morning the police had come to him. If he'd told them then, been honest, they would have checked the place out, might have found her, found her in time.

Oh, God, maybe he was responsible for Katy's death.

He looked again at Andrew. Andrew's face was a bland mask. But Andrew and his pals had taken Cal down an alley, systematically beaten him to within an inch of his life, left him unconscious and bleeding. If it hadn't been for a teenage couple looking for some place to make out, he may have lain there till morning. He had a head wound. There was blood. Would he have made it until morning? Would Katy have made it until Sunday?

His body jerked in terror driven spasms. He glanced again at Rigby. Rigby knew. That's what this was all about. Rigby knew they could have saved her, if only they'd got to her on Sunday. In his eyes Cal had killed her whether or not he'd inflicted the first blow.

He turned his head to the right and threw up; retched long past the point that his stomach was empty, conscious of five sets of eyes watching his every move. He wiped his chin on his shoulder and turned to face them. Spittle clung to the corners of his mouth, it was a struggle to stay upright on his knees, but what did it matter? All they wanted was a confession.

A confession.

Would they really let him live if he confessed?

His mind flashed back over the evening's events. The only time Rigby had hurt him was after he tried to hurt Rigby, despite Rigby's upper hand. Maybe Rigby wasn't a cold blooded killer and this was after all a ludicrous act to force Cal to confess.

But what about Chris? Chris looked like he would pull that

trigger without a second thought. Without any goddamn thought. Time was probably running out, whatever Rigby had planned.

Rigby was still standing over him. Cal tried asking with his eyes the question he was afraid to ask out loud. Rigby just nodded then hit him with another fake slap.

Okay.

Cal took a deep breath. "Alright, alright, I confess." He took another. "I killed Katy."

Nobody spoke. They were all waiting for more. Now… now he was going to have to lie. And hope like hell they fell for it.

Suddenly, something Rigby had said earlier came back to him. That and memories of a conversation with Pearson on the day he'd taken his anger out on his lunch. It was a huge risk, but at this stage anything was worth a try.

Another deep breath. "But it was an accident."

There was another momentary silence in the garage then Rigby shook his head. "You expect us to believe that?" He pulled a hypodermic needle from his pocket. "Well, let's see what you say after a little dose of this." He stepped behind Cal and stabbed the needle into Cal's left hand.

"He confessed. That's all that matters." Chris moved towards Cal, the gun aimed at Cal's head, his finger clicking back on the trigger. "Let's finish this now."

"No!" Rigby flung himself towards Chris.

Why not? Cal thought, as everything went black.

Chapter 53

It was dark and quiet in the garage when he came round. Too quiet. Had they left him out here in the middle of nowhere to die?

He was lying on the garage floor, his arms stretched above his head, his wrists still cuffed and tethered to something behind him. He tugged on the cuffs. No give at all, but from the creaking sound, he guessed he was fastened to one of the garage doors.

He listened. He heard only his breath.

He shivered, the already cold temperatures aggravated by an occasional thin draught. He was definitely near a door. And he could well freeze before he starved to death.

His initial instincts had been right on this time. The 'confess and live' line had been a ruse. Rigby was out for revenge, retribution that fitted the original crime. If Katy had died a lingering death then so would her murderer. But first, he'd teased Cal into believing that he still had a chance, given him one last straw for his desperate imagination to grasp onto. So much for trust. Maybe the bad news was that he was still alive, hadn't died in the initial scuffle, taken the easy way out.

He tried to swallow. His mouth was stale and dry from retching. He needed a drink. Well, he could forget that.

Shackled in an isolated garage, the last place anyone would think of looking for him. How long would he last? Dehydration or hypothermia? Which would get him first? Apart from aching ribs, his body felt okay so there were no unattended injuries to speed death on its way.

He shivered again. It was so goddamn cold.

How long had he been out? Minutes? Hours? There was no way of telling. The darkness was complete, no thin cracks of light outlining the doors. It must still be night.

He thought of Lily. She would be home by now. He hoped Pearson would be gentle with her, know that she had nothing to tell him about Cal's latest disappearance. At least Kieran would be there to help her through it. Cal couldn't bear to think of her having to cope on her own. What would the girls be thinking, their daddy gone, police swarming round the house, no chance for Lily to hide the truth from them this time?

He shivered again. A strange sensation tickled the base of his skull.

The sensation moved. Cal froze.

Something was crawling up the back of his head. Seconds of almost imperceptible movement followed by a pause, then the movement continued. Cal turned his head. The movement continued, over the crown, across the top of his scalp. He shook his head from side to side. The insect—a spider, a cockroach?—stuck to its path, allowing itself the odd little detour but seemingly headed for Cal's forehead.

He shivered again, this time not from the cold. He remembered once reading that cockroaches were attracted to the warm breath from human mouths. He clenched his lips together.

The insect kept moving. He closed his eyes just in time for it to scamper across his left eyelid onto his cheek, brush across the left corner of his lips and pause on his chin, interested in the now dried spittle.

One little bug. As long as it stayed away from any bodily crevices he could just about cope. As long as it was just one. Cal recalled the cobwebs he'd seen when he first walked in. He was lying in an empty dusty garage, a haven for bugs of all kinds. The longer he lay here, the more creatures would find him.

He clenched his lips even tighter, praying there weren't any ant colonies in the vicinity.

The insect decided to move on, across Cal's neck at an angle towards his back. Then it disappeared.

Cal sagged with relief. How stupid. He'd let himself get so

tense over one little bug. What about the fact that he'd been left to die? That... that was just too big to fathom.

How could you be going along, living a normal acceptable life, and one day, the chance introduction of a third party, from what ever source, could result in ruin? How were you supposed to know who these people were? Know to never let them into your life. They didn't come with warning signs, like movie ratings. They came in the guise of friends, employees, lovers and even family, but they were human time bombs counting down the seconds until they blew your ordinary life apart.

Katy had appeared at his office, a nice young girl looking to improve her prospects, like all nice young people are supposed to. Would he have still taken her on if he'd known about her past? Probably. After all it was in the past and he was a believer in second chances. He'd had to be, since he was living one himself. He tried to think back to the day of the interview. Was there anything at all, even the slightest hint, that might have warned him off? He didn't think so. Life was like a game of cards. You got to pick which card you pulled from the deck, but you couldn't turn it over until after you'd chosen, and God forbid if you pulled the wrong card.

Sally had been the wrong card and Sheila too. Lily and his career, those he'd got right. But Katy! She was the one that would finish him off.

Or perhaps it wasn't her. Perhaps it started before Katy, like with the move to Leyton. If he hadn't moved here he would have never met Katy. But if he hadn't had the affair with Sheila he might not have left Manhattan and if he hadn't chosen to be an accountant he would never have met Sheila. This was ridiculous. If he'd never been born, he wouldn't be dying.

He'd heard that if you die in an accident your life flashes before you in an instant. What happened when you died slowly? If his current thoughts were anything to go by, you were treated to an overlong B movie of all your flaws and mistakes. He had to switch movies. He had to think of the good things, of Lily, the girls, the family.

A shuffling sound broke the silence. Cal tensed. Too loud for an insect and outside. An animal? A human?

Cal swallowed hard, desperate to moisten his mouth so he

could call out.

There was a click to the left.

He turned his head. A sliver of marginally lighter air appeared. The door was opening. Cal's heart skipped a beat. Rescue? The sliver widened, followed by a pool of light from a flashlight aimed down onto the ground so that the carrier was invisible.

"Hello?" Cal's croaky voice was barely audible.

The light came closer, swept in arcs, searching but deliberate, coming to a stop over his body, shining into his face, forcing him to scrunch his eyes against the brightness. His rescuer was a dark blur surrounded by a halo of light. Cal offered him a weak smile. There was no movement, no attempt to free him from his bonds or even offer a kind word. The inaction panicked Cal, but the guy would need a key to free the handcuffs, so he was probably working out what to do next.

The figure crouched, coming into the circle of light.

Oh God.

Chris Shore smiled at Cal. "Still alive?"

Cal stared at the hand holding the flashlight. Chris was still wearing the latex gloves.

"Rigby thought sending you straight off to prison would be letting you off easy. He wanted you to suffer, like he thought Katy suffered."

Cal stayed silent.

"I couldn't see why we couldn't just finish you off there and then. But Rigby, he said a deal was a deal."

Cal tried to remember which part of the deal involved him being left to rot in an isolated garage. In his anxiety he must have missed that option.

"Lucky for you," Chris said, "he stopped me shooting. From that close a range you wouldn't have survived."

Cal remained silent.

"He was real pissed at me for trying. Thought he was going to shoot me for a moment, the guy was so out of his brains." Chris sighed. "He's going to have to do something about his drinking if he's going to stay on the force. He's hit the bottle real hard since Katy went missing. By all accounts, Pearson's ready to give him the boot. It's his first stint as a detective, I guess he's on some kind of probation, but I don't think this little stunt is going to save him, even if it does put someone behind bars for Katy's death."

Chris laughed. His face lit up as if he'd just been told a good joke.

"But you were good, real good." He leant towards Cal, his voice dropping in volume. "When you said it was an accident, well…" He sniggered. "I couldn't believe my ears. It was perfect, just perfect." Chris straightened up. "But how did you know?"

The breath stopped in Cal's throat. He stared at Chris, aware of the cold floor against his back, the strain in his inner arms from the constant stretch, the hollow in his stomach. And aware of the real meaning of what Chris just said.

"Because it was, you know. I never meant to kill her." Chris looked horrified by the idea. "She was my own sister, I just wanted to stop her from leaving, leaving us like my mother did. I was waiting for her here that Friday night. We had an argument, I tried to stop her getting in the car, there was a scuffle, I shoved her away from the car door. That was all. One hard push and she staggered sideways."

Chris' eyes widened as he spoke as if he was seeing the events replayed in his mind. Cal sensed it was the first time Chris had allowed himself to talk about it. He decided to keep quiet.

Chris swung the flashlight round the garage walls. He stopped at the tool rack, illuminating one by one each tool, the rakes, the shovels. And a gap where one was missing.

Cal closed his eyes, glad that his stomach was already empty.

"She fell and hit her head against a hoe," Chris said in a dazed voice. It just went straight into her skull, like something out of a horror movie." He paused. "I… I didn't know what to do. I knew she was dead because her eyes were wide open, her mouth too, even though she didn't scream, and this tool… This tool was lodged…" He wiped his nose with the back of his hand. "I tried to wipe up some of the blood but there was too much. When I tried to move her it only made it worse. I panicked. I picked up Katy's bag and ran."

For a second Cal allowed himself a sense of relief. The truth at last, this had all been about a goddamn accident. Then reality kicked in. Chris stood up, reached beneath his jacket and pulled a pistol from his waistband.

"But you confessed." He looked down at Cal with a mixture of pity and scorn. "The family, Rigby, they're happy with that. Now all you have to do to stay alive is repeat it to Pearson. Tell him you couldn't live with the guilt anymore." He laughed. "And don't even think about saying you were coerced into it. According to Rigby, with all the lies you've told so far, nobody's going to believe you...and why should they? Everyone just wants to see Katy's killer behind bars. So what if you needed a little bit of nudging to get to the truth? Far better than you get away with it. You in prison, the case would be closed, closed for everyone but me. I'd always be wondering... would the truth come out?"

He waved the gun towards Cal. "And now I've told you the truth. I've got no choice. They're going to get a shock when they find you've committed suicide after all, but what can they do about it, they're all implicated in your being here. Besides, they won't turn their own brother in, will they?" He sniggered again. "I'll probably even admit that I did it, just overcome by the temptation to put away Katy's killer once and for all. How can they blame me for that?"

They wouldn't. As plans went, it sounded waterproof, and if it wasn't, it was still going to be too late for Cal to care.

Oh, damn.

Chris crouched by Cal's shoulder.

"Now what did Rigby say? Right handed man, gun to right temple, angled up slightly so that the shot looks self inflicted." He pressed the cold metal barrel against Cal's head.

Cal tensed. *I love you Lily.*

There was a loud bang, a blinding flash of light and several armed men burst through the side door.

Chris jerked around.

"Drop the gun," Pearson yelled, "and step away from Mr. Miller."

The gun clattered to the ground. Within seconds Chris was handcuffed and hustled away.

Pearson holstered his gun, crossed to Cal and squatted down beside him. "Get a stretcher and some blankets in here now," he shouted over his shoulder.

Cal was shaking so much that he couldn't speak. Not even

when Rigby appeared, leaning over him to unlock the handcuffs, gently helping him bring his arms down from over his head, then sliding an arm under his shoulder and easing him up into a sitting position.

"Dammit, the guy's freezing," Pearson said. 'Couldn't you at least have made sure he was wearing a jacket?"

"You expect me to think of everything?" Rigby said.

"Yes. Something like this, yes."

Rigby reached into his pocket, extracted the hip flask, flipped the lid and held it up to Cal's lips. Cal took a sip, expecting the burning sensation of alcohol against his already raw mouth but desperate for any kind of moisture. Instead he tasted water. He snatched the flask from Rigby's hand, drank every drop, wiped his mouth with the back of his hand and turned to Pearson.

"I guess I owe you one." He exhaled heavily. "Talk about the cavalry arriving just at the right moment."

Pearson shook his head. "You may want to save your gratitude. We knew exactly what was going on." He pushed Cal's trouser leg up to the reveal the tagging bracelet. "Rigby put a small transmitter onto the back of the bracelet. We heard every word from outside."

"Every word?" Cal wanted to make sure he wasn't hearing things in his muddled state. "So... you know I didn't kill Katy?"

Pearson nodded. "Got Chris' confession on tape, loud and clear."

"How'd you know he would confess?" Cal frowned. "How did you even know he'd turn up?" He turned to look at Rigby. "And as for this guy... he was threatening to shoot me himself a few hours ago."

The paramedics arrived with a stretcher. Pearson and Rigby moved to one side to let them do their job. As the two medics fussed over him, Cal kept his gaze firmly on the detectives. He wanted to be warm, but even more he wanted to know what was going on.

Pearson held his hand out towards Rigby. "Give me your gun."

For a moment it looked as if Rigby was going to refuse, then with a pained expression, he took his gun from his holster and slapped it into Pearson's hand.

"Benson, Stockman." Pearson called to the two officers who were in a group still standing at the door. "Take Detective Rigby back to the station house." Pearson turned back to Rigby, "Consider yourself under arrest."

There were gasps of surprise from all around the garage. Cal peered past the paramedics, delighted by the stunned expression on Rigby's face.

"Under arrest?" Rigby said, "what for?"

Pearson didn't reply. Just gave him a look that would frighten most people into silence.

"Why?" Rigby was obviously immune to the look.

"Let's start with A shall we." Pearson's voice was calm and deliberate, and even more scary than usual. He pointed across at Cal as the paramedics strapped Cal onto the stretcher. "Abduction and assault. We'll work through to Z back at the station house. And when we're done with the civilian side of things, we can start on the police rules you've broken."

Rigby looked away, his manner a mixture of insolence and defeat.

Cal's spirits soared. He hoped Pearson threw the book at Rigby. The guy deserved it.

The paramedics picked up the stretcher.

"Well, what are you waiting for?" Pearson yelled at Benson and Stockman. "Get him out of my sight."

The two officers rushed to obey. To Cal's dismay, Rigby went without a murmur.

Pearson turned to Cal. "You, I'll see down at the hospital in a little while. I'll pick up your wife on the way."

One of the paramedics said something. Cal didn't quite catch it. Pearson nodded.

"Thanks," Cal said. He relaxed back onto the stretcher, a delicious wave of sleepiness sweeping over him. "Tell her I... I..."

"Don't worry," Pearson said, "she knows."

Chapter 54

"Did you think I'd run again?"

Cal tightened his grip on Lily's hand. Her presence by his hospital bed was like a happy dream. Touching her was the only way he could convince himself that his mind wasn't playing tricks on him.

Lily shook her head. "The note said you were helping the police."

"The note?"

"On the kitchen table, remember?" She shrugged. "I thought it was rather an odd time for you to have to go out, but it was signed by Rigby, so until the other officers turned up to find out why your monitor wasn't responding, I didn't think too much of it."

Cal was confused. Rigby had forced him out of the house at gun-point and then left a note for Lily? That explained the time lag between him locking Cal in the car and driving away, but why would he leave a note?

"Did the note say where we were going?"

"No. I assumed you were at the police station. When I showed the officers the note, they said Rigby had nothing to do with the case anymore." Lily paled at the memory. "It got crazy for a while. Pearson turned up. They'd dragged him out from a dinner date with his family so I knew they were worried. But when Pearson told me that Rigby was Katy's boyfriend, well then…"

Her eyes brimmed with tears.

"Hey, it's all over now." Cal squeezed her hand again, wanting to distract her from the memories. "And Rigby is under arrest."

"Did he hurt you? The doctor said you had another cracked rib."

"That was... sort of self inflicted. I can't blame him for that, much as I'd like to. Still, I hope they lock him away for years. Guys like that shouldn't be allowed on the streets, never mind the police force. He was willing to get me killed in order to get a confession from Chris Shore. What if they hadn't burst in on time? They might have had their man, but I would have been dead."

"No, you wouldn't," Pearson said from the doorway. "The whole thing was an elaborate set up. The gun wasn't loaded." He walked towards the bed. "If you remember, Rigby gave Chris the gun in the garage so Chris just assumed it was. You were never in danger."

"Well, I sure as hell thought I was. If you knew it was Chris Shore why didn't you arrest him?"

"Lack of evidence."

"So how did you know it was him?" Lily said.

"I know you've both been through a lot. But understand, the evidence all pointed to your husband. His reluctance to tell the truth didn't help."

Cal turned his head away in embarrassment.

"At the funeral though," Pearson said, "Chris Shore let slip a couple of details which we hadn't released even to the family. Rigby was the only one not working on the case who knew and he picked up on them. He combed through the evidence we did have to see if there were any links to Chris that we might have missed, but there was nothing."

"The handkerchief?" Cal said, "C for Chris, not Cal."

Pearson made a face. "Yeah, it was his. But when it turned up in your car, why would we connect it to him?"

"How did it get in my car?"

"Chris put it there."

"Why me!"

"You were an easy target. He knew the police were talking to you, that you were the last person known to have seen Katy. He even knew you'd driven her to the house." Pearson paused. "And he'd seen her journals."

Cal frowned. "All of them?"

"You knew there was more than one?"

"Rigby told me earlier, said the others were true therefore the one about me had to be true." Cal glanced at Lily. "I promise you it wasn't."

"I can vouch for that," Pearson said. "Or at least, if we can believe anything Chris is telling us at the moment. He claimed that he was arguing with Katy about leaving, he'd asked her how she was going to support herself, and she told him she'd made up some incriminating stuff about someone in the village and if necessary she'd use it for blackmail. When Chris left the garage in a panic, he grabbed Katy's bag. He had to get rid of it so he put all her things back in her room, making it look as if she'd never intended leaving and burned the letter to her father."

"So there was a letter."

Pearson nodded. "The police found the journals in the search, but not before he'd read them and realized it was probably you she was going to blackmail."

"Katy was prepared to blackmail me?" Cal shook his head. "And I was feeling sorry for her and trying to help her. I feel such an idiot. How did she take me in like that?"

"If it's any consolation, you're not the only one. Most people who knew her thought she'd reformed after her little wild streak. I guess she was just keeping it hidden and plotting all the time." Pearson grimaced. "She wanted out, knew once she was 21 there wasn't anything her family could do about her leaving. In a way, she didn't lie to you. What she told you about her family was how she felt. You appear to be the only one she confided in."

"Yeah," Cal said, "and look what that got me."

"Think how Rigby feels," Pearson said.

"Rigby? Why should I care about him?"

"He was in love with Katy," Pearson said. "Thought she was in love with him. First she disappears, then she's discovered murdered, then he learns she was leaving him anyway."

"No wonder he lost it," Lily said.

"Now you feel sorry for him?" Cal couldn't believe Lily's change of heart. "He kidnapped me at gunpoint, remember?"

"He put his career on the line to solve this," Lily said.

"Thanks to him this is over for us."

Pearson nodded.

"All the charges dropped?" Cal watched Pearson's expression. "Even the obstruction of justice?" Wasn't he still guilty of something? He felt as if he were.

"All of them," Pearson said.

Cal allowed the knowledge to wash over him, for the first time in months his muscles relaxing and the tension sweeping out.

Then he frowned. "What about the e-mail? Who sent that?"

"Chris."

"How?"

"He was looking for ways to implicate you. Somehow he knew Katy's computer password, had been checking her emails and came across yours, asking her to contact you."

"But that message had never been read. You were there the day we discovered that."

"He'd read it from a remote location, possibly the library. He was there that Sunday. Saw you at the computers. That's when he came up with the idea of sending the reply. He saved it as new mail so it stayed in the mailbox, appeared unread. Seems it wasn't the first time he'd done it. He'd been snooping on Katy for quite some time, which is how he knew she was going to leave."

"Why?"

"After his mother left he became fixated on Katy. If you asked him about his family he would always mention how wonderful Katy was, like he had this perfect sister to make up for not having a mother. Katy was the only female in the family. In one way or another she became the replacement for them all, even though she was the youngest. Dennis and Brad are married, but for the other two, Katy's leaving town would be like their mother leaving all over again, except this time there'd be no females left.

"But she was about to leave home anyway; marry Rigby."

"That was okay. Rigby was a local guy, a cop, a friend of the family, at least in their eyes. If she married him, yes she'd move out, but only round the corner or down the street. She'd still be there for them, to keep the family going, organize the holiday celebrations, whatever. She'd still be Mom, and that's just what she had to get away from. Chris couldn't cope with the idea that she was leaving town, was convinced that he'd be able to persuade her to stay. He found out about the car, so he started following her constantly. That was how he knew that you'd dropped her off at that house. And then they had the scuffle…"

"So it was an accident."

"I don't think for a moment Chris ever intended to kill her. Would rather defeat the purpose, don't you think? If only he'd notified someone of what had happened, he could have saved us all the worry and the investigation."

Cal looked at Lily. Thought of how close this had come to ripping them apart. Could only hope that they could heal the wounds they had inflicted on each other, and then thought of his business.

"The bastard should be shot," he said.

"Not necessarily a wise comment to make in front of the law," Pearson said, "but I can understand your feelings."

"Rigby too."

Pearson looked disappointed. "I wondered how you'd feel on that score."

"What do you mean?" Cal said. "The guy single handedly puts me through the worst day of my life, how do you expect me to feel? I thought I was dead. Why the hell didn't he just tell me the truth? I could have gone along with the set up, pretended, but at least I would have known in advance I wasn't really about to die."

"Well…" Pearson scratched his neck. "You really are a lousy liar. Rigby doubted you could pull it off, thought that your pig-headedness would make you more bolshie than you should have been under the circumstances, would have given the game away."

"It wasn't a game," Cal said.

"In a way, it was," Pearson said, "and I must admit, much as I don't like his methods, I have to agree with his arguments." He grinned. "Of course, it helps that it worked."

Cal looked at Pearson in amazement. "What would have happened if it didn't?"

"You'd still be under arrest and Rigby would be in big, big trouble. So would Brad and Dennis. Rigby had to tell them what was going on. As police officers they would know a coerced confession like that would never hold up in court. He couldn't risk them blurting that out in front of Chris. So he persuaded them to go along with his plan. And he wanted them there as witnesses if Chris did confess.

"Rigby knew that if Chris had been involved in Katy's death he'd see the chance to get rid of you as the closing step. As far as he was concerned, not only Rigby but all his brothers were willing to be implicated in shooting you if you didn't confess, so to his way of thinking he wasn't acting alone. Rigby hoped that Chris would accidentally confess in one way or another while they were trying to force a confession out of you. When that didn't work he had to give Chris a chance to get at you. That's when he came up with the idea of leaving you in the garage.

"At first Rigby stayed with you, set up the transmitter, contacted us. Then he told Chris he'd been called away on business, asked him to cover for him. He guessed the temptation would prove too great for Chris, after all if you were only in prison there was still a chance that one day the truth might come out."

"So basically you're saying that if Chris was guilty, you'd find our for certain," Lily said.

"Exactly. And because of the wire, we have an unforced confession from Chris."

"And Rigby?" Cal said. "What happens to him?"

Pearson paused. "If it's any consolation, he's still stewing in Leyton jail."

Cal glared at Pearson.

"He's probably calling me some choice names and giving his fellow officers a hard time, if I know him. It's a shame. He has the makings of a great detective, but he's hot headed and impatient, constantly challenging the rules. Of course this business with Katy would have been enough to send the sanest person off the rails. That's why I took him off the case. At first he said he could handle the emotions, but it quickly became obvious he couldn't."

"So now he's finished?" Cal said, impatient with all the excuses.

Pearson hesitated. "That's up to you."

"To me?"

Pearson started pacing back and forth. "As I said, at heart he's a good detective. I know he went out on a limb on this one, and I can't tell you how many police regulations he's breached, but the plan was brilliant and it worked. Given the emotional pressure he was under, I think he deserves another chance. I'm inclined to suggest he's suspended for a few weeks—he needs a break anyhow to get over Katy's death—and then reinstated."

Cal shook his head. "Are you kidding? After the terror he put me through?"

"Well, that is from the police point of view." Pearson stopped pacing. "If you want to press criminal charges against him, that's your right. We'd have to follow through on them."

Cal felt a flicker of satisfaction. A few weeks' suspension and a return to normal life? Cal wasn't going to let him off that easily.

"So think about it," Pearson said. "And let us know what you decide." He walked towards the door, a faint look of amusement on his face. "But don't feel you have to rush the decision. As far as I'm concerned that cell is the safest place for him to be at the moment. At least I know what the hell he's up to. I'll come back later. I just wanted to make sure you were fully briefed on what had gone down." He smiled at Lily. "Bye, Mrs. Miller."

He was gone before they had a chance to reply.

They both stared at the empty doorway, the flood of truths rendering them speechless. Then Lily turned to Cal, taking his hand in hers again.

"It's over," she said.

Cal eased himself into a sitting position. "I want to go home. I've had enough of hospitals and jails." He stroked Lily's cheek and then let his fingers slide through her hair. "Home with you and the girls. It will be even sweeter knowing Chris and Rigby are behind bars."

"Cal." Lily said. "If it hadn't been for Rigby you wouldn't be free."

Cal thought of Rigby's drunken performance. He had to admire it, the mock punches, water filled hip flask, the empty gun. Rigby certainly knew how to stage a realistic sting. He thought back to being tied up in the garage. Too realistic. "I'll be sure to send him a thank you note."

"Don't you have any compassion for him? He was going to marry Katy. He must be devastated."

"And I've lost most of my business." Cal stood up, pulling Lily up with him, and hugged her. "And almost lost you."

"You can't blame Rigby for that."

Cal was silent.

"If you'd told the truth in the first place this might never have happened."

Cal put his finger to Lily's mouth to silence her. "I've already been there, believe me. I don't want to talk about that now. I know how stupid I've been."

"Okay," Lily said cautiously, "But just don't try and blame anyone else. I don't want this to fester between us. There's been enough lies and deception. I'm not going to go tiptoeing round you, agreeing how badly you've been treated, letting people turn you into the victim."

Cal couldn't help but smile. "Since when did you get so tough?"

"Since I saw my future as a single mother with three children."

Cal looked at Lily's stomach. "How do you think number three is coping with all this upset?"

"Blissfully unaware, I hope."

"Shall we go home and find out how one and two are coping?"

"Good idea." She kissed him lightly on the lips. "Let me go and find the nurse so we can get you checked out of here."

Lily headed for the door. Cal sat back down on the bed.

"By the way," he said, just before she disappeared, "what was it that you told Pearson that you thought might help?"

Lily grimaced. "How Katy knew about your birthmark."

"My birthmark? How did she know?"

"Just after she started working for you I brought the girls into the office. I needed to change Sophie's diaper. Katy offered to let me use her desk. She noticed Sophie's birthmark, commented on how cute it looked. I remember making a joke about how it was a Miller brand, that you had an identical one."

Cal closed his eyes. "That simple."

"That simple."

Cal opened his eyes. "I don't remember you telling me about that occasion."

"I don't remember you telling me about the real contents of Katy's journal," Lily said. "Not until you had to."

"If I'd told you earlier, would it have made a difference?"

"Pearson seemed to think so."

Cal looked up at the ceiling, silently cursing his stupidity.

"That's the problem with silent lies," he said, "no one can dispute them."

"Fortunately, it's a problem easily solved," Lily said before walking off down the corridor in search of a nurse.

Cal watched her go. He was such a lucky man. He had a wife who loved him beyond expectations. It would have been so easy for her to walk away. Justified even, given how he'd behaved. But she was prepared to give him yet another chance.

He thought of Chris Shore, alone in some cell, very likely facing a lengthy prison sentence; abandoned by his mother at an early age, never having the courage to seek out a wife of his own and then being partly responsible for the death of the only girl who did mean anything to him. Or Rigby, also behind bars, having to cope with a double blow: the loss of a loved one and the discovery that the love he thought he had was all a masquerade.

Yeah, he was a lucky man.

He still didn't like Rigby. Pearson had called him hot-headed and impatient. He'd missed out arrogant. And short-sighted and self-involved. But after all, the same could have been said of him a few years ago.

Damn, how could he have missed it?

Looking at Rigby was like seeing a younger version of himself. And realizing how far short of his youthful ideals he'd fallen. Rigby was prepared to risk everything for what he believed in, while, ever since that fiasco with Sally, he'd chosen to face difficulties with denial and lies, never being completely honest if he thought it would show him in a bad light. As a strategy it had rarely worked, but he'd been slow to learn that.

Or that trust was a two way process.

He tried to list the slights he had against Rigby. He'd raised the issue of the affair with Katy in front of Lily. He'd harassed Cal in the bar all these weeks ago. He'd been condescending and sarcastic during the first interviews at the police station.

Was that it?

307

In light of the revelation that it was his girl friend that was missing, these reactions seemed almost understandable.

Last night though he'd trodden all over Cal's rights, held him at gun point, forced him to break bail, scared the wits out of him, drugged him and used him as bait in his unauthorized scheme to catch a killer. Cal could never forgive him for that.

He'd also cleared Cal's name, given him back his freedom and allowed him a future with Lily and his family. The guy deserved his unending gratitude.

Cal sighed. There was really only one decision he could make. He pushed himself off the bed and hobbled over to the closet to find his clothes.

But as Pearson said, there was no hurry.

Acknowledgements

Thanks to Det. John D'Angelo (retired) of New Castle Police Department for providing an insight into police procedure - I apologize for any liberties I have taken with that information in the name of fiction – and Dave King (co-author of Self-Editing for Fiction Writers) for editing and teaching me all I know about editing. Any mistakes are all mine.

Many thanks also go to my husband and daughter for their support and patience during the writing of this novel.

About the Author

Mel Parish grew up in Newcastle-upon-Tyne, England, and after many years in London and Hong Kong currently resides in New York. Married with one daughter, and the accountant for an international consultancy firm, Silent Lies is Mel's debut novel.

Visit: www.melparish.com

Made in the USA
Middletown, DE
30 September 2015